Praise for *Blacksnake's Path*:

Blacksnake's Path tells the remarkable story of William Wells, an Indian captive turned Indian fighter-scout-spy-translator-negotiator-agent, in a way that alters our sense of American Indian history. As a man in the middle of two cultures, Wells gives us eyes into the powerful role Native Americans played in diplomacy as well as battle. Novelist William Heath balances his astonishing portraits of Indian fighters like Mad Anthony Wayne and William Henry Harrison with equally stunning portraits of Little Turtle and Blue Jacket and Blacksnake to show us less recognized but crucial ways that Indians forged the larger history of the United States. —Frank Bergon, author of *Shoshone Mike* and editor of the Penquin Classics edition of *The Journals of Lewis and Clark*

William Heath's story of the life of William Wells rescues from obscurity one of the most dramatic episodes in the long struggle for control of the North American continent. Heath ably combines the craft of the novelist with the deep research of the historian to make *Blacksnake's Path* as informative as it is enjoyable.
—Andrew Cayton, author of *Frontier Indiana* and *The Frontier Republic*

Blacksnake's Path is one of the best books, perhaps *the* best book that describes the earliest, wild and bloody days of the American Midwest. William Heath portrays this area superbly from the point of views of the Indians as well as of the whites through telling the life of William Wells. The amazing Wells lived on both sides of the conflict from the first American settlement of Kentucky in the 1770s through the Fort Dearborn Massacre in Chicago in 1812. —Jerry Crimmins, author of *Fort Dearborn*

Born white, raised red, William Wells was a sometimes warrior, soldier, spy and agent provocateur who played on, worked both sides in the bloody, thirty year struggle between the allied Indian nations and the United States for control of the Ohio Valley and Great Lakes Country. Seemingly he was a complex character and had more picaresque adventures than Boone or Crockett. But in his own times he never encountered the sort of publicists who eventually turned Dan'l and Davy into semi-mythic figures. And so Wells has all but disappeared in the mists of the past. In *Blacksnake's Path,* William Heath retrieves for the moment this gaudy, always-on-the-make frontiersman. —Bil Gilbert, author of *God Gave Us This Country*

In *Blacksnake's Path,* William Heath dresses the dry bones of history with the richly colored story of a man living both in the raw new country of America and the ancient one of the Miami Indians. Exquisitely detailed and written with convincing grace, William Wells, as well as the flesh and blood of neglected events in American history, come alive in these vibrant and compelling pages.   —Toby Olson, author of *Seaview* and *Tampico*

With his encyclopedic grasp of the era and the territory, William Heath takes the reader back to the frontier Ohio Valley in the midst of its bloodiest war. As scenic and action-packed as the best adventure novel, *Blacksnake's Path* is a rousing, brutal use of American history.
—Stewart O'Nan, author of *A Prayer for the Dying* and *Songs for the Missing*

William Heath respects readers. In *Blacksnake's Path,* he doesn't tell us what to think of his remarkable story and allows its moral implications to fall where they may. This admirable reticence of both language and tone sets off, by contrast, the violent beauty of his subject matter, the series of conflicts between Native Americans and European-Americans in Ohio and Indiana after the Revolution. Heath uses this war to explore the cultural differences between white and Indian society and the psychological tension of a man who belonged to both cultures and therefore wasn't always certain where his loyalties lay. The result is a great read, an accurate and vivid fictional biography, and a sobering reminder of the tragedy at the root of America's westward expansion.
              —John Vernon, author of *Lucky Billy* and *The Last Canyon*

Any good piece of historical fiction introduces us into the strangeness and particularity of earlier worlds and this is what William Heath does in *Blacksnake's Path.* Both the real William Wells, and the William Wells imagined here, moved between two worlds, and Heath recreates those worlds and what was at stake when they clashed.
              —Richard White, author of *The Middle Ground: Indians, Empires, and Republics in the Great Lakes Region, 1650-1815*

Extensively researched and written with a feel for the times, *Blacksnake's Path* tells a compelling story of cultural contest and confluence and breathes life into a long-neglected but pivotal character in the struggle for the Old Northwest Territory.
 —Colin Calloway, author of *The Shawnees and the War for America*

Blacksnake's Path

The True Adventures
of
William Wells

William Heath

FIRESIDE FICTION
2008

FIRESIDE FICTION
AN IMPRINT OF HERITAGE BOOKS, INC.

Books, CDs, and more—Worldwide

For our listing of thousands of titles see our website
at
www.HeritageBooks.com

Published 2008 by
HERITAGE BOOKS, INC.
Publishing Division
100 Railroad Ave. #104
Westminster, Maryland 21157

Copyright © 2008 William Heath

The cover painting, *Signing of the Treaty of Greene Ville*,
by Howard Chandler Christy, courtesy of
The Darke County Historical Society, Inc.

The image of William Wells's tomahawk on page 356
by permission of the Chicago History Museum

International Standard Book Numbers
Paperbound: 978-0-7884-4649-8
Clothbound: 978-0-7884-7451-4

For *Roser*

Caminante, no hay camino.
Se hace camino al andar.
Y al volver la vistas atrás
Se ve la senda que nunca
Se ha de volver a pisar.

—*Antonio Machado*

Traveler, there is no road.
You make one as you walk.
And when you turn to look back
You see the pathway
You will never pass again.

Table of Contents

The word "savage" was common
usage on the frontier and so it appears
frequently in the dialogue and sometimes
in the narrative in order to express the
attitudes of the time, not those of the author.
This practice is also true of other terms
now in disrepute such as "squaw man,"
"brave," and "half-breed."

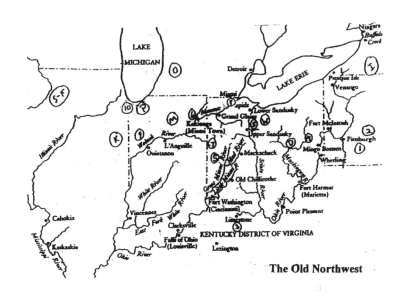

The Old Northwest

William Wells and the Wars for the Northwest Territory

Location of Indian Nations		Location of Battles	
I	Iroquois	1	Braddock's Defeat
M	Miami	2	Bushy Run
S	Shawnee	3	Blue Licks
D	Delaware	4	Gnatenhütten
W	Wyandot	5	Crawford's Torture
P	Potwatomi	6	Harmar's Defeat
K	Kickapoo	7	St. Clair's Defeat
O	Ottawa	8	Fallen Timbers
S-F	Saux-Fox	9	Tippecanoe
		10	Fort Dearborn

Part I

Deep in the wild and solemn woods,
Unknown to white man's track,
John Filson went one autumn day,
But never more came back.

—W. H. Venable

Tbe Ohio River: October 1788

When they saw his rusty red hair, they knew the boy was white. He was waist-deep at the edge of the river crying for help.

"Do something, John," a woman on the deck called up to her husband, who stood on the roof of the cabin at the back of the flatboat.

"It might be a trap," he said, keeping a steady hand on the steering oar. "Remember what we were told in Pittsburgh."

"I wouldn't trust the word of an uncouth stranger," the woman replied.

"Ask the boy to explain himself," the grandmother suggested.

"Man the sweeps," the father told his sons, and the boat began a slow swerve out of the main current and toward the northern shore.

Although the sun shimmered on the water and a warm breeze caressed their faces, the colors of the leaves—ocher, amber, russet and gold—betrayed the season. A turkey buzzard circled in the sky.

"Swim out," the man shouted. "We don't want to get too close."

"I think my leg's broke," the boy sobbed. "I can't swim."

"What in tarnation are you doin' on the Injun side of the river?"

"Me an' my brother come over to hunt an' he got caught but I run off. Oh please, save me or I'm done for. They'll kill me sure."

"What's your name?"

"William Wells, Sir."

"How'd you run if your leg was broke?"

"Don't argue with the boy," the grandmother scolded, "rescue him. Can't you see he's just a poor lost lamb?"

"Skin your eyes for the savages," the man cautioned as he guided the unwieldy craft in closer.

The Soldier had chosen his spot well: a sharp bend in the river and sudden headwinds created an eddy that drew the unwary traveler toward a stagnant backwater. A dozen Miami warriors hidden behind bushes and inside a huge hollow sycamore waited for his signal. As the long flatboat drifted closer, its strong odor carried across the river. The Soldier scrutinized the passengers and livestock. Only two men held rifles at the ready, three more were busy with the sweeps and steering oar, a youngster was uncoiling a rope. A slave family huddled under a makeshift tent in a front corner of the deck, near a pigpen and a pile of hay where three horses and a cow were feeding. Four females, gathered at the gunwale on the shore side, called encouragement to the boy in the water. One white-haired woman sat in a rocking chair, knitting needles in her hands and a cradle at her feet. A pig squealed, a dog barked, chickens cackled.

"God bless you," the boy cried out.

The Soldier raised his rifle and took aim through the willows, The Sleepy One and Cutfinger did the same. Their first volley dropped the two men with guns and the one standing on the roof. With a heart-stopping yell the other warriors sprang out of their hiding places and fired from the riverbank down into the flatboat. Those not killed by the first fusillade cowered behind the gunwale, only to be kicked repeatedly by a horse thrashing in its death agony. The shrieks and groans of the wounded were drowned out by the whoops of the warriors charging the boat with raised tomahawks. A white boy, bleeding badly, staggered to the shore and limped into the woods, closely pursued by William Wells, who had taken cover when the shooting started. One of the slaves leaped over the side and tried to swim for it, but two braves stabbed him in the back and took his hair. The bodies on deck were scalped and dumped into the river. A crying baby, cradle and all, was similarly cast upon the waters, followed by a crate of chickens. Two pigs and a dog were saved for the cooking pot.

The warriors scavenged the flatboat for plunder, tossing furniture, bedding, and supplies in all directions. He Provides claimed a long-barrelled rifle with a curly maple stock, a shot pouch, and a bag of powder; Sweating tried on a linen shirt with ruffles, a blue vest faced with white satin, and a macaroni hat set off with an ostrich plume; Buckfeet, Black Loon, and The Sleepy One had their taste for fancy earrings satisfied by silver shoe buckles, a gold watch, and a bejeweled snuff box; Cutfinger applied his tomahawk to a harpsicord and came away with useful keys and wires; Night Stander, sporting a silken robe de chambre, sampled a tin of chocolates; Earth settled for an iron kettle and a pewter tankard; The

Soldier eyed a scythe that he broke apart for the blade; The Cat wrapped himself in a patchwork quilt, waved a pair of scissors, and cut off the tails and manes of the dead horses; Thin Raccoon gave a tentative puff on an ivory flute; Two Lives discovered the best treasure of all: a keg of whiskey, which he would have to share. William Wells found the boy, who was about fourteen, hiding behind a fallen log. In his panic he had left a clear trail. His forehead was streaked with blood and he had been shot in the leg.

"Come with me," Wells said.

"What are they gonna do to me?" the boy muttered, his eyes wide with fear.

Wells pulled the boy to his feet and supported him with his arm so he could hobble back to where the contents of the flatboat were strewn on the muddy shore. The Soldier grunted approval when he noted the return of Blacksnake and his prisoner. Cutfinger, still grieving for his dead brother, stepped forward with a belt of black wampum and placed it over the boy's shoulders, claiming him for his own. The boy looked out at the river and saw the flatboat drifting away, followed by descending buzzards.

"You killed them all," the boy cried. "You killed my ma and my pa and you're gonna kill me too, aren't you?"

"I don't know," Wells stammered.

"You're lying. I can tell. You lied from the start. You do know. You're with them. You know what's gonna happen to me."

"No I don't," he insisted, shaking his head and trying to look sincere. "I don't know."

But, of course, he did.

Billy Wells: 1779

1

There was a man living on Jacob's Creek in southwestern Pennsylvania named James Smith; he had been captured by the Mohawks in 1755 while clearing the road for Braddock's doomed army. In an oak grove on a hill behind his cabin he had built a small bark-and-branch wigwam where he spent much of his time. Eight-year-old Billy Wells had heard his older brothers talk about this strange neighbor who kept to himself; one day he walked through the woods to spy on him. Playing Indian, he crawled on his belly under a clump of huckleberry bushes near the entrance of the wigwam; all he saw was a man lying on his back, reading.

"Why are you here, boy?" the man asked gruffly, without taking his eyes from the book in his hands. "Come on out so I can get a look at you."

Billy's heart jumped. He had an urge to run, but he did what the man said.

"What are they like?" he mumbled.

"Who?"

"The savages."

"The savages! Why do you want to know?"

"'Cause we're headin' west," the boy explained proudly. "We've got a flat in the makin' and come spring we're goin' down the O-hi-o."

"How far?"

"As far as the Falls."

"Are you afraid?"

"I ain't afeared a nothin'."

"Well, sometimes it pays to be a little afraid."

"How come you got your hair?"

"It grew back," the man said matter-of-factly; then he frowned, realizing what the boy meant. "They didn't scalp me, son. That's only for the dead, in the heat of battle. But they given me what you might call a close shave."

"Pa says they make people die real slow just for the fun a watchin'. Ma says they're bound sartin sure for hell. My brother Sam says they ain't nothin' but wolves that need killin'. What do you say?"

The man gave the boy a penetrating look; then paused a moment as if revisiting old memories and weighing present options.

"They're different," James Smith finally said with a wry smile. "Let's say they're real different and leave it at that."

2

The first William Wells, an English Puritan, had come to Virginia in 1636 and settled up the James River past Williamsburg, where sermons on God's omnipotence and salvation by grace yielded to talk of tobacco, slaves, fast horses, and loose women. In the late seventeenth-century the Wells clan moved to the Northern Neck frontier, St. Paul's Parish in Stafford County; there Billy Wells's father, Samuel, was born in 1734. When he was nineteen Samuel married Ann Farrow; they settled on the south bank of Quantico Run, in Prince William County, where their first four children were born: Sam, Carty, Hayden, and Elizabeth. Samuel came back from service in the French and Indian War feeling the lure of the backcountry; he was convinced that the best lands were farther west. And so, in 1768, the family began the arduous trek across the Allegheny mountains. Carty, already sparking a local girl, decided to stay behind.

They followed an old Indian trail, known as Nemacolin's path, which had been expanded into a muddy, stumpy, rutted wagon road that ended at Fort Pitt. There were a series of formidably steep ridges to ascend and descend along the way, creeks and rivers to cross, swamps and bogs to slog through, underbrush and fallen trees to clear. The difficulties and dangers of the journey were suggested by the place names: Big Savage Mountain, the Devil's Backbone, Satan's Hunting Ground, and the Shades of Death—the latter a dense glade of tall pine trees, where travelers, even at noonday, walked for miles through gloomy shadows. Finally, the Wells family stood on the western slope of Laurel Mountain and looked down at a vast forest, spreading as far as the eye could see. A few days later they selected a spot on Jacob's Creek, which emptied into the Youghiogheny River. That this area west of the mountains was claimed by both Virginia and Pennsylvania did not bother Samuel Wells; he simply blazed trees on the borders of the land he liked, cleared it for planting, and, with the help of a few neighbors, raised a substantial log cabin.

Billy Wells was born in August, 1770. His earliest memories dated from Lord Dunmore's war of 1774, when the Mingoes, in retaliation for the murder of Chief Logan's relativies, attacked exposed settlements. Once Billy was awakened during the middle of the night and, still half asleep, tossed across the back of a pack horse and rushed with the rest of the family to Crawford's Station, where they forted up in stifling quarters while Samuel and Sam went off to fight. Sitting around the fireplace in the evenings, Billy often heard his father and eldest brother swap stories of their adventures. They had marched with fat, old, gray-headed Dunmore, who, with an absurdly small gun on his shoulder, waddled along beside his troops. One day a few men opened fire at a bear swimming the Ohio.

"Well, did you get a shot?" Valentine Crawford inquired of John Moody, a Yorkshireman.

"Yes, by God, and I hit him too."

"How do you know that, John?" Crawford demanded, squinting skeptically at the far shore.

"Can't you see him switching his tail?"

Billy's father and brother laughed every time they told the tale. From that distance you could hardly see the bear, never mind its stub of a tail. They both had missed out on the desperate tree-to-tree fighting at the decisive battle of Point Pleasant, where, above the incessant rattle of gunfire and the shrill war whoops, the Virginians heard Cornstalk exhorting his warriors, "Be strong! Be strong!" By morning the battleground belonged to the Virginians, and so did Kentucky. Billy couldn't wait for the day when he would be an Indian fighter, too.

When word of Lexington and Concord reached Fort Pitt, Samuel and Sam went off to war again, this time against Lord Dunmore himself and his Tory allies. Ann was left to look after the family—which now included two more boys, Yelverton and Charles—on a frontier still exposed to Indian attack. When Samuel returned a year later, he had changed for the worse: surly, irascible, drinking more and more. With his mustering out money he had purchased a slave family—Jacob, Cate, and their three girls—and he was quick to whip them if he thought they weren't working as hard as he was. Then one day he came home drunk with Johanna Farrow, his wife's teenage niece. When Ann started shouting and throwing things, they beat her. Seven-year-old Billy tried to intervene; his father shoved him so hard against the wall his teeth rattled.

These backwoods Virginians were an unruly and un-churched lot. George Washington's friend William Crawford, the leading man in that part of the country, kept *his* niece as his mistress and shared her with his son John, his brother Valentine, and his half-brother. Even so, Samuel's behavior was sufficiently outrageous to draw complaints from his scattered neighbors; he was ordered to come to court at Andrew Heath's house and explain himself.

The threat of the whipping post sobered him considerably; after a long argument, Ann issued an ultimatum, either she goes or I go. Samuel made a counter-offer: Kentucky. Let's make a fresh start. Folks were all abuzz about the rich land there—word was that a planted crowbar would sprout ten-penny nails by morning. Ann was less than delighted by the prospect of moving further into the backcountry; but, like most frontier women, she had little choice.

3

The thaw came early in 1779; but what with heavy rains, high water, and last minute preparations, it was April before the five flatboats were ready to ride the spring freshets west. Samuel Wells—along with his cousin William Pope, Captain William Oldham, and several other Virginians—had his own oak-log ark laden with the family's earthly possessions. The slaves slept in a lean-to on the extensive front deck with the livestock; there was a cabin in the stern for everyone else. When the small flotilla reached Pittsburgh, and Billy saw the brick bastions of the star-shaped fort at the point and the clear waters of the Allegheny rolling in from the north to form the Ohio, all his senses came alive. Now they were at the mercy of the mighty river, drifting ceaselessly west into the unknown.

The Ohio was a beautiful river, wide and stately, flowing majestically down its verdant, thousand-mile-long valley to the Mississippi. Weeping willows fringed both banks beneath gigantic shaggy sycamores, their prodigious hollow trunks swollen with boles, their white limbs bent like beckoning witches' fingers. In the nearby hills magnificent oaks and poplars rose skyward, festooned with the thick vines of wild grapes and honeysuckle; the marshy bottomlands, inundated every spring, contained natural meadows of tall grasses and stands of hickory and beech. Billy's father and his older brothers, Sam and Hayden, eyed the trees with a woodcutter's craving to turn them into cords and cabins, fences and barns. The boy, more interested in wildlife and Indians, scanned the shore with his rifle by his side. Although he was only eight, he was already a good enough shot to bark a squirrel. His father had promised him he would see buffalo once they passed the settlements—probably savages, too.

When the war began between the British and the colonies, it wasn't hard to figure which side the Indians would take—the Americans wanted their land. That was why George Rogers Clark had led an expedition to the Falls of the Ohio and beyond against the British forts and trading posts the previous year. He knew the real fight was for the West. By joining him, Samuel Wells and his friends weren't avoiding the war; they were seeking out what would soon be a salient part of it.

To take advantage of the high water and avoid ambush, the families agreed to stop as little as possible, trusting the current to carry them safely past all obstacles. A long steering oar pivoted from a forked stick secured to the roof of the cabin in the stern; sweeps with substantial blades could be extended out the side windows to keep the boat away from shore and clear of numerous islands with their treacherous sandbars. Drifting along at about four miles an hour, with luck they would reach the Falls in less than ten days. Once, when the flat ran aground with a jarring thunk on a mud bank, Billy, Hayden, and Sam had to jump into muck up to their thighs to push it off. Another time they scraped a submerged tree, but no serious damage was done. Mostly they sat on the roof of the cabin, as far away from the slaves and livestock as possible, and marveled at the beauty and bounty of the land.

Sometimes the boats would get so close to each other that people would share food, exchange places, or at least talk across the water. Billy liked to jump over to play with Johnny Pope, who was his own age and smart as a whip. Captain William Oldham also sought occasions to visit the Popes's boat in order to regale Johnny's sister, Penelope, with stories of Morgan's riflemen and the fierce fighting around Freeman's Farm that led to Gentleman Johnny Burgoyne's surrender at Saratoga. Although only eleven, she was a dark-eyed beauty with a sparkling laugh, and all the young men—including Sam Wells and his friend Bland Ballard—vied for her attention. Billy had a crush on her, too, and wished *he* had some stories to tell, while his plain-faced and serious-minded sister, Elizabeth, who was seventeen, scowled with envy.

Beyond the recently constructed Fort McIntosh at the mouth of Big Beaver Creek, the river turned from its northwesterly direction and headed almost due south. Rocky palisades pressed in on both sides, casting long shadows on the water and quickening the current. Further down at Grave Creek, past the cluster of cabins at Wheeling, there was a tree-covered Indian mound—ninety-feet high, at least, Samuel estimated. A sixteen-mile straightaway known as The Long Reach, with rich black bottomlands along both shores, brought them to the Muskingum. Billy didn't see any live Indians, but he did notice abandoned campsites and more mounds. After the small fort at Point Pleasant, at the mouth of the Kanawha, not another soldier or settler was spotted.

What Billy did see was an astonishing amount of wild game. At the Big Sandy, more than fifty buffalo grazed along the bank. Buffalo traces, sometimes a quarter mile wide, led toward canebrakes, grassy savannahs, and salt licks. In the summer the herds swam or even waded across the river as they moved with the seasons. Occasionally Billy spotted an elk, a black bear, or even a bobcat; once he saw hundreds of squirrels, in a mass panic, swimming frantically toward the Indian side. Ducks, geese, swans, and wild turkeys were plentiful. Schools of bass, pike, and perch slapped against the underside of the flatboat. At dusk, when the deer came to the water's edge to drink, Billy heard the lament of the whip-poor-will and the shrill whistle of quails. The cacophonous love songs of frogs, the distant howl of wolves, and the hoot-a-hoot-a-hoo of owls filled the night. Those were the times when Billy's brothers told him tales of the catfish so big he drowned the man who caught him and of the dreaded bear-eating monster that lurked in the dark woods. Billy knew they were only joshing; whatever was out there, he wanted to see for himself.

The serpentine river carried them vaguely westward. Billy had the notion, as sharp bends to front and rear cut off the view, that they were gliding down a series of beautiful lakes. Trees blossomed—the redbuds were lavender, dogwoods displayed their stigmata—and the air was pungent with the promise of spring. At night the moon shone on the water and in the morning, as the mist rose and warblers sang, Sam would blow softly on a conch shell to let the other boats know where they were. Amid such soothing scenery, it was easy to forget that their watery path flowed through a predatory world.

They were now entering the most dangerous part of the trip. The confluence of the Scioto with the Ohio was a favorite Shawnee spot to waylay flatboats. Samuel Wells ordered his sons to load all the guns and keep a constant lookout. He also made sure that the flotilla stayed together, in the center of the river, and that no one fell behind. It seemed as if time and the current deliberately slowed down as they crawled along. Billy felt sure they were being watched; he strained his eyes in vain to discover painted faces hidden in the pawpaw thickets along the shore.

Everyone sighed when the danger was past. Then, after the next headland, they noted a dark congregation of buzzards gathered on a gravel bar jutting out from a small island near the northern shore. There, displayed on the mud, was the corpse of a naked woman impaled on a stake—belly pointed down river, head twisted to face whence she came. Even before his mother screamed, Billy, in the lead boat, saw it all. He smelled it too: the sickly sweet, putrid, penetrating odor of human death. The buzzards, as the flatboats drifted past, didn't budge.

The river wasn't the same after that. In spite of the clear sky and shining sun, the trees in bloom and the air filled with birdsong, around every bend they expected to see mutilated bodies or canoes of ferocious warriors. Billy and his brothers took turns keeping nightly vigil and watch by day. Mrs. Wells, her eyes downcast and her teeth clenched, stayed mostly in the cabin.

"I never wanted to come to this godforsaken place," she muttered to her husband. "I told you so before we left."

"It's no turning back now," he said with grim determination. "This land belongs to them what finds it first and I mean to get me some."

The flatboats drifted on. The skies lowered and darkened, a driving rain pocked the river and sudden gusts tossed the branches of the biggest trees. During a steady downpour, they rode the rising current, which swept them past the mouth of the Kentucky in the middle of the night. By morning the sun was shining, and, late in the day, they heard a soothing rumble, growing louder as they neared, that could only be their destination, the Falls of the Ohio—a two-mile stretch of rapids where the river dropped about twenty feet. The water widened into a deceptively placid lake; with shrill cries ospreys plummeted, feet-first, after fish near the surface and flocks of bright green and yellow parakeets swooped and hovered. A man in a canoe paddled out and warned them to head for the tall cane on the Kentucky side before the undercurrent pulled them into the suck of the rapids; and so the flatboats, plying their sweeps and steering oars, drifted toward the deep natural harbor where Beargrass Creek entered the Ohio, and came to rest.

Beargrass Stations

1

In the spring of 1779 the settlement at the Falls was a disapointment to Billy's eager eyes: a crude stockade with a two-story blockhouse at each corner, a scattering of rough-hewn log cabins, a few stump-studded fields, and a muddy road by the river. The new arrivals were offered temporary shelter in the fetid, overcrowed fort. All the talk was about General George Rogers Clark's daring capture of Vincennes. In late March, British Governor Hamilton, loathed as the "Hair Buyer" on the Kentucky frontier, had been brought to town in chains. Although the settlers hoped that the war would soon be over, for every man who swung an ax or a hoe another stood guard with a rifle, and at night they brought their cattle and horses inside the fort's palisades.

"Soon we'll have our own farm," Samuel Wells told his wife.

"I reckon maybe," she allowed in a voice that dampened her husband's enthusiasm.

Because of its location by the rock-strewn rapids of the Falls, the town was destined to become an important trading center; until then the site wasn't especially desirable to the prospective settler. The high level plain bordering the Falls was relatively safe from flooding, but scattered ponds and swampy areas nearby bred mosquitoes. The Wells family and their five slaves headed for the middle fork of Beargrass Creek, where an elaborate network of beaver dams, some higher than a man's head, helped sustain the fertile soil. Day after day axes rang and chips flew as everybody cut timber and cleared underbrush until they were bone weary. Billy's hands sprouted blisters on top of blisters and his poison-ivy-coated arms were a torment. Once, as he was gathering kindling, he almost stepped on a rattlesnake thicker than his leg. In a month they had a home: a two-room cabin with a mud-daubed stick chimney, a window covered with greased paper, and a cockloft of planks in the rafters where the boys slept on a moss-stuffed mattress. Behind it was a one-room, dirt-floored cabin for Jacob, Cate, and the three girls. There was also a corn field that the sun reached for a couple of hours around noontime before sinking behind the towering poplars.

Many of the settlers—including Billy's father and his brother Sam—volunteered to join Colonel Bowman in a raid on the Shawnee villages north of the Ohio. A captive had recently escaped and promised to show them the way. The Kentuckians rendezvoused at the mouth of the Licking in May and then marched up the Little Miami to the main town, Chillicothe. A squaw saw them first and screamed "Kentuck! Kentuck!" while the warriors raced to the solid-log council house, where they mounted a fierce defense. Sam told Billy that the shooting was so intense the bark flew from the trees; finally the warriors withdrew, but not before they'd killed nine Kentuckians. Billy's father brought home two horses; Sam was the proud owner of a linen shirt, covered with silver brooches, that he claimed belonged to Chief Black Fish himself. The settlers along the Beargrass braced for retaliation, but instead the Shawnees attacked Boonesboro.

When George Rogers Clark returned to Louisville in August, he called for a feast to celebrate his victories in the Illinois country. He had brought rum, sugar, and a French fiddler by keelboat all the way from Kaskaskia, and a new puncheon floor had been laid in Bachelor's Hall inside the stockade, so a shindig was in order. Billy begged his parents to bring him along; besides, wasn't it his birthday? He grinned when he saw that Clark's hair was redder than his own and he was astonished to see how nice the women looked decked out in their fanciest duds. The people kicked up their heels, swirled, shouted, cavorted about, and cut pigeon wings; the women sat in the men's laps between dances and sang "Green grow the rushes, O! / Kiss her quick and let her go." Billy drank too much rum toddy and awoke with his first hangover. He was nine years old.

One day in early November, as Samuel Wells and his sons were finishing a lean-to stable for the horses on the back of their cabin, a tall, slender, black-haired stranger rode up on a big horse.

"In the name of the Great Jehovah, what are y'all doin' on my land?" he demanded.

"We got the tomahawk rights to this place," Samuel insisted. "You kin see my blazes on the trees and the corn in the field."

"That doesn't mean spit in the ocean. My name is John Floyd and you're squattin' on my acreage."

"Damnation if it's yours. Me an' my sons have sweated our arses off to clear this land and build these cabins. Around here, mister, it's first come first serve."

"That remains to be seen," Floyd said, his black eyes burning. "The Virginia land commissioners will be at the Falls next week. They'll tell you whose land this is."

When the commissioners arrived they validated what he had said. Floyd was a Virginia aristocrat, a veteran of Lord Dunmore's War, a tall and handsome man of adventure whose straight black hair and dark, intense features betrayed a dash of Indian blood. Early in the Revolution he had led the privateering scooner *Phoenix* against the British, been captured and imprisoned at Dartmouth, and then, after charming the jailor's daughter, escaped to France. Marie Antoinette herself had presented him with an exquisite set of silver buckles and Ben Franklin paid his passage home. He had first visited the Falls in 1774 and staked out a claim. Samuel Wells and his family were indeed squatters. The problem was that winter had arrived with the commissioners; it was simply too cold to search for another place to live.

"Let them stay where they're at for the season," Floyd said nonchalantly. "I'll draw up a tenant's lease."

"We didn't come here to be beholdin' to no man," Sam shouted. "I'd rather die first."

"If you are a gentleman," Floyd retorted, "that can be arranged."

"Sam, you simmer down," Samuel ordered his hot-tempered son. "The snow's already a foot deep; we don't got no choice."

The snow kept falling, an unrelenting wind sliced like the Devil's own razorblade from the northwest, the cold got colder and didn't let up. The Ohio River was covered by ice two-feet thick; most of the streams and ponds froze to the bottom killing the fish. In the surrounding forests deer died in their tracks, wild turkeys toppled dead from their roosts, buffalos bellowed in the dark before they perished. The Wells family wrapped themselves in bearskins and huddled around the fireplace; their slave family did the same. In the night Billy would awake with a start whenever a tree, frozen to the heartwood sap, would split open with a resounding crack and crash to the earth. One morning he saw a full-grown elk leaning against the chimney for warmth. In December one horse died, in January they ate the last of their pigs.

Early in February Sam trudged to the fort through the thick-crusted snow to buy corn; he came back—his breath frozen on his beard, his eyebrows icicles—empty-handed; flour, John Floyd told him, was "as dear as gold dust," in depreciating Continental currency it sold for $150 a bushel. The people at the Falls had suffered terribly. William Pope's sister, Jane, lost three of her children to chills and fever; other people died of dysentery. One night it was so cold in the cabin that the whiskey froze in the jug. Every day Billy bundled up as best he could against frostbite and went out to knock the ice from the horses's nostrils, cut cane for fodder, and gather snow for drinking and cooking. By early March, they were down to their last johnny cake. When the weather finally broke and the men could go hunting, the buffalo meat they brought in was poor and stringy.

2

Spring that year was as splendid as the winter had been severe. A hot sun turned the snow to slush; everywhere Billy heard the gurgle of trickling water. So many trees, flowers, and shrubs burst into blossom that it made him forget the stench of the carcasses littering the woods. Hundreds of new immigrants, arriving with the warm weather, spread out into the forest to mark their chosen spots with tomahawk blazes. Samuel Wells and his sons reluctantly helped John Floyd and his brothers construct his station, a palisaded parallelogram set on a hill by a good spring. The backs of the cabins, with the high side out and the clapboard roofs slanted inward, formed two walls of the fort, completed by a stockade of pointed logs. The men mixed the hard work of construction with a lot of rough fun; they uncorked the whiskey jug they called Black Betty and vied to kiss her sweet lips. The crude jests that bandied back and forth sometimes led to no-holds-barred fights; the other men would drop their carpenter's tools to root for their bloody nosed favorite, rolling in leaf mold and mire.

Other stations were built further south, near the saltworks at Bullitts Lick. Soon it was common to see caravans of wagons on the rutted roads, based on old buffalo traces, going to and from the Falls. William Pope, accompanied by Captain Oldham, took his family to Sullivan's Station on the south fork of Beargrass; disconsolate over the loss of their three children, Jane and her husband Thomas Helm, simply left, vowing never to return. In April Billy's brother Carty and his family arrived from Virginia and settled near the Fish Ponds several miles below the town.

Daniel Boone's younger brother Squire was the most venturesome of all, leading a dauntless group of settlers to his Painted Stone Station on Clear Creek, over twenty miles east of Linn's Station, the last outpost on the Beargrass. Samuel Wells was tempted to join him, but what he wanted was his own station; after the planting had been done and the livestock replaced, he and Sam went scouting for prime timber, choice land, and a good spring. Because the warmer weather brought with it the danger of war parties, Billy was ordered to stay at home and help his mother.

His first job in the morning was to peek out of the cracks in the loft and look for Indians; then he would drive the cow into a corner between the cabin and the lean-to and hold its calf's ears while his mother did the milking; next he would tend to the fire and husk, silk, and shell enough corn for breakfast pone; after that he would help Jacob with the hoeing in the truck patch of vegetables and melons, try to keep the crows and squirrels out of the corn field, feed and fodder the livestock, tote water from the spring, or take turns with his mother, sister, and Cate churning butter or pounding corn at the hominy block by the front door of the cabin.

Since her marriage Ann Wells had known nothing but the labor of childbirth and the work of farming. Although she wore a kerchief on her head to hide her grey hair, there was no concealing her sallow face, gnarled hands, and gaunt form. There must have been days when she looked with a moist eye in the cracked mirror beside her bed and wondered what it would be like to live in a white frame house with plastered walls and glass windows.

The only time she enjoyed herself was when she was spinning the fine flax fibers into linen; then Billy would sometimes hear her singing above the lulling hum of the wheel about "Old Sister Pheby," or "Barbry Allen," whom love-lorn Sweet William died for. Billy helped his mother rake, dry, and break the fibers; then came the scrutching board and hacking out the coarser tow fibers from the finer ones and reeling them into skeins; after the spinning, the sheets of linen were spread out, weighed down with stones at the corners, and sprinkled for bleaching. The most readily available dye came from the inner bark of white walnut trees; it was a drab butternut yellow color that matched Ann's weather-beaten skin.

Ann had no kinfolk to keep her company; sometimes she and Jacob's Cate would sit by the front door snapping beans and talking; once on a whim she put on her best calico dress, picked up her shoes, and walked barefoot to town. She came back that night with a new silken sunbonnet tied by a band of red ribbon, which she hung on a peg beside her petticoats and bed gown, and rarely wore. What she usually served on the family's few pewter plates was the standard frontier fare: hog and hominy, cornmeal mush and milk, johnny cake and pone, grits and gravy, but on occassion she would outdo herself and come up with plum pudding, cherry pie, whipped syllabub, or, Billy's favorite, the handmade doughnuts known as "wonders."

Meanwhile, the settlers in pell-mell haste picked their spots and asserted tomahawk rights; before long conflicting claims overlapped like autumn's fallen leaves, a situation that soon made Kentucky an El Dorado for lawyers. Even the threat of war parties could not slow the land-mad urge to beat everybody else to the tallest timber and the richest bottoms.

Back at the Falls things were more organized; in May the town was named Louisville, in gratitude for France's support of the Revolution; seven Trustees were chosen—including John Floyd and William Pope—and three-hundred half-acre lots were surveyed.

"Couldn't we move into town," Ann pleaded, "at least until the war is over?"

"And live under the thumb of John Floyd!" Samuel growled.

"Ain't that what we're already doin'?" she replied.

Samuel Wells had a notion to take his family into the wilderness, even farther out than Squire Boone's place, but when word came from two escaped captives that over a thousand British and Indians were on the march to attack Fort Nelson at Louisville, they had to seek protection inside Floyd's Station instead. Billy didn't mind, he enjoyed having his playmates closer; but his mother quarreled with the other women and frowned with disgust at how filthy everything was: so many people and animals cramped up in so small a space! In late June, during a period of heavy rains, word came that Ruddle's and Martin's Stations, near the forks of the Licking, had been destroyed by an overwhelming enemy force armed with cannons. Men, women, and children had been massacred by the Indians, and two hundred more taken prisoner. None of the Beargrass stations could resist the firepower of a six-pounder, but miraculously the British commander Colonel Bird, horrified by the barbarity of his Indian allies and running short of supplies, withdrew to Detroit.

Once again Samuel Wells was ready to seek his fortune in the deep forests but now Ann came down with the ague. At first they thought it was just a case of the shakes; Doctor George Hartt arrived from Louisville, eyed her closely, sniffed the air, and pronounced it a bilious remitting fever and flux, prescribing a brisk cathartic of calomel and quicksilver to purge her body of corrupting fluids. She vomited up a dark green bile and held one hand to her throat as though she were choking—a draught of warmed goose grease didn't relieve the sensation. For fear of contagion, Billy wasn't allowed in the room, but he could hear her moaning day and night. When her skin broke out in festering sores, the doctor tried opening a vein. The blood ran black and viscous in the basin; her pulse softened; Ann fainted away for five minutes. The doctor shook his head, declaring that she was in the hands of God. Billy was brought to her bedside to say goodbye; she made a mighty effort to raise her head and reach out her arm, but they weren't allowed to touch. The next morning, he was told that his mother was dead.

She was buried in her calico dress and silken sunbonnet, the red ribbon tied in a bow under her chin. The mourners at the station prayed a little and drank a lot and said it was no surprise—hadn't they heard a hound baying that very night? Samuel Wells, blaming himself for his wife's death, sat down on a stump and wept; he fell into such a funk that his life was despaired of. Billy cried and cried, while his sister Elizabeth tried to comfort him. Sam sulked around the station and got into fights. He welcomed George Rogers Clark's call for another campaign against the Indians.

3

After the campaign Sam had a nasty argument with John Floyd, reproaching him for taking more than his share of silver brooches from a dead Indian to smelt into spoons; so the Wells family moved to Linn's Station, a few miles away. William Linn, a celebrated war hero, had single-handedly brought a thousand pounds of desperately needed gunpowder from New Orleans to a besieged Wheeling in 1777. A generous man, he had opened his station as a refuge; eighty people were crowded into the cabins facing the compound, which was more like a quagmire.

The mild winter that year was a mixed blessing, since the early thaw brought Indian raids. One day in March William Linn left ahead of a group going to court in Louisville. Shortly afterwards, Billy and the others at the station heard the report of rifles. A party of men set out immediately and soon saw Linn's horse, shot dead on the trail, but they couldn't find Linn. The following morning a wider area was searched and his mutilated body was discovered a mile away. From the blood on the leaves and the condition of the ground they could see that he had put up one hell of a running fight. The bond of grief helped Billy become friends with Will Linn and his brother Ashel. Not a week passed that spring without word of another bloody ambush; at Linn's Station alone there were already dozens of widows and orphans. In April, Squire Boone was in a skirmish; his right arm was shattered by one shot and he took another ball in his side. Boone's Painted Stone Station was especially vulnerable; one by one its people were scalped or captured. Yet in spite of the danger, the settlers continued to clear land, plant crops, and hunt for meat—even if they had to sneak out at night to do it.

Every morning at daybreak Billy and the other boys took their dogs to chase deer and wild turkey from the corn fields; later in the summer, when the ears were ripe, they had to watch for crows, squirrels, and the occasional hog. It was impossible to keep the coons out of the fruit trees; some would shake the boughs while others gorged on what fell. Once Billy brought down two with a single shot, but others took their place. The boys also had to listen for the bells of the browsing cows and bring them in to be milked. When they weren't working, they liked to gather berries and nuts, flip over rocks in Beargrass Creek looking for crawfish, or whittle sticks with their Barlow knives and boast about what they would do to the Indians when given the chance. Already accurate with rifles, they practiced shooting a bow and arrow or throwing a tomahawk. For all his brave talk, Billy sometimes had nightmares of rattlesnakes, copperheads, and Shawnee warriors.

As the summer of 1781 dragged to a close, the situation at the stations became more dire. The garrison at the Falls ran so low on supplies that men deserted; those who remained were forced to fend for themselves. There simply wasn't enough food or gunpowder left at the fort to make a campaign against the Indians feasible.

In late August George Rogers Clark returned to Louisville after failing to raise enough troops in western Pennsylvania to attack Detroit. A week later word came that about a hundred men under Colonel Lochry, who descended the Ohio a few days after Clark, were attacked by British and Indians as they were cooking breakfast at a small creek ten miles below the mouth of the Great Miami. A lone survivor reported that forty were killed, most after they surrendered, and sixty-four captured. John Floyd called for immediate retaliation; Clark argued that the real problem was with the Miami on the Wabash, but most of the Kentuckians were the Miami on the Wabash, but most of the Kentuckians were obsessed by the Shawnee. Clark declared he would lead them anywhere, no matter how desperate the venture, but the commanders couldn't agree and the troops disbanded, leaving all the Beargrass stations dangerously exposed.

A few weeks later, in mid-September, two couples at Linn's Station wished to celebrate the first legal marriages in that part of the country, so Sam's friend Bland Ballard set out to bring Reverend John Whittaker from Brashear's Station; on the way he came across signs of a war party and went to warn Squire Boone. The people at Painted Stone, who had already lost many of their best men, decided to evacuate. The Jefferson County militia, led by Lieutenant James Welsh, was sent out from the Low Dutch Station to escort them, accompanied by some of Clark's men from Pennsylvania. Because he was still weak from his wounds, and there weren't enough pack horses to carry him and his belongings, Squire Boone, his twelve-year-old son Moses, and a widow and her four children remained behind; the militia promised to return for them the next day. After a few miles Welsh suddenly became feverish; ten men stayed to contrive a litter and tend to him.

Meanwhile the column of settlers, pack horses, and militia got strung out along the trail, known as Boone's Trace. At the main fork of Long Run, they were attacked by about fifty Miami warriors. A few in the front panicked and fled. The rest took cover and opened fire on the enemy. Realizing that their position was untenable, Bland Ballard and Thomas McCarty decided to cut loose the packs, mount the women and children on the horses, and make a dash for Linn's Station about eight miles away. The Hansbury's old slave woman hoisted up her petticoats to run better and hollered, "Every man for himself and God for us all." The retreat quickly became a rout; a few escaped the scalping knife because the warriors stopped to plunder the packs.

The first thing Billy noticed was a cow with an arrow in its side and one horn shot off, looking back in bafflement as it trotted toward the fort. Then he heard distant gunfire and the cries of the women off in the woods. As the fear-stricken survivors staggered through the gate, Billy saw that their bloody clothes were ripped to shreds and that the shock of sudden death was in their eyes.

Floyd was furious when the first militia man rode in without a scratch.

"Where's the rest?" he demanded.

"I couldn't say."

"Have they all been killed?"

"I don't know."

"By God, man, if you've cut and run I'll see you hung!"

John Van Cleve lost his wife and two children. His eighteen-year-old daughter Rachel, who had witnessed the scalping of her older sister Sarah, couldn't speak or stop shivering. The only thing that had saved her from the same fate was the nick-of-time arrival of the militia who had been down the trail tending to Lieutenant Welsh. The widow Holt, whose husband had been killed in May, wept for the death of her children; Thomas McCarty had been shot twice in the face but was still alive; Joseph Eastwood's elderly parents and his pregnant wife were among the missing.

Isaiah Boone, Squire's nine-year-old son—sporting a gold-fringed, three-cornered cocked hat his brother had sent him from Kaskaskia—had accompanied the settlers. George Yount told how he had come upon the boy staring at something on the far side of Long Run.

"What is it?" he asked.

"That Indian's trying to shoot me," Isaiah said indignantly, motioning toward a clay bank.

"Why don't you shoot him?"

"My gun's wet and won't go," the boy explained.

"Where is he?"

"Over there." Isaiah pointed at the spot.

Yount waited until the Indian showed his head and shot him in the neck.

"Now you, boy," he shouted, "throw away your gun and clear yourself."

At first Isaiah didn't want to drop his treasured gun, but as he ran he found he had to. Then he dropped his shot pouch. Finally he hopped on a horse, swatting it so hard to make it run faster that he lost his prized hat, but at last he reached Linn's Station unhurt.

That evening John Floyd asked for a mounted force to bury the dead and rescue Squire Boone and the others, if it was not too late. So many horses had been stolen that only twenty-seven men stepped foward, including Samuel and Sam. Billy watched with pride as they cleaned their guns with a tow cloth, checked their flints, and filled their shot pouches and powder horns. They left before dawn, vowing to bring back the scalps of any lingering redskins. About noon Joseph Eastwood's parents straggled in to Linn's Station with grim news; they had heard a battle raging west of Long Run. Everyone primed their weapons and cast anxious eyes through the loopholes.

"I see Colonel Floyd," Billy was the first to cry out. "He's on Sam's horse and Sam's runnin' beside him, holdin' on to a stirrup."

A pitiful handful of men followed, some on horseback, several of them badly wounded.

"Where's everybody else?" a man demanded.

"Worse and worse, Mr. Campbell," Floyd snarled, his dark face working to control his emotions. "They cut us to pieces. There must have been over two hundred of 'em. They decoyed us at a ravine near Long Run and then ambushed us on the ridge from both sides. We held them off as long as our powder lasted, but then it was every man for himself. I'd be a goner myself, if it hadn't been for Sam here."

"Did you see my wife?" Joseph Eastwood asked anxiously.

"She's dead, Joe. Those execrable hell hounds butchered her. Horrible!"

"Where's Pa?" Billy asked.

"He's dead, boy. I'm afraid they're all dead."

It was true. Billy struggled to underestand; he was an orphan. As Floyd's men rode along in the early dawn, Samuel Wells had spotted Isaiah's hat, picked it up, and slid it inside his hunting shirt. "That's little Boone's," he told Sam, "if I live I'll give it up him," but he had fallen at the first volley. Only ten had returned to tell the tale; a dozen had been killed and five captured, and young Captain Peter Asturgus's life hung by a thread. During the night the Miami had been reinforced by Wyandot warriors led by the notorious Mohawk chief Joseph Brant. Floyd's rangers had been outnumbered almost ten to one. The hero of the day had been Sam, who seeing Floyd unhorsed, unarmed, and limping badly, offered his own mount and ran alongside him all the way to safety. Everyone agreed that it was a noble deed, especially in light of the two men's previous animosity. As a token of gratitude and a pledge of friendship, Floyd gave Sam a hundred acres of land.

Two days later, 300 armed men gathered from all the stations rode out to Painted Stone—where Squire Boone and the others, waiting in agonized suspense, were unharmed—and returned to the horrific scene of the slaughter. They buried the dead, so badly bloated and dismembered that many were unrecognizeable, in a large sinkhole and covered it with stones and tree limbs. They carved the names of the slain on a nearby beech tree.

After Sam's act of bravery, the eligible young ladies of the Beargrass cast admiring eyes in his direction. On December 30, 1781 he married Mary Spear, and they settled into their own cabin at Linn's Station. The orphans of that year's Indian raids were adopted by various settlers; Billy Wells, along with the Linn boys, went to live with William Pope's family at Sullivan's Station. Elizabeth Wells moved to Louisville; Hayden decided to try his fortune in Tennessee.

4

William Pope, like most of the men on the Beargrass, was preoccupied with the buying and selling of land. A melancholy brooder with a taste for Monongahela rye, he was often either too busy or too soused to be bothered by a gang of unruly and rambunctious boys. For the most part, Billy, his friend Johnny Pope, and the Linn boys were allowed to run wild. Old enough now to dress like men in leather breeches and shirts, they often hiked to an inter-linked series of sinkholes nearby known as the Fish Ponds, where the fishing and hunting were good. Billy knew how to skin and gut the game he shot and how to cut and pack the meat to carry it back to the settlement.

The Popes also had a house in town; frequently the boys would visit Louisville and hang out at Michael Humble's gunsmith's shop or watch the soldiers shoveling dirt in an effort to turn Fort Nelson into an imposing stronghold, surrounded by deep ditches and cannon-proof earthen breastworks, topped by a ten-foot picket of sharpened logs. Even more interesting to the boys was the sight of old Mr. Asturgus directing the construction of a seventy-foot-long row galley, which was supposed to float up and down the Ohio and provide a "roof" over Kentucky; in truth, it was more like one moving shingle trying to keep out the rain. The improved fort did protect Louisville; in August, however, after the war in the east had ended, the British and Indians struck Bryan's Station and then slaughtered some sixty of the Bluegrass's finest men at Blue Licks.

To revenge the carnage at Blue Licks, General Clark ordered an invasion of the Shawnee towns. William Pope was named a Lieutenant Colonel; William Oldham, Bland Ballard, and Sam Wells were part of his regiment. The plan called for the troops from Louisville to go up river in twenty boats to the mouth of the Licking, where they would be joined by more frontiersmen from the Bluegrass. Billy and the other boys watched the flotilla set off; for a month everyone anxiously awaited the outcome. Waving a few scalps and showing off their booty, the men returned in late November. The Kentuckians reduced five villages to ashes and rescued a few captives, including a black boy and girl who would be returned to slavery. Seven Shawnee were taken prisoner; Sam swore that one woman was the most beautiful squaw he had ever seen. Other than destroying the Shawnee towns, it wasn't much of a victory; nevertheless Colonel Floyd vowed that the survivors ought to hold a reunion at the mouth of the Licking in fifty years.

Before he left on Clark's campaign William Pope, in a moment of parental concern, announced that he wanted his son Johnny, and any other boys of ability at the station, educated. To that end he hired one William Johnson, at a hundred pounds specie per annum, to provide his paltry batch of backwoods scholars a smattering of learning. Billy squirmed among a row of boys on a log bench, shouting lessons by rote and scrawling simple sentences on slate. The schoolmaster—a sallow-faced man with small, calculating eyes and a wheedling voice—pushed his scholars hard, as if it were his mission to sweat from them the last beads of ignorance by spring. Billy perused *Robinson Crusoe,* cyphered to three, took a stab at spelling, made a goosequill pen, and learned to say, *veni, vidi, vici.* Whenever he faltered he had his palm smacked with a hickory stick

Johnny Pope, easily the brightest of the bunch, had a terrible accident that fall: his arm got caught in his father's cornstalk mill and was so badly mangled it had to be amputated.

"I reckon I won't be fighting any Indians," Johnny, in a characteristically calm and thoughtful mood, told Billy, "but at least I can still read."

A few months later Billy breathed a sigh of relief when the school year was brought to an abrupt end: the teacher, out botanizing in the woods, disappeared. Captured by savages was the assumption, since all that was found were his shattered spectacles.

Hope ran high when the new year arrived. Word came that the British had agreed to a peace. Whether the Indians would comply was the question. In February a war party stole several horses in Louisville; in March they did the same at Sullivan's Station; Billy was heartbroken to lose his dappled gray, a gift from Sam. One April day John Floyd put on the scarlet cloak he had bought in Paris and rode to the saltworks with his brother and three other men. They were ambushed about a mile from Clear's Cabins on the Salt River; Floyd, whose cloak made a perfect target, was shot twice and died of his wounds two days later. They buried him beneath a huge spreading black walnut tree beside his station. At the funeral, George Rogers Clark argued vehemently for one more retributive campaign against the Shawnee and Miami.

The settlers, however, had had enough of bloodshed and wanted to enjoy the fruits of peace. For them the big news of 1783 was the opening of Daniel Broadhead's retail store in Louisville. Here could be found everything from silks, satins, and the finest linens to linsey and broadcloth; there were farm implements and cooking irons; feed, seed, and groceries; china and glassware; furniture and frivolities; sipping whiskey, Madeira, and a good cigar. Customers exchanged prime peltry at John Sanders's "keep" (a covered flatboat stranded further down Main Street) for certificates of deposit, which were in turn accepted at Broadhead's store as currency.

Louisville was becoming a lively place. It seemed as if every other person in town ran his own tavern, one even had a billiard table. There was even talk of building with brick and paving the streets with cobblestones. On Sundays the women in their best bonnets strolled along the shoreline, while Billy and the other boys played marbles and mumblety-peg. The men indulged in rough and tumble wrestling matches, horse races, shooting contests, cock fights, wolf baitings, and gander pulls. The latter, a test of a man's insensate heart and sure grip, involved galloping past a live gander—neck greased, webbed feet tied to a branch—and, in one swift motion, yanking off its head.

In the fall William Pope moved his family to the Pond Settlment about five miles below Louisville. William Oldham, who had married Penelope Pope the previous year when she turned fourteen, lived nearby. Another neighbor was Nacy Brashears and his family, recently arrived from Maryland. One day Billy's vanished schoolmaster William Johnston showed up looking a little worse for wear; he had been ransomed after six months with the Wea Indians and wanted his old job back. Billy didn't relish the thought of more lessons, but at least it gave him something to do during the long winter months. Besides, he looked at his teacher with more interest now that he was a man who had lived among the Indians.

In the spring of 1784 Sam fulfilled his father's dream by establishing Wells Station by a good spring on Bullskin Creek, about four miles west of Squire Boone's Painted Stone Station, which had been rebuilt and resettled the previous year. Billy wanted to join him, but it was decided that he ought to stay with the Popes and continue his schooling, at least until there was a treaty with the Indians.

One day in early March, 1784, Billy Wells, Will and Asahel Linn, and Walt Brashears were camping at Robert's Pond not far from the Ohio River. It was a great place to hunt and fish; there were beaver dams and plenty of geese, swans, and ducks on the water. A light snow had fallen during the night; the boys came upon the tracks of a yearling cub, which they trailed and treed. Billy and Will, the oldest and the best shots, took aim, fired, and the black bear tumbled down. They yelped with delight—the smaller the cub the more tender the meat—and determined to carry their prize home. As Billy was tying a thong of rawhide around the cub's legs, he saw a pair of dark, intent, glittering eyes staring at him from the nearby underbrush. The warrior's face was painted half red, half black. Billy wanted to shout a warning, but before he could make his voice work a tall Indian with a raised tomahawk in one hand stepped forward, gripped him tightly by the wrist, and said, "Howdy-do, howdy-do."

Wild Carrot

When the other boys saw the tall Indian, whose name was The Soldier, take Billy Wells by the wrist, they tried to run. Will stumbled and fell; his younger brother Asahel was seized by Drifting Snow before he could take a step. Walt Brashears, a fleet-footed twelve-year-old, sprinted off at top speed. He made it to the edge of the woods before he was caught and brought back. The Indians named the boys on the spot; Walt was Swift Elk; sturdy but clumsy Will was Little Fat Bear; Asahel, who kept whimpering, was Cat Bird; and because of his red hair Billy was Wild Carrot.

"*Mili, mili!*" demanded Sees in the Dark, who tugged at Billy Wells's hunting shirt and offered in exchange a tattered buckskin vest stiff with crusted dirt that smelled of stale sweat and bear grease. Billy on impulse handed his hat and skinning knife to The Soldier, who laughed and said something to the other Indians that they didn't seem to understand.

The warriors stripped the boys down to their breeches and replaced their shoes with moccasins, fastened buffalo thongs around their necks as a kind of leash, and loaded them with plunder. Fond of Women inspected each one in turn before he asked Billy, "Where from?"

"Louisville," he replied.

"You lie! Too far."

"I ain't lyin'," Billy insisted.

Fond of Women put his left hand on Billy's chest and warned, "You lie, I kill."

Billy eyed the tomahawk in the warrior's right fist and felt his neck shrink.

"We're all from Louisville," he insisted, hoping that his heart would not betray him. He was determined to keep the Indians away from the Popes' house and the Pond Settlement nearby. "We hiked out here to hunt and camp."

"That's right," the other boys chimed in with counterfeit conviction.

Fond of Women paused for a moment, considering his options, before he said, with a loose, lopsided smile, "We go now. Hully."

The six Indians set off at a steady trot, with Swampy in the lead and a warrior following each boy, ready to strike anyone who didn't keep up the pace. Sees in the Dark lagged behind. It was his job to hide their tracks and watch for any clues the captives might try to leave to mark their trail. Before long they reached a creek that flowed into the Ohio River. Swampy waded into the water, bent over, and began tossing rocks on the shore. Suddenly he thrust both arms down and pulled up a hickory-bark canoe. The warriors emptied it, inspected it for leaks, and retrieved some paddles from a hollow log. Then everyone clambered on board.

"No sound, no halm," Fond of Women said.

They paddled down the narrow stream and into the broad Ohio, angling with the current for the mouth of a creek on the Indian side. This time they hid the canoe beside a fallen tree above the bank and covered it with branches and leaves. The warriors retrieved some stashed supplies from a hollow sycamore and added them to the boys' loads. Will had the bear cub strapped to his back; his brother and Walt carried blankets, food, and a cooking kettle; Billy had the heaviest task of all: lugging the extra muskets, wrapped in deerskin and bound with a rawhide cord.

The path they followed led almost due north, away from the river, over a range of hills called the Knobs that were covered with hardwoods and dense underbrush. The moment they entered the forest, gnats, attracted by their sweat, pestered their faces. As they jogged on, up hill and down dale, across creeks and through cane breaks, Billy felt a searing pain in his side and his legs ached. Although he was a tough, wiry kid with plenty of stamina, he couldn't last much longer. Fortunately, when they reached the next ridge, Swampy signalled a halt. The boys, gasping for breath, dropped their loads and sprawled along the trail. Drifting Snow climbed a tall tree and scouted the territory. Sees in the Dark arrived a few minutes later and conferred with the other warriors; apparently they weren't being followed.

"You hungly," Fond of Women asked.

"A little," Billy said.

"You eat by and by."

The boys were given a sip of water from a spring before being loaded up again and prodded with tomahawks to resume the relentless pace. As he struggled up the next ridge, Will, staggering under the weight of his burden, collapsed on the ground, the bear cub flopping down next to him.

"I can't go on," he muttered. Doing his best to put up a bold front, he gestured at his skull and said, "You can kill me if you want."

As Fond of Women gripped his tomahawk, Billy braced himself for the worst. But then Swampy pointed to the dead bear cub and the exhausted lad lying side by side, noting their similarities, and all the warriors laughed. They must have realized that the boys had reached their limit, for they let them rest; when they started again, the warriors carried the heavy loads, following a path only they knew, until the sun slanting through trees told them it was time to stop.

They camped on high ground, half a mile away from the main trail, near a spring. Drifting Snow built a fire with flint and tinder and suspended the copper kettle over it from a tripod of saplings. After fitfully singeing off the fur, he chopped up the bear cub and tossed everything into the boiling water. The Soldier retrieved a wooden spoon from his pack, dipped in, slurped greedily at the stew, wiped the greasy spoon on his moccasin, and passed it over to Wild Carrot.

Billy's stomach was tied in a knot and he didn't think he could eat, but one sip of the broth and he hungered for meat. He scooped out a tasty morsel, wiped the spoon on his moccasin, and handed it back to The Soldier, who grunted in approval. The other boys followed his example.

After the meal The Soldier reached for his pipe tomahawk. Billy couldn't take his eyes off his movements. With ceremonious precision he prepared a blend of tobacco and sumac leaves by rubbing them between his thumb and the edge of his scalping knife. Before filling the bowl, he tossed a pinch into the fire and whispered words of thanks. He lit up with a burning brand, sucked in the smoke, blew it out his nostrils, and sighed in satisfaction. With each puff he seemed to grow more at ease, until his flinty warrior's face, glistening in the firelight, was completely relaxed. Then he handed the pipe to Drifting Snow. In this manner the pipe was passed around the circle, and bowl after bowl was smoked out, while Billy watched in fascination.

This peaceful interlude abruptly ended when it was time for bed. The warriors cut hemlock boughs and spread deerskins for the boys to sleep on, but first each was tightly bound. The leash around Billy's neck, with a small silver bell suspended from it, was tied to a tree; his arms were pinioned behind his back with cords at his wrists and elbows, and his feet were fastened to stakes driven deeply into the ground. The other boys were tethered in the same way. All they could do was look at each other with woebegone eyes, since they knew it would be dangerous to talk.

Transfixed in this constrained position, Billy was sure he wouldn't sleep. Ants and ticks stung him so often he could feel his face swelling. When he jerked his head to shake them off, the silver bell rang and Fond of Women muttered, "*Sehe!* Be still." The Soldier came over and saw at a glance what the trouble was. He returned with a gob of bear grease, smeared it over Billy's face, and pulled his deerskin up to his chin. That didn't drive away the insects, he could still feel them walking on his eyelids, but at least they stung him less. He was in agony. The rawhide at his neck felt like it was shrinking and the cords at his elbows were so tight he feared his ribs would split or his arms would pop their shoulder sockets. The pain intensified until he wanted to scream; then, gradually, his senses blurred and it subsided. He wondered if he'd ever fall asleep. *If I can only twist my head*, he thought, *maybe I can chew through the cord.* It yielded to his teeth with surprising ease, and the bell didn't even ring. By wriggling his hands and arms he was able to free his wrists and elbows. Now it was simply a matter of sitting up to untie his feet. He slipped into the trees without a sound and raced back to the river, which he swam with rapid strokes all the way home, where his ma and pa were standing at the door waiting for him.

He awoke with dew on his face in the morning. His body ached and his feet were lacerated and swollen. The Soldier untied his arms and legs; it took an excruciating effort to stand. He tottered to the fire in a daze and rubbed his sore wrists, hoping that the warmth would loosen his joints. All four boys moved about painfully as if they were arthritic old men. Crooked Mouth came in from the woods holding several dead squirrels by the tail.

"Those don't look like deer," Sees in the Dark said.

"It's true."

"I wanted venison."

"Me too."

"Didn't you see any deer?"

"I missed him."

"A deer is larger than a squirrel."

"He heard me."

"What a shame!"

"Yes, yes."

Billy listened with interest, trying without success to understand what they were saying. He had overheard some Shawnees talking last summer at a prisoner exchange in Louisville; these Indians didn't sound the same.

"Are you Shawnee?" he asked Fond of Women.

"*Lennape n'hackey,*" he replied. "Me Delaware."

"Everybody?"

"He Miami," he said, pointing to The Soldier. "His name Soger."

But why are we heading due north? Billy wondered. He knew from talking with his brother Sam that the Shawnee villages were to the northeast, on the Great Miami and the Mad River, and he thought that the Delaware were east of them on the Muskingum. He didn't know that the tribe had recently accepted a Miami invitation to move west and settle in the White River valley. Anybody trying to rescue him would probably assume he had been captured by the Shawnee, since they were blamed for most of the raids on the Beargrass. If that were true, he was on his own, with no help to be expected. His only hope of escape, if they adopted him and didn't kill him, would be to become Indian—to learn everything they knew and then use those skills to run away. He had no choice but to prepare himself, to win their trust, and wait for his chance.

The countryside they passed through on the second day was as hilly as the first. On the third day the land flattened out and the trees grew taller; occasionally they came to oak openings, where the spreading branches of the huge trees shut out the sunlight and stunted the undergrowth, leaving a clearing. There were streams and swamps and wide stretches of prairie covered with grass higher than a man's head. The game was plentiful and the hunting was easy, so the captives were well fed. Generally they kept to the higher ground, but sometimes they had to cross creeks on fallen logs and wade in flooded bottomlands up to the armpits. At night the boys dried off their moccasins by the fire to avoid "scald feet"—a painful inflammation caused by wet skin rubbing against wet leather.

Because Fond of Women stopped speaking English to the boys, Billy had of necessity to learn some Delaware. He caught on quickly and enjoyed making the strange sounds: *lachpi* meant "quick," *pennau,* "look," and *matta,* "no." He knew the words for food, drink, sit down, be quiet, tie him, I have to piss, and give that to me, as well as the names of the sun and the moon and of many birds and animals. The Indians even taught the boys some songs and amused themselves by making them sing every evening. The warriors laughed when Billy tried to pronounce his new vocabulary; even though he spoke better than the other boys, he often left out or added a syllable that changed the word's meaning.

On the third day they camped by a river the Indians called *Muscatatuck*, where they were met, apparently as planned, by another war party of four Delaware returning from a Kentucky raid with several horses and one prisoner. Abijah Clay, a gaunt, gander-necked man whose Adam's apple bobbed when he talked, had been captured near Big Bone Lick. He had pale-blue protruding eyes and, although he was only in his forties, his hair was completely white. It was clear from the contusions on his face and the way he supported his left arm with his right hand that he was badly off. One of his captors, whose name was Smoke, called him "you son of a bitch," and hit him at random moments with a ramrod swung like a switch. The four warriors had taken three scalps, which they proceeded to scrape and clean, cut into shape, and then mount on slim, limber twigs bent to form circular frames. The finished product was placed by the fire to dry. Billy watched with horrid interest; each was about the size of the palm of his hand: one blond, one auburn, and one almost as red as his own tingling hair.

"That's my wife and my two daughters," Mr. Clay said in an unnervingly matter-of-fact voice. "Only my son escaped."

After they finished, the warriors came over and shook hands. Smoke pulled a loaf of bread from his baggy hunting shirt, broke off a chunk, and offered it to Billy. As he raised it to his lips he couldn't help noticing the faint tracings of a bloody thumbprint.

The warriors and their captives continued steadfastly to the north for several more days. Billy grew stronger as they went on; his body no longer ached and he had a spring in his step. The other boys were also holding their own. Not so Mr. Clay, who had punctured his foot with a cane stub and was limping badly. "Please dear God preserve me," he would cry out on occasion, and Smoke would swat him with the ramrod. The countryside remained the same; dark forests broken by scattered shafts of sunlight and expansive meadows with many watery places to cross.

Early one afternoon the warriors stopped by some ancient mounds and began firing their guns in the air and yelling their high-pitched scalp halloo. In a few minutes a runner came out from the nearby village and was told the good news. Smoke grew animated as he acted out the killing of Mr. Clay's family. Suddenly everybody became busy. Crooked Mouth stripped the bark off several trees to immortalize their exploits on the trunks. When Fond of Women and Sees in the Dark pulled out their scalping knives, Billy thought that his time had come; instead they shaved the boys' hair, leaving only a few tufts at the top, where they fastened hawk feathers. Then they stripped the boys of their remaining clothes and smeared them with vermilion from head to foot. Smoke cut Mr. Clay's hair, too, only he painted him black.

The warriors were meticulous in their own preparations, drawing distinctive designs on their faces and adding trinkets to their ears and outfits. The three scalps, hoisted on a long pole, were carried in triumph. The prisoners were handed deer-hoof rattles and instructed to shake them and sing the words that Swampy repeated. When the mothers, wives, and girlfriends of the warriors arrived, dressed in their finery and covered with brooches, they confiscated all the plunder, including the horses. Finally the whole party, chanting and dancing, approached the village.

The Delaware town, called Chestnut Tree Place, was beside the White River. As the procession came in sight, villagers shouted and dogs howled. Even the babies, strapped to their mothers' backs, screamed with glee. When Billy saw the women and children form two lines that extended to the door of the council house, he knew that they were in for the dreaded gauntlet.

The involuntary smile of a doomed man stretched across Mr. Clay's face. "Please, God, no," he cried. "I can't run."

Smoke pulled him aside and the boys were brought forward.

"Whatever happens," Mr. Clay warned them, "don't stop."

Will went first, and this time he didn't fall. With his stocky body he bowled a few women over as he charged through the crowd that flailed away at him with sticks and clubs. On an unspoken impulse, the other boys took advantage of the confusion to sprint into the melee together. Billy, following advice he had once heard from an old frontiersman, ran in a zigzag fashion, ducking and shoving so that nobody could bring him down with a deadly blow. That cleared a path for Walt, who raced past him at high speed. The smaller, frailer Asahel was able to slip through with relative ease while the others were being beaten. All the boys, panting from their ordeal, reached the council house bloody and bruised, but without serious injury. They collapsed against the far wall and listened to the hideous sounds outside.

Huddled together in a dark corner of the council house they heard the beating of drums, the ecstatic shrieks of the Indians, and the tormented cries of Mr. Clay, pleading with them to let him die. Later that evening three squaws brought food and clothing, cleaned their cuts and bruises, massaged their sore feet with buffalo-bone marrow, and showed them where to sleep. The boys had heard enough about Indian customs to know that they would probably be adopted. They talked into the night about how to make the best of things and learn all they could before they tried to escape. If they weren't careful, they'd surely end up like poor Abijah Clay. The next morning Fond of Women, Crooked Mouth, Swampy, Drifting Snow, Smoke, and about a dozen other Delaware came to the council house and shook hands with the boys. Fond of Women put his hand on each boy's head in turn and said, "Indian." Then The Soldier arrived, and everyone shook hands again.

"Swift Elk, Little Fat Bear, and Cat Bird stay here at Chestnut Tree Place," Fond of Women announced.

"Wild Carrot goes with me," The Soldier said, taking him once more by the wrist. "To Snake-fish Town."

Billy was too shocked by this unexpected turn to speak, but in his parting glance at his friends there lingered the hopeless hope that one day they would meet again in Kentucky.

Vision Quest

1

After a two-day journey through sedge meadows and swampy woods, The Soldier and Wild Carrot arrived at Snake-fish Town, located on the northern bank of the Eel River, six miles above its confluence with the Wabash. When they drew near, The Soldier fired his rifle in the air, shouted that he had come with a captive, and prepared for their entry into the village. Wild Carrot, painted vermilion and with a belt of white wampum draped across his neck, was given a turtle-shell rattle to shake. They walked a narrow path between thickets of black jack and brambles until the wigwams came in sight, wreathed in blue-grey wood smoke beneath the trees. Women and children, brandishing sticks and clubs, gathered to meet him. Wild Carrot's heart skipped and bumped in his chest. If he had to run the gauntlet again, he was done for!

As the crowd parted to form two lines, there was a commotion in the back. All at once a dozen men and women, their mouths smeared blood-red and shrieking maniacally, rushed toward him. One woman grabbed his wampum belt and threw it to the ground. This was the fearsome man-eating society, the *Onsewonsa*, come to claim another victim.

At that moment an imposing old Indian stepped forward; he was wearing a French fleur-de-lis flag as a shawl, a half-moon silver gorget around his neck, and an otter skin turban. "I give this boy his life," The Porcupine said in a commanding voice. "He shall replace my dead son."

Then four girls about his own age seized Wild Carrot by both arms and pulled him down the bank into the river. Assuming that they meant to drown him, he shouted and shoved and tried to squirm away, while the people on shore laughed.

"No halm you," Laughing Eyes said in English. "Go down white, come up red."

The smiling girls sang and laughed as they scrubbed his skin with handfuls of clay and shoved him under the water. He surfaced, spluttering and splashing, and dunked the girls in turn, much to the delight of their audience. When he waded back to shore, after the bath of his life, the wampum belt was returned to his shoulders and he was paraded to the council house.

While The Porcupine, The Soldier, and a few warriors looked on, Two Lives led Wild Carrot to the center of the room, where light streamed down through the smoke hole in the roof, and inspected his head. Not satisfied with what he saw, he dried his fingers in ashes and yanked out some hair, entwining a hawk's feathers, ribbons, and beads in the tufts that were left. With an awl of sharpened bone he pierced Wild Carrot's septum and ear lobes, inserting a silver ring in each puncture. Although he could smell the blood dripping on his chest, the boy understood that now was a time to be brave and not cry out. Next his body was smeared with bear's grease and his face repainted. He was given a new pair of moccasins, with diamond designs in quillwork, buckskin leggings, a mink-skin pouch, a breechclout, a belt, armbands, and a Lyon linen shirt with ruffles at the throat and wrists. The Porcupine led him by the hand to the door of the council house.

"The spirit of my dead son is now free to walk the spirit path," he told the people. "We will celebrate this evening with feasting and dancing. This boy, whose white blood was washed away today, will grow tall and become a great hunter and warrior. We hope that this will happen soon, because already the Big Knives are crossing the Ohio and killing our game. I thank the manitous for giving me a long life and a new son to provide for me and my wife in our old age. If anyone lifts a weapon against this boy, I will strike him down, for he is my son and under my protection."

Thereupon the whole village shook Wild Carrot's left hand with their left hands, Indian fashion, and embraced him with their right arms.

"I am glad you are a Miami now and not a white man," one warrior said to him in English. "Because I hate them with all my heart."

The Porcupine directed Wild Carrot to enter a nearby wigwam, where an old woman named No Nose was swaying from side to side in front of a stick fire and moaning to herself.

"This is our son," he told his wife.

"My son would have grown up to be a good man," she sobbed. "I miss him very much. You must be good like him and I will be your mother."

Wild Carrot sensed that she was muttering something about her dead son. Hand extended he stepped forward, discerning at the center of her round uplifted face in the firelight the reason for her name. She struggled to rise, trying to reciprocate his gesture, but she was too drunk to stand.

2

At dawn the next day The Porcupine awoke him by tapping his foot. Exhausted by the incessant chanting, dancing, and drums of the previous evening, he had slept well. The center of attention, he had danced around the fire himself and taken his first ceremonial puff of Indian tobacco. Remembering, he began to smile; the dried paint made his face as stiff as a mask and his nose and ears stung. He felt another sharper rap and realized that The Porcupine was talking to him. Wild Carrot vaguely sensed that this was a lecture on the duties of being a Miami. Within weeks he would know enough of the language to enjoy these morning exhortations, laced with cautionary tales and sage advice; today all he could grasp from this drone of unknown words was that he was expected to do his best at whatever was asked of him. But first he should run down to the river with the other boys and take a bath.

The Sleepy One and Thin Raccoon eyed him suspiciously as he stepped from the wigwam. They resented all the fuss over this scrawny boy with a freckled face, pasty skin, rusty hair, and blue-green eyes. If he wanted to become a warrior, as they did, he would have to prove himself.

"You walk like a duck," The Sleepy One said, waddling to illustrate his point.

"You're the one that walks funny," Wild Carrot said, turning his toes in until they touched.

"Ducks can't run," Thin Raccoon stated.

"You want to race?" The Sleepy One offered, indicating a place beyond the village where some boys were sporting in the water.

"Sure." Wild Carrot could tell by their gestures what the challenge was and started running at the same time they did.

All eyes were on them as they ran a zigzag route among the scattered wigwams, through an orchard of plum trees, and then across a trampled field of grass to the river's edge, with Wild Carrot a stride ahead at the end.

"I drank too much water," The Sleepy One explained, with a mixture of gruding admiration and sullen resentment in his eyes. "Next time I win."

"We'll see," Wild Carrot said as he rubbed the paint off his face with clay and water.

"My son is the fastest boy in the village," No Nose announced to anyone who would listen. "He can catch deer with his hands."

"You better treat him well, or he'll run away," She Takes Hold cautioned.

"My son will soon be a brave warrior," No Nose insisted. "He won't ever run away."

Wild Carrot's new status as a fast runner did not free him from his domestic chores. Every day he had to gather and stack kindling, tend the fire—stoking it just right so that it wasn't too hot or too smoky—carry water from the spring, husk, shell, and pound into meal the dried white corn that was distinctive to the Miami, repair any damage to the reed walls and bark roof of the wigwam. Many of these tasks were similar to the ones he had helped his mother with back on the Beargrass; only she was often alone, while the Miami women liked to work together, talking and singing. When he was finished he could play with the other boys, whose only job seemed to be to keep an eye on the grazing horses.

"How many winters have you seen, Wild Carrot?" Cold Feet asked one day. The Sleepy One, Thin Raccoon, Sweating, Plays Tricks, and Fooled by Owls gathered near, watching how the white boy who thought he was a Miami would react. Wild Carrot perceived the taunt and responded cautiously. Cold Feet was more muscular than the other boys and had a mean streak.

"Thirteen, brother."

"Me, too, but you don't see me planting pumpkins every morning. I am going to be a great warrior, not a squaw."

"Perhaps we should call you sister, brother," Sweating said, "like Kiss Me, who wears a woman's dress."

Wild Carrot had often seen Kiss Me, one of The Soldier's sons, hoeing corn with the women. He had shown a preference for women's things when he was young; once this was clear, his parents had raised him as a girl. Even though The Soldier was the war chief of the village, he felt no disgrace in having a son who was a white face, since they were known to have special powers. Kiss Me wore his long hair tied in the back, had tattoos on his cheeks, and spoke in a singsong accent as if he were a girl.

"I do what my father, The Porcupine, tells me to do," Wild Carrot said. "He is the headman of this village."

His reply stumped them for a moment, since every Miami boy knew that it was his duty to respect his elders, especially chiefs.

"I obey my father," Cold Feet said. "He told me to stop helping my mother and start training to be a warrior. Last fall I had my vision quest and received my name."

"I want to be a warrior, too," Wild Carrot asserted, bracing himself for the battle that he knew was about to begin.

"You are a girl," Cold Feet sneered. "You do not know how to fight. Go home and help your mother string beads."

Although he had only been an Indian for two months, Wild Carrot knew the art of surprise. He turned, as if downcast by the harsh words, and as Cold Feet stepped forward to hit him in the back of the neck, Wild Carrot spun to the side and tripped him, shoving him to the ground. Then he pounced on him and twisted his arm in a hammerlock, driving Cold Feet's face into the dirt.

"Had enough?" he demanded, but Cold Feet refused to give up until his arm was wrenched so tightly it almost slipped its socket. He screamed in sudden agony and clutched his shoulder. Beads of sweat formed on his forehead and involuntary tears rolled down his face until the pain subsided.

"You cheated," he said with hatred in his eyes. "Next time I will get even."

That was one of many fights Wild Carrot had with the other boys; although he suffered some severe beatings, more often than not his quick wits and wiry agility, as well as his feisty spirit and thirst for praise, enabled him to come out on top. When No Nose managed to learn of his triumphs, she boasted to the village about her valiant son. Inevitably, these victories made enemies. Cold Feet, Sweating, Plays Tricks, and Fooled by Owls resented his success and conspired behind his back; The Sleepy One and Thin Raccoon became friendly rivals, striving to outdo each other and achieve distinction.

All the boys devoted daily hours to mastering the bow and arrow. Since the others had been practicing for much longer than he had, Wild Carrot was at a distinct disadvantage. The Porcupine taught him to steady the arrow with two fingers while a third held the sinew cord taut, to keep his wrist firm at the center of the ash wood bow, to pull with the right arm and push with the left in one intent movement as he sighted along the shaft, and finally to release the arrow smoothly with a satisfying twang. To test their speed and strength, the boys competed to see how many arrows they could shoot into the sky before the first one landed. For accuracy in shooting at a moving object they tried to match the trajectory of a soaring arrow, or a boy rolled a willow hoop and they endeavored to shoot through it. To learn to make quick decisions in battle, one boy would turn his back until the others hid behind trees. Then they would present and quickly withdraw targets for him to hit if he could. The people in the village liked to watch, pick favorites, and gamble on who would win. The Sleepy One, who seldom missed his aim, was the best bet. Sweating, an excellent shot, was even better at throwing a tomahawk. Wild Carrot attained a middling proficiency with these weapons; his consolation was knowing that when they were old enough to have rifles he would show them a thing or two about marksmanship.

In short foot races, Wild Carrot was the fastest, although most of the other boys passed him over longer distances. To improve their speed on land, they snatched butterflies out of the air and rubbed them on their chests; to gain more power in the water they trapped beavers and smacked each other with their tails. Fooled by Owls was such a good swimmer people said he had wood chips between his teeth. All the boys loved to play a demanding game that Wild Carrot suggested: catching the eels, called snake-fish, which gave the river and the village their names, with their bare hands. Once caught, however, nobody wanted the eels, since they were not considered a delicacy.

Wild Carrot quickly learned the art of leg wrestling, too, and engaged in many memorable tussles with Cold Feet and Thin Raccoon. Sometimes they fought sham battles with mud balls and willow sticks, or they painted their faces and practiced stalking each other in the woods. Once they smeared themselves with bear's grease and sneaked up on a wasps' nest; in a rash act of bravado Plays Tricks grabbed it and ran to the river; afterwards the swollen-faced victors compared honorable wounds. They shot blunt arrows at squirrels and crows and set snares for rabbits and muskrats. Cold Feet in particular possessed a sadistic streak and took obvious pleasure in tormenting small creatures. Once with his knife he pried off the beak and poked out the eyes of a crow; then he fastened a thong to one leg and watched it starve. That taught the others, he asserted, to stay out of the cornfields. Sometimes, Fooled by Owls held smoldering coals in his hands and boasted that he was immune to pain.

Both boys and girls were taught to fast and fend for themselves. Many a morning Wild Carrot and his companions were told to blacken their faces and not eat anything until nightfall. This testing would continue until they turned sixteen. Laughing Eyes and the other girls her age daubed a black spot on each cheek when they went without food for a day.

The boys talked excitedly together about the animals and enemies they planned to kill when they became men. In the evening they would go from wigwam to wigwam, listening to The Old Wolf, Looking Over the Top, and other storytellers recount great hunts and battles. The boys couldn't wait for the day their own names would be spoken of with respect around campfires. When war parties and hunting excursions left the village, Wild Carrot longed to go with them. If only he could be a great warrior like The Soldier or a great hunter like He Provides! He rarely thought of returning to Kentucky, instead he dreamed of coming home to The Porcupine and No Nose with bear meat on his back or fresh scalps in his hand. The Porcupine noted with pride the zeal to excel in his son's eyes; perhaps he would soon be ready for his vision quest.

3

One morning The Porcupine told Wild Carrot: "Today I want you to go into the forest and bring me back a live quail."

"Can't I shoot one, Father?"

"No."

"Then how will I do it?"

"That will be up to you. But first I want you to blacken your face with soot and leave your bow and arrow behind. And do not eat until you have done what I asked."

After three days Wild Carrot returned, looking famished, with a live quail in his hands.

"Have you eaten?" The Porcupine asked.

"No, Father."

"Good. First we will talk, then you can eat."

"Yes, Father."

"How did you catch the quail?"

Wild Carrot detailed how it had taken him a day to find a covey of quail, and how he spent the second day chasing them and growing weaker from hunger. Then on the third day he decided to hide in a place where the quail fed and wait for them to come to him.

"You have done well, my son. Now tell me, where did you sleep each night?"

"Beneath a large tree."

"What kind of tree was it?"

"I didn't notice."

"Were there any large dead branches over your head?"

"I didn't look."

"Did you hear birds singing in the morning?"

"Yes, Father."

"Which ones?"

"I don't know."

"Was the land high enough to drain well?"

"I don't know."

"Did you cover your tracks coming home?"

"No, Father."

"Then how do you know that a ghost did not follow you?"

"I don't."

Wild Carrot could see the disappointment deepening in The Porcupine's eyes.

"Did you see anything unusual?"

"Oh yes, Father, I saw a big black bear."

"What was he doing?"

"He was sitting on his haunches making strange sounds."

"What did he say?"

"Say?"

"Yes, you did not speak to him?" he asked eagerly.

"No, Father."

"Did the bear see you?"

"Yes."

"What did he do?"

"He looked at me."

"He did not run away?"

"No."

"And you did not talk to him?"

"No."

"That is unfortunate."

"Why?"

"Why do you think the bear was there? He probably wanted to tell you something. Now he is offended and will say bad things about you to the other bears."

"I'm sorry, Father."

"It is not your fault. You have had the misfortune of being born white and so you do not yet know how to behave. You say the bear was making strange sounds?"

"Yes, Father."

"He might have been singing his medicine song and that is why he did not speak to you."

"I hope so."

"Yes, perhaps that is what happened. You must learn to be more like the fox who keeps his ears up and looks closely at everything— even as he runs away he takes a last sideways glance to remember what he has seen. Before a man goes into the woods he sharpens his knife, his arrows, and his tomahawk. You must learn to sharpen your senses also. If we were not the best people and our country the most beautiful, the Master of Life would not have placed us here in the center of the world. But you must be alert to appreciate where you are. It is not enough to strengthen your body, you must strengthen your mind, too. A keen mind is the source of all true power."

4

That summer The Porcupine taught Wild Carrot how to read the signs and hear the voices that were all around them. If the fish were restless in the water, breaking the surface, and the birds flew low and made no sound, then a storm was brewing. If the leaves suddenly turned, showing their pale undersides, and the doves perched close to the trunks of large trees, then there would be thunder, lightning, and strong winds. The Porcupine always smelled the rain coming; he could hear it too, way off in the distance, before Wild Carrot noticed a thing. From the tightness of the cornshucks, the height of the wasps' nests, the depth of the muskrats' burrows, when the white pelicans flew south, he predicted a hard winter. He inspected the leaves and bark of a tree to find directions. A glance at a deer track told him if it were a buck, doe, or fawn. He could even look at moccasin prints and distinguish the sex, age, and tribe of the person who made them. To learn how fresh the tracks were he got down on his hands and knees and inspected the smallest particulars: a bent blade of grass, some torn moss on a stone, a disturbed leaf.

Wild Carrot listened to him with fascination and absorbed all he could. His white parents, when they were alive, had never taken the trouble to teach him so many useful things. Every day The Porcupine would tell him stories to illustrate the points he was making. Later he would expect Wild Carrot to repeat them. At first he could not do it.

"You did not like the story?" The Porcupine demanded, his face showing the deep furrows of his displeasure.

"No, I did, Father. I liked it very much."

"Then why can you not repeat it?"

"I forgot it."

"Good stories are told to be remembered. Unless you carry a story in your heart, how can you call upon it to help you when you need it? Do you understand?"

"Yes, Father."

He liked best stories about how the cunning fox outsmarted the wolf and ones about the glorious and bloody wars of the past. He also liked tales about the Great Hare, who held the world on his back, and Trickster, who traveled around having funny adventures that explained why the world was one way and not another.

"Once this great island the world was a barren place," The Porcupine said, "there were very few trees and almost no animals. Trickster, with his penis slung over his shoulder, had to walk for many miles to find food. Finally, he came upon a small duck pond, and he told the ducks he would teach them how to dance with their eyes shut. But one dancing duck cried out as Trickster was wringing its neck and warned the flock to fly away. Several days later he came to a prickly shrub with one bulb left.

"'If you eat me,' the bulb said, 'you will get the shits.'

"'Shut up, I am hungry,' Trickster said, popping the bulb into his mouth.

"It tasted bitter and didn't satisfy his hunger. Every time he sneaked up on some small animal, crawling on his hands and knees, a little puff would sound from his anus and scare it away.

"'Even a great man breaks wind,' Trickster said, 'but at least I don't have the shits.'

"As he continued on his way the puffs became stronger and more frequent. He walked faster to escape the smell. When he could not stand it any longer he stopped to build a fire. Then he picked up a burning brand and shoved it where he should not have.

"'I am tired of your singing,' he told his anus, which shriveled up from the searing heat and became pink and wrinkled. The way it is today.

"The next morning his situation was even worse. He began to wish he had the shits to be done with his suffering. Suddenly his desire was granted. He felt a great release and a greater relief, which turned to alarm as what started showed no signs of stopping. When the ooze reached his knees he climbed a tree and clung to a branch. "'Now what do I do?' Trickster wondered. 'I can not go down and there is no food up here. I will either sink or starve.'

"Then he noticed a chipmunk chattering over his head.

"'You look like a fool and you smell bad,' the chipmunk said in his squeaky voice before retreating into a hole in the tree.

"Trickster thought a long time about how to catch that insolent chipmunk and make a meal of him. At last he decided to use the longest thing he had as a weapon; he pulled his penis off his shoulder and stuck it in the hole. Chipmunk didn't want to be squashed, so he took a bite out of the penis. He didn't like the taste so he spat it out. Then he took another bite, and another, and spat them out, too. Trickster felt an excruciating pain at the tip of his penis, but he endured it and pushed harder in order to kill that chipmunk. The pieces that the chipmunk spat out fell into the ooze and turned into grass and flowers, animals and birds. When Trickster looked down he smiled with pleasure to see the earth filled with everything the heart desires. When he saw his bloody stub of a penis and chipmunk laughing at him, he cried. And that is how the world became so beautiful and abundant a place. But that is also why a man's penis is so small."

Wild Carrot liked that story; it made him laugh just to think of it. He decided to tell The Porcupine about Adam and Eve in the Garden.

"The black robes tell that story and it makes no sense," The Porcupine said, scowling. "Forget such foolishness. Apple trees, snakes, beautiful women, and the urge to mate are good things. The white man's God does not understand the wisdom of snakes."

"Why are snakes wise, Father?"

"Because they are at home on or under both earth and water, and when they wish to fly they shed their skins and turn into birds. They curl in a circle, the most powerful shape, and move like a rippling stream. Their tongues flicker and their fangs sting like fire. Snakes know many secrets."

5

In early fall, the Moon of the Hard Corn, squirrels were busy planting trees and snakes turned into raccoons. Geese gathered on the water and debated whether to fly south or become beavers. Some days, when the Great Panther swished his tail, high winds blew, and

Thunder Bird swooped low with flashing claws and scratched the tallest oaks. Wild Carrot had participated in the Green Corn Dance, when the first ears are ripe for roasting, and he had helped No Nose gather in the harvest and store food for the winter. All summer he had proved his mettle and prowess to the other boys; even Cold Feet rarely taunted him. He was now free to go where he pleased; the small children who used to watch him had ended their vigil. He no longer thought of escape. He was a Miami, Snake-fish Town was his home, and Kentucky was far away.

One day The Porcupine told him he was ready for his vision quest.

"First you must purge your body and empty your mind so that you will be receptive to messages from the spirit world," he said.

The Porcupine led him to a low dome-shaped sweathouse by the river that resembled a beaver lodge and ordered him to strip. Once inside, he was handed a cup of bitterroot tea to sip and a bowl of water to toss on the red-hot rocks. As the steam rose from the hissing rocks sweat rolled down his body. The tea made Wild Carrot nauseous, but he remained calm and did not panic. Finally The Porcupine opened the door and told him to plunge into the cold water.

"Crush charcoal from the fire, mix it with bear grease, and smear it on your face and chest," The Porcupine instructed. "That will tell people that you are Nobody on a vision quest. Whoever meets you will act as if you were not there. If you hear anyone coming, hide."

"How long must I fast, Father?"

"Do not hurry. Everything must be done deliberately so that the spirits will see that you wish to become a serious person. On the first night you will hear strange voices—bad birds come to deceive you. On the second the same. But by the third or fourth night, you will receive a sign."

"What kind of sign?"

"That is the mystery. Sometimes the Great Hare or some other important manitou appears, other times something as insignificant as an insect may whisper in your ear. All things that live are our relatives and we never know who will speak to us."

"What will they say?"

"That depends on how pure your heart is. Some men are told what brave deeds they will accomplish and the manner of their death. A few, like Two Lives, are told what they have done in the past. But above all you must be attentive and do as I say, otherwise bad things will happen."

"What sort of bad things?"

"Let us not speak of that. You must find the right place and remain there until a helpful spirit takes pity on you and tells you who you are and why you have been placed upon the earth."

"I hear you, Father."

The Porcupine took his ceremonial pipe tomahawk, the one wrapped in silver wire, packed it with a mix of kinnikinnik, and offered it in the six directions.

"Now I call upon the manitous to help this boy. May the sun and moon in the sky, the standing trees and flowing waters, and all that flies, walks, or crawls watch over him. Give this boy a vision so that he may know his true path."

As Wild Carrot walked through Snake-fish Town, whose lodges and corn fields were haphazardly spread along the river for over a mile, villagers averted their eyes and said nothing. He entered a vast morass that bordered the town, wading in ankle-high muck until he discovered a trail. He had heard from hunters that to the north he would find a land of small lakes, boggy marshes, scattered forests, and tall grass prairies, where wildlife was plentiful. That was his destination.

The sun had dropped to the treetops on the horizon before he came to a large pond, dotted with lily pads and fringed with cattails, where he decided to camp. Because he carried no weapons and was forbidden to build a fire, it was important to find a dry, safe place. He selected a large sycamore sloping beside the water, with a soft bedding of leaf litter and bark duff between the protruding roots at its base. At least he was allowed to bring a blanket, for his hunger pangs made him shiver and there was a chill in the air. The Porcupine had told him he should stay awake as long as he could, so that he would sleep deeply and have profound dreams.

Except for the time he brought back the live quail, his previous forays into the wilderness had been short trips with the other boys. Now he was a full day's hike away from the village and completely on his own. What if something terrible should happen! What if a panther or bear attacked him? What if Potawatomi warriors, who had begun to intrude on Miami hunting grounds, captured and tortured him! A wing beat of fear fluttered in his heart; then his face flushed with shame when he remembered that self-mastery was expected of a brave.

As The Porcupine had predicted, the night was filled with strange noises. Croaking frogs, whirring insects, rustlings in the cattails, interrupted cries from the forest, and then the harrowing scream, which suggested a man being strangled, of a great horned owl. Wild Carrot leaned against the tree and tried to identify each sound above the muffled tom-tom in his chest. Mosquitoes swarmed and pestered, crickets creaked and rasped in the grass, the distant howl of wolves carried across the water, high overhead geese honked as they veered south. Around midnight he fell into a dreamless sleep, only to be awakened before dawn by the unearthly laughter of a loon that seemed to mock him. When the first rays of sunlight appeared a gray ghost of mist lifted above the brown cattails and the songbirds began to whet and sweeten in celebration of the dawn. Meadowlarks warbled, grackles shrieked, thrushes trilled, and sparrows jingled their small change. Occasionally he heard the resonant discords of the trumpeter swan.

At his feet he noticed a small furry ball, that, upon examination, contained tiny bones. Wild Carrot knew what it was. Could that be the sign—the remains of a mouse coughed up by an owl? No, it couldn't be. The Porcupine had warned about bad birds; everyone knew that owls were the sons of witches. Nonetheless, it was a potent omen, so he put it in his pouch.

For the next two days Wild Carrot stayed in his spot and observed the web of life around him. The pond was home to a slew of ducks; his favorites were the wood ducks, whose red-circled eyes and black and white striped faces suggested war paint. He saw a great blue heron wade elegantly into the shallows, stand on one leg as it surveyed its domain, and then with a quick probing jab come up with a squirming frog in its beak. He noted a line of painted turtles basking on a half-submerged log. Over his head gray squirrels squabbled in the branches, furling and unfurling their bushy tails and scolding everything in sight. The increasing heat of the afternoon sun brought swarms of insects and swooping birds to feed on them. Iridescent dragonflies droned and hovered, brightly colored butterflies flitted by on indolent wings, and dying locusts buzzed on the water, their cycle ending. Hawks turned haughty spirals in the sky, humpbacked raccoons scouted the shore for crawfish, and at dusk deer came to drink. Hour after hour Wild Carrot watched, the passing time punctuated by a woodpecker tapping a weathered tree. It was an eat or be eaten world, filled with small, silent kills, but he felt at one with its primordial rhythms of predator and prey. At last he slipped into a semi-conscious state where he thought the silky fluff of milkweed pods that skimmed the autumnal air were spots in his blurred eyes. He felt such a lassitude in his limbs he might have welcomed a gentle death, easing his body back into earth. In the night he dreamt of Trickster, that cunning shape-shifter, carrying a rainbow-colored serpent draped over his shoulder that bit him on the ear. Wild Carrot awoke damp and chilled, as though he were coated with dew, and felt a strange coldness along his left leg. With his eyes still shut against the morning light, he reached out his hand and touched something slimy. He looked down and his heart stopped: a large blacksnake was curled snugly against his body for warmth. Wild Carrot ran his eyes from the creamy blotch under its chin down its sleek scales of glassy satin. The snake wasn't poisonous, but it was the biggest he had ever seen, at least six feet.

Surely, this was his omen! He wanted to speak, but his tongue was a stone in his mouth. Sensing his anxiety, the snake lifted its head. For a suspended moment Wild Carrot stared into an unblinking amber eye; then as quick as a snapped whip, it slithered up the sycamore, disappearing among the branches.

Wild Carrot wasn't sure what he should do. This was the fourth day and something truly unusual had happened, yet no voice had told him who he was. He rose unsteadily to his feet; should he stay or return to the village? Then he noticed something translucent sticking to his moccasin. It was a snakeskin, which, when lifted, stretched from the top of his upraised hand to the ground. The snake must have used the edge of his foot during the night to rub its old skin off. That had to be a sign! He couldn't wait to show this omen to The Porcupine and learn what it meant.

He started back immediately at a rapid pace. The excitement of the encounter with the snake had given him renewed energy, but by mid-afternoon he was so tired and light-headed from hunger he could hardly walk, and Snake-fish Town was still miles away. He tightened the rawhide belt around his waist and doggedly slogged on. When he finally reached the village it was dark. Firelight glinted through cracks in the reed walls of The Porcupine's wigwam.

"Father, I have returned," Wild Carrot said as he pushed aside the bearskin at the entrance.

"I am glad you still breathe," he replied. "Come sit by my side."

No Nose smiled broadly in welcome and handed him a wooden bowl and spoon.

"You must be hungry, my son," The Porcupine said. "Eat first and then tell me what you have seen."

Wild Carrot told of his ordeal and showed him the owl ball and the snakeskin.

"These are powerful signs," The Porcupine said. "Had you only found this one, you would have become a witch and someone would have had to kill you. But the blacksnake is a creature of sacred power. I am not certain from this skin whether you met the one who is the friend of the rattlesnake and squeezes its prey to death, but I think it is the other one, his younger brother, the smartest of all the snakes, who crawls up a tree before it hunts to see exactly where the bird nests are and when their eggs are ready to hatch."

"But why didn't the snake speak to me?"

"Because it had already told you what you need to know by this sign," The Porcupine said, holding up the perfectly preserved skin. "You will walk a winding path, see what lies around the bend, and think twisted thoughts, but always you will be guided by the spirit of the blacksnake."

Wild Carrot felt a surge of pride. He couldn't wait to tell The Sleepy One and Thin Raccoon his new name.

Blacksnake

1

In the Moon of the Big Fire, after the last kernel of corn had been cached, the several hundred people of Snake-fish Town divided into winter hunting parties and dispersed into the surrounding wilderness. It was a beautiful autumnal day with argent clouds scudding across an azure sky. Many headed northwest, for the vast tall grass prairies between the Wabash and the Illinois, to live off the buffalo. Blacksnake's group, led by He Provides, went southeast, toward the hardwood forests along the Mississinewa River, in order to hunt deer, beaver, and bear.

The Porcupine and The Soldier deferred to He Provides, a great hunter with a special power over bears. Blacksnake was pleased that he wouldn't be separated from his friends, Thin Raccoon and The Sleepy One. Cold Feet, Sweating, his younger brother Fooled by Owls, and Plays Tricks went along, too. Now that Blacksnake and the other boys had completed their vision quests, they wanted to prove themselves as hunters. As they walked to their campsite, the girls their age—Laughing Eyes, White Swan, and Sitting Quiet— teased them about who would be the first to bring home big game. Cold Feet, who had gotten his name because he had touched a dead bear's paws, said with certainty that he would be the one.

"Soon you will surpass your father, He Provides," Laughing Eyes said with a wry smile.

Cold Feet realized his mistake. "I didn't mean to boast."

"I think it will be him," she said, nodding at Blacksnake. "What will you kill for us?"

"Whatever the Great Hare, the master of the hunt, offers." Blacksnake knew that his proper answer only sharpened Cold Feet's shame.

"I will dance at your feast." Laughing Eyes smiled playfully.

In the deep woods, dwarfed by the towering trunks, it felt as though they were walking on the bottom of the sea. Ocher and gold leaves, rocking gently as they fell, spiraled slowly down. The air was laden with the lush, almost sickeningly sweet aroma of overripe pawpaws. Everyone got black stains on their hands when they stopped along the path to feast on fallen walnuts.

No sooner had the women completed the sapling framework and shingled on the final slabs of bark than the skies darkened and the rains came. The people huddled around smoky fires inside the six small wigwams that made up the hunting camp and waited for the weather to let up. For three gray, dismal days a hard, cold, lashing rain tore the last leaves from the trees and rattled acorns on the roof. Tan sheets of seething water swept down from the hills, gutting the gullies, overflowing the riverbanks, and flooding the bottomlands. Their only food was parched corn, shelled nuts, and jerked venison. At night the eerie shriek of a screech owl and the melancholy howl of wolves carried through the dark forest. The men spent their time straining deer sinews through their teeth to make bowstrings and fashioning arrows out of hickory. These, too, were clamped in the mouth at the middle and bent back and forth to correct the slightest deviation. When they were perfectly straight they were fletched in a spiral pattern with the feathers of the sandhill crane—the signature of the Miami—and tipped with the appropriate arrowhead.

"Father, when the rain stops, I want to go hunting," Blacksnake told The Porcupine.

"Do you think you are ready?"

Blacksnake bristled at the suggestion he lacked the necessary skills of a Miami hunter.

"I can shoot an arrow, throw a tomahawk, and survive on my own in the woods."

"Do you feel that is enough?"

From listening to the hunting tales told around the campfire, he understood that spotting a target, pulling a trigger, and lugging home bear meat was not what a true hunt was all about. Hunting was not a sport and a pastime for the Miami, but rather a way of life and a system of belief. They had a profound respect for the game they hunted; if they behaved properly before, during, and after the hunt, they would propitiate the spirits of the game and the animals would *willingly* offer themselves to be killed. If they did not, the animals would stay away.

"I know I still have a lot to learn," Blacksnake said. "Will you teach me?"

"Others know more than I do," The Porcupine replied. "That's why I want to go hunting with He Provides."

"He Provides knows a great deal, but who do you think taught him?"

"Tell me, Father."

"His grandfather, Looking Over the Top."

"That blind old man who limps and never speaks!"

"He is not blind. He can see very far when he wishes, especially in his dreams. If you have not heard him speak, perhaps you never asked him a good question."

"Why does he know so much?"

"Because he was raised by the bears."

"Truly?"

"That is what I have heard."

"How strange!"

"In the old days it was common for us to talk to the animals. On occasion a boy would go to live with the bears. Sometimes one of our women would fall in love with a bear and give birth to his children. If you look closely at a bear's footprints, you will see that he is related to us. It is the same with the smartest of the other animals—the beaver and the raccoon—their tracks resemble a child's hands and feet. Most of what we know we have learned from them. The bears taught us what is fit to eat and how to cure diseases. From the beavers we learned how to chop down trees and build sturdy lodges, and from the raccoons how to fish and wash food."

"Who taught us how to hunt?"

"Now that is a good question."

Looking Over the Top lived with He Provides and Walks by the Water and their children. He sat in the position of honor at the back of the wigwam facing the doorway. A pair of small, lens-less spectacles sat precariously on the hook of his large nose; his white hair hung in matted tangles beneath a black silk turban; the drooping loops of his cut ears, bound with brass rings, touched his shoulders. His wife, First Snow, wrapped in a dark-blue blanket, was by his side. She held a turkey-wing fan in her right hand and waved it occasionally in front of his face.

Blacksnake circled around the central fire and sat down. The old man's chin rested above the bear-claw necklace on his chest; his eyes were shut. The only sound was the crackling of logs under the cooking pot. Finally, the boy could no longer contain his curiosity. "Grandfather, is it true that you lived with bears?" he burst out. Looking Over the Top expelled a sudden lungful of air with a kind of woofing sound. "Is that what they say?" "Yes. Is it true?" "That was a long time ago," he replied in a low, hesitant voice. "Everyone else is dead. Who can remember such things?"

Blacksnake didn't know how to interpret that answer, but he sensed that the subject, for now, was closed. There was a long silence until he worked up the nerve to ask one more question. "Who taught the Miami how to hunt?"

The old man turned his head and squinted at him. The boy gazed into a maze of wrinkles. In truth, he wasn't blind, but one eye was filmed over and the entire left side of his face sagged.

Looking Over the Top pulled on his ear lobes and deliberated for an expanded moment before responding in a hoarse whisper, "The panther."

Later that day Blacksnake asked The Porcupine: "Father, how can I learn to hunt from the panthers? I have only seen one once."

"They are very hard to find," he replied. "They are solitary and secretive and do not like human beings. They do not even like each other. The old males sometimes kill their own kittens."

"I have seen their prints in the woods; could I trail one to its lair?"

"You would find it empty."

"I could wait."

"He would not return."

"Then how?"

It puzzled Blacksnake why he should have to locate an animal as rare and elusive as the panther to learn how to hunt a creature as plentiful as deer.

"You must not seek the panther where it is but where it will be."

"How can I know that?"

"By thinking panther thoughts."

"I do not understand."

"Remember how you caught the quail. To see a panther, you must become one."

Blacksnake pondered The Porcupine's words for a long time before he spoke again.

"It has been raining hard for several days and I am very hungry for meat."

"What kind of meat?"

"Venison."

"Where will you go?"

"To a field at the edge of the forest where the deer are feeding."

"When?"

"Tomorrow morning, just before dawn."

"That is good, my son."

"Will you come with me?"

"No. This you must do alone."

2

Blacksnake set out that afternoon in a steady downpour, following a ridge beside the roaring waters of the Mississinewa River. He knew that a soggy day, when sounds and smells were vague, was the best time to move undetected in the forest. Just before dusk, after passing a prominent limestone ledge, he veered north until he came to a grassy area that was part muskrat marsh and part meadow. The Cat, the father of Sweating and Fooled by Owls, had suggested the place to him. He checked the wind and made his way around to the southeast side, where sheets of rain gusted into his face, and found shelter beneath a huge fallen tree tilting from its stump. The storm eased at dusk and changed into a light drizzle. The boy waited and listened to the dripping leaves. A water-soaked possum waddled by, totally absorbed in following its own pink nose.

Before dawn, Blacksnake crawled up the slanted trunk to the spot, about eight feet above the ground, where the tree had snapped. He pressed himself against the moss-slick bark, with only his head protruding, and waited. A thick clinging fog, like milky paste, hung in the air. The first gray glimmer of light enabled him to descry the shapes of several deer feeding in the grassy field. One by one they lifted their heads, ears wide and tails swishing, and nosed the breeze for messages. The only sounds were the twitter of songbirds celebrating a new day and the far cawing of crows.

Then Blacksnake noticed a slight commotion among a dark knot of vultures in a bare tree. What had they seen? He scanned the meadow's edge. Twenty feet from where he was hidden, a big chestnut-brown panther crouched in the bushes, the black tip of its tail twitching. Its upraised head, surprisingly small for its body, was focused intensely on the nearest deer. The boy was close enough to see the cat nervously working its front claws in the earth, in anticipation of the kill.

When the panther began its final stalk, its movements were so slow they were almost imperceptible. Although the ground was damp enough to muffle footsteps, Blacksnake was sure that on a dry day not a leaf would have crinkled. The big cat, belly to the ground so snugly that its elbows showed above its back, shifted its weight from paw to paw with such smooth precision that it seemed to pour itself from place to place. At mid-step it would freeze, sometimes with one curled paw suspended in the air, before it crept closer. Like all good hunters the panther knew the importance of stealing up to the keen-scented deer from the leeward side.

Suddenly with a blurred burst of speed the panther made a prodigious leap toward its unwary prey. The deer snorted in surprise and sprang straight up in the air, while the rest of the frightened herd high-scutted away. A second leap propelled the cat almost onto the deer's back—one large forepaw tore into a shoulder and the other gripped and twisted its head—as its teeth sought the neck. Blacksnake heard the spine snap before the deer hit the ground. With one swift swipe the panther ripped open the deer's belly and the prismatic entrails slithered out. These were scarfed up, the big cat growling all the while in satisfaction.

Next the panther dragged the gutted deer back into some bushes almost directly under the trunk of the fallen tree where Blacksnake lay in hiding. The stench of death wafted up to him. Wouldn't the panther catch *his* scent? If so, he was in trouble; his bowstring was tucked away in his hunting pouch to protect it from the rain. His other weapon was a knife, but spread-eagled as he was on his belly, it was hard to reach. Before today, he would not have thought it possible to move so stealthily or kill so quickly. Was that what The Porcupine and Looking Over the Top had wanted him to know? Having seen it for himself, he was sure he would never forget.

He was enough of a Miami to believe that it had not been merely fortuitous that the panther had come to this place. Surely the spirit master of the big cat had looked favorably upon him. All at once he felt an irresistible impulse to speak.

"Thank you, Great Panther, for teaching me how to hunt," he said softly, his voice breaking.

The big cat jerked its head up, fixed the boy with its fiery yellow eyes, bared its fangs, and hissed. The boy felt his heart lurch and thud in his chest as they exchanged a long stare. Then the panther snarled from deep in its throat and slipped as silently as drifting smoke into the underbrush.

3

When Blacksnake returned, He Provides announced that it was time for all the boys to assist the men. Blacksnake was elated—at last he would get to hunt with the hunters! After smoking for a long time in his wigwam and drawing pictures with sticks in the dirt, The Old Wolf, father of The Soldier and The Porcupine, predicted that many deer were in the area. It was the height of rutting season, so He Provides removed the musk glands from the hind legs of a doe that had been slain that morning and rubbed the scent on the boys' moccasins. He used the hanging carcass to show where to aim to kill quickly and he talked to them about the duties of a good hunter. As he put a small bag of magical animal charms around Blacksnake's neck, he told him to pretend he was merely taking a walk in the woods, since thinking too intently about one particular prey might spook it. Although each person carried a ration of parched corn, no one ate before they started out, because hunger sharpened the senses.

That night a golden full moon emerged from behind the departing rain clouds, casting a lambent glow through the bare trees. The sodden leaves made no sound under their feet. They walked in single file, stepping in each other's footprints, until they came to a clearing. He Provides took a set of antlers from his hunting bag and at intervals clashed and scraped them together. The hunters, hidden behind trees, waited. After a while they heard the snapping of twigs. Then a strange bellow followed by a series of grunts made them stir uneasily. Suddenly a surprisingly large shape charged arrogantly into the clearing. This was not a buck but *wapiti* himself, a bull elk in must, with his nose held high in regal disdain, his enormous neck thrust out, and his magnificent branching antlers swept up and back over his head. Reeking from the stinking mud of his wallow, the elk stamped the ground and bugled out a defiant challenge.

He Provides nudged Blacksnake, indicating that it was his shot. The boy put an arrow in his mouth, nocked another to the string, and pulled the bow taut, aiming along the shaft. The moment the elk turned sideways, he let fly. The arrow sunk up to the feathers in its side and the great beast dropped. While the other boys looked on with undisguised envy, Blacksnake approached the fallen animal, whose legs were still twitching, and touched the tip of an arrow to its eye to be sure that it was dead. Then he motioned to He Provides and said, "Father, skin your elk."

The men nodded in approval; this boy had been well taught and the appearance of the elk was a powerful omen. He Provides thanked him and stepped forward with his skinning knife. It was the end of the rutting season for elks and the old bull was spent; sperm dripped from his belly. To signify the importance of the occasion, He Provides cut the elk's throat and smeared blood on the boys' faces. Then he removed the heart.

"Eat this," he said as he offered it to each boy in turn. "It will strengthen your spirit."

Blacksnake looked uneasily at the still warm morsel that seemed to quiver in his hand; the tart, gamy taste made his cheeks tingle.

Later that evening The Soldier killed a fat buck in the same way, and at dawn they surrounded a small meadow and shot five does. Blacksnake and Thin Raccoon had to run back to camp to get horses to carry all the meat. That evening, after making offerings of thanks, they feasted on roast shoulder of venison with sweet corn, root soup, and sassafras tea. Blacksnake felt a surge of pride when The Porcupine placed the antlers of the elk on the roof of his wigwam and Laughing Eyes danced with the other women in his honor.

During the two moons named for the buck, Blacksnake and the other boys hunted with the men. He Provides taught them to recognize the distinguishing prints, scats, and signs of the various animals and how to stalk them with a slightly stooped walk, stepping softly and stopping frequently to look, listen, and check the wind with a moist finger. The trick was to keep one eye on the tracks at your feet while the other scanned what might lie ahead. When visibility was poor, he taught them the art of looking sidewise or cupping the hands around the eyes for better focus. To lure predators, they learned to imitate the bleat of a fawn and the plaintive whine of a dying rabbit. Before long they understood the habits and habitat of the game so well that they knew when and where to hunt.

Deer, for example, stayed in one locality—feeding in meadows on the edges of forests at dawn and dusk, usually drinking at the same spot, and bedding down in the underbrush during the day. Blacksnake didn't always bring down the deer he aimed at—killing the elk with one shot had largely been luck. Sometimes he missed completely or wounded his prey with a paunch shot. Then he would face the dangerous task of trailing the wounded buck or doe into the thickets. Above all, Blacksnake learned to respect the animals and to give thanks after each kill. Whenever he brought game back to camp, he was praised and the carcasses were hung on sapling racks to drain. The deer were fat this time of year and their fur was thick for the winter. The women cured the meat they didn't cook and made a paste of the deer's brains to soften and tan the hides.

Beaver was another preferred dish. Once a good pond had been found, the men would tap the dam, smash the lodges, and tomahawk the inhabitants. None were allowed to survive and spread the alarm. Even after a beaver feast—the tail, boiled or roasted, was a delicacy—when the last tidbit had been sucked from the last rib, the bones were carefully gathered and buried. It was forbidden to throw them in the water lest the spirit of the beaver warn the others. The growing piles of deer and beaver pelts at the camp would be traded at Vincennes or Kekionga in the spring.

Some days they hunted for duck, geese, quail, and other waterfowl along the river. The wild turkey were easy to shoot from their roosts in low branches; some were so fat they split open when they hit the ground. One day so many pigeons flew overhead they darkened the skies for hours. The women and children fished along the banks of streams, snared rabbits and muskrats, and gathered nuts and roots in the wetlands and forests. Because of the constant feasting, Blacksnake became drunk on wild meat. The smell of roast venison made him dizzy. He loved the taste of duck that had been slathered with a layer of clay and then baked in the embers, or wild turkey stewed in raccoon fat, or goose turned on a spit and basted with its own drippings. He even preferred deer guts boiled with frogs in a broth to the bland hominy he had eaten in Kentucky. And he knew that when winter came and the venison lost its savor, it would be time to go after bear.

4

One morning Blacksnake awoke to find the tree branches sparkling like crystal and the streams ice-tight. For two days a silver rush of snow fell, followed by frigid weather. Curled leaves clawed across the snow crust; bare trees, buffeted by grim blasts of artic wind, creaked in the night. Often a deer, browsing on whatever greenery was left, would bog down in a snowdrift; a hunter could walk up to the floundering animal and slit its throat. Everyone soon tired of eating lean venison that tasted like pine needles. Even though their ponds were frozen over, the beavers still weren't safe. The men would cut a hole in the ice near their lodges and snatch one out by its hind leg when it came up for air. Unfortunately, Night Stander, the father of Thin Raccoon and Laughing Eyes, grabbed a front paw by mistake and lost a finger.

"That is a bad sign," The Porcupine said. "It is time to change the hunt."

"Last night I dreamed about bears," Looking Over the Top announced.

"I hunger for dark meat," Two Lives added.

"Good. Tomorrow we will go to look for The Old Man of the Woods," He Provides said. His remarks met with a murmur of approval, since he knew the secret names of the bears and how to find their dens. After gorging on acorns all fall, the bears would be rolling in fat and their meat would be sweet and juicy.

He Provides asked the boys to stay behind so that he could instruct them. Blacksnake thought he already knew about bears; occasionally in berry season he had seen them shambling along; and hadn't he and his friends in Kentucky, on the day they were captured, killed a cub? Once in the fall he had followed a bulky fellow, who moseyed about, puttering here and there, thrusting his muzzle under overturned logs and stones to grub for bugs and beetles. He watched him cuff a crumbling stump to shreds and lap up a swarming nest of ants with his long pink tongue. Somehow the bear knew he was being observed. He rose erect for a moment, caught a whiff of man-tainted air, and lumbered off, his broad rump wobbling, into the undergrowth. In Blacksnake's experience, all bears were cowards, and that's what he told He Provides.

"Do not be so sure," He Provides cautioned. "I have hunted The Shaggy One all my life, but I never know what he will do next. Remember, he is superior to us in many ways: he is stronger and faster; he has the power to cause and cure disease; he can live all winter without eating."

"How?" Blacksnake asked.

"Everyone knows he sucks on his paws, one a month," Cold Feet said, glad for the chance to show up his rival. Although they had stopped fighting, there was still bad blood between them.

At first Blacksnake thought that Cold Feet was deceiving him, but He Provides assured him that what his son had said was true.

"Once the bears were bigger and stronger than they are now," He Provides continued, "and they ate us for food. A long time ago we went to war and fought them in battles until they asked for peace. That is why they are afraid of us and run when they see us coming;

but some rogue bears are in these woods that never surrendered and will kill us if they can."

"How do I know when a bear is dangerous?" Blacksnake asked.

"Most bears are big bluffers," He Provides said. "They huff and bluster and smack their paws on the ground, but they only pretend to attack. Sometimes they pick on the smallest person, so you boys must be ready. Be firm and show no fear; they will back down."

"What about the killer bears?" Blacksnake asked, troubled by He Provides's remarks.

"They don't bluff. They will ambush you if they get a chance, and if you meet one he will look you in the eye and charge. Do not run, he is too fast, and do not climb a tree for he will pull you down. Stand your ground and use whatever weapons you have. If you have a bow and arrow, aim for the mouth; if you have a tomahawk, crush the skull; and if you have a knife, stab for the heart. But you must know that these bears are hard to kill."

"If a bear comes after me," Cold Feet asserted loudly, "I will bite off his nose!"

"I hope your big words were not heard in the forest," He Provides said, scowling at his boisterous son. "The Shaggy One has very keen senses. We have a saying:

A pine needle fell:
An eagle saw it.
A deer heard it.
A bear smelled it.

When you go looking for a bear he will know about you before you know about him. We have another saying: *If you seek the bear, prepare to bleed.* The Old Man of the Woods is very strong of life; you must be the same if you wish to hunt him on his home ground."

He Provides led the boys to a sweat lodge built especially for the occasion. Looking Over the Top was already inside, grimacing and groaning as he struggled with the spirit master of the bears. When they were drenched with sweat, the boys were told to plunge into the river and stay submerged for as long as possible. The shock of the freezing water almost stopped Blacksnake's heart. He clung to a root on the bottom so that the current wouldn't pull him under the ice. *I must be strong of life, like the bear,* he vowed, as he tried to kindle within himself a spark of warmth. When he finally surfaced, He Provides, who had sat on the bank and smoked his pipe during his ordeal, told Blacksnake not to eat anything before the next day's hunt.

He Provides had already scouted out likely dens. Sometimes a bear holed up in an old tree, or inside a hollow log, or amid the tangled roots of a blow-down. Others hid in crevices beneath rocky ledges or snuggled into small caves in the limestone cliffs along the river. A few lazy souls simply scooped a shallow cavity in the earth and covered themselves with fallen leaves.

About mid-day The Soldier spotted a breathing hole concealed beneath a jumble of boulders. Blacksnake and the others formed a semi-circle facing the opening. Although they were all armed with bows and arrows, and some of the men had guns, He Provides insisted on hunting bears the traditional way—with a tomahawk and a knife. The plan was to rouse the lethargic animal from his winter torpor, lure him out of his den, and then, while the others distracted him, He Provides would dispatch him with a blow to the skull or a stab in the heart.

"Come out, Grandfather," He Provides said. "We have found you and it is time."

They heard a low grumble and what sounded like a stifled sneeze. Suddenly snow flew in all directions as a burly black bear rumbled into their midst, looking groggy and grumpy. He was panting heavily, with a kind of whistling snuffle, and he weaved his large head back and forth trying to make sense of what he saw. At that moment Blacksnake became aware that the bear's beady eyes were staring directly at him. The bear chomped his jaws, making an unnerving popping noise; then he let loose a resounding "woof," lowered his head, and charged. In spite of what he had been told, Blacksnake instinctively spun around and sprinted away in panic. He had raced fifty yards before he realized he wasn't being chased. When he stopped and looked back, he saw to his burning shame all the others gathered around a dead bear in the snow. They glanced down the slope to where he stood alone and laughed at him.

He Provides kneeled on the right side of the dead bear and placed his left hand on its neck.

"I am sorry I had to kill you," he said. "Do not think badly of us. Our women wanted the warmth of your coat and our children wished to feel your strength inside of them. We are honored that you came to meet us and we promise to treat you with respect. Ask your spirit to tell your relatives to come to us also. They will be welcome."

Six of the men hoisted the big bear on their shoulders. Blacksnake trailed behind, with his head hung low. No one had spoken to him since he had disgraced himself. He knew that Cold Feet, in particular, was gloating over his failure of nerve.

"We have a visitor," The Soldier shouted when they reached the outskirts of the camp.

The carcass was propped up in a sitting position before He Provides's wigwam. Looking Over the Top, The Old Wolf, and The Porcupine, their aged faces animated with strong emotions, were the first to inspect it. The Porcupine passed a tobacco pipe among the men; each one blew some smoke into the bear's nostrils. The wives of the hunters came forward, grasped its forepaws, and asked its pardon. After that, Looking Over the Top addressed the dead bear:

"Do not be afraid, Grandfather. We are about to prepare a great feast in your honor that will enable you to join the spirits of your ancestors. My grandson He Provides, the best hunter among us, is the worthy man who slew you, and I, Looking Over the Top, who am known to your people, will eat your heart. We love you and respect you, none of our dogs will touch your bones, we and our children will never forget you."

He Provides then punched out the bear's eyes with his knife, chopped off its head with his axe, made a slit at the chest, and stripped off the glossy hide, taking care to preserve the chin skin, tongue, and claws. Blacksnake was amazed to see how closely the corpse of a bear, once the fat and fur had been removed, resembled a barrel-chested, short-legged man. Perhaps bears and human beings were related. *Why did I run?* he thought with shame. *Somehow I must redeem myself!*

Next the women prepared a feast of roast meat dipped in bear grease. Looking Over the Top was given the heart, the men shared the head on a birch-bark platter, Blacksnake and the other boys ate the brisket, and the women and girls shared the flanks. The leftovers were tossed in the fire to feed all the dead hunters and the skull of the bear was scraped clean and hung in a nearby tree.

Later that evening The Porcupine motioned for Blacksnake to sit beside him.

"I am ashamed," Blacksnake said. "He Provides warned us that the bear might bluff a charge, yet I ran away and the others didn't."

"Every man feels fear—you need not be ashamed of that—but you are a Miami and you must act bravely. To be a hunter and a warrior, the first battle you must win is with yourself."

"I hear you, Father."

Cold Feet and the other boys were willing to give Blacksnake a second chance—but should he turn tail again he knew they would be merciless.

A few days later the hunters headed for part of the Mississinewa River where bears often hibernated in caves along the banks. Before long The Cat spotted a fissure in the rocks. He Provides bent over the opening and called three times for the bear to come out.

Nothing happened.

"The Old Man of the Woods is in there," He Provides said.

"Someone should go in and get him out," Two Lives suggested.

"I will," The Soldier offered.

"You are too big," He Provides said.

The hunters stared at the small black hole. Blacksnake knew that his opportunity was at hand; he had to struggle to make his voice work. "Let me," he finally stammered.

The men understood and made no effort to dissuade him.

"Go slowly," He Provides warned, giving Blacksnake a lighted torch. "Smoke him out."

The boy took the torch, squeezed into the crevice, and began crawling down the dark, muddy passageway. The space was so cramped that, should the bear decide to come out, he would find Blacksnake in the way. Flickering light from the burning brand revealed solid rock ahead. Apparently the cave was empty. What should he do now? As he paused to consider, he heard a faint sigh, as if someone were lightly wheezing. What was that? He inched ahead on his belly. When he was almost at the back of the cave he realized that it took a dogleg to the right. He eased his head around the corner and scrutinized the blackness. He heard a mumbling sound, almost like a cat purring, and then a faint whimper followed by another long sigh. As his eyes adjusted to the semi-dark, he made out the shape, a few feet away, of a recumbent mother bear. Snuggled beside her were two roly-poly cubs, covered with fluffy, down-like fur. They tussled and tumbled—showing their pink feet and noses, their pale blue eyes—without waking her.

Then, all of a sudden, she was awake, looking at Blacksnake with drowsy interest.

He froze and avoided her gaze. For a moment he thought she might doze off again, but then she made an uneasy, chuffing sound and shifted her weight. Blacksnake thought she must have heard his heartbeats, but probably what aroused her from her deep sleep was the odor of smoke from his sputtering torch. She sniffed the air, huffed an order that the cubs seemed to understand, and trudged out of the cave with the cubs toddling behind. Blacksnake lay gasping in the mud, trying to catch his breath from the weight of the mother bear's big paws on his back. She and the cubs had walked right over him without stopping.

When he emerged from the cave, once again he saw the hunters dancing with excitement around a dead bear, but this time the men looked over at him with admiration. Even Cold Feet, who held high a whining cub by the scruff of its neck, could not conceal his envy.

5

For the rest of the winter, during the appropriate moons, they hunted mainly for bear. Blacksnake never ceased to marvel at He Provides's uncanny ability to close in on a distracted bear from its blind side and plunge his long knife into its heart. Sometimes the wounded beast would bawl and sob in pain (when that happened He Provides would scold it for behaving badly), or swipe viciously at the nearest hunters; usually it would simply slump down and die on the spot. The other men were not afraid to stand their ground and sink a tomahawk into an angry bear's skull, but no one else attempted to kill a cornered bear with only a knife.

Blacksnake and the other boys compared scratches and hoped for scars. Cold Feet, who proudly displayed bear cub cuts on his arm, still sulked because he knew he wasn't the one who had crawled into a bear's den. As the son of He Provides, he was determined to excel over all the other boys as a hunter. One day in early spring Blacksnake, Cold Feet, and Thin Raccoon came upon a glistening pile of fresh bear scat. It was dark and runny and smelled foul. On closer inspection they noticed bone splinters and strands of hair. Clearly, this was a big bear that had been feeding on carrion. Although they had been told not to hunt for bear alone, the boys followed its tracks. The spice of danger added zest to their pursuit. At a tree with claw marks ascending the trunk, they looked up and saw the bear blissfully sprawled lengthwise on a large limb, paws dangling.

"Climb up and get him?" Cold Feet suggested.

"You are the brave one," Blacksnake taunted back.

The bear became aware of their presence and sought refuge in a bushy nest in the crotch of the large tree. This cowardly behavior gave the boys courage.

"Come on down, you old bear," Cold Feet shouted. "This is your day to die."

"That is not the proper way to speak," Thin Raccoon said. "I'll bring the men."

"Tell them not to forget their skinning knives," Cold Feet called after him.

The bear poked his head out and glared irately at the two boys. Cold Feet circled to get a better shot and fired an arrow that hit the bear in a haunch. Before their astonished eyes the bear skid hind-first down the trunk in seconds. Once on the ground he twisted back on himself, snapping at the feathered shaft in his hip. The huge bear surged to his hind legs and waved one forepaw in front of his tan snout while he held the other over his heart as if to protect it. He was a scarred old warrior, with a torn ear, a chipped tooth, and a nasty, J-shaped gash on his brow.

Cold Feet fired an arrow that pierced the bear's side. Eyes blazing, the beast dropped to all fours. He chomped his jaws, clacked his teeth, and made loud, blowing sounds. His upper lip curled exposing long incisors, his neck hairs bristled, and his ears flattened. Suddenly he ripped out an explosive woof that almost lifted the two boys out of their moccasins and charged. Before Cold Feet had a chance to shoot again, the bear was on top of him, raking his chest with his claws and sinking his teeth into his thigh.

"He's caught me," Cold Feet cried out. "I'm dead."

Blacksnake ran forward and threw his tomahawk with all his might at the bear's forehead, but the weapon merely glanced off. The bear pinned Cold Feet to the ground with one big forepaw, fastened his teeth in his thigh, and tore at the flesh. Blacksnake saw a bright red spurt of blood and knew the boy was done for. With shaking hands he nocked an arrow to his bowstring and aimed for the bear's rib cage. The shaft sunk home, but the beast didn't go down. Instead he rolled to his feet and came after Blacksnake. A swipe of the bear's paw and the boy slammed face-first to the ground. Blacksnake heard the bear's hoarse, labored breathing in his ear and felt sharp teeth scraping the back of his skull.

What a horrible way to die, he thought, and yet he felt no pain.

His mind was clear and his senses were keen. He smelled the bear's rank outrageous stench as he reached for his knife. He knew that he should stay on his belly to protect his guts, but in that posture he couldn't fight back. Then the bear bit him on the buttocks, shook him like a rag doll, and effortlessly flipped him over. For a moment they were face to face; Blacksnake saw bloody slobber bubbling in the bear's mouth. In desperation he thrust his knife into the bear's chest with one hand while he tried to push away its dreadful snout with the other. The bear moaned like a man with a mortal wound, coughed up a gout of blood, and collapsed on top of him.

Blacksnake was still lying prostrate beneath the dead bear when Thin Raccoon and the hunters arrived. Although he was covered with blood, both the bear's and his own, his wounds were not severe. Blacksnake looked with shock and remorse at the mangled body of his fallen rival, who was barely conscious. "I killed the bear," he told him, as if that justified everything.

"He attacked me first," Cold Feet mumbled in reply, grimacing as he tried to smile. "I saw you try to save my life."

He died a few moments later in his father's arms.

The bear was declared an evil-minded renegade and burned on the spot without ceremony. Cold Feet was carried back to the hunting camp to be buried in the proper fashion, so that his spirit could slip into the forest and be transformed into a bear. Perhaps some day, The Porcupine told Blacksnake, Cold Feet would return to the Miami and tell them what he had learned.

Warpath

1

One day in the summer of 1788 The Porcupine informed Blacksnake that his education as a Miami was almost complete. He told him to blacken his face one more time and helped him build a reed hut a few miles from the village.

"My son," he said, "I am happy I have lived to see you reach this day. All the manitous of the earth and sky have been observing you for many moons and they will reward you for following the advice I have given you. Stay here and fast until I return."

It was June, the month when the whippoorwills fly over and the fawns chase each other in the oak openings. Blacksnake performed his fast calmly, with practiced discipline, tightening the thong around his waist each day and paying close attention to his dreams. Thin Raccoon and The Sleepy One had gone through the same process in the previous months, so he knew what to expect.

Seven days later The Porcupine came for him, bringing the group of friends and relatives that composed their winter hunting band. They led him to the village, where his black paint was washed off in the cold waters of the river. A great feast had been prepared in his honor. They all stuffed themselves heartily except Blacksnake, who, to break his fast, was served small, specially prepared portions in a separate wooden vessel.

After the meal, The Porcupine handed him a looking glass and a bag of vermillion paint. "Now you are a man," he said, "with all the rights of any other man in our village. You are free to do what you want and go where you want."

The Porcupine looked at him so meaningfully as he spoke that Blacksnake understood that he could, if he wished, return to Kentucky. He hesitated only a moment before he responded, "Father, I want to walk in the footsteps of the warriors."

The Porcupine scrutinized him closely for a long time in silence.

"No one in this village would ever ask you to shed the blood of the Big Knives. I am a man of peace and I do not believe that we

can win this war. We are too few and they are too many. But
sometimes a man must fight, even though he knows in his heart he
will lose. Do you understand?"

"Yes, Father." Blacksnake understood, better than most of the
Miami, how hopeless the situation of the Indians was; but he also
knew that his years among them were the most intense and
rewarding of his life; they had adopted him fully, shared all they had
with him, and praised his accomplishments; he had reciprocated by
accepting their ways.

"In the old days you would follow your first warpath south,
against the Chickasaw, and you would come back with a fresh scalp
and tell us how you got it. But we have decided in council to stop
raiding our old enemies and only fight the whites."

"I hear you, Father," Blacksnake said. "I know what I must do."

"You are already a good hunter for our village. Two winters ago
I gave you a gun, and you have shown that you can shoot better than
anyone else. But there is more to killing men than killing animals,
and these things are not for me to teach you. That is a job for my
brother, The Soldier, and my wife's brother, Two Lives. I will see
what they have to say."

Blacksnake already knew the basic duties of a Miami warrior.
He had watched war parties return with scalps and prisoners, some to
be adopted, others painted black and burned at the stake; he had
spent hours around camp fires listening to The Old Wolf and others
tell of the heroic battles of the past; and he had heard many a warrior
sing the song of his deeds. Most importantly, he knew that Laughing
Eyes would not wish to marry a man with no scalps to his credit.

2

The Miami had a long history of fighting with the other tribes, as
well as the French, the English, and the Americans. In the mid-
seventeenth century, the Senecas of the Iroquois confederacy, armed
with English muskets, had swept west seeking new hunting grounds.
Shouting their dreaded war cry, "We have come to drink your
blood!", they annihilated the Erie, decimated the Illinois, and pushed
the Miami to the far side of Lake Michigan. There, armed with
French guns, the Miami regrouped and fought back. Blacksnake's
favorite war story, which Looking Over the Top would recite in his
hoarse, hesitating voice—with long pauses and occasional omissions
that only made it more spell-binding and suspenseful—went like
this:

"I tell the tale as my father told me: Once when we lived on the shore of Lake Michigan, in a place we call Chigagou because a plant there stinks like a skunk, one of our chiefs was captured by the Seneca. In his death-song, it shames me to say, he asked his enemies to spare him if he would show them the way to our village. When the Senecas found only women, children, and old men there, they killed some, took the rest prisoner, and headed back to their country in the east. When our warriors found the village in ashes, they set out at once, tomahawks in hand, to pursue their enemies. Each night the Seneca killed and ate one of the Miami children and left the bones in the cinders of their campfire; each morning they would kill another and impale the head on a stake. At these sights, our warriors became more enraged and ran faster to avenge the dead and save their families. When the Senecas came near their village, they sent a runner ahead to tell the people to prepare a large fire and a great kettle for the good broth they were bringing home. In those days the Senecas had more guns than we did, so our warriors sneaked through the woods ahead of them and hid along the trail.

"The next morning the Senecas came down the trail to their village. Our warriors attacked with clubs and tomahawks and slaughtered all but four of them. We chopped off the heads of two of these, ran bark strings through their ears, and strung them around the necks of the other two, whose hands, noses, and lips we cut off, and sent them home as a sample of Miami vengeance. When the two Seneca entered their village, the people were already dancing around a great boiling kettle. Then they saw—and all was horror and confusion. When we got back to our village it was our turn to dance, with many scalps to justify our war songs."

Once the Seneca had been defeated and driven back, the Miami returned to their homelands along the Wabash. Although they were all one people, with the same language and customs, the various branches of the tribe lived in different villages and, for the most part, went their separate ways. The Piankashaw, or deer people, located near the French trading post at Vincennes; the Pepicokia, or turkey people, settled on the Vermillion and intermarried with the Kaskaskias, a remnant of the Illinois; the Wea, or snake people, lived off the buffalo at Ouiatanon across the river from a Kickapoo village; the Kilatika, or bear people, were at Snake-fish Town on the Eel River; and the Miami proper, or sandhill crane people, occupied Kekionga, at the strategic portage between the Wabash and Maumee rivers. These were the main centers, but there were also smaller villages. Little Turtle, for example, the war chief of Dappled Fawn's Miami village at Kekionga, preferred to live about fifteen miles west of there, in his own town up the Eel River.

The Soldier and Little Turtle were about the same age, and they had shared, as their fathers had before them, many adventures on the warpath. Little Turtle's father was made a chief as a very young man, after leading a successful ambush of the Seneca. He had even traveled to Lancaster and signed a treaty with the British, who had better goods at lower prices. Miami braves took part in Braddock's Defeat at the start of the French and Indian War as well as Pontiac's Revolt following it; in 1763, when English traders raised prices and restricted the flow of rum, ammunition, and gifts, the Miami sacked the British fort at Kekionga in retaliation. During the American Revolution Little Turtle and The Soldier had fought on the side of the British; they were among Gentleman Johnny Burgoyne's Indian warriors at the battle of Saratoga.

In the fall of 1780 an opportunistic French cavalry officer, Augustin La Balme, led a mounted force of about sixty men from Vincennes on a vague mission whose ultimate goal may have been to retake Detroit for the French. When they arrived at Kekionga, which was largely abandoned, they ransacked the village. Meanwhile, Little Turtle assembled his warriors and, in a surprise night attack, slaughtered La Balme and at least half of his men on the banks of the Eel River. Because of this victory, Little Turtle was made a war chief; for the rest of the war he and The Soldier led a series of successful raids against the settlements in Kentucky.

After the Revolution, when the tribes of the Ohio Valley learned that their British allies had ceded all Indian lands south of the Great Lakes to the Americans, war parties into Kentucky—such as the ones that killed Colonel Floyd and captured Billy Wells—continued. Regardless of what the treaty said, the Indians vowed to keep the Ohio River as the boundary between themselves and the settlers. In order to hold on to the lucrative fur trade for as long as possible, the British refused to abandon their major post at Detroit and encouraged the Indians to stand firm.

3

Blacksnake had first become aware of how precarious his adopted Miami world was during the summer of 1786, when there was serious trouble in Vincennes. The French traders, who intermarried with the Indians and respected their customs, had lived there at peace for a long time; but the American squatters didn't know how to behave. They built a blockhouse, worked their cornfields under arms, bartered whiskey to the Indians, and were often more disruptive than the drunken tribesmen. One day in June a few warriors, maddened by watching the slow, monotonous plod of oxen dragging wooden plows across the prairie, attacked two farmers, scalping one William Donnally. In retaliation, the Americans abducted a sick Indian from a Frenchman's house in town. After Donnally's wife shot and scalped him, they tied his corpse to the tail of a horse and dragged it through the streets of Vincennes. Two weeks later, some Kentuckians fired on a group of friendly Piankashaws near the mouth of the Wabash, killing five.

When word of these outrages reached Snake-fish Town and Kekionga, the war and peace chiefs met in council and decided to drive the Americans out of Vincennes. Blacksnake watched in awe as The Soldier set off with more than 100 men to join Little Turtle's even larger force from Kekionga. Several hundred Miami warriors from the upper Wabash arrived at Vincennes in mid-July and stated their demands. After hours of high-pitched oratory and dire threats, calumets were exchanged and smoked, generous gifts were given, and the Miami agreed to withdraw.

"If there is more trouble here," The Soldier warned before leaving, "we will return in roasting-ear time and we will know how to enter your gates without asking."

In October word reached the villages that George Rogers Clark had arrived in Vincennes with 1,000 men to march up the Wabash and wipe out the Miami. Once again the chiefs met in council and even more warriors assembled, reinforced by hundreds of Shawnee from their villages on the headwaters of the Mad River. Blacksnake and the other boys were told to defend Snake-fish Town and evacuate it if necessary. Little Turtle set an ambush for Clark's troops in the defiles of Pine Creek, between the Vermillion River and the Wea stronghold at Ouiatanon.

Clark's expedition started badly and ended worse. The troops were quarrelsome and insubordinate, rejecting his plan for a direct, cross-country assault on Kekionga in favor of a more roundabout route to Vincennes and then up the Wabash. The Kentucky militia thought they would be better fed if they stopped in Vincennes, since supplies could be boated down the Ohio and up the Wabash to them. The beef, delayed by low water, arrived spoiled, dissension bred desertions, and Clark, in despair, was often in his cups. As his undisciplined and depleted force headed up the Wabash, rumors spread through the ranks that they would all be cut off and killed— thoughts to make a man's skin tingle and his step falter. When the militia reached the Vermillion, a resounding cry was heard, "Who's for home?" Little Turtle's advance spies watched dumbfounded as Clark's troops, a day's march from where the Miami and Shawnee lay waiting for them, retreated back to Vincennes.

The frustration of the warriors returning to their villages without scalps changed to fury when they learned that while they were away another force of Kentuckians, led by Benjamin Logan, had burned Meckacheck and the other Shawnee towns on the Mad River. Moluntha's friendly village suffered the most casualties. The old chief had recently agreed to peace at Fort Finney; when the militia arrived he came out wearing a cockade hat and carrying a copy of the treaty and a peace pipe. On a pole outside his lodge waved an Ameican flag. But Hugh McGary, a fiery-tempered Indian hater, grabbed a squaw axe and sunk it in Moluntha's skull.

Their towns burned, their livestock stolen, and their crops destroyed, the Shawnee were compelled to disperse into small hunting parties and scavenge to survive. In the spring they moved their villages further north into Miami and Wyandot territory, settling on the Maumee, at Kekionga, and along the Mississenewa River. One group of Shawnee declared they had had enough of the Big Knives and headed for Spanish Territory west of the Mississippi. The Delaware, already settled on Miami land, moved more people to their villages on the White River. These tribes, as well as the lake Indians to their north and west, knew that the time for a showdown had come and that their only chance of winning it was to join forces.

Clark sent word from Vincennes that he was willing to negotiate, but the tribes did not trust him. He gave paltry gifts and did not know the rules of diplomacy, waving the black wampum belt of war and the white wampum belt of peace at the same time and daring the chiefs to surrender or fight. That was no way to show respect. The Miami warriors continued to raid Kentucky, keeping an eye on the troops stationed at Vincennes. The American government, undergoing the transition from the Articles of Confederation to the Constitution, was too disorganized and in debt to mount a concerted offensive against the Indians. Thus, in the fall of 1788, as Blacksnake prepared for his first warpath, a bloody stalemate existed in the valley of the Wabash.

4

Two Lives, the brother of No Nose, was the proper person to instruct Blacksnake in the art of war. A young brave on his first expedition was expected to serve and assist his maternal uncle. Blacksnake found it difficult to grasp the complex clan system in Snake-fish town. When a person was present he or she was not called by name but rather by relationship. The confusing part came with the extended family. Sitting Quiet, for example, the daughter of Two Lives and his wife Snapping Turtle, Blacksnake called "mother" and her children would be considered his sisters and brothers. In addition, he was expected to joke with some relatives and be very reserved with others. He and his uncle Two Lives often exchanged derogatory remarks about each other's abilities as hunters, warriors, and lovers.

"You only want a scalp so you can mount Laughing Eyes," Two Lives teased him.

"The only thing you mounted this year was your horse," Blacksnake fired back.

"I have had a few cows in my time."

"I do want to marry Laughing Eyes," Blacksnake admitted with a laugh. "I'd also like to own a horse."

"I have watched you grow and I believe you are ready," Two Lives said, the bantering preliminaries now over. He went on to explain with great earnestness that the art of war was simple: to kill as many enemies as you can while losing as few men as possible. To do this successfully it was essential to use deception and surprise, strike with sudden fury and local superiority, and retreat quickly with all the prisoners, scalps, and plunder that could be carried safely. A Miami warrior must also be ready, if *he* is caught by surprise and trapped himself, to fight fiercely to the last and die like a man.

"How do you feel about fighting the Big Knives?" Two Lives asked gravely, averting his eyes to avoid offense.

"They are no longer my people," Blacksnake said. "I am a Miami." In truth, he was more conflicted than that, but those feelings were buried deep inside him and could not be expressed, even to himself. He rarely even thought about his past life in Kentucky. What he was most conscious of was a desire to excel and prove his bravery.

"There is one thing you could do, if you wish, to help us."

"What is that?"

"Do not cut your hair."

A warrior going to battle left only a small scalplock on top of his head, which was then painted and decorated with feathers and ornaments. The boys often did the same in imitation of the men. For the past six months, Blacksnake had let his red hair grow, because Laughing Eyes liked to run her fingers through it and praise its color and texture. He wondered why Two Lives had made this request. Then he thought he knew and replied, "I will do what you want."

"Since the whites are so many, our only chance of saving our land is to make them shake with terror and flee back across the mountains. To do this we must show no mercy. No one is to be spared. Do you understand?"

"I hear you, Uncle."

Blacksnake understood. He had sat at the back of the council house and listened to the chiefs debate. They had decided to establish a base camp near the Ohio and send repeated attacks across the river against the Kentucky settlements. When the question was asked whether the warriors should take captives and keep them at the camp until they could be brought back to the villages, to be adopted or ransomed to the British, a loud chant had gone up, "Kill all! Kill all!"

It was war to the death; there would be no prisoners.

Traditionally, a warrior who wanted to go on a raid would gather a few like-minded men and they would slip off in the night without ceremony. If they were successful, they would enter the village, with scalps held on high, singing; if they failed and suffered casualties, they would cover themselves with ashes and come back in mourning. Because this was a large operation, the preparations were more public and elaborate. For weeks the warriors gathered their weapons and supplies. Under The Soldier's keen eye they practiced maneuvers.

Most importantly, the *Natte* or sacred war pack was prepared. Each warrior contributed a personal amulet that gave him power and protection—a wolf's tooth, a panther's paw, an eagle's talon, a buffalo's tail, a dried human heart, a scalp, the feathers of some rare bird, the skin of a blacksnake. These were added to the totems of the Miami tribes, including a perfectly preserved sandhill crane and the claws of a black bear. This war pack, if treated with the proper ritual and respect, would precede the warriors into enemy territory, ensure victory, and lead them safely home.

To purge and purify themselves for their first warpath, Blacksnake, Thin Raccoon, and The Sleepy One spent a lot of time in the sweat hut drinking bitterroot tea. The warriors were required to fast—except for those of the wolf totem, who devoured everything in sight—and abstain from sex. Blacksnake had not yet slept with Laughing Eyes, but, on occasion, other girls in the village had opened their buffalo robes to him.

The night before they left, several hundred people gathered in front of the council house. Snake-fish town was spread along the river for over a mile; Blacksnake didn't know most of its inhabitants. He lived in a smaller village within the larger one, at the mouth of Muddy Creek, which consisted mainly of the winter hunting band. He seldom spoke with the town's five other white captives nor with the French traders that periodically passed through the town.

Large fires blazed on three sides of the dancing ground and the drums began to thump, resounding to the night sky. The war post, set upright in the center, was a man-sized log, peeled of bark and painted red, with a few scalps fastened on top. An excited cry went up from the crowd, signaling that the "Discovery Dance" that always preceded a major war party was about to begin.

A warrior named The Crow, stripped to his breechclout and painted for battle, entered with a huge war club shaped like a jawbone in his right hand and a crow skin in the other. He stood motionless at first, as if summoning his manitous for strength, then he gave a prolonged, soaring war cry, which quavered at its highest pitch, faded, and burst forth again at the end with a shrill, nerve-shattering shriek. He began a slow, almost sauntering walk around the circle, pausing on occasion to see if he were being followed. Then he became more cautious, adopting a stealthy, stalking, toe-heel step that suggested he was in enemy territory. He found a trail and followed it, dropping to the ground and lying as still as a stone for a suspended moment, crawling on his belly to scout out his target, and crouching like a panther for the kill. Next he sprang to his feet, jumping from one imaginary tree to another before he hollered his war whoop and charged with sudden ferocity. His bulging eyes, the grimace on his face, the lethal speed of his assault—The Crow had worked himself into a trance that was totally convincing. As he went through the quick, brutal motions of ripping off a scalp, it was easy to believe that the bloody trophy was in his upraised hand. He sprinted in furious pursuit across the circle, brandishing his war club in mock combat as he slew foe after foe. When he mimed the plundering of the enemy's village, the swift retreat, and the triumphal return home, everyone responded to his scalp halloo with shouts of their own. Finally he sang a long song that recounted in detail his past exploits on the warpath, whacking his club on the post for emphasis, while the other warriors responded with a deep, guttural, "Ho-ah! Ho-ah!" in confirmation of each of his deeds. When he was done, he handed the war club to another warrior, who repeated the performance. Before the night was over, Blacksnake, too, had danced and sung—not of what he had done but of what he aspired to do.

In the morning Blacksnake gathered up his shot pouch, powder horn, and gun and joined the other warriors. In the blanket over his shoulder he had wrapped parched corn and jerked meat, a few strips of leather to patch his moccasins, a bag of paint, and some herbs and ointments.

The Porcupine placed his hand on Blacksnake's shoulder and said to Two Lives before they left, "I give you my heart. I know he will be safe with you."

"I will guard him with my life," Two Lives responded with great solemnity.

The Old Owl, the medicine man, led the procession out of the village carrying the sacred war pack. The Soldier and the other warriors fired their guns in the air and sang the departure song:

> *Do not weep, women,*
> *We are ready to die.*
> *We are all brave men,*
> *None is braver than I!*
> *This land holds*
> *Our ancestors' bones,*
> *To keep it*
> *We must be strong!*

Blacksnake, Thin Raccoon, The Sleepy One, and the other young men had to conduct themselves properly. Nothing was more shameful than to lose a warrior during his first battle; a strict adherence to a set of ritual prohibitions was considered the best way to ensure that everyone returned home safely. They were never to scratch their heads or bodies with their fingers or eat, drink, or sit during the day's march; when they camped at night they should not step over anyone else's person or possessions or reach for anything across the fire. The fire itself was laid out from east to west, with a forked stick at each end and a pole between to suspend the cooking kettle; each warrior placed offerings to his manitou at the fire's edge before eating or smoking. The older men, "Those who are respected," slept on the south side of the fire; the young men, "Those who respect," on the north. Each warrior hung his powder horn and moccasins from a forked stick by his blanket and slept with his feet to the fire and his face turned toward his Miami homeland. No guards were posted at night, but if anyone heard anything suspicious, he tapped the man next to him who passed the warning on. The young men saw to the needs of the veteran warriors—tending fire, cooking food, bringing water, mending moccasins—and listened to their tales and heeded their advice. Above all, it was taboo to pass in front of the sacred war pack, which always led the way.

Blacksnake was not happy when Two Lives gave him one of the cooking kettles to carry, but he hid his feelings and obeyed. The younger warriors literally walked in the footsteps of the older ones as they moved single file through the woods. Around noon on the fourth day they came to their base camp, located on some good bottomland at a fork of Eagle Creek, three miles up from its confluence with the Ohio River. A Shawnee hunting party led by a brave named Tecumseh was already there, so the Miami warriors camped separately to avoid contact with women. The war chiefs of both tribes conferred that evening and decided to break up into several war parties of about a dozen each.

5

The next day the men in The Soldier's group swam the river, bringing their powder and guns across on a makeshift raft of logs fastened with grapevines. They followed a buffalo trace to Big Bone Lick, where Blacksnake was astonished to see the skeletal remains of mastodons—curved tusks as long as a man; huge vertebrae, many larger than a whiskey keg. From there they took another trace due south, camping that night in a sinkhole to hide their fire. The following day, they left the buffalo trace and followed a narrow trail that wound through high hills and camped again in a thicket, this time without a fire. In the morning they came to Elkhorn Creek and followed it to the southeast for a few hours. Then scouts, sent forward to reconnoiter, reported that there was a clearing with two cabins ahead.

While the warriors re-painted their faces and checked their weapons, The Soldier told Blacksnake, Thin Raccoon, and The Sleepy One what the plan was. They were not to take part in the attack, but withhold their fire, stay back, and watch. Their job was to catch stray horses, shoot down anyone trying to escape, and give warning if enemy reinforcements were coming. When the sun was down behind the trees, the war party glided off into the deepening shadows. Near the clearing they spread out and waited for dawn. Blacksnake, following Two Lives, crept through a canebrake until he could see in the glow of the moon the dim outline of a cabin. He loaded his gun, placed a musket ball in his mouth, and waited.

As the first pink light suffused the trees a rooster crowed and a dog barked. The clearing was shrouded in mist, which lifted slowly, unveiling to Blacksnake's eyes what might almost have been his former Kentucky home: a hewn-log, two-room cabin, a smaller, makeshift cabin behind it, a corn crib, a cow shed, a horse corral, an outhouse, and a pig pen. A truck patch bordered one side of each cabin and a stump-pocked cornfield spread out in front. The warriors had agreed not to attack, if possible, until the settlers were in sight.

A tall man with a gun stepped out of the larger cabin first, next came his teenage son, with an ax on his shoulder, and his unarmed, white-bearded grandfather. The man hollered and two strapping black slaves, bare to the waist, emerged from the other cabin, carrying a shovel and a hoe. The men walked to the opposite side of the clearing from where Blacksnake was hiding and went to work at rooting up a stump. A black woman then joined two white women, a mother and daughter, at a nearby spring to wash clothes. Finally a black boy of about six began to play with a much younger white boy in the dooryard. The moment the man leaned his gun against a sapling to help push on the stump The Soldier gave the signal—the gobble of a turkey-cock—and the warriors opened fire; then, with shrill war whoops, they charged into the clearing.

Everything happened so quickly that Blacksnake could not take it all in. The first volley felled five men and two women. Only the daughter was not hit; she ran screaming toward her badly wounded father, who unsheathed his hunting knife, cut away her petticoats, and shouted, "Run, Judith, run!" She sprinted in her shift toward the wagon road, but Cutfinger shot her in the back and Black Loon rushed forward to take her hair. The father, realizing he was a dead man, grabbed his gun by the barrel and, with the last of his strength, smashed it against the stump.

Blacksnake—heart beating like a drum, mouth dry as dust—saw the black boy leap to his feet and race in his direction; he raised his gun and drew a bead, but, because the boy swerved suddenly at the last minute, he had to swing the barrel to the left at the same time he jerked the trigger and shot over his head. In a flash the boy disappeared into the canebrake, with Thin Raccoon and The Sleepy One in hot pursuit. By the time Blacksnake had poured powder and spat a musket ball into a patch and rammed it home, eight warriors were waving dripping scalps on high in the clearing. The grandfather, strangely enough, didn't have a spot of blood on him; apparently he had died of fright.

Still not satisfied, Buckfeet and Night Stander butchered the white man, crammed dirt in his mouth, and festooned his entrails on the split-rail fence. He Provides shot arrow after arrow into an already dead cow, cut out its tongue, then proceeded to kill hogs. As The Soldier admired the fine polished brasswork of the white man's gun, stock irrevocably broken, Black Loon walked up with his scalp of long, golden-brown hair and said with regret, "She would have made a pretty squaw."

Next the warriors turned their attention to plunder. Earth and The Cat ransacked the cabin, while Blacksnake helped Two Lives rip up a mattress for the ticking, filling the air with feathers.

Suddenly a thin, plaintive voice sounded from under the bed, "Mommy will be mad at you."

Two Lives bent down and pulled out the small boy who had been playing in the dooryard. In the excitement of the kill, the warriors had forgotten about him. All he wore was a tow shirt. A few feathers clung to his sweaty face. His knees were shaking. He had run inside and hidden beneath the bed at the first shots and so he hadn't seen the gruesome slaughter in the clearing. What troubled him was the mess they were making of his mother's house. Blacksnake might have been looking at an earlier version of himself—young Billy Wells, who used to wear a tow shirt and play in the dirt outside a cabin on Jacob's Creek. What should he do?

Before he could decide, Earth buried his pipe tomahawk into the boy's skull to the eyes, spattering gore everywhere. Blacksnake, in a daze, almost retched and staggered outside. A moment later Thin Raccoon and The Sleepy One ran up with the black boy's scalp. The warriors set fire to the cabins and outbuildings, rounded up the horses, and beat a hasty retreat.

The entire attack had taken fifteen minutes, but Blacksnake knew he would never forget it.

The smoke from the burning cabins would soon spread the alarm—the Kentuckians certainly knew the direction of their retreat—and so the race was on for the Ohio river. Blacksnake and the other warriors followed the buffalo trace, since it was the most direct way, and took turns riding and running, pausing only briefly to rest. When they heard hoof beats gaining on them, they spread out into the trees to make a stand; it was The Crow and his war party, bringing enough horses for everyone to ride. They didn't stop until they arrived at the river.

Again they made a log raft to ferry their powder, guns, and plunder across, while the warriors swam beside the horses. They were catching their breath when seven white men on fine horses rode up to the Kentucky side. Seeing that they were outnumbered and that the Indians were beyond rifle range, one of them shouted across the water, "You thievin' yaller rascals, we'll get you yet."

"Go home," Blacksnake shouted back to the delight of his comrades, "you're too late."

"You talk too good for an Injun. Is that you, Girty?"

"My name is Blacksnake."

"You're a damned renegade. You know what we do to renegades? We flay them and make shot pouches out of their skin."

"You'll have to catch me first."

"Next time, we will," the man promised in parting, as the Kentuckians wheeled their horses around, apparently heading for home, and the triumphant warriors proceeded to their base camp.

The following morning Blacksnake, Thin Raccoon, and The Sleepy One went down to the branch that joined Eagle Creek to fetch water for the cooking kettles. Some Shawnee squaws were up stream from them, talking and laughing as they gathered firewood. Tecumseh and a few of his men walked past heading out to hunt. The bells of the captured horses jingled softly as they grazed in the bottomlands. Suddenly Blacksnake heard the loud popping of rifles behind him. Indians from both camps began to run toward the high bank across the stream, where there was better cover, but they were met with a volley from that side and several warriors fell. Blacksnake and his friends dove behind a fallen log; they carried knives in their belts but had no other arms. Attacked from both east and west, the warriors retreated through a grove of beech trees to a grassy hill where they regrouped and opened fire, stopping the charge of the Kentuckians.

Because Indians always used less powder than the whites, their muskets cracked flatter, with a kind of muffled whistle. Blacksnake, caught between the lines of fire, hugged the earth and listened to the guns. It sounded as if only six or seven of the enemy were on each side, while more than fifty Shawnee and Miami warriors from the two adjacent camps were gathered to confront them. If that was the extent of the Kentucky force, they would pay dearly for their zeal.

Regardless of the outcome of the battle, Blacksnake and his two friends were in a precarious situation. The decaying log they were hiding behind offered scant protection from the crossfire; if the Kentuckians made an effort to advance, their position would be exposed. They were poised to make a break for it when they heard the moans of a Shawnee warrior, whose bloody body was partly visible to their right. They knew what they had to do.

"I see a savage down there in the grass," Blacksnake heard one of the Kentuckians say. "Cover me, boys, I'm gonna get me a scalp."

Thin Raccoon sprinted off first, zigzagging wildly to elude the gun fire; then Blacksnake and The Sleepy One ran to the mortally wounded warrior, grabbed him by both arms, and began to drag him away. They were almost to the cover of the beech trees when The Sleepy One cried out, "I'm hit," and fell. Blacksnake dropped the now dead Shawnee, put The Sleepy One's arm around his neck, and carried him to safety under a covering fire from the warriors on the hill. Thin Raccoon, unharmed, was already there to welcome them.

While the medicine man tended to a ball lodged in The Sleepy One's left leg, twenty warriors retrieved the other dead and wounded. As the gun smoke drifted off, Blacksnake had a clear view of the Kentuckians, who had stopped shooting to pillage the Indian camps. He recognized several men on horseback from the previous day. The Soldier did not counter-attack, anticipating that the invaders would misread his restraint as timidity and try to take the high ground. Two of the enemy dead were left at the base of the hill as bait.

In an act of foolhardy daring, a handful of mounted men suddenly charged through the grove of beech trees. The Soldier gave the order to fire when they were at close range; three of them fell dead at the first volley. The others spun about and rode off in a hail of musket balls. The rest of the Kentuckians panicked when they saw their impetuous comrades drop. Each man grabbed the nearest horse he could find and high-tailed it toward the river with the warriors giving chase. Only the timely arrival of a flatboat allowed most of them to escape across the Ohio. Although The Soldier and his men had been victorious, four warriors were dead, two Shawnee and two Miami: there would be no rejoicing that night in camp. The Sleepy One had a wound and Thin Raccoon a scalp to display back at Snake-fish town when they sang of their bravery, but Blacksnake still had nothing.

6

The Miami abandoned their base camp and divided themselves into smaller war parties. The Soldier's band made another foray into Kentucky, taking a few scalps and stealing horses, but Blacksnake's job was still to stay back and watch until the killing was over. Although he was praised by the older warriors for trying to retrieve the body of the dying Shawnee at Eagle Creek, that wasn't enough. To be a true Miami warrior he needed to bring home a trophy.

Often the men sitting around the campfire at night debated the art of scalping. The Cat favored a frontal approach, with a knee on the chest; Black Loon placed a foot in the small of the back and worked from there; Two Lives advised sitting on the fallen victim's shoulders, locking the head between your thighs, and, after making an initial cut, tugging off the hair with your teeth.

In early October, they spotted a flatboat heading for the Indian shore. The Soldier was about to set up an ambush when a force of about thirty mounted Kentuckians rode up to greet it. Seeing that he was outnumbered, The Soldier signaled for everyone to spread out and wait until they had a chance to cut off any stragglers.

Blacksnake hid in a pawpaw thicket on a low ridge where he had a good view of the riverbank; the men's voices and odors wafted up to him. They were planning a settlement, because one of them unpacked his instruments and proceeded to make a survey, while the others haphazardly cleared away undergrowth. They were all very excited and exuded land greed, shouting back and forth in disregard of any danger. The leader they called "Symmes" and the surveyor was "Filson," a thin man with a high forehead whose frustration grew as various Kentuckians kept disrupting his methodical work by calling for him to measure first this and then that.

Blacksnake shared the rage of the other Miami warriors. After all their bloody raids, here were the Big Knives on the Indian side of the river blithely surveying lots and streets for a town! No matter how many whites they killed, flatboat after flatboat of settlers continued to come. Somehow, they had to be stopped.

The warriors surrounded the intruder's camp that night, but the horses became restive when they crawled near. In the morning the Kentuckians headed inland to survey some good bottomland up the Great Miami, while the warriors watched them from a distance. That night the whites posted guard and again it seemed unwise to attack.

In the early afternoon of the next day the Kentuckians spotted Tecumseh's hunting party. The white men primed their weapons and prepared to charge the unsuspecting band when Symmes, the apparent leader, interposed himself and argued against it. Killing women and children was not the best way to initiate good relations. After an exchange of hot words most of the Kentuckians turned around and cantered off, leaving Symmes and about a dozen others behind. Because this remnant was still well-armed, The Soldier advised his warriors to spread out and wait.

The whites that stayed behind debated whether to do more surveying or return to the Ohio. Again the group divided, with several more abandoning Symmes. Since these rode off at a slower pace, Two Lives, Blacksnake, and a few other warriors decided to follow them on foot. After a mile or so the riders stopped near the bank of the Great Miami River to eat some wild plums. Filson, the scholarly looking surveyor, wandered away from his companions, a plum in one hand and a compass in the other, toward the exact spot where Blacksnake was hiding. Moving from the sunny fruit tree clearing into the twilight of a grove of towering cottonwoods, all Filson could see in front of him were vague shapes. Blacksnake emerged from his cover and leveled his musket.

When Filson finally discerned that a red-headed man dressed like an Indian was pointing a gun at his chest, he raised his left hand as a sign of peace, offered the plum with the other, and smiled a wide, lopsided smile. Blacksnake froze for a moment—the man's large, mournful eyes were gazing at him with intense curiosity.

"Are you by any chance Welch?" Filson asked, his scratchy voice reminded Blacksnake of his schoolteacher back in Kentucky.

Because other warriors were nearby and Blacksnake didn't want to be seen talking to the enemy, he pulled the trigger. The man said "Oh" in surprise, gripped his stomach, and crumpled to the ground. At that, more shots rang out from the grove of plum trees and the rest of the Kentuckians galloped away.

Struggling to control his mixed emotions, Blacksnake pulled out his knife, kneeled beside his victim, and hesitated, unsure which scalping method to employ.

"You're white," Filson moaned. "Why did you shoot me?"

"I am Miami," Blacksnake snarled in sudden rage and plunged his knife into Filson's chest, feeling the hilt rebound against his hand when the blade hit the rib cage. But he still wasn't dead, he was trying to speak. Blacksnake bent his ear to Filson's faltering lips.

"Adieu, Amanda," he whispered, and then he was lodged in the land of silence.

Removing his scalp was a messy business. Blacksnake cut along Filson's receding hairline, scraping the skull, but the top of his head was bare and covered with scar tissue, as if he'd been scalped before; it was hard to decide how to get a grip. What he finally yanked away with a distinct popping sound was a sorry sight that would require careful repair to look presentable.

Blacksnake didn't feel any of the elation he had anticipated. He was aware of a rivulet of sweat spidering down his spine, a strange heaviness in his arms, and an urge to vomit. It was all he could do to search through the man's possessions—a compass, a ferule, a thermometer, a quadrant, a hat with a hole in it (had he been shot at before?), and a slim book, tucked under his belt, with a map inside it—to see if there was anything he could use. Black Loon came up and extracted a quill pen from Filson's jacket, which he proceeded to insert horizontally through his septum to replace his nose bob.

That night around a campfire kindled with the help of papers torn from a book and a crumpled map, Blacksnake recited his exploit, shaking Filson's flimsy scalp in the air as he spoke. He knew what was expected the next day, and, after a restless night of inner debate, had determined to prove, once and for all, that he was truly a Miami brave. At dawn The Soldier led his men down to the bank of the Ohio and ordered the warriors to conceal themselves inside a huge, hollow sycamore. The spot had been carefully selected, but success would depend upon a perfect ruse. Blacksnake dressed in Filson's clothes—his face washed, his red hair fully visible—was standing waist-deep in the river when the flatboat came around the far bend.

Laughing Eyes

1

On an opal-tinted day in October, when the last leaves were falling from the trees, the war party returned in triumph to Snake-fishTown. The assembled villagers shrieked as The Little Doctor, bearing the sacred war pack, led the way to the council house, followed by the paint-streaked warriors displaying on poles the scalps of their slain enemies. They danced the buffalo dance and each man sang of his exploits. When Blacksnake recited, in the high nasal voice proper to such an occasion, how he had killed a man he met in the forest and taken his hair and how he had lured the flatboat on the Ohio River to the shore, the crowd shouted "Ho-ah!"

"He went out a boy," Two Lives said to The Porcupine after the ceremonies. "He came back a man."

"My son," The Porcupine replied, resting his hand on Blacksnake's shoulder and pulling aside the bearskin hung in the doorway, "come smoke."

No Nose looked up as they entered the wigwam. "Now you can marry," she said, holding two fingers together in the air and smiling lewdly. "Who will you choose?"

"Don't rush him," The Porcupine said. "He has time."

"Maybe he does and maybe he does not," No Nose asserted. "Not if he wants who I think."

"What do you mean?" Blacksnake demanded.

"You are not the only one interested in Laughing Eyes," she hinted with the smirk of someone who knows a secret.

Everyone agreed that Laughing Eyes was pretty and would make a good wife, but Blacksnake hadn't really considered the possibility that he might have rivals. He had noticed the way she looked at him when she didn't think he was looking (or did she?). Wasn't that a sure sign? And wasn't he the son of a chief?

Even in the flickering firelight of the lodge No Nose could see his face and read his thoughts. "Have you slept with her?"

"No, Mother."

"Have you tried?"

"Not yet."

"Do you know how?"

"Of course."

"I am not so sure," No Nose said skeptically. "I will ask Two Lives to give you lessons."

Blacksnake found it perfectly normal to discuss his sex life with his mother but bristled at the suggestion that he didn't know what he was doing. Hadn't he already slept with Thunderstruck, Brings Joy, and Mist at Dawn?

A discreet promiscuity prevailed among the teenagers of the village; a boy would hide beside the trails the women took to cut and fetch firewood; when he saw a girl he desired walking alone he would step out, take her by the wrist, and pull her gently into the bushes. If she resisted he withdrew, but enough girls consented to keep the game lively. At night boys would slip into the wigwams and wake the girls of their choice, who would welcome them or tell them to go away. A few bolder girls like Brings Joy and Shadows on Treetops at Sunset sought out their lovers, but most were an alluring combination of modesty and flirtatiousness. Laughing Eyes certainly had the knack to keep Blacksnake guessing; he hadn't yet worked up his nerve to make his plea.

"Who?" he asked No Nose. "What do you know?"

"Today I saw Sweating giving Kiss Me a ruffled shirt and a feathered hat."

"Why?" Blacksnake sensed he knew the answer. Sweating resented Blacksnake's accomplishments and blamed him for allowing Cold Feet to be killed by the rogue bear.

"Why do you think? She's the best love talker in the village and makes the most powerful love potion."

Because they were a blend of male and female forces, the he-shes, or white faces, were respected as persons with special powers, although they were also the butt of much joking. Kiss Me was often consulted as a matchmaker, sang and danced at major ceremonies, and did not lack for sexual partners among the boys and men, who sometimes made offers of marriage. A few white faces had been known to go on war parties, dressing as men once they left the village but restricted to using only war clubs in battle.

For the Miami, sex among teenagers was a private matter and considered essentially frivolous, but marriage was public, serious, and concerned everybody. Now that Blacksnake and his friends had been on the warpath and brought back scalps, the whole village watched closely to see whom they chose to marry. Since it was taboo to select someone within your own clan, every wedding meant a new alliance of families and an increase of relatives.

Two Lives dutifully came by the next morning to make sure Blacksnake understood the rudiments of lovemaking. After some ribald banter about whether or not his nephew was equipped for the job, Two Lives promptly sat on the ground with his knees up and demonstrated the preferred Miami method for enjoying sex out of doors in the day.

"Do this properly," he said, "and she will ask for more."

Then he got on his knees and explained how he wrapped his arms around his partner's lower back to hold her in place.

"This is the best way at night," he instructed, "but you must only move in a careful and controlled manner."

"Why?"

"If you become too excited," he replied with a salacious leer, "the sleeping platform will collapse and everybody will wake up!"

Finally, Two Lives insisted that as a Miami man and warrior Blacksnake must not overindulge his appetites—too much sex would sap his strength.

"I know this is difficult," he added, "because a woman of beauty like Laughing Eyes has great power."

Blacksnake smiled and nodded his head in agreement.

"By the way," Two Lives remarked, "do you know why a woman wiggles when she walks?"

"Tell me, Uncle."

"It happened like this: When the Great Hare first created the world, he made a man and gave him a dog as a companion. He thought that they would hunt together and be always happy. But before long the man became depressed and hung his head and moped around and lost interest in the hunt. The dog, meanwhile, became more nervous and excited, yelping and wagging his tail to prevent his master from sleeping all the time and letting them starve. The Great Hare saw that this would not do, so he decided one day to make a woman. He took a rib from the sleeping man and set it aside to ponder what shape she should have. Sensing that he would soon have a rival and feeling terribly hungry, the dog grabbed the rib in his teeth and, tail wagging, ran away with it. The Great Hare had to chase that dog for a long distance before he finally caught him and took the rib back and made a woman. All the time he was shaping her the dog was by his side with his tongue hanging and his tail wagging. When the Great Hare had finished, he asked the man what he thought of the woman. 'I like her,' the man said, 'she lifts my heart and makes life worth living, and I especially like the way she wiggles when she walks.' The Great Hare was pleased when he heard these words and I think the dog was too, because he still wags his tail."

Blacksnake laughed at the tale and thanked Two Lives, admitting that his uncle had taught him a few things. His first sexual experience with Brings Joy had been a furtive and hurried affair in the bushes that left both flustered and unsatisfied. When he gave her a necklace of blue beads the next day, she threw them on the ground. Knowing that he loved another, the two other girls he had slept with turned their attention elsewhere. Now he had a rival for Laughing Eyes's affections in Sweating, aided by a white face's potent magic.

That afternoon he sought out Kiss Me, who was gathering wood with some other women.

"Have you found a husband yet?" Blacksnake blurted out.

"Still looking," Kiss Me answered in the lisping, singsong, almost babyish voice that Miami women used when they were in a playful mood.

"How about me?"

"Too short," Kiss Me teased.

"Why did Sweating give you presents yesterday?"

"He wanted some love medicine to make his dreams come true."

"What dreams?"

"You know. Laughing Eyes. If *you* want her, I can touch her heart and fill her with desire; she will tear off her clothes to come to you. Were she on a distant island, she would come."

"Is that what you already promised Sweating?"

"What I promise I perform. I have the power."

"Perhaps I could give you something."

"What do you have that I want?"

Blacksnake handed over the compass he had taken from Filson, the surveyor he had killed.

"Oh, I do like that!" Kiss Me exclaimed, slipping it inside her dress. "I will bring you what you need."

Blacksnake thanked Kiss Me and turned to go but felt a restraining hand on his arm.

"Why not marry me?" Kiss Me asked in a way that might almost have been sincere. "I will not only cook for you, but hunt as well."

"Can you kill a deer?"

"If he stands still in my path."

"I want Laughing Eyes."

"I am good. I can make a man happy."

"That is what they say."

"What you hear is true. You should give me a try," Kiss Me insisted mischievously. "You might find you like it."

"I have made my choice."

"Look for me after the dance tomorrow evening. I know what will charm her."

The young men and women of Snake-fish Town spent most of the next day preparing for the stomp dance. Blacksnake used a clamshell to pull any facial stubble he could find, combed his hair, oiled it with bear grease, and selected his finest calico shirt and linen leggings. Laughing Eyes plaited her glossy, black hair and adorned it with an eel-skin wrap; she fastened hundreds of silver brooches and brass thimbles to her sleek doeskin dress and little bells to her ankles, so that she jingled when she walked, and applied a daub of vermilion to her cheeks and eyelids; she wore her finest earrings and her moccasins were exquisitely decorated with beadwork.

The frolic began at dusk and went on for hours. Usually the women danced in an inner ring with the men circling around them, but sometimes they would interweave and find individual partners. Although a few bold souls whispered wanton words when they had a chance, the pounding drums and constant movement permitted little chance to talk. The spice of the courtship was in the way bodies swayed and eyes beguiled.

Blacksnake positioned himself behind Laughing Eyes as often as possible and strived to match her rhythms with his own, but so did Sweating and a few other potential rivals. Whenever Blacksnake passed by her he put as much meaning in his glance as he could, which more than once made her cinnamon-brown face break into a smile that displayed her white teeth. Was that a good sign or did she think him a silly lovestruck fool?

When the drums stopped well after midnight, a few couples wandered off into the dark while most returned to their wigwams. Laughing Eyes seemed to tarry a moment at the edge of the dancing ground, but before Blacksnake could muster the resolve to approach her, she turned and walked slowly away. At that moment Kiss Me, whose dancing had won praise all evening, came up to him.

"Look what I have for you," he said, holding out a small bark torch.

"I could have made that myself," Blacksnake replied scornfully.

"Not this one," Kiss Me insisted. "I used specially prepared strips from trees known only to me; it has an aroma no woman can resist. Go to her tonight and you will see that what I say is true."

Blacksnake grasped the torch and strolled, as if he had no destination in mind, toward Laughing Eyes's wigwam and stood perplexed at the doorway. What if her parents, Night Stander and Burns the Meat, weren't asleep? Or, worse yet, what if she rejected him and everyone woke up and saw his shame? He looked at his torch, a scanty twist of bark, and wondered if he should trust in Kiss Me's magic. Yet there was something in Laughing Eyes's smile and the way she had lingered after the dance that gave him courage. Perhaps it was the wiggle in her walk as she sauntered off.

He took a deep breath and stepped inside. At the low embers of the fire pit he lit his torch and began to grope his way between the sleeping platforms along the walls. He shielded his eyes from the glare with one hand, straining to see her face in the semi-dark. He was reminded of one night during hunting season when they had set a burning brand in the bow of a canoe and drifted downstream watching for the ocular reflection of staring deer along the bank. In his reverie, he thought for a second that he had encountered a curious doe, but it was Laughing Eyes, peering coyly up at him with an ardent smile.

"I dreamed you would come," she whispered, lifting his spirits and giving him hope.

"I do not speak from the lips outward," he said softly, "but from within. If you are willing, I wish to take you as my wife."

"You have spoken good words and my heart is glad," she replied, her eyes sparkling; and with that she touched his hand, brought his flaming torch to her face, and blew his light out.

2

At dawn Blacksnake slipped from Laughing Eyes's embrace and stepped to the door of the lodge. He waited there until Night Stander woke up and noticed him.

"I have been with Laughing Eyes," he stated, as was befitting a man of honor. "It is at her fire only I wish to warm myself."

"I have heard you," Night Stander replied.

Blacksnake returned to his own lodge to retrieve his gun, powder horn, and shot pouch. It was a brisk autumnal day when the wind seethed in the trees and whispered in the grass; a chill in the air seemed to invite the first snowfall. After last night's frost, pawpaws and crab apples would finally be ripe. Soon the villagers would divide into winter hunting bands. Fluttering leaves—golden, crimson, scarlet, deep purple, and maroon—gave the forest a festive hue. Only the grove of shrub oaks, a natural windbreak on the northwest edge of the village, refused to surrender its brown and sear foliage. On the leeward side of a nearby hill Blacksnake found what he sought, a grazing buck, and brought him down with one shot. He hefted the carcass on his shoulders and carried it back to the village where he dropped it at the doorway of Laughing Eyes's wigwam. Then he went home and told his mother what he had done.

No Nose talked to The Porcupine, and the two gathered suitable gifts—furs, guns, and household goods—that represented a selection of the best of all they possessed. These were wrapped in a bearskin and presented to Night Stander and Burns the Meat.

"We are come to make you easy in your old age," The Porcupine announced. "We bring you fire, water, and moccasins. My son, Blacksnake, loves your daughter, Laughing Eyes. He can kill any animal and he will fill your kettle to the top."

"I have heard what you say and I like your talk," Night Stander answered.

The next day Night Stander and Burns the Meat processed to the lodge of The Porcupine and No Nose, bearing reciprocal gifts; Laughing Eyes, dressed in her finest, walked between them; once inside, she was seated on a buffalo skin in the place of honor.

"I thank you for choosing my daughter," Night Stander said to Blacksnake. "She is a good girl and she will not shame you."

"Her heart is like the sweet sap that rises every spring in the sugar tree," Burns the Meat added.

"I thank you for taking pity on me and letting me warm myself at your fire and bring you fresh meat," Blacksnake said.

"You will be proud to marry my son," No Nose asserted. "He has taken scalps."

"One, Mother."

"There will be many more."

The two families shared a meal and Laughing Eyes's parents returned to their lodge. The next morning Blacksnake gave a horse he had stolen in Kentucky to his good friend and her brother, Thin

Raccoon, who, in the spring, would present his sister with the choicest cuts of his winter hunt. That afternoon, Sweating, accompanied by The Sleepy One and Plays Tricks, saw Thin Raccoon with Blacksnake's horse and realized what had happened. In a blind rage he drew his knife and, before anyone could stop him, stabbed the horse several times in the side. Thin Raccoon picked up his gun and leveled it at him.

"I have been shamed in front of my friends," Sweating cried. "Now shoot me."

Instead Thin Raccoon pointed his gun at the head of the horse and put an end to its suffering. Sweating, now feeling doubly shamed, returned to his lodge and swallowed a poison made from the root of the May apple.

Fortunately, his mother Corn Woman saw him do it and ran to get The Little Doctor, who administered an antidote. Sweating fell into a coma in the evening, but by morning he regained consciousness and seemed fine. The Soldier gave Blacksnake two horses, one to replace his gift to Thin Raccoon and the other for Sweating, who, after conferring with his parents and friends, declared that his rage was spent.

After that near tragedy, the other young men Blacksnake's age quickly selected their mates: The Sleepy One married Apple Tree in Blossom; Thin Raccoon, Thunderstruck; Plays Tricks, Moonlight; Fooled by Owls, Sitting Quiet; and Sweating, Brings Joy. White Swan, the daughter of He Provides and Walks by the Water, became the second wife of Cutfinger and had to take orders from his first wife, Cat Bird. It wasn't unusual for important men, especially chiefs and leading warriors, to have more than one wife; A Wave, for example, when his first wife Humming Bird died, married her two younger sisters, Pumpkin Woman and Spring Deer. There was even one woman in the village, Three Thighs, who had four daughters by two husbands, Buck Feet and Black Loon, and divided her time between their lodges.

Not all of these domestic arrangements proved to be durable. It was rare for a man to leave a woman, because he would have to contend with her male relatives, but it was common for a wife to abandon a husband. One day in the fall of the following year Sweating came home and found that his lodge had been stripped of all but his gun, shot pouch, and powder horn. He'd been divorced. Brings Joy had moved in with The Muskrat, a warrior from the other end of the village. Everyone held their breath to see if Sweating would seek revenge or attempt suicide again; instead he quickly found another mate, Mist at Dawn, one of Three Thighs's daughters. Miami men made jealous husbands and adultery was punished severely. When The Porcupine and his wife were young and hot-blooded, he had caught her in the act and, in a frenzy of revenge, killed the other man and bitten off her nose. Given how close and loving the couple was now, Blacksnake found the story hard to believe—even though the evidence was in her name and on her face. Why, The Porcupine even helped with her daily chores. And wasn't he esteemed by all as a man of imperturbable calm and contemplative wisdom? But, then again, perhaps what happened in the past explained why she drank.

Everyone knew that on top of Hanging Rock, a prominent limestone out-cropping beside the Wabash, a fickle maiden named Wynusa had once encouraged two suitors to fight for her; but when the victor tossed his rival's lifeless body into the waters below, she suddenly realized which man she truly loved and leapt to her death after him.

Once the honeymoon was over, Blacksnake and Laughing Eyes settled into an easy, unreflective, and mutually sustaining domestic routine. He did what all the other Miami men did: when they weren't out hunting or on the warpath, they hung around the council house gambling, playing games, repairing their equipment, and speculating endlessly about when the Big Knives would attack. She, in turn, was usually with the other women, talking and singing as they shared their common work. In the winter hunting camp, she was often busy with her knife, skinning Blacksnake's kills and cutting up the meat. In the evenings he smoked his pipe and watched her scrape and shape and stretch the hides; to prepare deerskins she would rub them back and forth on a wooden post and knead deer brains into the texture; then, with her eyes rolled back as if in a trance, she chewed on the skin until it was soft and pliable. She also spent a lot of time making jerky to store for hard times, slicing meat into thin strips and placing them on a grid-work of saplings to dry over a low smoky fire. Once this slow process was completed, the meat was wrapped and packed away. When needed it would be pounded into a powder and added to the broth.

Blacksnake was delighted that Laughing Eyes, unlike her mother, proved to be an accomplished cook. Their typical meal was sagamite, a stew made of corn and the meat of the day; she could also prepare, when given the opportunity, a series of succulent delicacies: beaver tail, buffalo tongue, fawn in the bag, bear steaks, and roast turkey. In every Miami wigwam, during good times, the cooking pot was always simmering and people helped themselves whenever they wished. The hunt was abundant that winter. In the spring Blacksnake and some of his friends loaded their peltry on pack horses and made the long trek to Vincennes to see what they could get in exchange. The situation there was still tense. The town itself was a ramshackle affair, a few hundred houses along a couple muddy streets, yet it was bigger than the Louisville that Blacksnake vaguely remembered. He was impressed by the view across the vast prairies, the finer French houses, which featured whitewashed walls and backyard orchards in full blossom, and the new fort, with two-story blockhouses at every corner, that the American army had recently erected. The commandant, Major John Hamtramck—happening upon Blacksnake haggling in English with one of the traders—scrutinized him closely and asked his name.

"Blacksnake," he replied in Miami.

"No, I mean your English name."

Preoccupied at that moment with what he could get for his skins, he responded offhandedly, "William Wells."

Hamtramck looked him over one more time and then left him to deal with the traders. They were a shrewd lot and pretended to spot flaws in furs where there were none, but Laughing Eyes had done her work well and Blacksnake was prepared to argue his case.

When they returned to Snake-fish Town, Blacksnake and his friends brought with them the manufactured goods that had become, over time, Miami necessities: steel needles and knives; brass kettles and bowls; woolen strouds, calico dresses, and linen shirts; lace, thread, porcelain beads, and silk ribbons; casks of rum, kegs of powder, bags of shot and, most important of all, a few rifles that were more accurate than their old muskets.

In early summer The Sleepy One led a small band across the Ohio. Blacksnake stole three Kentucky horses, enough to repay The Soldier and keep one for himself. Like all Miami warriors, Blacksnake had abstained from sex both before leaving and during the weeks he was away on the warpath. Now that he was back, he longed for Laughing Eyes as never before.

"Tonight," he promised, "I will love you until the dawn."

"No," she said firmly. "I am carrying our child. He spoke to me in a dream."

"My heart is glad," he said, placing his hand on her slightly swollen belly, "but why not have sex?"

"Do you want him to be born bald?" she replied, as if stating the obvious.

Blacksnake thought he knew by now all the ways of the Miami, but his wife's answer took him by surprise. Nevertheless, what she stated was indeed the case; she wouldn't sleep with him until after the baby was born.

He lit his pipe, trying to calm himself, and considered his options. Sexual restraint was essential on the warpath; the village was a different matter. He knew of a few widows whose husbands had died recently, two of them still young, but they, like most Miami women, looked older than their years. All the girls his own age had married last fall, with one notable exception—Shadows on Treetops at Sunset, the pretty daughter of Cloud Catcher and The Names of the Beautiful Animals Invoked by Our Ancestors, a respected chief and the uncle of The Soldier's wife. The next afternoon Blacksnake approached her on a path near the village, filled her ears with pleading words, and she relented. After each rendezvous, he gave her tokens of his affection; she would half-smile and walk back to her father's lodge.

When Laughing Eyes's time drew near, she developed strange cravings for fruits out of season and exotic decoctions. Blacksnake rode all the way to Kekionga to bring her some dried cranberries and English tea. On the way back he stopped in the village of Little Turtle, the leading Miami war chief. His small town, which included a prosperous trading post run by chief Pacan's sister The Other Side, was an easy day's walk or an urgent two hour's run from Kekionga. Little Turtle had a teenage daughter, Sweet Breeze, whose quick wit and stunning beauty caught Blacksnake's attention immediately and made him wish that he could stay.

As he rode along the river on his return, lost in lustful fantasies of Laughing Eyes, Shadows on Treetops at Sunset, and Sweet Breeze, his horse almost stepped on a dead rattlesnake, whose drab, flabby length extended across the trail—a good sign. It was forbidden to kill grandfather rattlesnake, but his tail played a vital role in the birth process. Blacksnake cut off the powerful omen and placed it carefully in his hunting pouch.

One day in late August, Laughing Eyes said that it was time. Leaning on the arm of Burns the Meat, she walked to the birth hut where that night, bathed in sweat, she squatted down—clutching a wooden post with one hand and shaking the rattlesnake tail with the other—and, assisted by her mother, delivered her baby. After the cord was cut, she rested for a few hours before carrying the child to the river for bathing. Then she returned to her lodge and informed Blacksnake that he had a son.

Laughing Eyes named him "Speaks in Dreams," but, at that exact moment, Blacksnake thought he heard a small voice at the back of his head whisper, "His name is Samuel."

That year the winter was hard. Fearing an attack of the Big Knives from Kentucky, the villagers had delayed planting corn in the spring; then late rains and early frosts made for a small harvest. Because white settlers were driving more Shawnee and Delaware onto Miami land, the winter hunt was poor. By January they were chewing on boiled bark, turkey quills, old bones, acorns, cattails, roots. Some of the elderly, weakened by starvation, suffered from chills and fever—and The Little Doctor's cures of sweating, fasting, and purging only made them worse. Several died, including Looking Over the Top, the wise old man who had lived with the bears. Blacksnake had to resort to killing animals the Miami usually refused to eat—foxes, muskrats, wolves, and wildcats. Only the tribe's distant relatives, groundhogs and rabbits, were exempt.

To make matters worse, Laughing Eyes told him that sex was still forbidden.

"Why?" he demanded incredulously.

"Do you want to spoil your son's milk?" was her answer, and that settled that. Then she added with downcast eyes, "It is not easy for me either."

Blacksnake knew that he was being selfish and self-indulgent, but he was only nineteen.

Sugar weather came just in time. In early March, during a period of sunshiny days and frosty nights, the hunting band packed up their peltry and moved to a maple grove. Knives were driven at a slanting angle through the bark and reed spouts placed in the slashes. The slowly dripping sap water was caught in containers which, when full, were emptied into large brass kettles kept at a constant boil over blazing fires. The syrupy molasses from these was then transferred to long wooden troughs. At night the water in the troughs would rise to the top and freeze, leaving a thick brown residue of maple sugar at the bottom.

After all the privations of the hard winter, tears of joy squeezed from their eyes when they tasted the skin-tingling sweetness of that sap. They added it to every broth, slathered it on meat, chewed it like candy, and sucked it like honey until they were strong and happy again.

One day Blacksnake was sitting inside the bark and branch hut he and his family called home during sugar season, when Thin Raccoon pulled aside his bearskin doorway and announced, with a concerned look in his eyes, that a man, a white man, had come to see him.

He was short, stocky, dressed in fringed buckskins, with a bushy reddish beard and beady blue eyes.

"Billy," he said in a scratchy voice, "do you recognize me?"

Blacksnake looked him up and down and said, "No, I don't."

"I'm your brother, Carty Wells. Don't you remember?"

Billy Wells hadn't yet been born when his family moved to Jacobs Creek, leaving his brother Carty behind in Virginia. He had only seen him twice after Carty moved to Coxe's Fort, south of Louisville, a few years before Billy was captured. Therefore, Blacksnake spoke the truth when he looked the strange man in the eye and repeated, "No, I don't."

They sat down and shared a pipe and Carty did his best to convince Blacksnake that he was who he claimed to be. He certainly knew the names of all his brothers and sisters and he could describe in detail the pond south of Louisville where Billy Wells and his friends had been taken prisoner. As he spoke one of Blacksnake's dogs came into the hut and began gnawing on the man's boot. The man kicked him away, as was proper, but there was something in the way he looked at the dog that was troubling. Blacksnake had always taken the Miami's ubiquitous dogs for granted. They were a scrawny, sharp-nosed, pointy eared, whiny, ravenous lot—a cross between a fox and a wolf—always snarling and grinning and scrounging after any scrap they could find. Certainly, they were pesky and insatiable, but the man's lips, half-hidden by his beard, curled in obvious disgust. Blacksnake looked around his hut as if for the first time, seeing it as that white man must: a filthy hovel, clogged with suffocating smoke, that reeked of sweaty leather, spoiled meat, rotting wood, and rancid bear grease.

Suddenly he understood that the man's disgust was not only for his mangy dogs but also for him and all the Miami. He saw them as the same—dirty animals.

"I have listened to your words," Blacksnake said coldly, with deliberate formality, "but I do not believe you are my brother. I ask you to go now and not come back. These are my people."

"What about Sam?" Carty entreated. "Surely you'd recognize him! If he came, wouldn't you listen to him?"

The white man was weeping—tears that could have come from genuine emotion or merely the smarting of wood smoke. At that moment, remembering the world of Billy Wells, Blacksnake captured a vivid image of his brother Sam, clinging to the stirrup of his horse, upon which Colonel Floyd was mounted, and running for dear life, as he escaped from the battle where their father had been killed.

"I might," he said.

Part II

...the gradual extension of our settlements will as certainly cause the savage, as the wolf, to retire; both being animals of prey, though they differ in shape. In a word, there is nothing to be obtained by an Indian war, but the soil they live on, and this can be had by purchase at less expense...

—George Washington

Harmar's Defeat

1

In the spring of 1790 Sam Wells, guided by a trader from Vincennes, made the perilous trip to Snake-fish Town and asked his brother to come home with him. Blacksnake recognized Sam's pocmarked face instantly; after a long discussion, in which Sam evoked memories of their shared past, he reluctantly consented to visit, provided he could bring along Thin Raccoon and Fooled by Owls. The plan was to meet in early July at the mouth of Clark's Creek, on the Indian side above the Falls of the Ohio. In the days leading up to his departure, Blacksnake agonized over his decision. He was happy in his present life, but he knew in his bones that it couldn't last; after his brother's visit many long-repressed memories began to haunt his dreams. He thought that if he could return to Kentucky and see his white relatives, he might be able to decide what he should do. As they shared a last pipe together, The Porcupine was his stoic self and wished Blacksnake well. Sure she would never see him again, No Nose screamed and pulled her hair. Laughing Eyes, Speaks in Dreams in her arms, gave her husband a cold look of reproach.

"Your son needs a father."

"I will return," he promised, striving to hide his conflicted feelings.

"I do not believe you," she said and began to weep.

"I need to decide who I am," he struggled to explain.

"I thought you already knew."

After swapping their Kentucky-stolen horses for Indian ponies, the three friends rode to the place of rendezvous where Sam was waiting with a skiff to carry them across the river. Since friendly Indians bartering their furs and prisoner exchanges were a common sight in Louisville, the party was able to pass through town without incident.

Sam had sold his Station to Squire Boone and established a plantation north of Louisville. He built a substantial hewn-log house with a fieldstone foundation, a brick chimney, glass windows, and a puncheon floor. There was also a barn, a corncrib, stalls, a stone spring-house, and small cabins in back for the slave families that worked his several hundred acres of cleared land.

Mary Wells, in a loose-fitting homespun dress with a blue kerchief spread across her shoulders, met them at the door. Childbearing had aged her considerably. Her narrow, creased face had a sickly pallor, her breasts sagged, she walked with a slight stoop, and spoke with a twisted, thinning smile. Her feverish eyes, which reminded him of his mother, made Blacksnake nervous.

"A brand plucked from the burning," she cried, wrapping her skinny arms around him.

The pride of the family was a new daughter, Rebekah, born that spring. Blacksnake took an instant liking to her; whenever he put his hand in her cradle she would wrap her tiny fingers around one of his. Her two young sisters were more enthralled with the baby than with having Indians in the house. In fact, Thin Raccoon and Fooled by Owls preferred to sleep in a makeshift lean-to and eat under a spreading elm tree. Blacksnake tried the feather bed in the back room, but in the night he felt suffocated and joined his friends outside. He enjoyed being near Sam and his family, watching them and touching their possessions—he even tried on Sam's boots, heavy as millstones, and some of his clothes—yet he didn't feel comfortable talking with him.

The next day Sam took Blacksnake and his friends to visit the pond where Billy Wells had been captured. It all came back to him vividly, although now he could picture it from both sides. The Soldier must have been elated at how smoothly the boys were taken prisoner.

"You just missed the wedding of a friend of yours, Billy," Sam remarked with a note of sarcasm in his voice. "Will Linn married Absalom Keller's widow last week."

Blacksnake's heart jolted. His look was enough to tell Sam to go on with the story.

"The Linn boys and young Brashears stayed with the Delaware until the fall and pretended to adopt their ways. Then one day they saw their chance when they was left alone with an old couple. They grabbed the squaw's axe, knocked 'em both on the head, and skedaddled for the river. When they finally reached it they was in bad shape and Brashears couldn't swim a lick, so they made a raft and paddled across to Louisville."

"Did they kill them?" Blacksnake could not imagine raising a tomahawk against The Porcupine and No Nose.

"Hell, I don't know, they done what was necessary, I reckon."

An uneasy silence followed. Although Blacksnake felt no regrets, somehow the fact that his former friends had run away made his own choice seem less secure. What if *he* had? What would his life have been like then? He noticed Thin Raccoon and Fooled by Owls staring at him, so he quickly translated for them.

"This is where I was captured by The Soldier."

Whenever Blacksnake spoke Miami, Sam always looked surprised, almost shocked.

"You know, if you stayed, you could find work as an interpreter. General Harmar would pay top dollar for someone like you."

"I'll never fight against the Miami."

"I didn't say that. There's other things, treaties and such."

Again, Blacksnake translated: "My brother says the Miami should sign a treaty."

Thin Raccoon and Fooled by Owls frowned at the suggestion.

"The Miami won't sign a treaty with the Americans," Blacksnake told Sam, "unless the Ohio River is the boundary."

"It will be a cold day in Hell before that happens," Sam drawled. "Congress has passed laws and surveyors are sectioning the land north of the Ohio into squares."

"They had no right to do that," Blacksnake protested.

"They had every right in the world," Sam said heatedly. "The Injuns sided with the British and the British lost. It's that simple. Don't you see? This country don't belong to Injuns, it belongs to us. Once we get the land, they'll be gone, then watch us grow! Their way is doomed. You better get out while the gettin's good. You're not a squaw man yet, there's no blood on your hands, won't you come back to your own people, Billy?"

Since Sam had only spent an afternoon in Snake-fish Town, he assumed that Blacksnake had not yet taken a Miami wife—or white scalps. He believed in his heart that what his brother should do was too obvious to merit debate.

Blacksnake, for his part, didn't know how to begin to tell Sam about his life as a Miami; both men rode back to the house in silence.

Blacksnake and his two friends stayed around the Wells's place for the next several days. They went fishing and squirrel hunting, played with the children, met various visitors, including a doctor to check on the baby and Mary's minister, curious to see if they had souls worth saving. Sam didn't press his brother to leave the Miami, but in their small talk they couldn't avoid disputes.

Seen through Miami eyes, white people were often offensive: they smelled bad, walked funny, and had defective teeth; they shook with the wrong hand and mounted horses on the wrong side; they had hairy faces, seldom bathed, wore uncomfortable clothes, ate poor food, and talked too much, too loud, all at once, without listening to each other; they hoarded their excessive possessions and the males, black and white, worked in the fields like squaws. Why should a few have so much and most so little? It didn't make sense.

"They are clever at making things," Thin Raccoon granted. "If they had stayed on the other side of the mountains and sent a few traders among us, they could have been a useful people."

Fooled by Owls was puzzled by doctors and ministers.

"Why do the whites need both?" he asked.

"One is for the body, the other the spirit," Blacksnake said.

"How can you cure the body without seeking the spirit that caused the sickness?"

"They think they are separate."

"Is that why the ministers do not have sex?"

"That is only the blackrobes. They believe that sex is bad."

"Truly! Have they never tried it?"

"No."

"Well, that explains it. But why can not the blackrobes and the others agree on anything?"

"Each one reads a book called the Bible differently."

"Why do they look at books anyway?"

"To learn how to behave."

"Do not the old ones tell them?"

"No, they need to read it on paper."

"I do not like it," Fooled by Owls concluded. "When the white man makes marks on paper, we lose more land."

Sam suggested a trip to Louisville on Saturday; Mary said it would be too dangerous. Finally, they agreed that only Blacksnake, dressed like a white man, would accompany his brother into town. With his freckled face and thick red hair covering his slit ear lobes, wearing a linsey shirt, flannel breeches, and leather boots, he certainly didn't look like an Indian. Only a savvy frontier veteran would have noted his erect posture, toe-in walk, and quick eye. In Blacksnake's memory the area had been mostly forest. Now a smoky haze hung in the air from all the timber and underbrush being burned away; scattered everywhere he saw cleared fields and cabins. Half-wild hogs foraged in the woods and no signs of game were visible along the old buffalo trace that led to town. It seemed to Blacksnake that the quality of the settlers had declined. Gaunt, dispirited people—gaping and scratching, stretching and spitting—lounged outside their ramshackle shanties and didn't appear to be doing any work. The barefoot women wore shapeless tattered smocks, passels of children ran around naked as jaybirds, and the men had small, narrow-set, weasel eyes filled with suspicion.

"Damn bog-trotting Cohies are taking over this country," Sam said of these Scotch-Irish newcomers. "Sometimes I'm of a mind to pull up stakes and move on."

Louisville was still a small town. Many of the original log cabins had been replaced by frame houses; there were even two houses made of brick, a few stores, and a two-story stone courthouse. The largest Indian mound remained untouched, although several of the smaller ones were gone. The two brothers hitched their horses in front of Patton's Tavern and walked inside.

"What's yourn, stranger?" the bartender asked Blacksnake with a snaggle-toothed grin.

"Mike, this here's my brother Billy."

"The one what got taken across the river?"

"The same."

"We thought ye was daid."

Whenever white people talked about him, Blacksnake felt disembodied, as if he were and were not there at the same time; he knew that the "Billy" they referred to was him, and yet it wasn't. At such times he would smile and nod and say nothing.

Sam pulled a cob stopper from a small jug of whiskey and introduced his brother to some men drinking and talking at a table by the fireplace. Robert Kirk, a rubicund-faced man in a plum-colored coat with clubbed hair, was an Ulster Scot who believed in keeping the Sabbath and anything else within reach. Blacksnake remembered Sam's buckskin-clad friend Bland Ballard, a dark-browed, battle-scarred Indian fighter of the old school; he wore his hair long, a taunt to his savage foes; a large bone-handled knife in a leather sheath hung from his beadwork belt. Garth Rutherford, freshly arrived from Virginia, was a Tuckahoe aristocrat in a scarlet waistcoat, skin-tight white pantaloons, and a full-bottomed blond wig. A slave boy in a blue jacket with gold buttons stood by his side holding his plumed hat. Peter Smith, a pig-eyed, pug-nosed, broad-shouldered bully, whose scraggly beard was streaked with tobacco juice, slouched in a chair tilted against the wall and didn't bother to shake Blacksnake's hand.

Only Bland Ballard cast a curious eye at the man he had known as Billy Wells, estimating if he could be trusted. The others carried on their conversation as before, never once asking Blacksnake what the Miami were like, but more than willing to share their opinions on everything.

"Have you seen General Clark lately, Bland?" Sam asked.

"Tutherday."

"How is he?"

"More of a sot than ever."

"What's his opinion?"

"The same—extirpate them root and branch."

"Egad, he can't mean it," Rutherford said.

"He means it all right," Ballard said. "Once you've been here a while you'll mean it too."

"Give them a good drubbing," Kirk declared, his face turning a deeper shade of red.

"Gentlemen, draw it mild," Rutherford protested.

"Would you have this country left a wilderness?" Sam demanded.

"Better a charnel house, I suppose," Rutherford remarked sardonically.

"I'd rather kill the devil than have the devil kill me," Ballard said.

"They ought to be cut from the face of the earth," Smith shouted and stomped out in a huff.

"I sure as hell didn't come all this way to raise horses for the thievin' savages," Sam stated.

"It's the decree of Providence that those that cultivate the earth shall have it," Kirk asserted in pious tones. "Your savage lives only for the day's pleasure, he does not plan for the future."

Blacksnake, glumly silent during the conversation, felt a sudden impulse to speak.

"Is that why you always raid in the fall?" he blurted out, fixing Kirk with an unsettling gaze.

"What do you mean?" Kirk asked.

"When the corn is ripe," Blacksnake said, struggling to control his emotions. "That's when you raid. You destroy it...the winter food...and you burn the villages."

"It's the truth," Ballard acknowledged. "With Logan the last time we did exactly that: we burned the buggers out and shot them down as they ran. Same thing with Clark."

"That's why we need a treaty," Sam added, casting a troubled glance at his brother. "If the Miami sign, what happened to the Shawnee won't happen to them."

"The chief who signed the treaty was killed," Blacksnake said.

"You mean old Molunthy," Ballard said. "He run afoul a Hugh McGary. You may think what you're hearing at this table is pretty harsh, but they's plenty what hate Injuns like hell itself. McGary come up to the chief after he had surrendered and asked him if he had been at Blue Licks. Well, the old coot didn't understand a word, he jist nods his head, so McGary flew into a rage, grabs an axe, shouts 'I'll show you Blue Licks play!' and sinks it in his head. Then he turns on Colonel Trotter and said he'd chop him down, too, if he tried to stop him from killin' savages whenever he pleased. Why, that man feeds dead Injuns to his dogs to make them fierce."

"I wonder if Trotter wants him along this time," Kirk said.

"The Colonel will have to take what he can get," Sam said. "There's a lot of good men that plan to sit this one out. I say let the Cohies earn their keep."

Blacksnake realized that the men were talking about the next invasion of Indian territory, just as if he wasn't in the room.

"Why's that?" Rutherford inquired.

"Would *you* want to risk your hair for two dollars a month?" Ballard said. "I'll fight for Colonel Shelby and Kentucky, not General Harmar and the United States."

"A lot of us here in Kentucky wonder if maybe we ought to declare our independence not only from Virginia," Kirk explained, "but the United States as well, and go our own way."

"That's right," Sam added. "Why not form our own country and run it as we see fit?"

With that question lingering in the air, Sam and Blacksnake took their departure and once again rode home in silence.

The next morning Sam showed no surprise when his brother stated that he was going back to his people. Mary cried and said that their latchstring would always be out for him. Blacksnake told them that he had a wife and child to care for; Sam made no mention of General Harmar's planned invasion. Nevertheless, as the three friends mounted their ponies and headed north, in the back of his mind Blacksnake kept hearing Sam's voice, on the day they visited the pond where he was captured, pleading with him, "You better get out while the gettin's good."

2

At the end of the Revolution, the Treaty of Paris of 1783 had stipulated that Britain should abandon her frontier forts and cede the land south of the Great Lakes; the United States, in turn, would compensate the banished loyalists for their losses. When the new nation refused to make restitutions, Britain decided to keep her forts and retain the lucrative fur trade. To establish a tribal buffer zone between the Ohio River and Canada, they re-armed the Indians. In 1784, therefore, a reluctant Congress authorized the recruitment of 700 soldiers to defend the western frontier. The call went out for men of high caliber—free of disease and preferably sober—but most were flotsam and jetsam from the jails and gin mills of eastern port cities. Many were immigrants fresh off the boat, or drunks and drifters from the slums, shanghaied into service on the promise of grog, grub, clean clothes, and a trip to the West. Because Pennsylvania supplied more men than any other state, she had the dubious honor of selecting one of her own to lead this rag-tag army of riffraff.

Thirty-one-year-old Josiah Harmar was a rather bland man who at least looked the part: he was tall and well-built, with steely blue eyes and the deportment of an aristocrat; a cockade hat, graced by an ostrich plume, sat on the pig-tailed, powdered wig that concealed his bald head. By the time the raw recruits reached Pittsburgh, General Harmar had laced their bare backs with the stripes of discipline and named them The First American Regiment. Over the next several years Harmar's army moved slowly downriver, building forts, evicting squatters, surveying land, and signing treaties with any tribesmen who were short on supplies, thirsty for whiskey, and weary of war. These farcical treaties were dictated not negotiated; the intimidated Indians were told that they were now "a subdued people," who, because they had sided with the British, had forfeited their lands. By 1789, only one key tribe had refused to sign a single treaty—the Miami.

The grand design of Congress was that the Northwest Territory above the Ohio River should be settled in an orderly manner, in contrast to the pell-mell rush of selfish squatters that quickly turned Kentucky into a free-for-all of pettifogging litigants. After an official survey, range by range, dividing the acreage into squares of exact dimensions, the land would be sold to settlers, who would live in townships, each with its own school. The model was New England at its best: the wilderness would yield to cleared fields, church spires, and children playing on village greens.

When Washington became President in 1789, the United States was a vulnerable country surrounded by potential enemies; the army was too weak to fight a war and the treasury too depleted to finance one. A policy of peaceful coexistence with the Indians made sense. Through treaties the tribes would relinquish their lands. When the settlers, often former soldiers, moved in, felling trees and driving off the wildlife, the savages would remove into the illimitable regions of the West. Henry Knox, Washington's Secretary of War, whose department oversaw Indian Affairs, agreed with his commander-in-chief: resorting to force might stain the new nation's honor; it was cheaper to treat with the separate tribes than to fight them. If everything went according to plan, soon America would be as though the Indians had never been.

The Indians had other ideas. For years they had tried to establish a confederation that would unify the tribes on the warpath and at peace treaties. If they could set aside their inveterate rivalries, act in the common defense, and refuse to sign any treaty without the consent of all, then perhaps the white settlements could be confined to Kentucky. The British encouraged the belief that the Americans might accept an Ohio River boundary and that His Majesty's troops might fight shoulder to shoulder with the warriors. Every year the Indians met in Detroit to renew their pledge of unity; but periodically exposed and exhausted tribal factions surrendered more territory.

All Indian men were warriors, but no one expected them, even in the midst of an emergency, to be warriors all the time. Therefore, the most imperiled tribes agreed to live close together, along the Maumee River, with a concentration of Delaware, Shawnee, and Miami villages at Kekionga, where Little Turtle was the leading war chief.

The American policy of divide and conquer had been so successful Arthur St. Clair, the governor of the Northwest Territory, informed Washington that "the general confederacy is entirely broken." If that were true, all that remained was to identify the renegades and deal with them accordingly. The President ordered St. Clair to send an ambassador up the Wabash to find out which Indians wanted peace or war. In April, 1790, a month after Carty

Wells had visited Blacksnake, Antoine Gamelin of Vincennes made
that trip, delivering speeches at the villages of the Piankashaw, Wea,
and Kickapoo, as well as Snake-fish Town (when The Soldier and
Blacksnake were away on the war path) before reaching Kekionga.
At every stop he was chided for his bad manners: Why hadn't he
brought rum to humor the old people and powder and ball for the
young hunters? Didn't he know the women and children would
starve without good broth? Didn't he know a bearer of speeches
should never come with empty hands? Again and again various
tribes told him that no decision could be made without consulting
their brothers, the Miami. Finally, at Kekionga, both The Dappled
Fawn, the head peace chief, and Little Turtle, along with Blue
Jacket, the war chief of the Shawnee, explained to him that they
could not decide until they had conferred with their English father at
Detroit. After he received a report of Gamelin's failed mission,
Washington resolved to chastise "certain banditti of Indians" from
the northwest side of the Ohio. Secretary of War Knox concurred;
in June he ordered General Harmar to send a strike force of 400
mounted men "to extirpate, utterly, if possible, the said banditti."

Governor St. Clair took Washington's plan a precipitous step
further, raising 1,500 militia to supplement the regular army. The
recruits that answered the call were not the frontier veterans they
expected, rather a motley jumble of substitutes—mostly old and
infirm or young and inexperienced—unfed, ill-clothed, under-
equipped, and untrained. Many had never discharged a gun or an
order. And the pride of Kentucky colonels who purported to lead
them bickered bitterly over who was in command. St. Clair and
General Harmar favored a simultaneous, two-pronged attack,
sending 500 men from Fort Knox in Vincennes against the Wabash
villages and 1,500 from Fort Washington in Cincinnati to destroy
the Miami and their allies at Kekionga. Washington approved this
expanded operation, staking the moral, military, and political
prestige of the United States on what amounted to a full-scale
invasion of Indian country. Thus, what began as a peace initiative
had quickly become a punitive expedition, which the Indians could
only perceive as total war.

3

Upon his return from Kentucky, Blacksnake stayed only two
days in Snake-fish Town, enjoying a brief reconciliation with
Laughing Eyes and his young son, before riding off to tell Little
Turtle that the Big Knives were coming. Since the British had been

warning him for months, the chief was not surprised by Blacksnake's message, yet he did take a keen interest in the messenger.

"I once took a white boy with me on a raid into Kentucky," he said with a slight smile. "We hid in a corn field to wait for dawn; as soon as the sun came up he ran to the cabin shouting '*Indians! Indians!*' and spoiled our attack." Little Turtle chortled heartily at that part of the story, raising his voice to convey the boy's cry and waving his arms to mimic his frantic gestures. "I vowed never to take a captive on the war path again."

The two men exchanged a long, penetrating gaze. Little Turtle, at five feet ten, was an inch or two taller than Blacksnake and had a stronger build; in his early forties, his face suggested a philosopher more than a war chief. His large, black, tranquil eyes seemed to absorb everything they saw, while the wide, thin-lipped mouth moved easily between frowns and laughter. He spoke with a natural dignity that commanded instant respect.

"You speak and understand English well. Perhaps you can be of use to us." Blacksnake could feel the chief's mind considering alternatives and planning ahead. After a pause, Little Turtle squinted at him and asked, "Would you spy for me?"

At that moment, under the sway of Little Turtle's powerful presence, Blacksnake did not question his loyalties. "What would you like me to do?"

"When the soldiers march, capture one and make him talk. We will need to know how many and where they are headed in time to send runners to all the villages."

That evening Blacksnake stayed in Little Turtle's lodge beside the Eel River and again he found he could not take his eyes off the chief's beautiful teenage daughter, Sweet Breeze. Although they did not speak, something in the way she moved told him that she was pleased he was watching her. In the morning the two men rode off to confer with tribal leaders.

In the summer of 1790, Kekionga was the sprawling home of several tribes. The main town, led by Dappled Fawn, overlooked a bend where the St. Joseph from the north and St. Marys from the south came together to form the Maumee, which flowed northeast to Lake Erie. About two dozen French and British traders, several with families and some with Indian wives, lived there as well. On the opposite bank of the St. Joseph sat a smaller Miami village, where The Wildcat, also known as Jean Baptiste Richardville, nominally ruled in the absence of his uncle, Pecan, who had taken about forty of his followers into Spanish Territory. The Delaware had left the White River and settled on both sides of the St. Marys, four miles below Kekionga, while the Shawnee had built a new Chillicothe and Piqua three miles down the Maumee near the road to Detroit. In all, about two thousand people, including 600 warriors, lived in the various villages, each of which was surrounded by extensive cornfields.

Blacksnake found Kekionga a remarkably distinctive place. The hewn-log houses and stores of the traders—although clustered at the southern end of the village near an apple orchard, a cemetery surrounded by a picket fence, and the landing place—blended with the wigwams and cabins of the Indians; the old French post and British fort, sacked twice by the Miami, both lay in ruins. As peace chief, The Dappled Fawn gave orders to all residents, while The Wildcat spent much of his time at the card table with a group of young men that styled themselves "the Friars of St. Andrew" or "the Miami Recollects." The real power in the town belonged to The Wildcat's mother and Pecan's sister, The Other Side, who spoke for her bashful son in council. She had married a French nobleman, who had returned to Quebec; now she was the wife of another trader, Charles Beaubien, and controlled the portages, via the Little and Eel Rivers, to the Wabash. This gave Kekionga, that glorious gateway linking the St. Lawrence seaway with the Mississippi, its crucial strategic importance.

On the road by the river one Miami warrior doffed a powdered wig as Blacksnake passed by, another displayed a dried human heart skewered on a stick; a few steps later a French woman in an apron and cap gave him a *marron glacé.* As the shrieks of a prisoner from the Ohio being burned at the stake reached his ears, Blacksnake looked out on the water and saw three swains from the village rowing two damsels beneath pink parasols, whom they serenaded with bawdy lyrics accompanied by flute. That evening, as warriors inside the council house were striking the war post and working themselves into a frenzy, at Mr. Barthelme's place a fiddler played and guests walked a minuet or enjoyed a *dance rondy,* while the ladies sipped tangrie and the gentleman swigged cherry bounce— until one Mr. Abbott, drunk as a skunk, began offering his buxom daughter Betsey to all comers. Next morning the ringing of three cowbells called the still inebriated and often squabbling whites to prayers, led by Mr. Louis Payet, whose obese wife had to be trundled to matins in a cart. Blacksnake stayed in the lodge of The

Dappled Fawn and his brother the Deer, where the cooking pot was always simmering and the men shared pipes and stories. After breakfasting on English tea and scones with clotted cream at John Kinzie's house, Little Turtle presented Blacksnake to Blue Jacket, war chief of the Shawnee, a tall, strong, fiery-eyed man, resplendent in a gold-laced scarlet coat with gold epaulets and sporting a large silver gorget in front, and Buckongahelas (The Agile One), war chief of the Delaware, whose ear lobes, torn in battle, dangled like dead worms over his shoulders. With two of the notorious Girty brothers, George and James, serving as translators, the chiefs listened to what Blacksnake had to say and discussed strategy. Since warriors could not stand the monotony of waiting for something to happen, it was unfeasible to guard the paths to their villages. They wanted to fight once and go home. An invading army would have a hundred-and-fifty-mile march through uncharted territory—surely stray hunters would sound the alarm. Then spies could be sent out to stalk their progress. After promising to return in September, the month of the hard corn, Blacksnake went back to Snake-fish town.

In early October a Shawnee hunting party sent word that Harmar's army had reached Old Chillicothe, the target of Clark's raids in 1780 and 1782; they were encamped on a tributary of the Little Miami at the edge of a beautiful prairie and numbered about 1,500, mainly militia, with seven times more infantry than cavalry, and three brass cannon. Blacksnake located the troops a few days later, as they approached Lorimier's abandoned trading post, known as the French Store; he killed a bear cub in a clearing, cut the skin into little pieces, and scattered them on stumps for Harmar's men to find—an omen that many soldiers would soon lose their scalps.

Because the army kept a close two-column formation—with scouts and surveyors in front, flanking squadrons, and rear guards—it was difficult to take a prisoner. At night the army bivouacked in a defensive square with a posted perimeter and supplies inside. In late October ten mounted men searching for lost horses stumbled upon a Shawnee boy, armed with only a bow and arrow; one of the horsemen gashed his face with a sword, slicing off the top of his ear and injuring his eye, before taking him alive. Apparently he talked; Blacksnake, hiding in a tree, saw the soldiers hobbling the horses and selecting 600 light troops for an early start the next morning. He immediately rode off to tell Little Turtle that General Harmar's army was only two days away.

When Blacksnake arrived, Kekionga was in chaos. Major Hamtramck was also on the march from Vincennes; 600 Wabash Indians, including The Soldier's men from Snake-fish Town, had set an ambush for him in the ravines of Pine Creek below the Wea village at Ouiatanon. Meanwhile, the eagerly expected warriors from the Three Fires—Ottawa, Potawatomi, Chippewa—had not yet arrived at Kekionga. Faced with an insufficient number of defenders, Little Turtle and the other war chiefs called for an evacuation. Everything that couldn't be carried was buried; the women hastily harvested corn while the men dug holes to hide it in. The war chiefs confiscated all powder and ball from the traders' stores, and the tribes withdrew in three directions: the Delaware to the White River, the Shawnee down the Maumee, the Miami headed northwest to the Elkhart River. Seeing that several of the French traders' log stores and warehouses might serve as enemy defenses, Little Turtle ordered them burned.

After an arduous march through beech forests and swamps in a cold, drizzling rain, Colonel Hardin's advance troops reached Kekionga in the early evening of October 15th; the main force arrived two days later. The militia immediately separated into gangs of pillagers who raced from one village to the next searching for loot. Two stray Shawnee boys, found hiding beneath a river bank, were shot at; one escaped and the other, before he died, mortally wounded a soldier. Harmar's men lost no time ravaging all the towns and surrounding cornfields; they girded the fruit trees, trampled the gardens, dug up the cached food, and torched wigwams. Two nights later a Delaware chief, Captain Punk, was waylaid while attempting to steal horses and killed. Two triumphant Kentuckians, McClure and McClay, brought the severed head back to camp, stuck it on a stake in front of Harmar's marquee, and crammed tobacco plugs in both sides of its mouth.

Blacksnake, concealed with Little Turtle and other Miami warriors in a clump of trees, saw the smoke rising from Kekionga. From high ground across the river he could see how quickly the unruly militia had ignored commands and broken ranks in a frantic hunt for plunder.

"They are greedy and want blood," Blacksnake noted.

"We will give them some," Little Turtle replied.

The next morning Colonel Trotter led a detachment of several hundred Kentucky militia and thirty federal troops on a reconnaissance mission. After crossing the St. Joseph's River at the ford, they picked up the Indians' trail and began moving toward where Blacksnake and the others lay in hiding, their paint-streaked faces matching the fall foliage. Little Turtle instructed two mounted men to draw the cavalry into a wild goose chase that would leave the infantry exposed. The first brave was quickly intercepted and killed by a few horsemen; when the second was spotted, the four commanders of the militia themselves rode off in hot pursuit. Unfortunately, the leaderless infantry stayed put in the wide prairie, out of the range of Blacksnake's rifle. He could only watch helplessly as the cornered brave tried his best to elude the Kentuckians on fast horses, wounding one of them, before he, too, was overtaken and killed. When a small escort was seen moving to the rear with the injured soldier, Little Turtle told his warriors to circle around and cut them off, but a savvy army scout warned Trotter in time to send reinforcements. The cat-and-mouse game continued all afternoon as Little Turtle tried to lure the skittish militia into his trap. Toward sunset Harmar ordered a cannon fired three times, a signal for all looters to return to the main camp; Trotter and his men welcomed this as a summons to abandon their three-day expedition.

Little Turtle had traversed much of the area between the Ohio River and the Great Lakes; as a young man he had seen New Orleans and Quebec, yet the place he knew best was the upper Eel River. If Harmar persisted in sending detachments in that direction, Little Turtle was sure he could find a spot for an ambush. After Trotter's force withdrew, he led his men down a side trail through a narrow, boggy prairie, telling them to make no effort to hide their tracks, and encamped at the far end. Then he instructed Blacksnake and some other braves to go back and scatter trinkets along their route. That night the painted warriors danced to throbbing drums and chanted their feats of valor. In the morning Little Turtle positioned his men in the tall grass and trees on both sides of the path and left a campfire smoldering. Two men on horseback and four on foot were sent out as bait.

General Harmar was irate at Colonel Trotter for returning early; his rival for command, Colonel Hardin, demanded that the disgraced militia be given a chance the next day to save face. The men, however, were reluctant to follow the hard-charging Hardin, whose derring-do might cost them their scalps; many dropped by the wayside. When Hardin's detachment, now down to 200, reached the wide prairie where Trotter had dallied the previous afternoon, his scouts discovered the wooded knoll that had concealed Little Turtle's warriors. Hardin halted while Captain Faulkner's company of infantry reconnoitered the land on the left and Major Fontaine's cavalry inspected the main trail. At about this time three spectral Indian dogs loped out of the woods, sniffed around, and ran off, spooking some of the soldiers. Half an hour later Major Fontaine reported fresh signs on a side path two miles ahead—apparently the terrified savages were in full retreat. Hardin galloped forward to lead his troops; he was in such a rush to pursue the foe that he forgot all about Faulkner's company until he arrived at the fork in the trail; then he dispatched Major Fontaine and his cavalry to retrieve them.

"Wait until they are between our lines," Little Turtle told his warriors, gesturing vigorously to illustrate his plan. "Those on the hill, take trees, aim for their chests, and fire first. Those on the other side, lie flat in the grass until the shooting starts, then rise up and fire. If they make a stand, fire again in turn; if they break and run, chase them down with tomahawks. The quicker we kill them, the greater their fear and the more complete our victory."

Blacksnake checked and rechecked his flint, patches, powder horn, and pouch.

"A Kentucky rifle," Little Turtle said, hefting it and drawing a bead down the trail. "How accurate is it?"

"That depends on who pulls the trigger."

"Are you a good shot?"

"Yes."

"How good?"

"I can hit a man at over a hundred yards." It was not the Miami way to boast, Blacksnake knew, neither was it appropriate for a brave to understate his skills.

"If you do not want to be in this fight," Little Turtle said, "I will understand."

"I am here to defend my people," Blacksnake replied calmly, trying not to think about the fact that some of the men he was about to shoot at were probably people he knew in Kentucky—maybe even his brothers!

"I have heard you. When they come, aim at those who are far away, beyond the range of our muskets."

Blacksnake wasn't convinced that the troops would walk into the trap being set for them until he heard the absolute certainty in the chief's voice—not "if," but *"when* they come."

Little Turtle inspected the positioning of his men again and then stood in front of the smoldering fire where all could see him. He took off his bear-claw necklace and dropped it on the ground and tossed his King George medallion a few yards away.

"When their advance scouts on horseback see these," he told his men, "they will stop and dismount to pick them up. Those behind them will stop, too. That is when we will open fire."

Blacksnake thought that he spoke almost in a detached manner, as if recalling a fleeting dream, yet his words gave the warriors strength and patience.

Hardin's force, deprived of Fontaine's cavalry and Faulkner's company of infantry, was now less than 150. They followed the side trail, which evinced fresh tracks in the mud and trinkets dropped in haste, across the Eel River and up its north bank. Two Indians, spotted ahead, instantly dropped their packs and fled into the thick underbrush. The troops entered a narrow, bushy prairie, with dense forest close to the trail on one side and marshland on the other along the river. To keep on dry land, the soldiers had no choice but to advance single file down the path. Then the retort of an Indian gun sounded from the woods, a lone rider galloped away in the distance, and Hardin, riding in front, saw smoke rising at the far tree line.

"Come on, boys," he shouted, "they're on the run and won't fight."

Hardin and the others on horseback rode to the smoldering campfire and stopped, followed by a strung-out line of militia and regulars on foot. The Colonel saw Little Turtle's bear-claw necklace and medallion in the dust, raised his hand for everyone to halt, and dismounted to pick them up. At that point the warriors back in the trees opened fire on one flank with devastating effect. Hardin's men scrambled for cover in the marsh, only to be met by a second deadly volley from the warriors hidden in the tall grass. This threw the remaining militia into a total panic; without firing a shot, most dropped their guns and scrambled in terror back down the trail, colliding into the more disciplined regulars attempting to form a line of defense. Seeing the confusion, the warriors gripped their tomahawks, gave a spine-tingling shout, and closed in through the thick clouds of gun smoke for hand-to-hand combat. Only about forty of Hardin's force, mainly regulars, held their ground and put up a desperate fight, a few escaping into the nearby swamp; several Miami warriors, in the frenzy of the kill, were fatally stabbed with bayonets before the last dripping soldier's scalp was held aloft with a triumphant yell.

After the first withering volleys, Blacksnake joined in the pursuit of those that fled—not recognizing among them his younger brother Charles and his older brother Sam. The warriors chased the militia back across the Eel River, cutting down stragglers, before they encountered sustained fire from Major Fontaine's cavalry and Captain Faulkner's infantry, returning too late to help prevent Little Turtle's ambush, let alone halt the retreat of the militia. One panic-stricken soldier, who probably didn't stop running until he reached Kekionga, shouted to Fontaine as he raced past, "For God's sake get out! You'll be killed! Yonder is Indians enough to eat you all up!"

4

While Little Turtle defeated Hardin's detachment along the Eel River, General Harmar moved his main force to the Shawnee towns down the Maumee from Kekionga and systematically destroyed them. Two days later—a warm, sunny, teasingly pleasant interlude of Indian summer—he began the march back to Fort Washington, camping beside Nine-Mile Run near the Black Swamp. That evening a scout covering the army's withdrawal reported that about 100 Miami warriors had returned to Kekionga to scavenge in the ruins for buried provisions. Still smarting from his defeat, Colonel Hardin pleaded with Harmar to send a quick strike force back in the night to take the Indians by surprise.

A force of 400 left around midnight beneath a full moon. When they came within a mile of Kekionga, they halted while Hardin and Major John Wyllys agreed upon a plan: Hardin with Major Horatio Hall's battalion would circle to the left, cross the St. Mary's, and come up behind Pecan's town on the west bank of the St. Joseph, near the shallow ford to Kekionga; at dawn Wyllys's regulars, Major John Fontaine's cavalry, and Major James McMillan's battalion of militia infantry would initiate the engagement by crossing the Maumee ford and attacking Kekionga from the south. Caught by surprise in a synchronized pincers movement the Miami warriors would be given a taste of their own medicine and slaughtered. Harmar would have his victory, Hardin his revenge, and the savages their retribution.

Early in the morning of October 22nd, as Blacksnake was standing beside Little Turtle—who held in his hands the charred fragments of two chests that had contained the wampum belts recording Miami tribal history—they heard gun shots from the west side of the St. Joseph River. It was Hall's battalion opening fire on some Indians near the stream behind Pecan's village; when the Indians fled to the north, the militia disobeyed orders and went after them. At almost the same time a brave ran up shouting that the Big

Knives were coming—several hundred infantry and some cavalry had been spotted south of the Maumee. Little Turtle improvised on the spot, sending horsemen off to rally the Delaware and Shawnee warriors at their nearby towns. "Take some riflemen down to the orchard," he told Blacksnake. "Do not fire until the soldiers reach the middle of the ford. Hold them as long as you can and keep moving from tree to tree so they cannot outflank you."

As if he had all the time in the world, Little Turtle walked over to a group of men sitting and talking around a fire at the edge of the town. "Stay where you are," he said softly, "the Big Knives are coming. They can see you from the hills across the river; do not act alarmed. When you hear gunfire from the French orchard, take cover behind those hazel bushes and wait until they are close before you shoot."

Next he ordered a dozen braves on horseback to ride down to the Maumee ford, and, when the soldiers came, to divert their cavalry off to the northeast, toward the Shawnee towns and away from Kekionga. The chief then gathered about a hundred Miami braves and positioned them in a burnt cornfield and some elevated, brushy ground above the town and distant from the two fords.

Blacksnake steadied the long barrel of his heavy rifle in the crotch of a fruit tree and drew a bead on the Maumee ford, off to his left. He held his breath through a sustained, eerie quiet as McMillan's militia waded into the river in the hazy early morning light. When the first line of soldiers reached the middle of the water, the warriors opened fire, cracking the silence. Several men screamed and swore, gripped the place where they were hit, and dropped; the rest either retreated in fright or rushed toward the northern shore; this confusion gave the Miami marksmen time to shoot again before receiving a return volley. Blacksnake was startled when the young warrior beside him cried out, "I'm shot," threw a futile hand at the sky, and fell dead—it was Little Turtle's favorite nephew. The Wildcat, who was as wide as he was tall and very strong, lifted the body in his arms and they all retreated back through the charred logs and creosote stench of the French village and took cover behind the banks of the St. Joseph.

When Major Fontaine saw the militia floundering and a circle of savages sitting in plain sight around a campfire ahead, his blood boiled. "After them, boys!" he shouted and charged toward Kekionga alone, leaving his men in his wake. As he rounded a hazel thicket, waving his sword, several warriors shot him at point blank range; somehow he clung to his saddle while his crazed horse ran in circles, until five of his men, who were also shot at and wounded, rode up to retrieve his body. The now leaderless cavalry spotted some Indians on horseback and gave chase. Upon reaching the lower end of Kekionga, McMillan's militia infantry were immediately engaged by the first of Blue Jacket's Shawnee warriors arriving from their villages down the Maumee; a tree-to-tree battle then spread out through the swampy forests east of the main town.

Blacksnake fired from behind a fallen log with unthinking, automatic precision. The last to cross the ford were Major Wyllys's sixty regulars, already deprived of the militia who were supposed to protect their flanks; in their buff and blue uniforms they marched in a disciplined hollow square formation, meeting only sporadic fire from Blacksnake and the other Miami riflemen on their left flank. They proceeded through Kekionga and arrived at a cornfield near the ruins of the old British fort; at this point Little Turtle's concealed braves shattered the air with their war cry and tore the soldiers to shreds with a withering volley from three sides.

Major Wyllys tried to maintain an orderly line of battle and fight for better ground, but his situation was too exposed and the Miami braves, infuriated by the destruction of Kekionga, gave him no reprieve. Blacksnake advanced with the other marksmen along the river bank, aimed for the officers and saw Wyllys himself clutch his chest and fall—soon a brave was sporting the major's large cockade hat. After a flurry of volleys that shrouded the battlefield in gun smoke, a swift and deadly, strangely muffled struggle began; Little Turtle's warriors, brandishing their scalping knives, tomahawks and war clubs, fearlessly rushed in among the remaining soldiers, who defended themselves as best they could with bayonets. The desperate position of the surrounded men quickly became impossible as more warriors swarmed in from the nearby villages. Only seven regulars and a few of the militia escaped across the low waters of the St. Joseph.

Just when it looked as if the Indians' victory was complete, Colonel Hardin and Hall's men, who had been engaged in a separate battle with Delaware and Miami warriors in the vicinity of Pecan's village, arrived at the west bank of the St. Joseph and opened fire on Little Turtle's men as they were fording the river. Blacksnake saw a young brave, accompanied by his father and brother, get shot in the middle of the stream; when the father dropped his gun and stooped down to help his son, the other son fell by his side. The old man dragged them both to the shore and sat down between them, waiting to be shot in turn. The ferocious fighting along the river intensified, lasting over an hour, until the carcasses of dead horses and the mingled bodies of soldiers and warriors clogged the darkening water. Finally remnants of McMillan's battalion, whose running skirmish with Shawnee warriors had carried them around to the right and away from the other fighting, appeared on the scene, throwing both sides into disarray. The startled militia, thinking they saw more Indians, fired a volley at their own men, and retreated, leaving their dead and wounded behind; while Little Turtle, assuming that Harmar had committed the rest of his army, broke off the engagement and his warriors dispersed into the trees.

Hardin's and Wyllys's disjointed and ill-conceived plan, which called for undisciplined troops to march over unfamiliar terrain and attack in unison, had, in a sense, worked, bringing the battle to a close. Blacksnake had no doubt that the victory was Little Turtle's. The army's losses were triple those on the Eel River three days before. The warriors also had reason to mourn: the Miami, Delaware, and Shawnee had lost twenty-five braves.

Blacksnake knew that all those dead warriors cried out for revenge. Around noon contingents from the Ottawa, Pottawatomi, and Chippewa had arrived in time to take part in the last phase of the battle. By evening, more reinforcements from the Three Fires marched in. The war chiefs of the various tribes immediately met to plan an attack on Harmar's demoralized army camped nine miles away. There were dozens of locations between Kekionga and Fort Washington that were ideal for an ambush. The only questions were where and when.

That night, however, a strange thing happened. A little after sunset, Blacksnake watched the moon come up blood red and stay that way for almost an hour. He knew what this omen meant: if they attacked the Big Knives soon many warriors would die. The Ottawa conjurers, awestruck with fear, issued dire warnings.

When Little Turtle awoke in the morning, all the men of the Three Fires were gone and the chance to attack Harmar's retreating army was lost.

"Harmar was a fool," Little Turtle told Blacksnake later in the day. "He was like a bear hiding under a rock who sticks out one paw at a time to be cut off. Did you see the way the Kentucky men ran for their lives when we attacked but the soldiers stood their ground until they died? The white generals always think the next battle will be like the last. When they come again they will not send out small war parties. They will stay together in a big group, like the flocks of pigeons that always nest in the same place—then it will be easier to kill them all!"

St. Clair's Defeat

1

As soon as the tattered remnants of the militia brought word of Harmar's Defeat, which they blamed on the general's drunkenness not their own lack of discipline, the Kentuckians began plotting a retaliatory strike. No one spoke more profusely or wrote more prolixly in favor of another expedition than James Wilkinson—since he aspired to lead it. A Maryland man of small stature and charming manners who craved wealth and power, he knew that the best way to stand tall in the eyes of Kentuckians was to kill savages.

At the start of the Revolution, he had apprenticed his ambition to Benedict Arnold and served under General St. Clair at Ticonderoga, Trenton, and Princeton. But Wilkinson always knew where his loyalties lay: he was a patriot and partisan of the glorious cause of himself. By betraying both friends and enemies, he rose in the ranks and married Ann, of the Philadelphia Biddles, thus adding a dollop of class and a fat dowry to his rising fortunes. Appointed Clothier-General, he displayed more aptitude for lining his pockets than outfitting the army. When word of his dubious bookkeeping reached General Washington, he resigned before he could be dismissed.

In 1784 Wilkinson moved his family to Lexington and began to upstage and backstab his Kentucky rivals. Soon he was surrounded by a coterie of young male sycophants enticed by his prodigal parties and grandiose designs and ready to do his bidding. To finance his vast, ambitious enterprises, Wilkinson contrived his most devious scheme to date. In those days Spain controlled both banks of the lower Mississippi, cutting off Kentucky farmers from the lucrative markets of New Orleans. A gratuity of a pair of blooded horses to the proper authority in Natchez smoothed his way downriver to a meeting with Esteban Rodríguez Miró, a man susceptible to towering tales and low deals. When Wilkinson returned to Lexington, by way of Charleston, South Carolina, he made his triumphal entry in a carriage drawn by four prancing fillies with two slaves in silken livery as outriders. New Orleans, he announced, was open to trade—but only in his boats. What he failed to mention was that he was now a spy in the pay of Spain.

Everything worked as planned, for a time. Profits rose for Kentucky farmers, produce from Wilkinson's cargo boats lined the docks of New Orleans, and packhorses laden with the coin of the realm made their way up the Natchez Trace to his fancy Lexington home. But Kentucky did not secede, as Wilkinson had promised; Rodríguez Miró began to wonder if maybe he hadn't been duped. When Spain decided to open its market to anyone willing to pay a 15% tax, Wilkinson lost his monopoly and his debts soared. He decided that the best way to save his honor and stave off his creditors was to revive his military career. After all, Kentuckians still called him "General" and what were redskins to a man who had fought the redcoats! Wasn't a name in arms the best way to become the Washington of the West?

In May 1791, a mounted force of 800 Kentucky militia crossed the Ohio led by Brigadier-General Charles Scott—Wilkinson had to settle for second in command. Their goal was Ouiatanon, the main Wea town on the Wabash, and their mission was to destroy it and the surrounding villages, kill any warriors who offered resistance, and capture the women and children, in order to demonstrate to the savages that they were at the mercy of the United States.

After days of riding through mud and rain, the militia saw in the distance smoke rising from the campfires of Ouiatanon, which was largely undefended. Scott sent a detachment under Col. John Hardin to attack some smaller villages on the left while Wilkinson was ordered to surprise the main town. The Indians tried to flee in canoes across the swollen waters of the Wabash to the Kickapoo village on the opposite bank. Wilkinson's men killed some boys and old men protecting the retreat and opened fire on the last canoes, filled with women and children. By the time Scott arrived, their bodies had all drifted downstream, enabling Wilkinson to assert that only warriors had been shot. Next the militia crossed the river at a fording place and sacked the Kickapoo town. Hardin had caught the smaller Wea villages completely by surprise, killing six and taking fifty prisoners.

After releasing the elderly and ill among his prisoners with a message to their people that unless they signed a treaty they would be humbled in the dust, Scott and his militia headed back to Louisville. Along the way they happened upon a British trader accompanied by The Wasp, an important Wea chief. The Kentuckians confiscated the trader's goods and killed and skinned the Indian to make razor strops as mementos of the campaign—a small detail Scott left out of his glowing report. Forty-one women and children were left as hostages at Fort Steuben.

Pleased by Scott's success, St. Clair did not want the martial ardor of the Kentuckians to cool, so he authorized a second expedition—this time with Wilkinson in charge—to attack Snake-fish Town. His instructions were not to scalp the dead and to bring the women and children back alive. A force of 525 men headed north. It was an arduous trek through uncharted territory. The only person along who had ever seen the village was Sam Wells, and he had traveled with a trader from Vincennes by way of the Wabash. For days the militia struggled through tangled underbrush and a labyrinth of bogs bisected by an occasional Indian path. On the afternoon of August 7th they arrived at the Wabash and crossed to the far shore. Here they found numerous signs of Indians, including a well-trodden trail and freshly painted war posts. They rode north for a few miles before they heard the sounds of laughter. Coming closer, they saw children playing tag on the roofs of the cabins; it was the time of the green corn ceremony and everyone was in a festive mood. The village was situated in an oak barren along the west bank of the Eel River.

A woman screamed "Kentuck! Kentuck!" and everything was confusion. Wilkinson ordered a charge and his men spurred their horses across the shallow waters of the river into the heart of Snake-fish Town. A few shots were fired by a handful of warriors and three soldiers fell. The return volley killed men, women, and a baby. Some squaws and children were captured. The rest of the Indians sought refuge in nearby swamps; they cowered all night in cold water as their village was burned and their crops cut down.

Although the people of Snake-fish Town feared invasion and had been making preparations to pack their possessions and bury provisions for winter, Wilkinson's attack had caught them by surprise. The Soldier had taken sixty men down the Wabash, expecting an attack from that direction; the rest of the warriors, including Blacksnake, had ridden off that morning for Kekionga to get ammunition; The Porcupine and two-dozen others were out in the countryside digging roots. There was nothing they could do but wait in hiding until the Big Knives left.

2

It took two days for Plays Tricks to run all the way to Kekionga with the news that Snake-fish Town had been destroyed. "We are dead," he cried and began calling out the names of those killed and captured. The Old Wolf, Black Loon, The Cat, The Quail, The Lead Mine, Cutfinger, Corn Woman, Cloud Catcher and her baby boy Too Many Questions—all were slain by the soldiers. Among the women and children taken captive were No Nose, Laughing Eyes, and Speaks in Dreams—Blacksnake's mother, wife, and son. Wilkinson had left Looking Over The Top's old widowed wife, First Snow, behind with a message that the hostages would be held at Fort Washington until the chiefs of Snake-fish Town signed a peace treaty and surrendered land.

Blacksnake felt bereft; he paced listlessly back and forth beside the river and wondered what to do. Within a year all the major Indian settlements along the Wabash and Eel Rivers, as well as the Delaware, Shawnee, and Miami villages at Kekionga itself, had been leveled. He had lost his white family long ago. Did he now have to give up his Miami family too?

Little Turtle walked up to Blacksnake as he stood in the old French orchard near the partially rebuilt Kekionga.

"I want you to stay here with me," he said.

"My wife and child," Blacksnake replied in tight-lipped anger, "I need to do what I can to free them."

"Nothing can be done for them," Little Turtle stated with characteristic assurance, "until we have fought the army again."

"How do you know?"

"The whites will not accept what happened to Harmar. They will think we were lucky or he was a bad leader. These raids on the Wea and your people will convince them the fight has gone out of us and we will run. That is why we must defeat this next army. After they count their dead, they will agree to return the prisoners and respect our lands."

"What about The Porcupine?" Blacksnake asked. "I should be with him."

"The Soldier will look after his brother. I need you here."

"Why? What can I do?"

"I watched you when we fought Harmar's men. Your rifle reaches a great distance and you hit what you aim at. We have a hundred Kentucky rifles. I want you to stay in my lodge and teach my men how to shoot."

Although slower to load than a musket, the rifle's longer range and greater accuracy made it the frontiersman's weapon of choice. Billy Wells was already a skilled marksman by age ten, and as Blacksnake he welcomed the chance to show the Miami warriors how it was done. Many of them were good shots, but few knew how to clean and oil their rifles or the finer points of fixing the sights and regulating the powder. Before long they were riddling targets the size of a man a hundred yards away.

Blacksnake spent many lonely days and restless nights thinking about Laughing Eyes and his son. When the impending battle was over, he would go to Fort Washington and gain their release. Nevertheless he could not keep his eyes off Sweet Breeze, who had a sidelong way of glancing back at him that was at once modest and enticing. One afternoon she came up to him while he was sitting on a split-log bench in front of Little Turtle's lodge and began combing his hair. She had two combs, a coarse one of wood and a fine one of ivory; first she worked through the matted tangles of his long red hair, being careful not to jerk too hard and laughing when some strands pulled away; then she used the fine one to finish the job, massaging his head with bear's grease at the end and combing in the sheen.

"It is hard for a man to lose his wife," she said softly. "Do you miss her very much?"

"Yes, I do," he replied, "but I am glad to be here with you."

"People say that now that your wife is gone you will return to the whites."

"I am a Miami." His answer had become axiomatic.

"They say that you will never love another and do not wish to marry again."

Among the Miami it was quite common for distinguished warriors to have more than one wife; or for a man who had lost his wife to marry her younger sister. Since Laughing Eyes had no sisters, Blacksnake, as a favorite of the chief Little Turtle, was expected to select another mate.

"Do not listen to the twittering of passing birds," Blacksnake protested. "The truth is that I love you."

Throughout their conversation Sweet Breeze had held her face in a demure, downcast way, as if to belie the boldness of her words, but now she broke into a wide smile that displayed a dazzling set of small white teeth and her black eyes sparkled.

"My heart soars at your words," she said, "but we must not talk of love in the daylight. I will speak to my father."

The next evening Little Turtle, with Blacksnake sitting by his side, assembled the members of his clan and announced, "I have given my daughter to this man, who is now my son. He will care for her and keep her safe and she will work for him and bear his children. Now I invite all of you to a great feast."

Sweet Breeze, a bride at eighteen, wore a white doeskin dress, laden with silver spangles that hung from one shoulder and clung to her hips, and her long glossy black hair draped over her small, shapely breasts. Her eyelids, cheeks, and the rims of her ears were tinged with vermilion and she had a tiny tattoo on her chin. After the feasting and frolic dancing, snuggled together under a feather blanket, Blacksnake smelled her hair scented with spruce wood. In the morning the other women in the lodge teased her as one who had enjoyed an obviously good experience.

As her name suggested, Sweet Breeze was amiable and eager to please; sitting on a cornhusk mat and eating a savory bowl of bear meat stew, Blacksnake could only wonder how a man's whole world might suddenly fall apart and then, astonishingly, in the blink of an eye, come together again. In his present smug contentment, Blacksnake let whole days slip by without thinking of Laughing Eyes and his lost son.

3

By the fall of 1791, Arthur St. Clair was a veteran of many battles. Born in Scotland, he came to America as a British soldier and fought under General Wolfe on the Plains of Abraham outside the ramparts of Quebec. After the French and Indian War he married Phoebe Bayard of Boston; a legacy she inherited aided his rapid rise to prominence in Pennsylvania while she slowly sank into insanity. During the Revolution he was court-martialed but exonerated for his failure to defend the supposedly impregnable Fort Ticonderoga; after distinguishing himself at Trenton and Princeton, he became a member of Washington's inner circle and was promoted to Major General. An autocrat by nature, St. Clair's effort to cultivate the common touch—by dressing simply, speaking frankly and permitting the middling and meaner sort access to his person—was rebuffed by the people of Pennsylvania, who rejected by ten to one his bid to be their governor. He fared better in Congress, which elected him President, and named him governor of the Northwest Territory.

After Harmar's ignominious defeat, St. Clair was ordered by President Washington to lead a second campaign. In March 1791 Congress authorized the enlargement of the United States Army to 3,000 regulars, mostly six-month levies, supplemented by State militias. Since the Indians at best could only gather 1,500 warriors, and lacked the logistics to keep them together for long, St. Clair assumed that it would be easy to march to Kekionga and establish a permanent fort there, compelling the Indians to flee or surrender and the British to relinquish their post at Detroit.

The formidable task of equipping the army was awarded to a private contractor, William Duer, a corrupt crony of Secretary of War Henry Knox. Already up to his neck in stock and bond speculations that would soon land him in debtor's prison, Duer purloined as much cash as he could to keep his creditors at bay. When military supplies finally began to reach Fort Washington, they were often defective. For an army that planned to cut a road through 150 miles of wilderness and build three forts, there was an insufficient quantity of axes, and saws that proved to be soft and dulled easily. The troops were issued haversacks without straps and waterproofing; shoes were outsized and weak in the seams; tents leaked, clothes shrank, hats didn't fit; the two forges sent to repair muskets lacked anvils; the powder, shipped in kegs from Pittsburgh, dampened from exposure on the way; the ammunition had to be fixed, shells and cartridges filled by hand; damaged field artillery carriages had to be replaced; four-pound shot was provided for three-pound cannon; packhorse saddles were ideal for elephants; the scrawny nags themselves—un-belled and un-hobbled—were left free to forage and many were lost.

The troops were a motley lot, the dregs of seaboard cities, who knew nothing of muskets or woodcraft. As soon as the difficult march across the mountains began, they got drunk and deserted at every opportunity. Irate officers laced the backs of the worst offenders with a liberal number of stripes and made them dance to "Laura Grogan," but no amount of punishment could turn these miserable wretches into disciplined soldiers.

Although the expedition had been planned for early August, not until September did troops from the East began to arrive. They fell far short of the projected 3,000 men so reinforcements of 400 Kentucky militia infantry were sent for. Since veteran frontiersmen preferred to ride to battle on their own horses, under their own leaders, and kill savages in their own fashion, most of the militia were greenhorns. When General Harmar, whose own expedition had hardly been a model of efficiency, saw how ill-prepared St. Clair's troops were, he was appalled. To march blindly into Indian territory and fight their finest warriors on their own ground with such men was to invite disaster. How could St. Clair risk so many lives with so little chance of success? The wiser strategy would have been to wait for spring and a fresh batch of recruits who could be properly trained and equipped.

The troops spent late September building Fort Hamilton, twenty miles north of Cincinnati, and waiting for the militia to arrive from Kentucky. In early October, the army crawled northward into unknown territory, following a conjectural compass-course toward Kekionga. Although most of the militia were not experienced frontiersmen, they were relieved of fatigue duty and given the job of scouting ahead. Then came the surveyors and road cutters, who felled trees, cleared underbrush, and built bridges for the infantry and the lengthy supply line of packhorses, bullocks, and oxen drawing ten cannon. About two-hundred camp followers went along, including drivers and drovers, wives and children of soldiers, as well as assorted mistresses, nurses, cooks, washerwomen, and prostitutes. By mid-October the weather turned cold and stormy; the carcasses of dead horses marked the army's route as frosts killed the last of the forage; a combination of steady rains, leaky tents, and chilling winds caused an epidemic of flu. When an expected supply train of packhorses was delayed, everyone was put on half rations. Frequent desertions further depleted St. Clair's troops, who had stopped to construct a second fort, named for Secretary of State Thomas Jefferson.

Even though General Richard Butler, who was second in commander, held St. Clair in contempt, he felt compelled to seek out an interview. "General," he said, "I request permission to lead a thousand hand-picked men on a rapid expedition against the Miami towns."

St. Clair's eyebrows went up in astonishment. "What are your reasons?" he demanded.

"Winter will soon be setting in," Butler said, stating what he felt to be obvious, "and the enlistments of the levies are almost over. If we wait any longer, all the packhorses will die, the levies will demand their discharges, the militia will desert in droves, and the savages, who must know we're coming, will ambush and annihilate the remainder."

"And what would you have me and the rest of the army do while you are winning your great victory?" St. Clair asked disdainfully.

"The troops can finish the fort and you can bring them on at your leisure."

St. Clair told Butler he would consider his proposal and inform him of his decision tomorrow. The audacity of the man! For a subaltern to make such a blatant bid for power to his face was enough to make him laugh.

"Your request is denied," St. Clair told him curtly the next morning. "Resume your duties."

The affronted Butler was more convinced than ever that the general was a damn fool who knew nothing about fighting Indians.

St. Clair understood that he had to act promptly. Already an entire company of levies from Virginia had been discharged and the mutterings of discontent among the militia were verging on mutiny. If he didn't restore discipline and engage the enemy soon, the entire expedition could become a fiasco. In late October two deserters and a man who shot a fellow soldier and threatened an officer were hanged before the entire army. The next day St. Clair marched his troops out of Fort Jefferson, leaving a garrison of 120 invalids to defend it. His plan was to move his troops so deep into enemy territory they wouldn't dare desert and to precipitate a confrontation with the Indians before all the levies left.

During the evening of October 30th, the encampment was caught in a major storm; gale-force winds blew down dead trees and branches, bolts of lightning split the tallest oaks. In the morning the commander of the Kentucky militia, Colonel William Oldham—the same man who had rafted down the Ohio with Billy Wells in 1779 and married Penelope Pope—reported to St. Clair that half of the militia had deserted in the night, vowing to plunder provisions from any packhorses they met. Oldham warned that the rest of the militia were likely to follow.

Throughout the campaign St. Clair had been far more preoccupied by the problems of maintaining his own army than those of encountering the enemy—he never really knew how many warriors he might face, where they might be, and who would lead them. He detached the First Regiment, his 300 best troops, with orders to chase the fleeing militia, return as an escort for the convoy of provisions, and deter other potential deserters. Apparently the general planned to "awe" the militia, not the Miami, with a show of force. By now his army, deprived of its only battle-tested troops, was reduced to less than 1,400 men.

St. Clair felt certain his force was clearly superior to his savage foes. As for the occasional skirmishes his scouts had had, they were nothing but run-ins with wandering hunting parties; the men who disappeared almost daily were no doubt deserters. Wasn't his force far larger than either the Scott or Wilkinson expedition in the summer and hadn't the savages fled from them? Surely when he reached Kekionga, the warriors would run and later the chiefs would show up to sue for peace, and then he could resume his job as governor. What concerned the grossly overweight general the most was a worsening case of the gout; his body ached so badly he could no longer sit upon a horse; a litter was made, which he referred to as his bier—and thus lying prostrate and wrapped ten-fold in flannel robes the fat, pain-wracked general was trundled forward into November.

4

All summer Little Turtle and the other war chiefs had been meeting in council and making trips to Detroit to ask for British aid. Without more guns and ammunition their men wouldn't be able to fight the United States army. Runners carrying black wampum and tobacco painted red had gone off in every direction to tell the warriors of the scattered tribes to gather at the Maumee Rapids. When word came of Scott's attack on the Wea and Kickapoo towns, those braves left as well. Blacksnake was the only Eel River man who had stayed in Kekionga after Snake-fish Town was destroyed in early August. Little Turtle simply didn't know how many warriors he could count on or how many troops he would have to face. He hoped that the army, whatever its size, would march slowly, giving him time to prepare.

The celebrated Mohawk leader Joseph Brant argued that now was the time to negotiate, not fight; he renewed his plea that Little Turtle and the others abandon the Ohio River and accept a boundary line at the Muskingum. He even traveled with some chiefs to Quebec to see if the British would mediate such a treaty. The Miami and Shawnee, however, were in no mood to compromise away their lands and the American army was already on the march. In mid-October scouts reported that the soldiers had finished one fort and were building another deep in Indian territory. After eagerly awaited armaments arrived from Detroit, the war chiefs decided to move their warriors to Kekionga, where an inter-tribal council would select a commander.

Some favored Buckongahelas, the Delaware whose courage in battle was legendary; others, Blue Jacket, the great Shawnee war chief; many wanted Little Turtle, because of his skillfully planned ambush and improvised on-the-spot decisions at Harmar's two defeats. Finally, after hours of orators singing the praises of each, Buckongahelas himself rose to speak.

"Little Turtle should lead," he said simply. "I would be proud to fight for him."

The Delaware chief's gracious words settled the issue. The next day all the warriors assembled on a grassy plain along the St. Mary's River south of Kekionga. Little Turtle was now the commander, but the braves would fight alongside their own tribesmen and under their own leaders. Since the warriors shared the same assumptions about how to fight—attack by surprise in a half-moon formation, moving from tree to tree to flank the enemy— the basic problem was agreeing on what signals the braves should use to coordinate their actions.

Little Turtle had learned a few things from fighting Harmar that he wanted the warriors to know. He told several hundred men to go cut sticks as tall as they were and then return.

"The soldiers put a long knife on the end of their guns," he said. "Braves eager to take a wounded man's scalp have been killed by them. Remember, the dying rattlesnake is dangerous, beware of his fangs. Sometimes the soldiers with knives on their guns run forward in a group to drive off our warriors and stab those who are reloading. This is what we must do: those they run at should wait for a good target, shoot straight, then withdraw to a safe spot to reload; if they keep coming, repeat this pattern. Those who are not attacked should only give ground if they have to. Once the soldiers have run a little way, they will tire and become confused, then we will turn on them and strike from three sides. Now I want us to practice; the men with long sticks will do what the soldiers do and the rest will respond in the proper way."

Even though what they were acting out was deadly serious, the warriors laughed as they imitated the soldiers and charged at the semi-circle of men spread across the open field. Some of the braves put powder in their muskets, but no ball, and startled their attackers by firing point-blank in their faces. If Little Turtle's plans were executed correctly, the charging soldiers would be trapped. Each time they raced forward, the line of warriors bent but did not break and then closed in again. Of course playing at war against men with sticks was not the same as repelling a trained army's bayonet charge backed by muskets and cannon.

Little Turtle ordered any braves possessing good rifles to practice with Blacksnake's Miami marksmen. Cockade hats and jackets with insignia, trophies from Harmar's Defeat, were displayed to help the warriors identify and target officers.

One afternoon a band of Delaware scouts brought in a soldier taken outside Fort Jefferson three days before. His captors had stripped off his clothes, leaving him with nothing to wear but a tattered hunting shirt, and painted his face part red, part black. Many warriors wanted to burn him on the spot, but first he must run the gauntlet. A loud halloo sounded and two parallel lines formed from the center of town to the river. The poor man was knocked to the ground and kicked and clubbed until he almost lost consciousness; finally he staggered to the door of the council house, where he was, at least temporarily, safe.

Blacksnake was waiting with several others to interrogate him. He looked the man in the face, which appeared to have been dipped in blood; the soldier wiped his eyes, saw a red-headed man in front of him, extended his hand to shake, and burst into tears.

"Do not weep like a woman," Blacksnake warned, "or you will be killed."

The man tried to control his emotions. Blacksnake gave him a cloth to clean his face.

"What is your name?" Blacksnake asked.

"Matthew Bunn."

"Where are you from?"

"Brookfield, Massachusetts."

"Where did you enlist?"

"Providence, Rhode Island."

He answered every question as briefly as possible, but his terse description of troops in disarray—plagued by sickness, desertion, and lack of supplies—substantiated what the scouts had reported and convinced Blacksnake that Little Turtle's determination to ambush St. Clair's army on its way to Kekionga was correct. For almost a week the war chiefs debated this plan—some favored defending the town, others fighting another day—but finally Little Turtle prevailed.

"We will go and meet St. Clair," Little Turtle told the assembled warriors, "wait for him to make a big mistake, then attack him with all our might."

Blacksnake took reluctant leave of his young bride of two months and joined the other warriors preparing for battle by fasting and abstinence. Little Turtle divided the braves into groups of twenty and told them to spread out and take separate routes toward the approaching army. Once they were near St. Clair's troops the war chiefs would gather and decide when to strike.

By the end of October all the war parties had reunited a few miles from St. Clair's army; scouts returned that evening with reports that sixty Long Knives had deserted and 300 soldiers had gone after them. St. Clair had made the same mistake as Harmar— he had divided his forces. Some of the chiefs wanted to attack him at dawn, but Little Turtle argued that they should wait. Let him march a few more days, until he is too far away for anyone to come to his rescue. It was difficult to restrain the braves; they wanted to kill the army's scouts and sentries and steal their horses; but if they did, and St. Clair became alarmed, the all-important element of surprise would be lost.

5

On November 3rd, the army had begun to camp; but when St. Clair arrived he noted that the land was exposed to flooding and ordered a search for a better site. The weary men marched on and by the early evening were pitching their tents on high, lightly timbered ground—surrounded by swampy lowlands and dark forests—beside a river that was assumed to be the St. Mary's.

The deployment of the troops was based on St. Clair's order of march; three of General Richard Butler's battalions formed one line facing west across the stream; seventy yards behind and parallel to them was an equally long line of two more battalions and the Second United States Regiment, facing east. Four cannon were positioned in the middle of each line. The riflemen protected the north side of this rectangular formation; the cavalry the southern end; the officers' marqees and their servants, the women and children, the drivers and drovers, the packhorses and supply wagons were crammed together in the middle. Six outposts of sentries defended the perimeter. Because of insufficient space in the main camp and to prevent further desertions, the militiamen were sent across the river to an open prairie, scattered with trees—a spot that showed fresh sign and the remains of many old Indian camps. A light snow began to fall.

Captain Jacob Slough, a red-faced, scraggly bearded levy in Major Thomas Butler's battalion, was pitching his tent when Lieutenant-Colonel George Gibson walked up holding a dead raccoon by the tail.

"Come to my tent," he said, "and I'll show you how to dress this critter Injun fashion."

Captain Edward Butler, the youngest and best-looking of the three Butler brothers in St. Clair's army, soon joined them for a taste of raccoon stew.

"I reckon that if a few boys was sent out tonight," Butler observed, "they'd catch some of them rascals stealin' our horses."

"I'd gladly lead that party," Slough asserted on impulse, "if they give me some good men."

"You can have your pick," Butler said, and called for volunteers from Gibson's regiment.

Slough stopped by Colonel William Oldham's tent to tell him about the night patrol.

Oldham was lying down, wide-awake, with his clothes on.

"I wouldn't go if I was you," he advised. "You've got a right smart chance of bein' cut off."

"Do you think they're out there?"

"I'm sure of it," Oldham replied with stoic fatalism. "I know they've been watching us. I saw fresh tracks in the mud by the river. I expect the whole army will be attacked in the morning."

"Well, I've got my orders," Slough muttered, regretting his impetuous offer to lead the scouting party, "so I've got to go."

Oldham told Slough the watchword for his sentinels and wished him well.

Slough and his men made their way slowly in the dark a mile up the Indian path that led northwest from the militia campsite. The patrol halted and spread out on each side of the trail, lying flat on the frozen ground. After a few minutes six or seven Indians passed within fifteen yards of them; Slough's men opened fire and the rest ran off. The men reloaded and again lay in hiding.

Half an hour later a large party of Indians appeared to the left of the path, gliding like ghostly apparitions through the trees, in the direction of the army encampment. Then another force of similar size moved with silent stealth across the snow-spotted forest to the right. George Adams, an experienced Kentucky woodsmen, whispered, "Boys, it's time to skedaddle," and so Slough and his men made their way cautiously back to camp.

When they reached Oldham's tent around midnight, he was still awake.

"Colonel," Slough said, his voice breaking with emotion, "I think you're right about the savages wanting to fight. The woods is full of 'em."

"I probably should inform Butler of my suspicions," Oldham said. "Tell the general that I think the army will be attacked in the morning."

Slough saw that the light was out in Butler's tent so he asked Lieutenant-Colonel Gibson to help wake him.

"I'm not dressed," Gibson protested. "Your orders were from him, make your report."

Slough was returning to Butler's tent when he saw the general step out and go stand by a fire where some sentries were warming themselves.

"Come over here, General," Slough said softly, "I have something important to tell you."

"What's all this secrecy?" Butler demanded, as he moved away from the other men.

"We went up the path about a mile and saw two large war parties of savages," Slough said. "Colonel Oldham told me to tell you that he thinks we will be attacked in the morning."

"Does he now." Butler stood a long time, stroking his chin; finally he added, "Thank you for your attention and vigilance."

"If you wish, Sir, I will inform General St. Clair."

"No, no, that won't be necessary," Butler replied sardonically. Simply hearing his commander's name seemed to upset him. "You must be fatigued. Go get some rest."

6

As Blacksnake knew, Little Turtle's decision to make a surprise attack at dawn was standard Indian procedure, but that tactic had never been attempted against a large military encampment in battle formation on high ground. The warriors of the Three Fires—the Chippewa, Ottawa, and Pottawatomi—would advance on the left flank, the Wyandot, Mingo, and Cherokee on the right, with the Miami, Shawnee, and Delaware in the center. Blue Jacket, in a bright, red British coat that belied his name and mounted on a fine horse, was given the honor of leading the attack against the perilously isolated Kentucky militia, while other warriors would over-run the sentry outposts. Blacksnake's riflemen were divided, one group on the east and the other on the west. They were to position themselves behind trees near the cannon and pick off the officers and men of the artillery.

"When we ambushed Harmar's men," Little Turtle said, "the militia ran like rabbits into the soldiers and caused great confusion. They will do that again if we strike terror in their hearts. Once the warriors are in place, just before the sun rises, I want all the tribes to give their war cries."

"That will spoil our surprise," Blue Jacket protested.

"No," Little Turtle replied with conviction, "it will only make it greater. The soldiers' legs will shake when they realize they are surrounded. Then we will attack and kill them all!"

The forest was almost pitch-black, illuminated only by patches of snow; in the dark the warriors were able to creep past the perimeter outposts of St. Clair's camp—some crawling on their stomachs through the grass, others hiding behind trees and shrubs in the marshlands. During the night sentries who thought they saw suspicious movements or heard strange sounds fired random shots into the obscurity, but the soldiers, accustomed to perturbed sentries, rolled over and slept on.

The shrill piping of fifes and the rat-a-tat-tat roll of drums sounded reveille before the first daylight filtered through the trees. As was their custom, the troops paraded under arms until sunrise. They were dismissed a little early that particular day; St. Clair had not compelled his weary troops to dig earthworks the previous evening and he wanted to turn this ground into a base camp and deposit for his final assault on Kekionga, which he assumed was only twenty miles away. In truth, the army was not encamped beside the St. Mary's as he thought but rather at the headwaters of the Wabash, and Kekionga was still fifty miles distant.

Little Turtle and his warriors were considerably closer.

The militia had just returned to their tents and were kindling fires to take off the morning chill and cook their scanty breakfasts when the forest on every side came alive with an unnerving mix of horse-bells, howling wolves, and human cries. The startled soldiers looked wildly around; all they saw was a pervasive gray gloom broken by glimmering traces of sunlight.

Then one sentry thought he saw a painted face and pulled his trigger; suddenly Blue Jacket's Shawnees discharged a thunderous volley from their hiding places and surged forward, supported by Miami and Delaware warriors. The frenzied panic of the militia was quick and contagious; some fired once or twice; most dropped their guns as if they were the cause of their danger and sprinted in helter-skelter confusion over the marshy bottomland and across the shallow river that separated them from the refuge of the main camp. Colonel Oldham ran after his fleeing men, shouting futilely, "Stop, you cowardly rascals, stand and fight!"

From his hiding place in the woods, Blacksnake saw the terror-stricken militiamen race headlong into Major Thomas Butler's levy battalion, and, as Little Turtle had predicted, throw it into disarray; they didn't stop running until they collided with the levy battalions in the second line, already engaged with Chippewa, Ottawa, and Potawatomi warriors attacking from the east.

St. Clair's drummers vigorously beat the alarm and those troops who were not disrupted by the flight of the militia took their battle stations. Although the soldiers held the high ground, the fact that their camp was not fortified and lacked trees left them vulnerable to enemy fire. The Miami, Shawnee, and Delaware warriors had pursued the militia across the bottomlands and taken cover in the tall grass, behind scattered sugar maples, and under the steep bank of the Wabash before opening fire on the first line of levies. The braves fought in silence now, seldom shooting twice from the same spot and only showing themselves when they darted forward to other hiding places or lifted their heads to draw a bead on the exposed troops.

Blacksnake's sharpshooters rested their rifles on fallen logs and picked off the artillerymen one by one. This deadly methodical work filled Blacksnake with a strange exhilaration—a greedy need to kill and keep killing, combined with a pride in his unfailing aim—as officers and soldiers fell steadily, replaced by others who fell in turn, leaving a pile of tangled corpses beside the big guns. Although the cannons continued their deafening roar, their placement on a knoll prohibited bringing them to bear on the warriors in the bottomlands in front of them; as a result, round after round of canister and ball sailed harmlessly over the heads of Little Turtle's braves, crashing into trees and smashing down branches in the encircling forest. The incessant gunfire created a dense cloud of white, sulfurous smoke that hovered three feet above the ground, making it harder for the soldiers to see their enemy and easier for the Indians to advance.

In a desperate effort to break the encirclement and turn the enemy's left flank, Lieutenant-Colonel William Darke ordered the Second United States Regiment to fix bayonets and charge. The soldiers, supported by two-dozen men on horseback, gave a spirited cry, rushed down a slope, and plunged through a small creek directly toward a squad of Wyandot. The braves yielded ground, as Little Turtle had instructed, and retreated to a driftwood-filled ravine where they reloaded and waited. The small company of cavalry quickly became impeded by a swampy thicket and lagged behind; the elated foot soldiers, thinking they had won the day, ran forward across a hundred yards of grassy bottomland until they were panting for breath. At that point the Indians opened fire from all sides with lethal effect. Darke's men defended themselves as best they could against the pitiless snipers and tried to fight their way back to the main camp, leaving the bottomland strewn with the bodies of their fallen comrades.

Meanwhile, Wyandot and Mingo warriors infiltrated the gap in the second line left by Darke's charging regiment and overran the artillerymen, killing and scalping everyone in sight and silencing the smoldering cannon. Their incursion carried them into the center of the army's position, where they wreaked havoc among the horrified camp followers, before the soldiers regrouped and drove them back.

No sooner had the remnants of Darke's men returned than the entire left flank of St. Clair's second line began to collapse, which was only prevented by a timely bayonet charge by Lieutenant-Colonel Gibson's levies, who fought furiously hand to hand with the warriors before they withdrew.   Then the first line, under a relentless siege by the Shawnee, Miami, and Delaware, started to weaken, and another bayonet charge was ordered against the braves that had advanced to the very mouths of the cannon.   Major Jonathan Heart of the Second Regiment and Major Thomas Butler of the levies led their men directly into the swarming warriors and were met with a devastating volley.   Heart was shot dead immediately, yet the troops pressed on, taking casualties at every step, until they had crossed the Wabash and were compelled to stop. Within minutes all the officers, conspicuous in their plumed cockades and decorated jackets, were either killed or seriously wounded, and the surviving soldiers struggled back to what was left of their camp.

When the first line gave way, Blacksnake pressed forward with the other braves and took the scalps of dead artillerymen until his arm ached. One, however, gave him pause. He knew that face! *Who was it?*   In the heat of battle he couldn't recall the name. As he hesitated, another brave finished the work that he was about to begin and waved the trophy aloft with a victorious shriek. Blacksnake stood staring blankly at the corpse for a moment, as if he didn't know where he was.

Little Turtle's warriors now held half of the high ground. Using flour bags and supply wagons as a makeshift breastwork, they poured their fire into what remained of St. Clair's army—where pandemonium reigned. Frightened, uncontrollable militia, along with other panic-stricken soldiers who abandoned the battle, had pillaged the officers' marquees, scavenging whatever they could lay their hands on; now they huddled sullenly together like a herd of cattle, waiting in a stupefied daze to be shot down. Various stages of hysteria prevailed among many of the women camp followers: some wandered in circles, wringing their hands and screaming; some stood petrified with clenched fists and fixed eyes; some kneeled and cried out for God's mercy; some sobbed in each other's arms; a few dropped to the ground in a deathly swoon; others found guns and fought back. Any wounded who could be carried were gathered in the center of the camp, where with groans and crys for water they, too, awaited the bitter end.

General Richard Butler, shot in the side earlier in the fight, had been brought back to his tent and propped in a sitting position against some knapsacks. At the height of the action, St. Clair sent his aid-de-camp, Lieutenant Ebenezer Denny, with his compliments to inquire about his condition. Butler insisted that all would be well and his wound was not serious. At that moment a spent musket ball smacked the kneecap of a Virginia cadet attending the general and the young man yelped. The comic incongruity of this trivial incident in the midst of so much mayhem struck Butler as so funny that his considerable flesh shook with laughter, causing Denny to conclude that indeed the general's injury was not severe.

St. Clair himself had been miraculously rejuvenated by the battle. The gout-ridden commander was resting when the shooting began. Immediately he rose from his sickbed, donned a coarse cappo coat and his tri-cornered beaver hat, and called for his horse, which was shot before he could mount. A second horse was brought forward, and it too was shot along with the servant holding the reins. Then a third horse was shot. Seemingly oblivious to his chronic pain, St. Clair proceeded to hobble up and down his beloved order of battle, attempting to rally his men. The fact that he wasn't mounted or in his officer's uniform saved his life. Even so, during the fight his cheek was grazed by one ball and his coat perforated by seven others. When first the rear and then the front lines began to crumble, he ordered charge after charge to firm them up, but now, three hours after the shooting began, his entire army was on the point of collapse. If something weren't done soon, they would all be dead.

The scene Blacksnake beheld was one of utter chaos. Shrouded in a pall of drifting powder smoke that afforded him the briefest glimpse of friend or foe, the cries of dying men and the crack of muskets rising to a maddening din, the soldiers appeared to be too stunned and exhausted to save themselves. St. Clair ordered Lieutenant-Colonel Darke to attempt another desperate charge; only a dispirited handful obeyed his command and they were repulsed after a short advance. A drummer beat out the call to retreat; in the uproar and confusion no one responded. Finally the wily George Adams, a veteran of Harmar's campaign, shouted to the men in his battalion, "Boys, let's make for the trace," and with a supporting yell soldiers dashed toward the forest. The warriors of the Three Fires positioned there were caught by surprise and fell back. All of St. Clair's decimated force who were able to move made a break for this narrow opening in the Indians' encirclement, crashing through the thick underbrush of the forest until they found the road. Blacksnake fired a shot at the wobbly figure of St. Clair himself— astride a sway-backed, butt-sprung old packhorse, too burdened to achieve a trot—as he was slowly joggled, bounced, and jolted from the field of his defeat.

The precipitous flight of the survivors brought them to Fort Jefferson, thirty miles away, that evening. Since it was too small to hold everybody, the remnants of St. Clair's beaten army pressed on through the night and didn't stop until they arrived at Fort Hamilton the next afternoon.

The advance had taken a month; the retreat, two days.

7

Blacksnake had joined in the pursuit of the fleeing army, which instantly disintegrated into a formless, frantic mob, with every man vying to leave his fellows behind. Whatever prevented a soldier from running faster was thrown away, until the road of the retreat was littered for miles with muskets and cartridge boxes, knapsacks and regimentals. Most of the horses that could be found had two or more people clinging to their backs and others clutching their tails. A few courageous souls tried to carry wounded comrades, but most were abandoned to share the same grisly fate as any stragglers overtaken by the warriors, who gave up the chase after a couple of miles in order to gather plunder.

Blacksnake saw one tall woman racing down the road with a child in her arms and her long, auburn hair streaming out behind her. She had outrun many of the men but now was at the last of her strength and in her terror dropped her baby in a snowdrift and hurried on. A Wyandot warrior picked up the child, who already had a few wisps of red hair, and he and Blacksnake brought him back to what remained of St. Clair's camp.

What Blacksnake saw there defied description. Any wounded who had been left behind had been butchered by the warriors, as had many of the camp followers, and these, added to those who fell in the battle itself, left the ground covered in every direction with stripped and scalped corpses. Some had been singled out for special torment. A few women had been horribly mutilated and impaled on stakes, so that even in the spirit world they could not give birth to more whites; handfuls of earth had been crammed into the mouths of many of the dead soldiers to signify their insatiable hunger for tribal lands.

General Richard Butler, still propped against some knapsacks outside his tent, had been tomahawked along with the other wounded soldiers; since he was recognized as an important man who had once lived among the Seneca, his carefully preserved scalp was sent by runner to Joseph Brant, in order to chide the chief and his warriors of the Six Nations for shirking the battle. Because Butler was a brave man, his heart, cut into as many pieces as tribes who had fought that day, was eaten.

A few wagons laden with kegs of corn liquor were discovered by the overjoyed warriors—with the expected results. The fat oxen that had pulled the cannon were slaughtered and roasted over the soldiers' campfires. There was more than enough plunder for everyone: tents, blankets, shirts, hats, axes, muskets, and swords. Soon hundreds of drunken warriors in war paint were swaggering and staggering around the camp—most gripping fresh scalps in their bloody hands, some wearing the epauletted coats and cockade hats of United States army officers—displaying their spoils and celebrating their victory.

Blacksnake and Little Turtle walked along the edge of the high ground, where St. Clair's cannons, now almost buried beneath a heap of the dead, still pointed west. Blacksnake stopped and gazed vaguely at the bodies until his eyes rested on one face.

"You and your men shot well," Little Turtle said.

"Yes," Blacksnake replied abstractly. After the frenzy of killing earlier that day, he was emotionally drained and walked around in a kind of daze.

"What are you looking at?"

"I know that man." Suddenly he had a flashback to the moment he paused before scalping an officer by the cannon and another warrior had done the deed. As if in a dream he saw the man's face and recognized him. "His name was William Oldham. He was a friend of my family."

Blacksnake wondered if anyone else he knew had been in the fight. If Oldham was present, what about his brother Sam? Was he, too, among the dead? Then he thought again of the redheaded woman leaving her baby behind in the snow. Why did she trouble his thoughts now?

Little Turtle put his hand on Blacksnake's shoulder and squinted out on the scene of the battle—the greatest victory the Indians had ever won and the worst defeat the U. S. army had ever suffered—where more than half of St. Clair's army lay dead. A reeking vapor rose visibly from each scalped head in the frosty air; to Blacksnake at a distance they resembled nothing so much as hundreds of strangely smoking pumpkins left out in a winter field.

"We have killed too many," Little Turtle said, voicing Blacksnake's thoughts and acknowledging that even in war there were balances to be respected. "Yet it is not enough."

Vincennes

1

News of St. Clair's defeat reached Philadelphia in December. Washington excused himself from the dinner table to receive the courier and returned to his guests as if nothing had happened. Later that evening in the library, with only his private secretary Tobias Lear as witness, the President began striding up and down and wringing his hands. "God damn that man to hell," he raged. "Didn't I tell him, in this very room, to beware of surprise! 'You know how they fight us,' I said. 'In a word—beware of surprise!' And yet! To suffer that army to be cut to pieces, hacked, butchered, tomahawked by surprise—the very thing I warned him against! Oh God, Oh God, he is worse than a murderer! How can he answer his country? The blood of the slain is upon him—the curse of the widows and orphans—the curse of Heaven! I say again, God damn that man!" Lear had never seen the President so angry or heard him use such profanity. Red-faced and shaking, Washington sat down on the sofa, trying to master his emotions; finally, after a long silence, he fixed Lear with a stern gaze and spoke slowly, "This must not go beyond this room," he cautioned. "General St. Clair shall have justice..."

The magnitude of the disaster shocked the country. Two armies obliterated in two years! Many in the East said that now was the time to treat fairly with the Indians and purchase a just peace. Many in the West wanted an end to federal restraint—turn the Kentucky militia loose and drive the savages from the land! Washington knew he had a full-scale war on his hands, but he also knew the tatterdemalion remnants of St. Clair's army were in no condition to fight it. The United States needed to buy time while it trained and equipped a superior force.

After heated debates in secret sessions, Congress approved a substantial military escalation—an army of 5,000 men with a budget of $1,000,000 financed by revised tariffs, new loans, and a tax on whiskey. St. Clair was eased out of his command and replaced by Mad Anthony Wayne, a high-strung Revolutionary War veteran whose vanity and ambition were only surpassed by his bravery and bull-headedness. To secure votes for an enlarged army, Washington promised a significant peace initiatve. He would offer an olive branch while he sharpened his sword.

Several agents that Secretary of War Knox had sent to make peace with the hostile Indians had either been turned back or murdered. In a last-ditch effort, Knox persuaded Major Alexander Trueman, who had led St. Clair's cavalry, to carry another peace initiative to where the hostile tribes were gathered. The veteran Kentucky Indian fighter Colonal John Hardin was sent with the same message to the Wyandot villages on the Sandusky.

Trueman, accompanied by his servant William Lynch and interpreter William Smalley, left Fort Washington on May 20th, 1792, and proceeded up the road Harmar's army had cut less than two years before. On the eighth day, they met three Delaware hunters—an old man, a young brave, and a boy of twelve. They seemed friendly and offered to share their camp. Lynch broke out some chocolate for supper. Afterwards, with Smalley interpreting, Trueman read parts of Knox's speech to them: "We should be greatly gratified with the opportunity of imparting to you all the blessings of civilization....repair to Philadelphia to meet President Washington in person....there make a peace founded upon the principles of justice and humanity...."

"How will it be received?" Trueman asked anxiously.

"I am not a chief," the old man said. "You must go to the Auglaize towns and see."

Trueman and the old man, who seemed cheerful and laughed easily, sat by the fire smoking and talking. When Trueman indicated that he and his servant were tired, the Indian spread skins for them. Smalley stayed up and continued the conversation.

The old Indian fell to brooding and finally he said, "Ask your captain if his man could be tied. Because there are three of you, my boys are frightened and can't sleep."

Smalley conveyed this request to the half-asleep Major, who without deliberation ordered his servant to submit.

The Indians bound Lynch's elbows tightly behind his back and fastened his feet together with a bridle strap. Then everyone lay down.

After a while the old Indian picked up Smalley's gun and set the breach.

"My gun is ugly and no good," he complained. "I can't kill enough deer."

Then, as if on a whim, he shot Trueman in the chest, who groaned once before he died.

Smalley jumped up, ran behind a tree, and pleaded for his life. He said he had lived among the Indians, his Delaware name was "White Warrior," and he could be of use. Meanwhile, Lynch was dragged by the old Indian to the fire and shot in the neck.

"You have killed them both," Smalley shouted.

"Sit down," the old Indian said as he walked toward him.

"If I do, you will tomahawk me."

"Sit down. Sit down. I will not harm you."

"If you sit down," Smalley said, "I will."

They both sat down and talked while Smalley tried to decide what to do.

"What did you kill them for?" he demanded.

"They had fine horses, good things I needed. If I had taken them to our village, I would get nothing. Now I have all."

The old Indian stripped the fancy uniform off Major Trueman and the younger man helped himself to Lynch's clothes.

"Scalp them," the old Indian said.

The younger man did as he was told; the boy went and got some supple twigs to make hoops. Trueman's hair was dark, Lynch's was light, sandy, almost golden. The Indians threw whatever they didn't want into the fire, including all the papers except the speech from Knox, which was attached to a belt of white wampum. They divided the rest of the plunder and sat down and smoked. Relucantly, Smalley joined them.

At daylight they wrapped the bodies of Trueman and Lynch in a worn-out blanket and placed them beside a rotten log, concealing the spot with leaves and underbrush.

For breakfast they ate the rest of the chocolate.

Two days later, with Smalley in tow, they reached the Auglaize. The old man showed Knox's speech to Buckongahelas, the celebrated Delaware war chief.

"You should not have killed them," he said. "They should have been brought to the towns. If we did not like the message, we could have killed them here."

2

On July 12th, 1792, the interpreter from Louisville that General Rufus Putnam had sent for stood before him in the Quartermaster General's house at Fort Washington. He was of medium height with curly reddish hair and a deep tan that almost hid the freckles on his face. His boyish features were vaguely simian, with a shrewd look in his blue-green eyes and a stubborn set to his jaw. He wore the standard frontier garb of fringed hunting shirt and leggings, but his moccasins displayed the tell-tale diamond-pattern beadwork of the Miami. John Heckewelder, a Moravian missionary who had spent many years among the Delaware, occasionally joined in questioning the young man, who stood very straight, gazed directly at them, and spoke calmly and frankly. He said his name was William Wells and that he had been captured by the Miami when he was thirteen, adopted by the chief, and lived among them on the Eel River for eight years.

A solid, no-nonsense New Englander of fifty-four, Putnam was a tall, imposing man with a round, rubicund face whose weak chin made his large nose even more prominent; he wore a velvet jacket, a lacey white shirt, and his brown hair was drawn tightly back in a queue. A former millwright and surveyor who had risen to the rank of brigadier-general in the Revolution, Putnam had founded the first permanent settlement north of the Ohio, Marietta, in 1788. President Washington had personally convinced him to take on this risky peace mission.

"Why did you leave?" Putnam peered at the young man with bemused curiosity.

This was the question Wells had been dreading. On the trip from Louisville to Cincinnati he had debated with himself how to answer. He did not want to say that his two homes, Snake-fish Town and Kekionga, had been reduced to ashes by American forces, or that he had two Indian families; he certainly didn't want them to know that one of his wives was Little Turtle's daughter, for that would make them doubt his loyalty; nor that his other wife and child were being held prisoner at Fort Washington, which would also make his motives suspect. He didn't want to talk about his own confusion and inner torment. Since his visit to Sam's home in Kentucky two years before, he had felt a growing dissatisfaction with Indian life—sometimes they *were* dirty, envious, superstitious, and vain; they lived for the moment, never making provision for the future—was that a life he wanted? Both The Porcupine and Little Turtle were about as important as men could be among the Miami, but what did they have to show for it? Whatever possessions they accumulated, they gave away. Wells knew that the Indians were determined to fight a war for the Ohio River boundary; he also knew that no matter how just their cause, they were certain to lose. Those who didn't die in battle would succumb to drink, disease, starvation. He didn't want to admit how much of an opportunist he was being by following his brother's advice to "get out while the gettin's good." Was he a rat abandoning a sinking ship? Better to say he was doing the civilized and sensible thing.

"I have kin in Kentucky," he explained.

"I've been told you're from a good family," Putnam said.

"Yes, Sir. My brother Sam has a fine farm outside Louisville and Carty works in the Indian trade. They talked me into coming home."

"When did you leave?"

"In June."

"And the Indians let you?"

"Yes, Sir. I'm the adopted son of the chief and free to go where I please. The Porcupine, that's the chief's name, is a very important man. He has a lot of influence and he favors peace."

"You say The Porcupine is for peace, did he go to Vincennes in March?"

"He sent his brother, The Soldier, and another chief."

"And you accompanied them?"

"Yes, Sir. I have been to Vincennes before and I know Major Hamtramck. He told my brothers where to find me."

"What did they tell you?"

"They said I needed to think of my flesh-and-blood kin, and that there was a good chance I could find a job as an interpreter for the United States and help make peace."

William Wells had not told his brothers about Sweet Breeze, with whom he had spent the past winter in Little Turtle's hunting camp. She was obviously pregnant when he traveled to Vincennes in the spring. There he had sold his peltry and served as an interpreter in a tentative peace agreement that Hamtramck had asked several Wea and Eel River chiefs to sign.

"Did you stay in Vincennes?"

"No, Sir, I went back to the Eel River."

"Did you tell The Porcupine you were leaving?"

"He had gone to a council at the Glaize with the other chiefs."

"Wasn't that a war council?" Putnam asked with concern. "We've tried several times to send messengers bearing white flags to the Glaize and we fear all of them have been killed. How do you know he's for peace?"

"He's told me many times."

"Maybe he just wants to get the hostages back," Heckewelder suggested. He had a long, thin, almost emaciated face, but kindly eyes that, although they had witnessed thirty years of frontier iniquities, still seemed somehow naive.

"It's possible," Wells granted. "Some Indians are great liars, but I think he's for peace."

"What can you tell us about the engagement of November 4th?" Putnam asked.

"I was in it," Wells admitted, in spite of his resolve to conceal his participation. "What do you want to know?"

"Where are the cannon?"

He almost flinched at the question, whose answer he knew all-too well.

"They were too heavy to transport, so they were left. Some are buried in the bank of the creek, others are inside hollow logs."

"How many Indians were involved?"

"About fifteen hundred in all."

"Did the British direct the attack on St. Clair?"

"Little Turtle of the Miami led; it was his plan. The warriors fought under their war chiefs. Some Canadians were there; Simon Girty was with the Wyandots."

"And what is the general sentiment among the Indians now?"

"They mean to fight for their land. Since they've beaten you, I mean us, twice, they're sure they can do it again."

"You could prove to be a very valuable man, Mr. Wells," Putnam said, smiling with satisfaction. "We know very little about the Miami and the Wabash Indians; if you help us, we will pay you handsomely. Is there anything we can do for you now?"

"I'd like to see the hostages. My Indian mother and sisters are among them."

When Laughing Eyes saw a man with reddish hair walking toward the hostage compound inside the stockade, she shrieked with joy and ran to him with open arms.

"My husband," she cried, "you have come for me."

"Do not tell anyone we are married," he whispered in her ear as he held her. "It must be kept a secret until everyone is freed."

Before they could say another word, No Nose rushed over carrying Speaks in Dreams, who gazed at his father without recognition. In a moment Blacksnake was surrounded by the women of Snake-fish Town, laughing and crying and asking when they could go home.

It had been almost a year since Blacksnake had seen his wife and son and adopted mother; although it was unmanly to cry, the tears came to his eyes and he could not speak. So much had happened since his family was taken into captivity and brought to Fort Washington, how could he even begin to explain?

Laughing Eyes stepped back and examined him closely.

"Why are you dressed like that?"

"I work for General Putnam now. I am his interpreter. Soon we will go to Vincennes and sign a peace treaty and all the prisoners will be freed."

The look Laughing Eyes gave him mocked her name.

"Are you already free? What about your other wife, Sweet Breeze?" She pronounced her name with disdain. "Did you think I would not hear? Do you know you have a daughter?"

Wells stood dumbfounded—how could Laughing Eyes, held hostage at Fort Washington, have learned these things? He had the uneasy feeling that she knew more about his life and who he truly was than he did.

"You are not the man I thought you were," she said, quickening his own doubts, and turned away.

3

Ten days before William Wells presented himself to General Putnam at Fort Washington, a delegation of leading citizens had arrived from Vincennes, together with six Wea Indians who had relatives among the hostages. They urged Putnam to come to Vincennes, which they called "the O post," to make peace with the Wabash Indians.

This resolve became more urgent when Jean Krouch, a Wea chief visiting his captive wife and children, suddenly took sick, died, and was buried with full military honors. The next day Wells translated for a Wea spokesman who begged Putnam to release the hostages before they became sick too. "If we must die," he said, "we would rather die in our country."

In keeping with Indian custom, Putnam took a day to consider the request before responding. After expressing once again his grief over the death of the Wea chief, he said, with Wells interpreting, "I wish to make you happy in every respect. Your women and children are under my care and protection. I am making the necessary arrangements for our journey to the O post, where I hope to make a lasting peace. In thirty days, we shall all set out together."

The Indians were unhappy about this delay, but they had no choice in the matter. It took time to prepare for the treaty. Seven or eight hundred Indians were expected in Vincennes, and provisions and presents for all of them were required. Putnam also clung to the slim hope that yet another peace messenger, the Mohican envoy Captain Hendrick Aupaumut, would return from the Glaize or that Knox might send him revised orders.

On his next visit to the stockade, Laughing Eyes told Wells she still loved him and wished to see him but that she no longer considered him her husband. Although he had wondered over the past year how he might make a similar declaration to her, Laughing Eyes's statement took him by surprise and hurt his feelings—the woman he had once longed for and lived with was lost to him. Or was she? In truth, her words served to clear the air. Now that their separation was acknowledged, they actually found it easier to be together. Wells began to stop by the hostage compound in the evening—sharing a meal, playing with his son, talking and laughing, sometimes staying the night. He spent the rest of his time either out hunting or inspecting the settlements. Already there were several thousand people living in towns north of the Ohio, between the Big and Little Miami Rivers; and Newport, across from Cincinnati at the mouth of the Licking River, was growing fast. This area alone, if it had the will and the weapons, could muster more soldiers than all the warriors gathered at the Glaize. When Wells saw with his own eyes how quickly the country was being settled, he knew in his heart that the Indian way was doomed. He felt relief, tinged with an aching sadness, to be no longer a part of it.

The upper town of Cincinnati occupied a grid of streets on high ground back from the river. Most of the dwellings were log cabins, plus a smattering of two-story frame houses, painted red, with stone chimneys. Stores and taverns faced the public square. Fort Washington, whose shingle roof and front palisade were also painted red, loomed over the town. Warehouses and repair shops lined the riverbank, as did several groggeries with crib girls.

When the flatboats were ready, Wells and the hostages, escorted by sixty soldiers, headed down the Ohio, reaching Louisville three days later. Putnam, Heckewelder, and some other gentlemen arrived in a barge the next day. Because the water was low and the channel narrow, the baggage had to be unloaded and transported to the other end of the rapids. The hostages camped on the north shore near Fort Steuben.

Wells took the opportunity to visit Sam, whose plantation was clearly prospering. He had bought more slaves, who had cleared more fields, and now was adding rooms to the main house (Mary was expecting again) and building a front porch. Rebekah, already walking and talking, called him "Uncle Billy" and liked to be carried on his shoulder.

"This is the life," Sam told him several times a day. "This is what our daddy died for."

Louisville had erected another brick house since Wells had seen it last, and the two-story limestone courthouse had a belfry but no bell. Along the road by the riverside, wagons and two-wheeled carts lugged cargo from the wharf above the rapids to the quay below it—a place where hogs gathered to feed on dead fish. Two of the taverns in town boasted billiard tables and a Mr. Nickle had opened a dancing school for would-be debutantes. One day Wells's heart sank when he recognized Penelope Pope, William Oldham's widow, walking in black down Market Street with her three children. The image of his dead body, sprawled beside a cannon, flashed before his eyes. The big news was that Kentucky had officially become a State in June; now the question was whether Louisville or Lexington should be the capital.

On Sunday, the journey continued: 140 people divided among four flatboats, three barges, and six canoes. For five days they drifted down the wide, slow-moving Ohio beneath towering poplars and didn't see a single settlement until Henderson, with thirty cabins, twenty miles below Green River. Every morning herds of buffalo and numerous deer grazed by the river bank. Pleased that game was yet plentiful in this part of the country, Wells and Heckewelder liked to take a canoe and join the hunters.

One day Wells shot a large bear, which sat down on the spot and whined in pain with a plaintive, almost human sound. To Heckwelder's astonishment, Wells stood in front of the mortally wounded bear and lectured it sternly in Miami on how to behave.

"Do not be a coward," Blacksnake scolded, swatting the bear on the nose with his ramrod for emphasis. "Today it was your fate to meet a great hunter and you ought to die like a man, a hero, and not weep like an old woman. If it had been your good fortune to triumph over me, and I had fallen under the power of *your* medicine, I would not disgrace my people. I would know how to be strong and die with courage, as a true warrior."

Afterwards, Heckewelder asked Wells what he had said.

"Do you think he understood you?" he couldn't resist adding.

"He understood me all right," Wells replied. "You saw how ashamed he looked."

That same day Wells shot a buck, turned to Heckewelder, and said, "Friend, skin your deer."

"Why did you give your kill to me?" Heckewelder asked.

"It is our custom," Wells replied simply.

As they packed the meat to bring back to the boats, Heckewelder wondered if the young man at his side could ever stop being a Miami even if he wanted to.

In many respects Wells and Heckewelder were an odd pair. The younger was a sinewy strong, robust man of action, not given to reflection or spiritual questioning, who had shed blood and taken scalps; the elder was thin, frail, sensitive and retiring; his life had always revolved around his Moravian faith; yet as a youth he had been impulsive enough to become a missionary. Despite his failing health, he still managed to do an astonishing amount of traveling. He felt a strange affinity for Wells and enjoyed their talks as they drifted down the Ohio.

When the subject was religion, Wells's eyes glazed over; he did take a keen interest in how the Moravians had had success in teaching the Indians how to live like whites.

"You say the men worked in the fields with the women?" Wells asked incredulously. "I'd have to see that to believe it."

"It's true," Heckewelder insisted with animation as he elaborated on how the missionaries had transformed Indian life. "The men tended the chickens, hogs, and cattle too. Some learned carpentry, masonry, blacksmithing, weaving, milling. The Indians lived in square houses on straight streets and dressed as we do. They didn't paint their faces, wore their hair long, and renounced the warpath. Adultery, drunkenness, gambling, stealing, lying, heathen feasting, dancing, and witchcraft were forbidden. Everyone worked hard for six days and kept the Sabbath holy. We prayed in Delaware, preached in English, and sang in German."

"Where are the Moravian Indians now?"

"In Canada."

"Why did you leave?" This was the question Wells had been waiting to ask.

"I haven't." Heckewelder nodded his head toward the hostages on the nearest flatboat. "Look around you."

"But why did you leave the mission towns?"

"Gnadenhütten."

The word was notorious on the frontier.

"Tell me about that."

Heckewelder, a German although born in England, told Wells how he had joined the Moravian mission while he was a teenager living in Bethlehem, Pennsylvania. In 1772, David Zeisberger led his mainly Delaware converts to the east branch of the Muskingum—the Tuscarawas. Schoenbrunn, "the beautiful spring," was the first town; ten miles downstream was Gnadenhutten, "the cabins of grace." During the Revolution the Moravian Indians tried to remain neutral, but Matthew Elliott, the British agent, thought they were spying for the Americans and forced them to move to Upper Sandusky, where they were left to shift for themselves.

Heckewelder paused at this moment in his account and began to fidget with his shirt collar. Wells observed this nervous gesture and had a sudden insight.

"You *were* spying," he said on impulse.

"I, I, I am an American, a patriot." Heckewelder looked at Wells with stricken eyes. "If I knew war parties were heading for the settlements—I wrote letters. I wanted to save lives."

"But that's why the British made you abandon your towns."

"Yah, I suppose," Heckewelder admitted reluctantly. "All winter we suffered. When the cattle died, they lived on roots. The corn was still standing in Gnadenhütten, so in February many decided to return. On March 7th, 1782, over a hundred militia arrived in Gnadenhütten. They accused our people of harboring war parties and held a vote whether to kill them on the spot or deliver them as captives to Fort Pitt. Sixteen frontiersmen stepped forward in favor of mercy, the rest were for death. They murdered ninety-six, thirty-four were children. We lost most of our finest people— old Abraham, Isaac and Anna, Christian and Augustina, Philipus and Lorel, Samuel, Johannes, Tobias... All gone!"

Killing on the frontier was commonplace, but this was a cold-blooded massacre. Suddenly Wells remembered with painful vividness his first raid on Kentucky, and how Earth had tomahawked the little boy who hid under the bed. "How did you learn what happened?" he asked. "Did anyone escape?"

"One boy, Thomas, hid in the root cellar. When the killing began, the blood streamed down on his head. He managed to squirm out a small hole in the back and made his way to Sandusky."

"Was anything done to the leader?"

"No, no, not him. I met him once. David Williamson. He was from Catfish. I asked him if the land across the Ohio was as good as people said; 'far too good for its present inhabitants,' he replied. No, nothing happened to him, it was Colonel Crawford who paid the terrible price...

"Why, I was in Catfish two months ago—they call it Washington these days—and dined with Mr. Van Sweringen. We got to talking about the massacre and at one point he threw up his hands and said, 'I have heard from the lips of the murderers themselves that they killed them while they were praying, singing, and kissing! It doesn't surprise me that St. Clair's campaign ended in disaster. There is a great blood guilt on this land that must be atoned for.' Those were his words. I wonder if Williamson or any of the rest ever feel remorse."

4

On September 3rd the small flotilla reached the mouth of the Wabash, where six pirogues and an escort of soldiers from Fort Knox were waiting. That evening a makeshift table was set for a sumptuous feast of turtle soup, buffalo tongue, bear steaks, pike filets, pork chops, roast venison, turkey, and duck, as well as assorted wines. All officers and gentlemen were invited; Wells was not. He shared a bowl of sucotash with No Nose, Laughing Eyes, and Speaks in Dreams. He felt the snub keenly and longed for the day when he, too, would be considered a gentleman.

Ten days later they docked at Vincennes, near the sally port of Fort Knox. When the Eel River and Wea Indians saw their relatives, they ran down to the bank of the river singing songs of joy and firing guns in the air. On the way up the Wabash, Putnam, who was impressed by Wells's knowledge of Indian customs, asked his advice. The two men had agreed that an immediate freeing of the prisoners would demonstrate from the outset the government's good intentions.

Wells surveyed the crowd while he translated Putnam's words: "Brothers, I thank the Great Spirit that has given us this opportunity to see and speak to one another. For a long time you have been mourning for your friends and relations. This day restores them to your arms."

Putnam told the Wea that he lamented the death of their chief in Cincinnati, expressing his wish to wipe the tears from their eyes. Next, he issued an address to the people of Vincennes, reminding them that he was here on serious business and that no spiritous liquors would be sold to the Indians until the treaty was concluded.

Vincennes was situated on the east bank of the Wabash in the middle of a beautiful prairie; the land on the west bank, which stretched as far as the eye could see, was a savannah inundated each spring. Ever since he became a Miami hunter, Wells had bartered his peltry at Françoise Bosseron's store in Vincennes; he knew the narrow, pig-littered streets of the town well. The one-story, hewn-log houses of the French Creole settlers were unmistakable: bark roofs, whitewashed fronts, vine-draped arcades, and mud-daubed chimneys. Their skinny cattle grazed on scant grasses in a common pasture; a few men with gumption farmed long, strip patches with crude, wooden ploughs pulled by plodding oxen and brought their produce to town in two-wheeled carts. Most of the men were vaguely connected to the fur trade or sold liquor to the Indians. The husbands did much of the domestic work, milking cows, churning butter, cooking, fetching and carrying, everything, it seemed, except the washing. Their wives, so deeply tanned it was hard to distinguish the Piankshaw squaws from their Parisian sisters, wore sandals and short, brightly colored petticoats, with their glossy, well-groomed hair in silk kerchiefs. They shashayed around in small groups, laughing and chattering, or sat together on shady front porches to nurse their children and comment on the passing scene. As in Kekionga, Wells felt at ease among these French settlers who loved festive evenings of drinking, gambling, and dancing.

The more recently arrived Americans were a mixed lot. Some saw Vincennes as a place outside of human laws and civilized restraints and behaved accordingly. Others, as if to compensate for the bad examples of their countrymen, were models of honesty and hard work who took pride in turning the rich, black, sandy soil into fields of wheat and barley.

Fort Knox, at the foot of Buntin Street, with a two-story blockhouse on each corner, was by far the largest and tallest structure in town, surpassing some nearby Indian mounds. The St. Francis Xavier church had been rebuilt in 1785, including a bell brought all the way from Philadelphia (what an ill omen that Louis Derroyan, who swung it, fell to his death from the scaffold!).

Within a week nearly 700 Indians were camped outside of town, anxious to start the treaty before hunting season began. The Porcupine, who had been ill, was one of the last to arrive. On Monday morning, Putnam addressed thirty-one chiefs from the Eel River, Wea, Potawatomi, Kickapoo, Piankashaw, Mascouten, Kaskaskia, and Peoria in the council house at Vincennes. Before he spoke, there was a profound silence:

"Brothers! Let us smoke a pipe of friendship," he said, while William Wells moved around the room passing out tobacco and lighting pipes. As Putnam shook the chiefs' hands, many of them blew smoke in his face. He told them that he had seen the great Chief of the United States, General Washington, sign treaties with the Iroquois and Cherokee and that he wished all the Indian nations would come to his council fire in Philadelphia, to talk, smoke, and be happy. Unfortunately, a dark cloud had divided the United States from their brothers on the Wabash, and in darkness and confusion they had fought and tomahawked each other.

"Brothers! The great Chief wishes to disperse this dark cloud— to withdraw the tomahawks from our people's heads and bury them—to take you by the hand in lasting friendship. He appointed me his Agent for this purpose. I speak to you from my heart, not my lips only. Speak also from your hearts—tell me the cause of your uneasiness, and I will endeavor to remove it."

After each phrase, Putnam paused to let Wells and three other interpreters translate his words. When he finished, The Porcupine rose and spoke.

"My Older Brother, I am sorry that I have been sick and my voice is weak. All I will say is that I rejoice in what you have said. We shall give you our reply tomorrow."

At first it felt very strange to be translating his adoptive father's words to Putnam, but Wells soon warmed to his task. His voice gradually rose and gained inflection and emphasis. Because he could not articulate his own conflicted feelings, he felt a kind of elation in speaking the words of others. At the moment, what he was doing seemed right—who better to stand in the middle and make clear to each side what the other wanted?

"Why did they blow smoke in my face?" Putnam stormed at Wells later that evening.

"It's supposed to be an honor," Wells said. "They like you."

"If that's how they treat their friends, thank God I'm not their enemy!"

"I think they'll sign, Sir, provided you don't want their land. Do you have that authority?"

"Indeed I do. I'll even show you my instructions from Knox. Here, look at this paragraph: 'You will make it clearly understood that we want not a foot of their land, and that it is theirs, and theirs only—That they have the right to sell, and the right to refuse to sell, and that the United States will guarantee to them their said just rights.' Does that suffice?"

Wells certainly found the words satisfactory, and the fact that Putnam had showed them to him even more so. *He treats me as an equal,* he thought; *if the United States really means what it says, peace is truly possible.* And if that were so, Wells felt less regret that he had switched sides.

Because The Porcupine had been ill, the Indians selected a relatively young and unknown chief, Jean Baptist Ducoigne of the Kaskaskia, to speak for the tribes. He blamed the English for giving the Indians the tomahawk and expressed a desire to live at peace. Several other chiefs seconded his words. Finally The Porcupine rose and shook hands solemnly with Putnam.

"My Older Brother!" he said. "The hearts of us Indians are all placed on the left side; therefore I shake hands with the left hand. I speak with my mouth but the sentiments are from my heart. You disturbed my bed! My village was destroyed!"

The Porcupine held up two strings of black wampum while Wells translated his angry reference to Wilkinson's raid to Putnam. For a moment it looked as if the council would break into mutual recriminations, but then the Eel River chief presented two white strings and said:

"My Older Brother! The sky is clear, the darkness is gone, and I speak with a cheerful heart. You have told us good things. You wish to bury the tomahawk. Now we will bury it deep. Our Father the French never craved our lands. Why should any person want what is not his? The Great Spirit placed us here. We think it best for you to live yonder, with your faces toward us, and we shall live here, with our faces toward you. When we want to see you, we can go there; if you want to see us, you can come here. Let us have peace and may the road between us always be open."

After two days of meetings, in which the boundaries were discussed to everyone's satisfaction, it was Putnam's turn to speak again, with Wells travelling as easily from one language to another as he had crossed the border between his two worlds. "Brothers! I believe all parties are now agreed. The white people commit to writing what they transact, that the paper may speak when we are dead. Your custom is to record by belts. We shall do it both ways."

He then read the articles of the treaty, which acknowledged that the lands belonged exclusively to the Indians—*that they have a right to sell and a right to refuse to sell*—and put the tribes under the protection of the United States.

"Brothers! We have wiped off the blood. We have buried the hatchet. All that is past shall be forgotten. I now present this belt of peace to you in the name of the United States.

"Brothers! We both hold this belt in our hands—*here* at this end the United States hold it. You hold it by the other end. The road, you see, is broad and level and clear. We may now pass to one another easily and without difficulty." Wells reflected on how those words captured his own experience. "The more firmly we hold this belt, the happier we shall be. Our women and children have no more reason to be afraid. Our young men will observe that this is a job that their wise men have done well."

In proclamation of the peace, Putnam personally fired one of the cannon and had the head chief of each of the nations who signed the treaty do so in turn. Then he ordered four large oxen slain and bread and brandy for everyone.

On Saturday afternoon, the Indians held a feast followed by an evening dance to celebrate the peace treaty. Dressed in their finest, the tribes paraded through the town, beating drums, shaking rattles, and singing. At the council house, with many soldiers and settlers as spectators, they performed for their guests traditional seasonal dances, finishing with a war dance. As each warrior circled the fire and smacked the war post with his tomahawk, Wells had to repress a strong urge to step forward and shout, "My name is Blacksnake and these are the scalps of the men I have slain!" But this dance was all for show, merely a spectacle to entertain white people; the warriors had feasted, not fasted, and that night they would not walk the warpath but continue drinking; the only blood shed would be from drunken mayhem among themselves.

On Sunday Putnam was bedridden with the flu, so Major Hamtramck distributed the presents, Wells served as his assistant, and Mr. Prior, the commissary, kept a written record of who got what. To avoid a chaos of needy hands, the Indians were divided by tribes, separated by sex, and lined up. The chiefs came first and received scarlet coats, tricorner hats, and various silver ornaments—medals, arm bands, nose and ear bobs, brooches; next came the men, who received linen shirts, stroud breech clouts and leggings, blankets, vermilion, gun flints, hunting knives, and small hatchets; the women were given calico shirts, scarlet broad cloth, blankets, brass kettles, scissors, thread, needles, ribbons, combs, and looking glasses. When he saw that only 120 Eel River Indians were there, Wells was appalled; Snake-fish Town had numbered over 400 a few years earlier and The Soldier could always count on at least 100 warriors. Now only forty men stood in line, several quite old.

"Where are the others?" Wells asked Thin Raccoon, who had remained his friend in spite of the fact that Wells had left Laughing Eyes and now worked for the Americans.

"Dead," he replied, and began to recite the names.

5

Although Putnam's fever broke a few days later, he was still too weak for the trip to Philadelphia; in his place Heckewelder agreed to accompany the delegation as far as Carlisle. Because The Porcupine remained in poor health, The Names of the Beautiful Animals Invoked by our Ancestors and The Soldier would represent the Eel River tribe. The party of sixteen Indians and seven whites set out on horseback for Louisville the next day.

Putnam asked Wells to come see him. He had lost a lot of weight and his drawn face made his nose larger, but the sparkle was back in his eyes.

"I want to thank you," he said. "You've served me well. I believe it's a good treaty."

"I think so too, Sir," Wells said with genuine pride in what had been accomplished.

Unlike all the previous treaties that the United States had dictated to the tribes above the Ohio, this one did not assert that the Indians had forfeited all their lands because they had sided with the British during the Revolution. Instead it stated that the Indians were the rightful owners of the lands and could not be forced to sell against their will. If the United States meant what it said—the Senate still had to ratify the treaty—then there was a real possibility for peace.

"For this good work to continue," Putnam said, "I would like to bring all the hostile tribes within the protection of the United States. We have tried all year to send peace messengers, but you know what happened to them."

Wells looked glum; he could see where this conversation was going.

"Trueman and Hardin were soldiers," Putnam continued, "who had fought against them—no wonder they were killed! You're different. You have lived among them and speak their language. When St. Clair marched against Kekionga, he could not find one person who knew the way. Well, *you know the way*! You can go where others can't. If you will carry a peace message to the Glaize—at least to the Delaware and Miami if not the Shawnee— you will do this country and the cause of peace a great service and you will be richly rewarded. I am prepared to pay you one dollar a day, plus three hundred dollars to cover your expenses and those of whomever accompanies you, and I will increase this to five hundred dollars if you succeed in inducing the chiefs to come to Marietta to sign a treaty. I doubt if there is another line of work for a man in your situation that would pay so well."

"If I live to spend it." Wells smiled grimly, unwilling to admit that the danger of the job appealed to him more than the dollars. "I'll need a horse."

"You'll have one," Putnam said, shaking his hand again. "Mr. Wells, you're a godsend."

"A pleasing thought, Sir. The Miami may have other notions."

From *Au Glaize* to *Roche de Bout*

1

Before he left Vincennes as a peace messenger for General Putnam, William Wells had a sad parting with The Porcupine, No Nose, Laughing Eyes, and his son Speaks in Dreams. Instead of returning to the ruins of Snake-fish Town, they planned to join the winter hunting camp of He Provides on the Mississinewa and in the spring establish a new village.

"When you first came to us I saved your life and raised you as my son," The Porcupine said in a strained voice. "I had hoped you would look after me in my old age, for you are a good hunter. Now you are a man and choose to walk a different path. I hope you will work for peace and teach the Big Knives to behave the way our fathers the French once did."

"I will return with a present for you," Wells promised, gazing fondly at his adoptive father.

"I would be glad to see another spring." The Porcupine spoke abstractedly, as though he had not heard a word. "I believe I will die before the first snow."

Wells wanted to say something reassuring, but he could see signs of death in the old man's eyes and said nothing. They shook left hands and gripped each other's shoulders with their right. No Nose and Laughing Eyes gave him long hugs and wept bitter tears; Speaks in Dreams, who somehow already knew that weeping was only for women, simply looked up at him as if he were a stranger. Wells mounted his horse, took one last backward glance, and headed up the Wabash trail toward the Glaize. He was accompanied by Laughing Eyes's brother Thin Raccoon and a delegation of chiefs who had signed the treaty: A Wave of the Eel River, Smoke of the Wea, The Little Left Handed Man and Yellow Beaver of the Piankashaw.

October, the month of the low fire: a time when the leaves, in their last days, achieved prismatic splendor and glided earthward. Crimson sumac, golden birch and maple, deep-purple ash, garnet oak, bright-yellow hickory, maroon dogwood—on and on they rode through the mellow, autumnal world. Deer, bear, ducks, and geese were plentiful near the river. Acorns cracked under the horses' hooves, sending alarmed otters splashing into the water. Wild cherries and hawthorn berries were ripe; after the first frost, so were pawpaws and crab apples. Screaming flocks of green and yellow parakeets filled their days with raucous serenades; one afternoon the sky darkened as a host of passenger pigeons roared overhead; at night wolves howled, owls hooted, foxes barked, and occasionally a panther shrieked. Wells could almost believe the land was as it always had been, except when he passed through the charred remains of once thriving villages. From Vincennes to Kekionga, the home ground of the Miami, not one town was left standing along the Wabash.

Finally they came to Little Turtle's new town, on the north bank of the Maumee just west of Bean Creek. Wells was delighted to see Sweet Breeze and their baby, Ahpezzahquah, whom he promptly named Ann in honor of his mother; he felt awkward holding his wife and daughter in his arms with Thin Raccoon scowling down at them from his horse. Little Turtle had left two weeks earlier with a war party of several hundred Shawnee and Miami—that boded badly for Wells's peace mission. The villagers were packing to move to their hunting grounds; before they left, Wells assured Sweet Breeze that he would spend the winter with her at Little Turtle's camp.

Wells went to the lodge of Dappled Fawn and told him that the treaty the Wabash Indians had signed with Putnam at Vincennes acknowledged the Ohio River boundary.

"Your good news comes too late," the peace chief said. "We have already met in general council and sent a message with the Seneca to the Fifteen Fires in Philadelphia."

"What did it say?"

"Painted Pole of the Shawnee spoke for all the tribes. Let him tell you."

The Glaize, an old buffalo wallow at the confluence of the Auglaize River with the Maumee, had replaced Kekionga as the gathering place of the hostile tribes. Since ancient times it had been a campsite on an old warpath, stretching from Lake Erie to the Ohio River. The Shawnee had three towns—two downriver from Little Turtle on the Maumee, led by the war chiefs Blue Jacket and The Snake, and Captain Johnny's town on the east bank of the Auglaize near its mouth. A small Delaware village stood directly across the river; eight miles below on the Auglaize was the tribe's main town.

Scattered among these villages were renegade Cherokee from Chicamauga, refugee Conoy and Nanticoke from the Chesapeake Bay, and families of Mohawk, Cayuga, and Seneca referred to collectively as "Mingo."

Dappled Fawn brought Wells and his delegation to the council house in the main Delaware town, where Big Cat was the civil chief, to meet with Painted Pole, the Shawnee spokesman, and Buckongahelas, the Delaware war chief Wells knew from Kekionga.

Wells explained the provisions of the treaty at Vincennes to the chiefs; he also translated a speech from Putnam to the tribes at the Glaize: "I wish to see your women and children go to bed without fear, and your hunters succeed in the chase, so that all of you, young and old, may live in comfort.... Send some of your wise men with my messengers to meet me at the mouth of Muskingum, that we may speak together and shake hands in friendship."

Buckongahelas repeated what Dappled Fawn had said: "You have come too late. We who are all one color now are of one head and one heart. We can not go to Muskingum until we see how Washington responds to our message."

"Other birds have sung these sweet words to us before," Painted Pole added. "I have told Washington that we do not want compensation; we want the return of our lands, which he has no right to hold. The Ohio River must be the boundary; to demonstrate his good faith, he should remove his forts from our country. If he agrees to these conditions, we will meet with the Americans at Lower Sandusky in the spring."

"Washington must give us some reason to believe him," Buckongahelas added. "He has lied to us before. Joseph Brant's son told us he saw Washington pick up a handful of dust and say he would not restore even this much to the Indians. Others have warned that if we meet with the Americans they will poison our rum and put sickness in our blankets. When have the Americans ever dealt fairly with us?"

"Every time the Big Knives plan to attack us, they first send messengers of peace," Big Cat said, his voice deepening in anger. "They speak good words before they do bad deeds. If the Americans want peace, why are they strengthening Fort Jefferson? Why did they murder the Shawnee chief Moluntha under an American flag? If they truly, as they say, want to civilize us and teach us to worship their God, why did they fall upon the Christian Indians and kill them all? Do they think we are fools that forget what they have done?"

Wells had nothing to say to refute these arguments—a few months before they had been his own. Clearly his mission was at an end. The Indians at the Glaize would not consider peace offers until President Washington would agree to their preconditions.

"I will go to the Muskingum and tell Putnam why you can't come," Wells said.

"We know you are under Little Turtle's protection," Buckongahelas replied sternly, "but you are no longer one of us. We do not want you to travel the bloody road between this place and the Ohio—only our warriors can do that. Remain here, or go back the way you came; if you try to go to the Muskingum you will be killed just like the other messengers."

Wells could see that it was useless to protest; in fact, he was relieved—now he could stay the winter and not break his agreement with Putnam. His career as a government emissary was over, almost before it had begun, and perhaps that was all for the best. Soon he would hold Sweet Breeze in his arms again.

Several days later Wells went to visit the traders' town, on a high bluff south of the Maumee overlooking the Glaize, where many of the men he knew from Kekionga had moved their stores. The largest was a hewed-log structure containing George Ironside's warehouse, store, and home. John Kinzie, the silversmith, was next to him, then the French baker and the Miamis Company agent, and Antoine Lasselle, the fur trader. The thirty-two-year-old Ironside was the man Wells knew and liked best; he had been educated at King's College, Aberdeen, and, after coming to America, had married a Mohawk woman and prospered as a fur trader at Kekionga before Harmar's invasion drove him to the Glaize. Ironside told Wells about a boy his wife's brother, White Loon, had captured, pointing across the Maumee at a lone cabin where he lived.

Wells encountered the boy one afternoon walking in a lovely white oak opening above the point where the traders' town stood. The place was the highest ground in the vicinity, providing an impressive view of the bottomland at the Glaize, covered with cornfields. A few Indians had waded into the Maumee to gig for fish; their laughter, whenever they hit or missed, drifted up to them.

"What's your name?"

"Oliver Spencer."

"How old are you?"

"Thirteen."

Remembering another boy captured at the same age years before, Wells felt his heart flutter as he scrutinized the youth.

"Where were you taken?"

"On a creek, between Columbia and Cincinnati."

"And your father is?"

"Colonel Oliver Spencer," the boy stated proudly. "He fought the British."

Wells recalled conversations while he was at Fort Washington about the boy's capture. An Indian war party, out stealing horses, discovered four people in a canoe returning from Cincinnati to Columbia. They killed one man, wounded another, and, when the canoe tipped over, an old lady fell into the water—her voluminous skirts fortuitously carried her downstream and out of danger. Young Oliver had been taken prisoner.

"Does your Indian mother treat you well?"

"Sometimes she gets drunk and beats me."

Wells walked with the boy back to his cabin and met Cooh-coo-cheeh, the squaw that looked after him. She had the intense, piercing look of a seer; her face was twisted into a grimace, yet she seemed to care for her adopted son. Two of her grandchildren also lived there; one a sly-eyed spoiled brat she called "Simo-ne," reputed to be Simon Girty's bastard, the other a good-humored teenage girl who was obviously fond of Oliver.

"Will you tell my parents where I am," the boy pleaded. "I so want to go home."

"I'll do what I can." Wells resolved to act quickly on the matter, while the boy was still sure where his true home was.

Outside the cabin, which stood beside the ancient warrior's path, he saw a post, painted red, about four-feet high, with a crudely carved human face on one side. It was the grave of a great warrior, Cooh-coo-cheeh's dead husband, killed at Kekionga during Harmar's defeat. Dangling from a long pole slanted above the post were nineteen scalps; the hair—of differing colors, textures, and lengths—waved gently in the autumn breeze. Wells stared at the scalps for a long time in a kind of reverie. Yes, among them was one of reddish hue. Whichever side he took, was he destined to kill (or be killed by) his friends and relatives?

The next day the Little Left Handed Man started back to Vincennes, carrying a message from Wells to Major Hamtramck that the treaty at the Muskingum would not take place and that young Oliver Spencer was safe and well at the Glaize.

A week later Little Turtle and his warriors returned in triumph. They had captured two prisoners who told them that a supply convoy would be returning soon from Fort Jefferson. On November 6th, 1792, while the convoy was camped outside Fort St. Clair, Little Turtle had attacked the hundred-man escort at dawn.

"They were Kentucky militia," Little Turtle said, becoming more animated as he described the battle. "Half of them threw down their guns and ran for the fort; the other half made a stand in a stable outside the walls. They fought bravely, but we outflanked them, captured their packhorses, and brought back six scalps."

Wells told him about the treaty at Vincennes and his failed mission to the Glaize.

"Now that we are united is the time to work for peace," Little Turtle said with cogency and conviction, "but my voice is not listened to here. Buckongahelas and Blue Jacket speak in council—I am not heard. The British agents have Shawnee wives and favor the Shawnee. Often I have shown the tribes how to fight, but I also know when not to fight. If the British would give me big guns, I could destroy the American forts and drive the settlers back across the Ohio. If they do not, all we can do is ambush Wayne's supply convoys and wait. The terms we have sent to Washington are too strong; he will not accept them; next year we shall have war."

Wells was glad he had been forbidden to cross the bloody ground to Marietta; otherwise, he would have had to report Little Turtle's gloomy words to Putnam. For a few months he would live at Little Turtle's camp, hunt for his family, and be Blacksnake again; in the spring he could decide, one more time, who he was.

2

Eight months later, on July 10, 1793, William Wells arrived at Roche de Bout, the foot of the rapids of the Maumee, where the Indian confederacy was holding a general council prior to treating at Lower Sandusky with three commissioners of the United States. He was on another risky mission—this one proposed by Major Hamtramck to Wells when he had returned to Vincennes back in February—to serve as a confidential American agent, observe the deliberations of the tribal council planned for that summer, and report to General Wayne at Fort Washington.

"If you live, you will be paid three hundred dollars," Hamtramck had assured him with a sardonic smile. "You should know that the Indians have expressly forbidden the presence of any American citizens on their sacred council ground."

"My name is Blacksnake," Wells had replied somewhat hesitantly, as if auditioning an identity. "I am a Miami."

"I certainly hope so," Hamtramck said in a skeptical voice. "For your own good."

When he arrived at the Rapids, accompanied by Yellow Beaver of the Piankashaw, Wells thought there was a good chance that the Indians might sign a treaty similar to the one Putnam had negotiated at Vincennes—one that recognized the Indians' rights to the soil. He did not realize that he was walking into a labyrinth. The tribes had become wary when the United States agreed to a negotiation at Lower Sandusky without acknowledging the Indians' preconditions for a treaty. A few days before Wells reached the Rapids, a delegation of two Indian chiefs from each nation had been sent to the American commissioners, then at Niagara, to ask why General Wayne continued to prepare for war and whether they were authorized to make the Ohio River the boundary line. Already 1,400 Indians had gathered, over 1,000 of them warriors. That most of the Indians had not brought their families along was a clear sign a peace treaty with the Americans was not expected. This would be a council where war chiefs and warriors took precedence over peace chiefs and families.

In his Indian garb Wells did not find it hard to blend in with the throng of warriors and observe their moods, which ranged from joyful camaraderie when sober to maniacal enmity when drunk. Every day more braves arrived from distant places. A band of Creek and Cherokee marched in, displaying fresh scalps on poles and passing out pieces of tobacco, painted red as a declaration of war, to all the tribes. They boasted of their conquests in the South and encouraged everyone to fight the Big Knives. A few days later some Chippewa from beyond Lake Superior arrived, astonishing Wells with their wild appearance. They all wore nose and ear bobs and painted their faces with weird designs of red, black, green, and blue. Armed only with bows and arrows, they wrapped feathers, skins, and tails of birds and beasts in their long, out-jutting hair.

A rum-soaked fellow, playing a wooden flute with his nose, staggered up to Wells and peered at him curiously. A curly blond scalp hung from his left ear and a wolf's pelt, head and all, draped from his own head down his back, with the bushy tail touching the ground. He was painted in such a way that Wells could not bring his whole face into focus; it was as if he were the one who was drunk—all he could see were kaleidoscopic slivers of eyes, nose, mouth, and chin.

"My name Devil," he mumbled to Wells in vaguely audible English. "I am a devil. I am a man. I am a warrior." He pounded his fist on his chest and shouted, "I am a great man! I am a great warrior! I am not afraid of the Big Knives! I will drink their blood and eat their hearts!" Finally he simply stood, silently swaying, showing Wells the leering glint in first one eye, then the other, while a malign grin spread across his face.

Had the man had accosted him because he knew he was white? Wells backed away warily and made a point of avoiding drunken warriors thereafter.

When the delegation sent to the American commissioners at Niagara returned, Wells could see the dissatisfaction on Little Turtle's face. Word spread quickly that Joseph Brant, who spoke for the tribes, had not insisted on the Ohio River boundary.

At the council two days later, while Brant was explaining that his omissions had not been deliberate, Buckongahelas jumped to his feet and, against all tribal protocol, interrupted him.

"You speak big words to us now," the Delaware war chief snapped, "but your words to the Americans were small. Tell me, why was that? When we fought St. Clair, I looked for you but did not see you. Tell me, where were you? We sent you a scalp from that battle. Did it enliven your spirit as a man? We were very clear in council what we wanted to say to the commissioners. We insisted that the Shawnee were to speak for us. Tell me, why did you talk instead and why did you not say what you should?"

One of the interpreters stood up and scolded Buckongahelas for not waiting until Brant had finished speaking—instantly the council house was swept with a firestorm of disagreement as to whether Brant had deliberately misled the commissioners. Wells was alarmed; he had never seen the formal deliberations of an Indian council in such turbulent disarray.

The debate over Brant's actions divided the tribes into two factions. The Iroquois, Ottawa, Potawatomi, and Chippewa held private meetings where they decided that negotiations without preconditions ought to take place. The Miami, Delaware, Shawnee, and Wyandot chiefs also met as a group and vowed not to treat unless the Ohio River was accepted ahead of time as the boundary. After days of contentious deliberations, the tribes, with Brant and the Iroquois dissenting, agreed to send the Wyandot chief Carry-one-about with a written message that demanded the removal of all settlers north of the Ohio.

In early August the Indians met in general council to hear the results of Carry-one-about's embassy. This time the Americans had been told unequivocally what the Indian confederacy wanted. One of the commissionrs, General Benjamin Lincoln, in an effort to salvage the peace talks, responded at length. Concessions on both sides would have to be made, he said, and the exact location of the boundary line would be the great topic of face-to-face discussions with the Indians. He reiterated the terms of previous treaties, noting that large tracts of those ceded lands had already been sold and settled. The United States, however, was prepared to give an unprecedented sum of money in compensation. He granted that at the treaty with Great Britain the King had not given away Indian lands, since he did not own them in the first place; having *conceded this great point*, by acknowledging that the Indians possessed the right of soil to their own country, General Lincoln still asserted that the United States could pre-empt tribal lands. In effect, he admitted that all past treaties were invalid yet insisted that their terms must be respected.

For a week the Indians met in council almost daily to discuss how to respond. These heated debates made the disarray Wells had observed earlier seem minor. He sat uneasily among the Miami, watching and listening and thinking that nothing good could come of this.

"Would the Americans ever accept the Muskingum?" Little Turtle asked Wells one day.

"No. I am certain that they will not. I have been to Cincinnati and seen all the people. Even if the government ordered them to move, they would refuse."

"The whites spread like oil on a blanket," Little Turtle said sadly. "We melt like snow in the sun. Unless something happens soon, we will disappear."

"What do you plan to do?"

"Blue Jacket has gone to Montreal to learn if the British will join us in war."

"Is that what you want?"

"Yes. I wish to fight, but I only fight to win; we can win with British help. If we cannot win, then I do not want to fight; I prefer to work for peace."

Wells knew that Little Turtle was an eloquent speaker whose powerful words might sway some tribes toward peace, but he also saw daily how Alexander McKee and the other British agents along with their Shawnee allies were manipulating the council and keeping the Miami chief from asserting his leadership.

"But what if the council votes for war?"

"Then I will fight and die for my people."

"Why not speak up for peace at the council?"

"It is not my place, and they would not listen."

After a week of debate, the council voted to stand by the terms they had set the previous October at the Glaize. An ultimatum to the Americans was drafted, with Captain Johnny of the Shawnee speaking and Lieutenant Shelby of the British Indian department writing down his words:

"Brothers, money, to us, is of no value. Divide, therefore, this large sum you have offered to us among the poor white settlers north of the Ohio to help them move. We want peace. Restore our country and we shall be enemies no longer. We desire you to consider, brothers, that our only demand is the peaceable possession of a small part of our once great country. Look back, and review the lands from whence we have been driven to this spot. We can retreat no farther; the country behind hardly affords food for its present inhabitants. We have therefore resolved to leave our bones in this small space where we are now confined."

The speech was approved in council and the tribes made their marks: Wyandot, Seven Nations of Canada, Delaware, Shawnee, Miami, Ottawa, Chippewa, Seneca, Potawatomi, Conoy, Nanticoke, Mohican, Mississauga, Creek, and Cherokee. Only Joseph Brant and most of the Iroquois refused to sign, but the protracted disputes had left all of the tribes deeply divided.

Two Wyandot runners brought the speech to General Lincoln and the other commissioners; they quickly dismissed it as contemptible impertinence and declared the negotiations at an end.

"We have received just such an answer as I could have wished," General Lincoln remarked. His Bible had taught him that a benevolent Deity favored industrious settlers not idle hunters who, unless they learned to till the soil, were destined to dwindle away— with a little help from General Wayne, who was now free to attack with his American Legion.

3

A few days after the collapse of the peace talks, Wells and Little Turtle walked along the Maumee. At a quiet spot beneath a shady elm tree they sat down for a smoke.

"Father, I have decided to go back to Kentucky," Wells said. "I want to take Sweet Breeze and my daughter with me."

"Will they be safe there?" As always when he was thinking deep thoughts, Little Turtle squinted in concentration.

"They can stay with my brother Sam until the danger is over."

"What will you do?"

"I am going to report to General Wayne on what happened here."

"This was our best chance for peace," Little Turtle said solemnly. "If we had met with the commissioners, perhaps we could have agreed on a compromise. The Ohio River was the last great natural boundary between our two peoples, that is why we wanted it as the line, but already it is too late. We have gone down a bloody path that has no end. The whites are like the leaves on the trees. When the frost comes they fall and are blown away. When the spring returns they are more plentiful than before. Although the British have put the tomahawk in our hands, they will not support us with soldiers and big guns. We can not win this war, yet we must fight it. The Americans have given us no choice."

"Father, when we fought Harmar and St. Clair, I might have killed my brother. He told me later that he was in those battles. His hair might have hung in my lodge. Now, if I fight for Wayne, we might kill each other."

"We have shared many things; you know the feelings I have for you. If we meet in battle, I swear I will not try to kill you."

"Father, I swear I will not try to kill you," Wells said with strong emotion.

"My son, we will not seek each other's death, yet death may find us." Little Turtle looked at Wells a long time before he continued. "This may be the last pipe we smoke together. Since there will be war, I must fight, but if I can I will work for peace."

"Father, I will do the same. Let us sit here as friends until the sun reaches the top of those trees. Then I will leave, and we will be enemies—until this war is over and the path to peace is clear."

Fallen Timbers

1

Except for his red hair, the young man who stood before General Wayne on that balmy September morning looked like an Indian. His weather-beaten face was as brown as a cured ham and his buckskin clothing, complete with breechclout and moccasins, was the same as that of any savage. He had the Indian way of standing perfectly straight without stiffness. An exhausted William Wells had arrived at Fort Jefferson three days earlier. He had rested overnight before Colonel Hamtramck sent him on to Hobson's Choice, Wayne's riverside camp near Cincinnati, to report that the American Commissioners had failed to sign a peace treaty with the Indians gathered at Roche de Bout.

"How long were you there?" The overweight and gout-ridden Commander-in-Chief was seated behind a desk. He wore a freshly pressed teal-blue coat faced with scarlet, featuring a tall, starched collar and golden epaulets. A white-powdered wig, perched above a high forehead, accentuated his pitch-black eyebrows; a pair of dark hazel eyes gazed at Wells with keen curiosity; a firm, determined mouth compensated for his slack double chin.

"From July 10th until it ended," Wells replied. "I was at all the tribal councils."

"How is that possible? I thought Americans were expressly forbidden to attend."

"I've lived among the Miami since I was a boy," Wells explained. "They've adopted me; I'm considered one of them."

What he neglected to say, because he knew it might discredit him, was that he was married to the daughter of Little Turtle, Wayne's most gifted opponent in the art of war. Wells was perfectly willing to tell what he had learned about the Indians' plans in general, but he avoided the specifics of his close relationship to the Miami war chief.

"Were any other white men present?"

"Simon Girty sat in all the time, along with two British officers—one was Lieutenant Silby of the 5th Regiment; but the man to blame was Colonel McKee."

"The Head of the British Indian Department?"

"Yes, Sir. Every night he met with the principal chiefs of the Shawnee and Delaware and promised them all the arms they wanted if they'd fight for the Ohio River boundary."

"Were you at those meetings?"

"I heard about them," Wells answered, deliberately omitting that Little Turtle was his source. "On three different occasions the council decided for peace, but each time Colonel McKee made promises to certain chiefs overnight and the next morning they changed their minds. If it wasn't for him, most of the Indians would've met with the Commissioners and signed a treaty. The western Indians wanted peace; only the Shawnee, Wyandot, and Delaware favored war. After the Commissioners left, a few British agents painted up like Indians and joined in a war dance. McKee passed out rifles, fusils, ammunition, scalping knives, and tomahawks—the chiefs got swords and pistols—and the tribes agreed to meet in late September at the Glaize to plan strategy."

"It requires no microscopic eye to see through their insidious designs," Wayne declaimed, his voice rising with his rhetoric. "We must scourge these heathen caitiff! I have a mind to dispatch my own twenty-five hundred 'Commissioners' and settle the issue at bayonet point!"

"It's too late in the season to do that, Sir," Wells stated. He was astonished by how quickly the impeccably pressed and powdered general turned red-faced and enraged.

"How many warriors could they bring against us?" Wayne asked to test how trustworthy this newly arrived man of dubious background was.

"Let's see." Wells's eyes narrowed as he pictured in his mind's eye the assembled Indians. "You've got about three hundred Shawnee, at least that many Delaware, a couple hundred Wyandot, a hundred Miami, the Three Fires—that's the Ottawa, Potawatomi and Chippewa—have four hundred warriors in the area, and another hundred strays and renegades, mainly Cherokee and Mingo. What does that add up to? I'd say roughly fifteen hundred, in all; plus five hundred more Lake Indians who might get involved if the army moves as slow as St. Clair did."

"That is something the Legion will never do!" Wayne snapped. "I'll show the savages the way a real army marches—and fights. What route do you recommend to the Indian towns?"

"I'd take St. Clair's road to the site of his defeat, follow Delaware Creek to the Auglaize, then go down that river to where the villages are clustered along the Maumee."

"What is their plan against us?" Wayne's black brows lowered.

"They'll keep spies out to report on your movements. They'll cut off your convoys, kill the packhorses, steal your supplies, and pick off soldiers at every opportunity. Once you're beyond St. Clair's battlefield, and if they've got enough warriors, they'll try to catch you by surprise."

"That's where *you* come in," Wayne said, giving Wells a final, satisfied scrutiny. The slow and sure way the young man spoke inspired confidence. "Colonel Hamtramck tells me that you are acquainted with every inch of ground, that you know every trail and all the lairs of the savages."

"The Colonel exaggerates, but I do know the country."

"It is not my intention to march into an ambush," Wayne asserted. "St. Clair's men paid the ultimate price for his blindness. I will *not* make the same mistake. He once told me that there wasn't a man on the frontier capable of spying out the camps of the savages; and if there were, no reward could induce him to attempt such a risk. I believe that you, Mr. Wells, are just such a man. I am prepared to pay you forty dollars a month plus rations, name you Captain of a company of spies of your choosing, and promise you a position in the Indian Department when this war is over. Will you accept?"

"It will be an honor to serve you, Sir," Wells said calmly; he was not surprised by the offer; Sam had often told him that his experiences could prove invaluable to the army. The two men shook hands; then Wayne asked his newly appointed Captain for more details about the Indians.

"When the Legion reaches Roche de Bout, what do you think the British will do?"

"I reckon they'll fight. They've got several hundred regular troops and Colonel McKee commands a thousand militia in Detroit. From what I've seen, he sure wants war."

"Good, that's what we're here for." Wayne's eyes lit up at the prospect. "During the Revolution, General Washington would gather us officers in his marquee to discuss strategy. I always waited until the end, after the others had spoken, and made him ask me directly for my opinion. 'Well, General Wayne,' he would say, 'you've been very quiet this evening, what do you think we should do?' 'Fight, Sir,' was invariably my answer." Wayne laughed heartily at his own laconic reply. "I believe that's why the President appointed me Commander-in-Chief of the Legion—he knows I never run from a fight."

2

In truth, Washington had been reluctant to select Wayne to lead the newly expanded and reorganized American Legion, preferring instead his own good friend "Light-Horse" Harry Lee. Although "Mad Anthony" had made a name in arms for himself during the Revolution—by battling the Hessians at Germantown, the British at Monmouth, and Creek warriors in Georgia (and especially by a swashbuckling bayonet charge at the storming of Stony Point)— Wayne was vainglorious, headstrong, hot-tempered, and addicted to drink; yet the President knew that he was a man who did not flinch.

In the wake of St. Clair's disastrous defeat, Congress had authorized doubling the size of the United States Army to 5,000 men, composed of four Sub-Legions, each of which would include companies of riflemen, musket-men, artillery men, and dragoons. If anything, the dregs that could be cajoled and coerced into joining Wayne's Legion were even poorer specimens of humanity than the unfortunates who had marched and died for generals Harmar and St. Clair. Given what had happened to them, a man would have to be a damn fool or suicidal to enlist to fight the Indians. Wayne proved to be a relentless taskmaster determined to turn this sodden rabble into resolute soldiers, even if he had to flay every back and stretch several necks to do it.

For a year Wayne, stationed near Pittsburgh, drilled the sorry recruits who trickled in from the East while he waited to see if the Indians of the Ohio Valley would sign a peace treaty. A dozen soldiers who had had the audacity to desert were shot or hanged, with the whole army drawn up to witness punishment, and many more joined the "Damnation Club," reserved for those boasting the most lashes and the deepest scars. In the spring of 1793 the Legion rafted down to Cincinnati, where their rigorous training continued at their riverside camp, Hobson's Choice.

Wells saw his first sample of Wayne's hash discipline a few days after he agreed to scout for the army. A man named James Irvin, found guilty of desertion, had been sentenced to walk the gauntlet through the entire Legion, have his head and eyebrows shaved, be branded on the forehead with a capital D, and drummed out of camp with a rope around his neck. All of which he suffered with remarkably little protest—it was almost as if by his silence he were saying, "Sure, this is bad, but I'm the lucky one, because what the savages have in store for you will be far worse!" That same day Wells watched four other men receive 100 lashes each for habitual drunkenness, sleeping on guard duty, attempted desertion, and striking a sergeant.

"I would much rather lead gentlemen by a silver thread," Wayne remarked to Wells when he saw his pained reaction, "but this rabble requires a strong flogging through the small guts, on occasion even a liberal dose of niter, to put them in awe and turn them into a fit fighting force. I want them to fear *my* wrath more than the savages."

Indeed, the men both feared and hated Wayne as a meticulous martinet and an implacable perfectionist, while several officers—led by the ever-scheming Brigadier General James Wilkinson, whose envy and ambition could not rest until his Commander-in-Chief was undone—rankled under what they took to be Wayne's pomposity and arrogance and accused him of playing favorites.

Wayne was often rash, acerbic, volatile, and bombastic, but he could also be prudent, persistent, and innovative. He was certain that once his troops were properly trained no savages could withstand their assault. Wells could picture Wayne's plan: a synchronized use of sharpshooters, howitzers, bayonet charge, and mounted swordsmen would rouse the Indians from their chosen hiding places and rout them entirely.

"The Legion must be made superior to insult," he told Wells, showing him how he had ordered the touchholes on his men's muskets rebored so that they could be loaded on the run without priming. Although his preferred method of combat was the bayonet charge, Wayne had not neglected his riflemen, awarding a gill of whiskey to the best marksmen and consigning the worst to do the drudgery of the camp. He engaged his troops in mock combat, so that they could practice wheeling into formation and maneuvering over rough terrain.

Wayne was a stickler for appearances. The four Sub-Legions wore color-coordinated uniforms trimmed in white, yellow, red, or green, fancy hats peaked by ostrich plumes and tumbling tufts of black horsehair, and each followed its own legionary standard with a life-size silver eagle on top. The dragoons were divided into four troops mounted on sorrels, grays, chestnuts, and bays. Peter Wals, the Legion's barber, was in a constant frazzle keeping the longhaired officers and men properly primped and powdered. Wayne, dubbed "Dandy Tony," always dressed immaculately—and woe to the soldier who wasn't. Once the real shooting started the clothes of many a soldier would be soaked with blood, but the fastidious general was appalled by the least speck of dirt.

"Have you no pride, man?" Wayne shouted at soldier after soldier as he inspected his troops. "Clean up that uniform!" Those who failed to comply were strapped to a wagon wheel and whipped.

"In my experience it usually takes three years to train a man in this dreadful trade of death," Wayne told Wells in all seriousness, "so he can live on his ration and take proper care of his arms and uniform. In half that time I have taught the soldiers of the Legion to believe in their united prowess. If the riflemen will rely on their accuracy, the dragoons on their broadswords, and, above all, the infantry on their bayonets, no foe can insult us with impunity! Tomorrow we advance."

Wayne's order was no sooner given than it had to be rescinded. An epidemic of influenza swept through the Legion, leaving many officers and men bedridden. The local quacks attacked the disease with their usual ghastly repertoire of bloodletting and blistering, vomiting and shitting, scarifying and cauterizing. The purgative of choice was calomel; once the body was drained of almost all its fluids, and the patient was too weak to protest any further, the system was restored via some charlatan's celebrated elixir. Remarkably, in spite of these ministrations, only a few soldiers died. By October 7th, the Legion was ready to march.

3

The advance was brought to an abrupt halt six miles north of Fort Jefferson a week later when Wayne realized that his army lacked adequate supplies to proceed. He ordered the Legion to fortify the place—situated on high ground beside a creek in a beautiful, wide prairie—while he waited for more provisions and the Kentucky volunteers to arrive. Wayne named his new fort, which took months to complete, after his good friend from the Revolution, General Nathaniel Greene (or was it his vivacious widow Catherine?). The fifty-acre oak-log stockade included huts for the soldiers, barracks for the officers, a sizable home for the Commander-in-Chief, bastions, blockhouses, sentry boxes, storage buildings, an armory, and shops.

No matter how strong Fort Greene Ville was, the vulnerability of the Legion's position was quickly brought home to Wayne one day in mid-October when a convoy of wagons, laden with corn and escorted by infantrymen, was ambushed by over 100 Ottawa warriors led by Little Otter. Most of the American soldiers fled for their lives; of the few who stood and fought, ten were captured and fifteen killed, including their commander Lieutenant John Lowery. The victorious Indians carried off what they could, leaving the wagons and several teams of oxen standing in the road, and stole more than sixty horses.

The previous day, Cornet William Blue and thirty of his dragoons had been out in the prairie a few miles from camp grazing their horses; two Indians were observed in the middle distance hurrying away. Blue drew his sword, shouted "Charge!" and rode off at top speed to run them down. Before he reached the tree line, Wyandot warriors rose up from behind a fallen log and fired, killing two sergeants. Blue spun his horse around, looking for his other men, and found to his dismay that only one private accompanied him—the rest had panicked and returned to camp. That evening, after the two bodies had been retrieved and buried, Wells watched an irate Wayne order the entire army to be paraded by the bank of the creek to witness a drumhead court-martial of the soldier held responsible for the retreat; throughout his summary trial, which sentenced him to be shot, his grave was being dug. As the firing squad prepared arms, Wayne castigated his troops with a tirade on the contemptibility of cowardice but in the end pardoned the man.

Wells spent much of October interviewing soldiers who wanted to join his company of spies. He was looking for a select group of men like himself, escaped captives or experienced woodsmen, who had lived with the Indians long enough to learn the language and know their ways. His most impressive recruit was Robert McClellan, a pack-horseman reputed to be the fastest runner and the highest jumper at Fort Greene Ville. For a gill of whiskey he would outrace any man who challenged him; for another he would jump over his horse. Once Wells saw him speed across the parade ground and leap over a covered wagon about eight feet high! McClellan was of medium height, slim and wiry—but every muscle must have been of steel.

In late October almost a thousand Kentucky volunteers led by General Charles Scott rode into camp, including Sam Wells, who was a Major now, and the legendary frontiersman Simon Kenton with his own hand-picked company of spies. Although these mounted men augmented his numbers and improved his mobility, Wayne was disdainful of the undisciplined and unreliable militiamen; he suspected, with good reason, that most had come merely for plunder. In order to take advantage of Kenton and his experienced scouts, Wayne sent them, along with Wells and eighty regulars under Major William McMahon, on a reconnaissance mission.

"Keep going until you find something to fight," Wayne told them.

A few days later, Wells and Kenton were able to crawl up close to Big Cat's Delaware village without being detected; Wells was impressed by how the tall, raw-boned, older man moved with an agility equal to his own.

When the two reported back, the hotheaded McMahon was all for an attack. "They're outnumbered," he insisted. "Let's catch 'em by surprise, hit quick, then cut and run!"

"Not far down that river," Wells warned, "are some five hundred warriors who will swarm after us at the first gunshot."

"I sure didn't come here to make a present of my hair to some savage," Kenton drawled as he inserted a pinch of snuff in his left nostril and snorted it in a way that hitched up one side of his face; then he added, with a devilish glint in his light blue eyes, "I'd rather it was the other way around. As I see it, there's too many of us to stay a secret for long and too few of us to fight. When I was a boy I thought I could swat a wasps' nest with a stick and outrun the inhabitants. Well, I was wrong, and I ain't a boy no more. We've had our scout, now let's skedaddle."

No one could doubt the bravery of the savvy old Indian fighter; clearly this was a situation where discretion was the better part of valor; so the expedition returned on October 30th and informed Wayne that the enemy was assembled in large numbers at the Glaize. When the Kentucky volunteers realized that Wayne planned to settle into winter quarters, they began to grumble.

"If something isn't done soon," Wells remarked to Wayne, "those men are gone."

"I'm all for disbanding the damn rascals," Wayne muttered in reply, "but I'd like to get a modicum of use out of them in the meantime. Isn't there some way they can lift a few scalps for souvenirs on their trip home?"

"The Delaware villages on the White River might not be completely deserted," Wells offered, deliberately steering Wayne away from the Miami towns on the Mississinewa.

"How far away is that?"

"I reckon a two or three day march."

"And you have been there?"

"Yes, Sir, when I was first taken captive." Wells hadn't been back to Chestnut Tree Place since, but he could still picture it and figured he could find it.

"Ten days of provisions should be adequate," Wayne said, smiling with satisfaction. "Take them on an excursion and return by way of Fort Hamilton; even if they don't see any savages, at least they'll have had some exercise."

Word spread quickly that Wayne intended to send the volunteers back to Kentucky via a roundabout sortie into Indian country; that night half of the militia abandoned camp and made a beeline for Cincinnati. Those who remained left Fort Greene Ville on November 5th, heading northwest along the overgrown road built by St. Clair two years earlier.

Wells was happy for a chance to spend time with his brother Sam; typically, they traveled in silence, only exchanging occasional comments on the land and the weather, yet they were both content; finally they were on the same side. They rode through brushy woods, towering oak openings, and flat, boggy beech land; a heavy rain began about noon and turned to snow by early evening. The next day they headed southwest, slogging through swamps and crossing creeks.

"Are you sure you know where you're goin', little brother?" Sam remarked.

"More or less."

In the afternoon they reached what Wells thought was the White River. At a fording place he saw the tracks of Indian horses.

Wells ordered a halt; he and Sam went on foot to scout upstream. As they came around a bend they saw an Indian couple in a canoe paddling toward them. The two men crouched behind a fallen log and prepared to fire. Wells heard Sam cocking his rifle at the exact moment he recognized The Porcupine and No Nose in the canoe.

"Don't shoot," he hissed, pushing Sam's barrel aside just as he pulled the trigger.

"What the hell did you do that for?"

"Those are my Indian parents," Wells whispered tersely. "They raised me."

Wells quickly stood up and shouted in Miami, "I am your son, Blacksnake, do not be afraid. The gun fired by accident."

He hurried down a slope to the side of the water and told them to flee as fast as they could because soldiers were near. There wasn't time to talk, or explain why *he* was there; he cringed in shame when he saw how much they had aged and the scorn and sorrow in the eyes of The Porcupine before he and No Nose paddled away.

"This must be the Mississinewa, not the White River," Wells told Sam, who hated savages as much as any Kentuckian but in light of his brother's feelings kept his own counsel.

Wells couldn't prevent the soldiers, who had heard the shot, from searching for Indians; they found a small hunting camp, where they confiscated a few old blankets; later they caught a horse with deer skins strapped to its back; but fortunately The Porcupine and No Nose had vanished.

Wells regretted that he had suggested the expedition and vowed to steer the Kentuckians due south away from both the Mississinewa and the White River. Over the next three days they rode along a series of creeks through some beautiful bottomland filled with enormous maple, walnut, buckeye, and oak trees. They found several abandoned hunting camps, but, to his enormous relief, saw no more Indians before their arrival at Fort Hamilton.

In late December, noting that the ground was clear of snow, Wayne led an expedition to the site of St. Clair's defeat. The troops reached the battlefield on Christmas Eve. The sight of bare black branches stretching skyward as if in mourning and white skeletal remains scattered everywhere filled Wells with dread. Before the men could pitch their tents and spread their bedrolls, they had to scrape the ground clear of bones. Captain Edward Butler rode to the spot under a spreading oak where the marquee of his brother General Richard Butler had stood.

"I left him here," Butler stated, "propped against that tree with a loaded pistol in each hand. He knew he was a goner. We were surrounded. My other brother was badly wounded; I helped him mount, and, with me hanging on to that horse's tail, we barely saved our skins."

Butler stooped down and lifted a long leg bone to inspect in the twilight. "That's him," he said solemnly. "See that crack? He broke his right thigh when he was a boy."

Wells stood in a semicircle of men staring grimly at the other thighbone on the ground, part of a rib cage, and a crushed skull.

That night Wells dreamt he was a boy drifting with his family on a raft down the Ohio River and that William Oldham was still a dashing young man courting the beautiful Penelope Pope; all of a sudden the dream changed and a ghostly Oldham was standing before him, holding his own bloody entrails in his outstretched hands, and looking at him with unspeakable reproach. Wells awoke with a start and, peering outside his tent, saw General Wayne pacing the skeleton-strewn battlefield in the moonlight, keeping a lone vigil.

The next day Wells pointed out two brass cannon sunk in the creek and another inside a hollow log. The men were so excited by the discovery that none thought to ask Wells how he happened to know their location.   The cannon were in surprisingly good condition; with a little cleaning, they would be fit for use. The men collected all the bones they could carry into a huge pile.   Even though it was two years since the battle, and predators had scattered the remains, 600 skulls were found, each bearing the tell-tale marks of tomahawk and scalping knife.

Wayne ordered one big grave dug and the remains were buried with the honors of war, including three rounds from each refurbished cannon.   Then the troops built a small but sturdy fort with the burial site in the center, an out-jutting blockhouse on each corner, and the cannon positioned to defend the log walls.   Two companies of infantry and twenty-six artillerymen would man the garrison, led by Captain Alexander Gibson.

"Thanks to you," Wayne told Wells, "we have recovered three of General St. Clair's lost cannon.   They may yet do us good service. I shall name this place 'Fort Recovery.'"

4

In January of 1794, Robert Wilson, an Irish merchant who lived and traded with the Delaware, accompanied by an old Stockbridge Indian, arrived unexpectedly at Fort Greene Ville under a white flag. They had come in response to a message Wells had sent to Little Turtle and The Porcupine via a Delaware squaw he had previously captured, saying that the United States was yet willing to treat and urging them to respond.   The next day two Delaware warriors joined the delegation; Wells recognized young George White Eyes and a son of Buckongahelas. Although their immediate objective was the release of a few Indians captured by Wells, the talks quickly expanded into an exploration of peace terms.   General Wayne insisted that before serious negotiations could begin the Indians would have to demonstrate their good faith by bringing all their prisoners to Fort Recovery by February 15th.   When the Indians left, hopes were high among the soldiers that a peace treaty would be negotiated and a bloody war avoided.

One person who was decidedly unhappy about the prospect of peace was the Seneca warrior Big Tree, called "Stiff Knee" by the soldiers because of a past battle injury. He was a long-time friend of the late General Richard Butler and had vowed to kill three Delaware to avenge his white brother's death at St. Clair's Defeat, but so far he had only killed one. If the peace treaty took place, he might lose his chance to keep his pledge. As the days passed, he drank more and his face froze into a permanent grimace; some men commented on how strangely he was acting. One afternoon Big Tree staggered onto the parade ground and shouted, "If I cannot kill for my friend, I will die for him!" Before anyone could intervene, Big Tree pulled out his knife and plunged it into his own chest, dying a few moments later. He was buried that evening with military honors; afterwards General Wayne invited the officers to his newly finished home for a glass of wine. February 15th came and went and no Indians with captives arrived at Fort Recovery. The entire frontier was quiet—no raids or skirmishes were reported.

"I fear their silence," Wayne told Wells.

"I don't figure they'll attack until the leaves are out," Wells replied.

The months of anxious waiting cooped up inside a stale, malodorous fort frayed the garrison's nerves. One morning Wells was awakened by pistol fire; he stepped outside and saw two men sprawled several paces apart on the parade grounds. Lieutenant John Bradshaw and Lieutenant Nathaniel Huston had shot each other; both were mortally wounded and died the same day. They had exchanged drunken insults the previous night and other officers had egged them into a challenge. This was the fifteenth duel of the past year, and it would not be the last to have fatal consequences. Like other veterans of the Revolution, Wayne saw dueling as a sign of aristocratic high spirits and made no effort to stop the practice. The two promising young officers were buried side-by-side in their uniforms. No volleys were fired over their graves as a final salute.

Given how touchy everyone was at the fort, Wells welcomed his dangerous missions as a scout. One day in early March, General Wayne summoned him to his house.

"Captain Wells," Wayne said, "I want you to go to Sandusky and bring back a prisoner."

"I can bring you a prisoner," Wells replied, "but not from Sandusky."

"Why not from Sandusky?"

"Because only Wyandot are there."

"Well, why won't a Wyandot do?"

"For the best of reasons," Wells answered. "A Wyandot will not be taken alive."

"What do you propose then?"

"I reckon the Delaware and Shawnee have hunting camps up by the French Store."

"Then take some of your men and go there. I want to know what the copper-colored gentry are up to. And if you should see that goddamned rascal George Loramier, I want you to be the last person he ever sees. Do you understand?"

Wells understood. For many years the Loramier family had run a trading post at the portage place between the headwaters of the Great Miami and the Auglaize; Wayne suspected they had become McKee's agents for arming the savages. Wells picked his best men—Robert McClellan, Paschal Hickman, Dodson Thorp, William Ramsey, and William May—and the six spies, along with a select detachment of Major McMahon's dragoons, rode off to reconnoiter the portage. True to his word, Wells and his men captured a Delaware warrior and his squaw. The Indians told them that a large council had met to consider Wayne's offer to negotiate, but, before they brought in all their prisoners, several chiefs would be coming to Fort Greene Ville carrying a white flag. The next night, lax sentries let the two escape into the forest.

McMahon and his dragoons returned to Fort Greene Ville while Wells and his spies continued to scout along the Auglaize. In the early evening Wells, accompanied by McClellan and Hickman, spotted smoke rising from the middle of an oak opening. Crawling closer, he saw three Indians sitting around a small campfire. They were on high ground, clear of underbrush; it would be very difficult to sneak up without being seen. Wells spotted a fallen log on the far side of the Indians' camp; the men circled around and crept on hands and knees until they were concealed behind a large, rotting tree trunk. The Indians were roasting a shank of venison over the open fire and seemed to be in great spirits, laughing and playing tricks on each other. Wells whispered that he would shoot the one on the left, Hickman would shoot the one on the right, and McClellan would use his speed and agility to race forward and take the third man alive. It was a very risky enterprise, but Wells was determined to have a prisoner.

Wells and Hickman primed their rifles, propped them on the log, and took steady aim. On an agreed upon signal, they both fired; in that split second, and taking advantage of the cloud of powder smoke, McClellan sprang forward, tomahawk in hand. The Indian who had not been shot gave a shout of surprise and bolted like a startled deer, heading for the river. He leaped into the water and quickly found himself mired in several feet of soft mud. McClellan jumped in after him. The Indian drew his knife, but after a brief scuffle, McClellan was able to subdue him.

Wells and Hickman soon arrived, made their way down the slippery bank, pulled their captive out of the wallow, and tied him up. He appeared to be in his early twenties, about the same age as Wells; he was sulky, lowered his head, and refused to speak. While Hickman went back for the horses, Wells scrutinized the prisoner. Then he dipped a bandana in the water and washed the mud and paint off the young man's face. He was white! Wells and McClellan exchanged uneasy glances as they thought about how close they had come to killing him. He still refused to say a word about who he was. After scalping the two Indians, Wells gathered his band of spies and rode back toward Fort Greene Ville with the silent prisoner.

"I have lived with the Indians, too," Wells told him first in English, then in Miami, Delaware, and Shawnee.

Even though the man did not move a muscle or betray the least surprise, Wells could sense that his ability to speak several Indian languages had made an impression on the captive.

"Where were you taken?" he asked with seeming casualness.

"Brew Ricks," the prisoner mumbled.

Wells hesitated, then he understood. "Blue Licks?"

The young man nodded. As they rode on, he slowly—in broken English mixed with Shawnee—told the story of how as a boy he had ridden off with the men from Bryan's Station and been captured along with his older brother at the Battle of Blue Licks in 1782. Several years later his brother decided to escape back to Kentucky, but by that time the young man had become so fully a Shawnee he refused to join him.

"What's your name?" Hickman asked with sudden curiosity.

"Christopher Miller."

"Your brother's name is Nicholas," Hickman stated matter of factly. "I know him, I know your family, your ma and pa, too."

The young man, as Wells could understand, was torn by emotions that finally broke through the stoic mask of his face.

"I want to see my folks," he said.

Wells questioned Miller again at Fort Greene Ville in the presence of General Wayne, who wanted to know if the Indians' peace overtures had been sincere.

"No," Miller said, in slow, stumbling, but discernible English, "the white flag was a decoy to spy on your fort and gain time to assemble the warriors in force. Colonel McKee warned the chiefs that your peace offers were a trap; he continues to supply the tribes with provisions, arms, and ammunition."

Based on the similarity of their experiences, Wells and Miller quickly developed a strong affinity; even though Miller was actually a year older, Wells became his mentor and taught him what he could about adjusting to life in the white world. Wells was immediately aware that Miller would be invaluable as one of his scouts; with Wayne's somewhat skeptical approval, he asked him to join his company of spies.

"The Indian way of life can't last," Wells argued. "That's simply how it is. Too many whites want their land. Visit your folks in Kentucky, you'll see what I mean. They'll tell you that you've got one skill that people want—you know as much about the Shawnee as I do about the Miami. General Wayne will pay you well for your services. And after the Indian wars are over, you won't be a renegade, you'll be a hero. That's how I see it."

"I'll ride with you," Miller said after a brooding silence, "but first I must go home."

5

A month later, Christopher Miller and his brother Nicholas returned from Kentucky and entered Wells's company of spies. That spring the scouts, in a series of sorties, reconnoitered the territory, occasionally fighting brief skirmishes and taking prisoners. During these incursions Wells played such a conspicuous role that the Delaware, Shawnee, and Miami complained to McKee about his depredations. Whenever they lost a warrior, they blamed it on him. How could the Indians send a large force to surprise Wayne if the ubiquitous Wells spied out their every move?

For his part, Wells repressed any remorse he might feel about fighting the Indians. He had a dangerous job to do, which required his full concentration and abilities to accomplish and come back alive. He also had a strong desire to impress his demanding commander, who trusted his judgment, usually accepted his advice, and sometimes confided in him.

Wells, McClellan, May, Hickman, and the Miller brothers scouted for an early June expedition to the Auglaize under Captain Alexander Gibson, the officer in charge at Fort Recovery. As usual, Wells's spies were dressed and painted as Indians and mounted on good horses. When they neared the river they came upon a lone Potawatomi warrior. Since he was outnumbered six to one, they called upon him to surrender. Instead he raised his rifle and fired at Wells, who felt the ball whiz past his ear. Then he dove into the underbrush and scrambled out of sight. In a flash, McClellan was after him, hurdling over bushes and logs. Sensing that he would soon be overtaken, the warrior turned and began to reload, but McClellan swatted the rifle aside with his tomahawk and, assisted by Christopher Miller, wrestled him to the ground.

They brought the Potawatomi back to Fort Greene Ville for questioning. During the last moon, he said, Buckongahelas, Blue Jacket, and Little Turtle had sent messengers to all the Indians, urging them to take the warpath against the Americans. More than 1,000 warriors had assembled at Roche de Bout, where the British were making haste to complete a large fortification, manned by 400 British troops, across the river from McKee's house and stores; in addition, 1,500 militia from Detroit were also ready to fight. Governor Simcoe had sent speeches to the tribes, accompanied by wampum and feathers, war pipes, hatchets, and tobacco—all painted blood red. One of the speeches was from Lord Dorchester himself, who predicted that Britain would be at war with the Americans "in the course of the present year." Encouraged by this promise of British support, Little Turtle hoped to assemble 3,000 warriors and attack the Legion by the beginning of the next moon.

Late in June, Wells and his spies went on a mission with some scouting parties of Choctaw and Chickasaw braves who had volunteered to fight their traditional enemies the Shawnee and Miami. At Wells's suggestion, each wore a yellow ribbon in his scalp lock to signify his allegiance. Although Wells knew the Auglaize and Maumee area much better than these natives of the South, their woodcraft and tracking skills were invaluable. One day at dusk, Wells and some Choctaws spotted a war party near the abandoned site of Girty's Town. When Wells saw the long line of warriors walking single-file through the trees, he realized from his experience with Little Turtle during the St. Clair campaign that this would be only one of many columns advancing through the wilderness. They were headed in the direction of Wayne's most exposed outpost, Fort Recovery.

Taking advantage of the twilight to hide both their numbers and location, Wells and the Choctaws spread out and opened fire, exchanging several volleys with the warriors, killing five and losing one Choctaw; then they slipped away into the dark forest. Wells ordered most of the Indians and ten of his men back to Fort Greene Ville to warn Wayne that the enemy was advancing in great force. The next day, close to the shore of Lake St. Mary's, a few spies and several braves had a skirmish with a Wyandot scouting party, in which a white soldier was killed and a Chickasaw wounded. Wells sent Jemmy Underwood, a Chickasaw chief the soldiers called "Joe," ahead to warn Captain Gibson that Fort Recovery was in imminent danger, while he and a few others stayed behind to spy on the flanks of the Indian army, which included a handful of armed white men with blackened faces and three British officers in scarlet coats.

Before dawn on June 30th, 1794, Joe staggered into Fort Recovery and was brought to Major William McMahon, whose riflemen and dragoons had escorted a convoy of oxen and packhorses to the fort the previous day. Joe was so exhausted his broken English was incoherent; the Major laughed in his face when he made signs that the woods were full of Indians.

Before returning to Fort Greene Ville, McMahon had ordered his packmen, accompanied by a small front guard, to graze their horses on some lush grassland half a mile away while the officers finished breakfast inside the fort. As soon as the men and animals disappeared into the trees beyond the clearing, the Indians opened fire from ambush, killing several of the front guard and two packmen with their first volley and scattering the horses in all directions; the survivors raced for their lives back to the fort.

In the midst of this confusion the fiery, six-foot-six McMahon rushed out of the fort hatless, literally with egg on his face, his long red hair blowing in the wind, and shouted for Captain James Taylor and his mounted dragoons, supported by Captain Asa Hartshorne and sixteen riflemen, to charge the foe. When the cavalry galloped toward a nearby creek, hundreds of Indians concealed behind the bank rose up and fired, killing McMahon and nine of his men, and wounding Taylor. Hartshorne was hit in the thigh; two of his men tried to carry him to safety, but he was cumbersome and their progress was slow; seeing that the situation was hopeless, Hartshorne ordered them to put him down, handed one of them his watch, and said, "Save yourselves, boys, I'm a dead man." Before his men were out of sight, a fatal arrow struck his chest.

To cover the chaotic retreat of the dragoons and infantry Captain Gibson ordered Lieutenant Samuel Drake's company of riflemen to take positions on the brow of a nearby hill. After firing one volley, *they* became the focus of another furious attack; when, moments later, Drake was wounded in the groin, he and the rest of his men were forced to retreat to the besieged fort.

The first fifteen minutes of the battle clearly favored the Indians. In the estimation of Little Turtle, however, nothing had gone as planned. His original intention had been to ambush the convoys that supplied both Fort Recovery and Fort Greene Ville in order to strand the Legion in its outposts. Over 1,000 warriors—well armed by McKee, led by their tribal war chiefs, and accompanied by several British officers—had left Roche de Bout in mid June and made their way in twelve separate columns through the wilderness. Once they reached Girty's town, the warriors of the Three Fires, especially Chippewa from Saginaw and Ottawa from Mackinac, began to criticize Little Turtle's strategy; they wanted to grab some quick plunder, take a few scalps, and return home. When a spy reported that packhorses laden with sacks of flour and kegs of whiskey had reached Fort Recovery, they insisted on making the fort itself their target. Buckongahelas had not yet arrived, but Blue Jacket supported the plan in order to solidify his power at Little Turtle's expense; the Bear Chief of the Ottawa was chosen to lead the attack.

Inspired by their initial success, the impetuous warriors of the Three Fires, goaded on by the Shawnee, rushed forward in a frenzy to storm the walls of the fort, only to be met with withering rifle fire as well as a devastating shelling from the cannon recovered in December by Wells and two others found later. Leaving their dead scattered on the open ground, the stunned warriors were forced to retire to better cover. For the next four hours, both sides exchanged heavy, largely ineffectual gunfire, followed by an eerie lull that lasted until evening. Once night fell, dark and foggy, warriors carrying torches approached within range of the fort to retrieve their dead, only to lose more men to the American sharpshooters. In the morning the Indians staged a retreat to lure the soldiers out of the fort; when Gibson didn't fall for the ruse, the warriors were compelled to retreat in earnest. Fort Recovery, built on the site of Little Turtle's great victory, defended by the very cannon he had captured from St. Clair, was now the scene of a major Indian defeat. Forty had been killed, more warriors than in any previous battle with the army of the United States. That evening the tribes fed on roasted horse and oxen and pointed the finger of blame at each other. The next day, the demoralized warriors of the Three Fires, clutching a few scalps and riding some captured horses, headed home, vowing never to return. Little Turtle saw clearly that the confederation was doomed unless the British provided them with cannon to reduce Wayne's forts to splinters.

When the remnants of the dispirited Indian army returned to Roche de Bout, their best opportunity squandered and their vital unity gone, they did have one piece of good news to report: the dreaded William Wells had been killed.

"All is not lost," McKee assured them. "You have plucked out Wayne's eyes."

6

A few days later a defector from Fort Greene Ville informed McKee of his error: William Wells had not participated in the defense of Fort Recovery and was alive. Wayne would march within the month.

The mounted volunteers from Kentucky began to arrive in mid-July; Wells scanned the faces in vain for his brother Sam, but he did recognize Bland Ballard and two of Squire Boone's sons. That evening Wayne offered Wells and his spies $100 for the next Indian prisoner and $50 for each subsequent capture. Within a week Wells, May, and McClellan bought in two Shawnee, who confirmed that the Three Fires had abandoned the confederacy and that the remaining warriors were gathered along the Maumee.

The Legion left Fort Greene Ville on July 28th, marched twelve miles, and camped beside a small muddy creek. By noon the next day they passed Fort Recovery, receiving a fifteen-gun salute from the garrison. Wayne's force was twice as large as St. Clair's had been, and he drove them twice as hard, hoping to catch the enemy by surprise. When he saw how quickly the flanking troops became strung out and disorganized as they struggled through the tangled underbrush, Wells became convinced that the Legion, in spite of its rigorous training and the vigilance of his spies, was still very vulnerable. Only the fact that Little Turtle's forces were depleted preserved them from a deadly ambush deep in the woods.

Not even Julius Caesar would have faulted Wayne's method of defending the legionary encampment each evening. After the quarter-master-general, usually on Wells's advice, selected the spot, the men pitched their tents and cleared away all underbrush, digging trenches and cutting down trees to build a formidable breastwork, which was protected, in turn, by outposts of guards and a wider ring of sentinels. The Kentucky volunteers, who camped separately, had learned nothing from St. Clair's defeat, since they disdained these back-breaking precautions.

After five days of trudging through thickets of brambles and bridging mosquito-infested swamps, Wayne's army entered a majestic prairie, covered with flowers and dotted with small copses of trees. The weather was sultry and the troops were tired. Wells was struck by the beauty of the place and welcomed the rare chance to look around and see the Legion and the Kentucky volunteers in their entirety; the vista also lifted the men's spirits and a great cheer rose toward a blue, cloudless sky from more than 3,000 throats. How could the Indians resist such a force?

On the other side of the prairie the army forded the St. Marys River and cleared an encampment on the north shore. The men were placing the last logs on the breastworks when Wayne changed his mind and ordered the army to recross the river and build another camp as well as a blockhouse on the south shore.

"Hope it don't rain," Wells cautioned Wayne. "I've seen this ground knee-deep in water."

The general, in an impetuous mood, ignored the advice of his chief scout and the mutterings of his bone-weary men and retired to seek relief for his gout. Soon the woods were filled with the whack of axes and the earth-shaking thunder of felled trees. Suddenly, a gigantic beech came crashing down on Wayne's tent. The general was dragged unconscious from the wreckage; Doctor Richard Allison, the senior surgeon, administered a few volatile drops that brought him to his senses; he was badly bruised but otherwise unharmed. An old stump had caught the brunt of the huge trunk and saved his life.

Wells had no time to brood about Wayne's brush with death; a deputy quartermaster named Robert Newman had disappeared that same day and the scouts were sent out to search for him. Wells discovered tracks of a horse and footprints of four men; they had approached the army's encampment and then headed back toward the Auglaize. Had the Indians taken Newman prisoner?

Although the ever-ambitious and conniving Brigadier General Wilkinson, the same man who had taken Wells's family prisoner, had been instigating dissension in the ranks by spreading slanderous innuendo about Wayne, Wells had no idea how insidious his machinations were. Wilkinson's grand design was predicated on the failure of Wayne's campaign. As the senior officer, he would then assume command of the army, defeat the savages, and succeed to the Presidency as the Washington of the West; or, if his election were not assured, he might lead a secession movement in Kentucky and, with the backing of England or Spain, establish a new country in the Ohio valley. The reason Wayne had been unable to start his expedition sooner was because of Wilkinson's mutinous schemes. He had connived with the contractors to delay his supplies; the tree that had fallen on Wayne's tent was perhaps no accident; and certainly Newman was no captive but a cat's-paw sent by Wilkinson to warn the British of Wayne's advance.

When the blockhouse was completed, Wayne named it Fort Adams after the Vice President and left forty invalids to defend it. The officer in charge of the inadequate garrison grinned bleakly at Wells and quipped out of the side of his mouth, "If I'm lucky the savages will lift my hair before I slit my own throat!" Wells had no word of comfort to offer. The prospect was indeed grim.

Wells and his men scouted ahead, through high scrubby and low swampy lands, until they came upon Delaware Creek, leading to Big Cat's village at its confluence with the Auglaize. Wells returned and asked Wayne for a mounted force to take the town by surprise. Major William Price and a select group of Kentucky volunteers, together with Wells's spies, rode forward rapidly but the Indians had already abandoned the place, burning their homes behind them. Wells and McClelland did manage to seize an aged Delaware couple too infirm to escape.

The Legion proceeded down one side of the Auglaize river with the Kentucky volunteers on the other—an ill-advised tactic, Wells thought, that invited an ambush. It was an overcast day of hard rain; for miles the men marched through flourishing cornfields interspersed with clusters of smoldering wigwams and cabins. When they reached the Maumee and ascended the bluff on the southwest shore, the spot where Wells had met Oliver Spencer the previous year, Wayne was astonished to see the extent of the settlement. Beyond the ruins of the traders' houses and the main village, the bottomlands were cultivated as far as the eye could see with green fields of corn and an abundance of vegetables—peas, beans, cucumbers, potatoes, squash, and pumpkins. Buried in caches or concealed in the weeds the soldiers found many bushels of stored corn as well as brass kettles, pewter plates, iron hammers and chisels, wooden barrels and kegs.

"I congratulate you on taking possession of the Grand Emporium of the hostile Indians of the West," Wayne told his men.

"Tomorrow we will begin erecting a fort at this place, and I defy the English, the Indians, and all the devils in Hell to take it!"

As the Legion set to work building Fort Defiance, Wayne sent Wells and five of his men on their most dangerous mission yet: they were to spy all the way to the British fort beyond Roche de Bout, reporting on its readiness and the number of warriors in the area. Wayne told Wells to free the old Delaware couple he had captured so that they could return to their tribe with a message that a peace treaty was still possible.

The scouts rode all day and night, circling around the south side of the Maumee in order to cross the river and approach the camps of the warriors from the north. Pretending they were a vagrant band of Indians coming to join the confederacy, they would try to mingle with the enemy and gain as much information as they could. At first, the plan worked to perfection. In the early afternoon Wells and his men skirted a large Indian encampment without arousing suspicion and from a distance they observed several hundred British soldiers working furiously to complete the defenses of Fort Miamis. At dusk, after passing through a small Delaware village, they happened upon a Shawnee couple carrying baskets of corn and beans and took them prisoner.

"Let's tie these two up and go back," McClellan suggested. "I've got a hankering for a Delaware scalp."

"How many warriors do you figure we'll face?" Wells asked.

"I only saw one or two," McClellan replied. "I reckon a few more were inside."

"I'll do the talking," Wells cautioned. "At the first sign of trouble, shoot and run."

Feeling exhilarated and invincible after surviving so many risky exploits, Wells couldn't resist one more act of daredevil bravado. Leaving Nicholas Miller behind to guard the captives, he and his men returned to the Delaware village. With his rifle across the pommel of his saddle, Wells rode boldly up to a large pitched marquee, a trophy from St. Clair's Defeat, to parlay. When a dozen well-armed warriors stepped out of the large tent and into the firelight, he had to make a concerted effort to keep his face impassive.

"Have you anything to eat?" Wells asked in Delaware.

"Plenty," one of the warriors replied, motioning toward an old squaw who was stirring the cooking pot; then he gave Wells a close scrutiny. "I have seen you before."

"We passed this way earlier."

"Why did you return?"

"We did not want to hunt at night," Wells explained. "The shots might have caused alarm."

"You are not Delaware," the curious Indian said, still not offering him any food.

"I am Miami." Wells spoke with the conviction that he could be either white or Indian whenever he wished. "We have been to Detroit to sell skins and now we have returned to fight. When will the Americans come?"

"In a few days many will die."

"Do we have enough warriors?"

"When the Three Fires return we will attack and kill them all."

"I know that man," another Indian said, pointing toward Christopher Miller.

"We passed this way earlier," Wells repeated.

A moment later he heard the same man whisper the word "Washington." Sensing that they were discovered, Wells gave the signal to open fire. The five scouts shot at the nearest Indians. Then, crouching low in their saddles with their heads tucked behind their horses' necks, they galloped off. Before they reached the safety of the dark forest, McClellan shouted, "I'm hit," and Wells cried out in pain as his right wrist was shattered, knocking his rifle out of his hand.

There was no time to retrieve his beloved gun or dress his wounds; Wells and McClellan rode on in excruciating agony until the scouts were sure they were beyond pursuit. McClellan had been hit in the shoulder, close to the neck. Although the wounds of the two men were not life threatening, both needed urgent medical attention. After reuniting with Nicholas Miller and the two captives, Wells sent Christopher ahead to fetch the surgeon.

When Doctor Allison, escorted by a company of dragoons, arrived sometime later, he took one look at Wells's wrist, shook his head, and said, "You've done the Legion good service, Captain Wells, but I believe you've fought your last Indian."

7

No matter how serious his injury, Wells refused to abandon the campaign. Even if he could not fight or scout the territory, he knew the Indians better than anyone else in the Legion, and Wayne still valued his advice. Doctor Allison made a splint and a shoulder sling to hold his injured wrist in place; Wells knew from his years with the Miami which tree barks made the most soothing balms.

Although the wound continued to fester and rendered his right hand almost useless, he could mount his horse unassisted—which was more than could be said for the gout-plagued Wayne. When the troops left Fort Defiance in August and began their march down the Maumee toward the waiting warriors of the Indian confederacy, Wells rode with them.

On the same day that the scouts returned to Fort Defiance, Wells had interrogated the captured Shawnee man. He had been remarkably forthcoming, giving the numbers of the British at work on the fort (200), of warriors already present (700), of others expected soon (540), and of militia coming from Detroit (800).

"Where do the Indians mean to fight?" Wells asked.

"At the foot of the rapids; the white man who came in told Colonel McKee that the army was headed for that place."

"What white man?" Wells demanded.

From the Indian's description, Wells knew it was Robert Newman; what he did not know was that he was Wilkinson's secret agent. Newman had warned the Indians to abandon their villages and had informed them of the strength of Wayne's force, explaining how to distinguish officers from regulars; he had even urged them to attack the Americans in the morning when they were on the march, not at night in their fortified encampment.

The next day, Wayne sent Christopher Miller, accompanied by a Shawnee prisoner, back to Roche de Bout with a final offer of peace, warning that if Miller were harmed, the seven Indians still held prisoner would be put to death. Wells knew that, but for his wound, *he* probably would have been the person carrying this dangerous message.

While the Legion was camped near Snake's Town, Miller returned with a counteroffer from young George White Eyes: "Brothers, if you are sincere in your hearts you will set down where you are and not build forts in our village—in the space of ten days you shall see us coming with the flag before us." Miller reported that he had been well treated, but it was his impression that the Indians intended to fight.

"What's your opinion, Captain Wells?" Wayne asked.

"I reckon they're stalling until the Lake Indians and the Detroit militia arrive. If you stop, they'll see that as a sign of fear."

"My sentiments exactly," Wayne said. "We're marching."

On the 18th the Legion arrived at Roche de Bout, where a craggy island of prominent rocks and scrub cedar marked the end of the rapids. They were now less than a day's march away from Fort

Miamis. Wayne ordered a crude stockade built for the army's excess baggage and sent several scouting parties forward to ascertain the size of the enemy force and the nature of the terrain. Wells could only look on in frustration as Captain George Shrim led his spies off on their mission.

Major William Price, at the head of his select Kentucky volunteers, reported that the warriors had taken up positions in the tall grass near an area that had been hit by a tornado years ago and was now an almost impenetrable maze of fallen timber. Shrim's men, however, had not been able to do much scouting; rather they had engaged a large body of Indians. One of Wells's best spies, William May, had been captured; the next day he was tied to a tree and used for target practice.

In the eleven months since he first met him, Wayne had learned to value Wells's advice. That evening Wayne once again asked for his thoughts. Wells knew the importance of the situation and he weighed his words carefully.

"They expected you'd fight today, but you didn't. They'll be certain you'll fight tomorrow, so I wouldn't if I was you. Warriors fast before they go into battle to purify their spirit and protect them in case they're shot in the guts. They fasted today, they'll tighten the rawhide strap around their waist and fast tomorrow; by the next day, they'll have to go back for food. If the warriors abandon their positions, or feel weak from hunger, that'll sure disrupt their plans."

"I don't think we should bring on a large engagement," General Scott offered. "We might start a war with Great Britain."

"By God, General," Wayne raged, "I don't understand you! You've heard what Captain Wells said. The enemy is in front of us and I mean to find them and fight!"

The next day Wayne sent out Major Price to reconnoiter the ground again. He reported that the warriors had withdrawn from their former position and were probably now concealed in the fallen timber. Many soldiers assumed that the Indians' pullback meant that they were fleeing, but Wells was certain that they intended to fight. What he didn't know was whether Little Turtle was still their leader. He doubted it, because it wasn't like him to give battle from a fixed position, no matter how strong; furthermore, the presence of the river on one side made his favorite half-moon formation untenable. Was Blue Jacket in charge? Or Buckongahelas? Or the British?

In fact, Little Turtle had traveled to Detroit to ask for twenty men and two cannon. When the British commander refused, Little Turtle decided that it would be unwise to fight.

"We have defeated the Americans under different commanders twice," he told the assembled chiefs and warriors as they discussed the peace offer that Christopher Miller had brought. "We cannot always expect the same good fortune. The Americans are now led by a chief that never sleeps. He has more men than we do and we can never catch him by surprise. The British have promised to fight with us, but instead they have used us like their dogs to set upon the enemy. When the Americans advance, we should step aside and see if the British will keep their word. I do not think they will. Now is the time, while we are still strong, to seek for peace."

"If the American commander never sleeps," Blue Jacket sneered, "we know who his eyes are. Who taught him how to see day and night? Perhaps you are afraid of your son, Blacksnake. Perhaps you feel fear in your heart. When the Americans came before, we drank their blood. The more men they send against us, the more we will kill and the greater our victory!"

The Shawnee and Delaware braves shook their weapons in the air and roared their approval; it was clear who would lead them into battle.

"I fear no man," Little Turtle said calmly, refusing to take Blue Jacket's bait. "If we must fight, I and my Miami warriors will fight."

8

The morning of August 20th began with showers and an occasional crack of thunder. Wayne's men were summoned by beating drums and blaring trumpets at five. The general straddled a campstool in front of his marquee as an aide powdered his wig, brushed his coat, and polished his boots, while the soldiers prepared their guns and Wells primed his pistol—a tricky task for a man with only one good hand. Doctor Allison wrapped Wayne's gout-ridden legs in flannel and three soldiers helped him mount his horse. Because of the rain, it was after seven when the march began. The soldiers traveled light, leaving their knapsacks behind at Fort Deposit; each man carried only his weapons, a blanket roll, and two days of rations. Wells rode alongside William Henry Harrison, a tall, sallow, rail-thin Virginian whose face was dominated by a large, aquiline nose and a supercilious smile. Many of the other officers resented the fact that young Harrison owed his commission as Wayne's aide-de-camp to his politically prominent family; Wells liked him because he helped him learn to write correct English and asked questions about the Indians; Wayne enjoyed his company since they shared a taste for the Latin classics, especially the campaigns of Julius Caesar and *his* Legion—*veni, vidi, vici.* Today would tell the tale.

Major Price and his mounted Kentucky scouts led the way, followed by a front guard of infantrymen; behind them, at a considerable distance from each other, came the long double-file columns of the Legion, with Wilkinson commanding the right, Hamtramck the left, and Wayne in the center, which included the artillery, packhorses, and more troops—the whole force flanked by riflemen. The rest of the Kentucky volunteers, over 1,000 strong but still not trusted by Wayne, brought up the rear. The skies cleared as they marched through the wet woods; it was going to be a hot, humid day.

After several hours of slow riding through thick woods broken by steep ravines leading to the river on their right, Price's men came to an opening covered with tall grass and scrub brush; ahead they could see a mile-wide swath where the tornado-torn forest was twisted into a tangled maze of blown-down trunks, jagged branches, upturned roots, and dense undergrowth, forming a natural defensive position that appeared to be impenetrable. Two volunteers moved cautiously forward, with the rest spread out behind them to prevent being flanked. In spite of the steamy heat, it was a beautiful late summer morning; the sun-splashed field was alive with acrobatic grasshoppers, flittering brilliant-hued butterflies, darting green hummingbirds, and a host of swarming bugs. A lone vulture, as if forewarned, hovered overhead.

Suddenly the sultry air was split by shrill, tremulous war cries as Ottawa fighters with painted faces rose from their hiding places in the tall grass and fired point-blank at the most exposed of Price's men. Several were shot from their saddles and riderless horses dashed in all directions. These were experienced frontiersmen, not raw recruits, but the shock of the Indian attack was unnerving; although Price called upon them to resist, most, without firing a shot, wheeled their frightened horses and dashed into the forest, with the Indians close behind. The retreating Kentuckians collided with the front guard of the Legion, throwing them into disarray.

Obeying Wayne's orders about anyone abandoning the field of battle, Captain John Cooke told his infantry to fire on the fleeing Kentuckians, who halted briefly before veering off to the right.

Cooke rallied a remnant of his company, sending three well-directed volleys at the advancing braves, forcing them to stop and seek cover; finally his men, too, broke and ran back to the main army. When Wells saw them, he realized that if the Indians could take advantage of the spreading panic in the ranks, they might drive a wedge into the middle of Wayne's Legion and cause a general collapse—thus repeating the pattern of St. Clair's defeat.

At the first sounds of gunfire, Wayne sent his aides-de-camp riding off to find out what was happening. Within minutes, one of Price's retreating men reported that the Indians were deployed in an oblique line that started at the river and reached across the bottomland but was concentrated in the fallen timber on the highland beyond the bluff. At least several hundred warriors were now rushing forward to attack the Legion itself, clashing with Wilkinson's right wing, which was putting up a stiff resistance.

Wells could see Wayne's eyes blaze as he sent skirmishers ahead to protect his troops while they maneuvered into battle formation—this would be the crucial test of their hard months of training. Because of the morning's dampness, the dull thud of the drums beating out Wayne's commands were too muffled to reach the ears of Hamtramck or Wilkinson, leaving them to improvise on the spot. As much as Wilkinson might have wished to sabotage Wayne, in the heat of battle and to save his own skin, he had no choice but to fight as hard as he could.

"Don't let them circle you," Wells shouted in warning.

Harrison rode up and urged Wayne to stay out of the line of fire, but his words of caution were brushed aside. Heeding Wells's advice, Wayne told General Scott and his mounted Kentucky volunteers to sweep around to the left and outflank the enemy on that side, sent Captain Robert MisCampbell's dragoons to the right to disperse the Indians defending the ravines by the bluff and the bottomlands along the river, and directed the artillery to shell the fallen timber in front. Then he turned to the lines of infantry forming behind him.

"Charge the damned rascals with the bayonet!" Wayne shouted, waving his own sword in the air. "Drive them, drive them, drive them to Hell until their legs stick out!"

A "huzza" rose from hundreds of throats as the men moved forward at a brisk walk with trailed arms and fixed bayonets. The attack of the Ottawa had already spent its momentum. Their two war chiefs had both been badly wounded; the scattered warriors who clashed with the main army quickly gave way when faced with the disciplined double lines of Wayne's advancing men.

Meanwhile, Captain MisCampbell and his dragoons had come galloping through Wilkinson's right wing, riding into the marshy tall grass prairie beside the river. Seeing that this charge was premature and unsupported, Wilkinson ordered his own dragoons into action and his infantry to advance. Although they did so with alacrity, they could not possibly keep up with the mounted men, who pressed ahead and were met with a lethal fire from the concealed enemy. MisCampbell and several of his men were killed by the first volley, but Lieutenant Leonard Covington, his broadsword flashing in the sun, rode on, killing two warriors himself; his display of bravery inspired the dragoons to breach the thinly spread Indian defenses, forcing several warriors into the river where they were cut down. Wilkinson's infantry augmented the advance as they marched with fixed bayonets toward the fallen timber upon the bluff.

Hamtramck had also told his men to charge; and so, in spite of the confusion in orders, the entire Legion was on the move in unison. The impetuous assault of the Ottawa, joined by other warriors of the Three Fires, had created a gap in the Indians' defenses. When the warriors saw the plumed-helmeted men of the Legion emerging from the rolling white clouds of powder smoke and advancing inexorably toward them in sweeping lines, a long shining knife projecting from the end of each musket, they fired a few, sporadic volleys and fell back. Only the Wyandot, true to their reputation for unrelenting courage, made a stand, supported by fifty Detroit rangers. With burning throats and bursting hearts, soldiers and warriors grappled in deadly hand-to-hand combat that cost the lives of eight warriors, as well as five rangers, before they finally gave up the battleground.

The retreating warriors ran to Fort Miamis, three miles away, where the British, refusing their pleas for assistance, locked the gates in their faces, thus adding humiliation to defeat—an act that none of the Indians present would ever forgive or forget.

Wincing with each jolt of his horse, Wells rode across the battleground strewn with downed trees and dead or wounded men. As far as he could tell, the losses of the Indians had been low, perhaps twenty killed in all. Much to his relief, he didn't identify any of the dead as Miami; surely Little Turtle was still alive. In truth, more United States troops had died than warriors, yet

Wayne's victory, thanks to the refusal of the British to participate on the Indian side, had been decisive.

The Legion pursued the fleeing Indians for over a mile before Wayne called a halt and ordered a half-gill of whiskey for each of his men.

"I have always flogged the British and the Indians," Wayne boasted as he rode among his exhausted yet elated troops; then, noting that a few of his sweltering soldiers had taken off their shirts, he instantly flew into a rage. "I have fought under the hottest and coldest suns, and such a thing shall *not* be permitted. It's damned cowardly!" he growled. Wells had the impression that a sweaty chest was more abhorrent to him than a bloody one.

Wayne was so insulted by the sight of the cross of St. George still flying above Fort Miamis, which was clearly visible on a commanding bluff overlooking the now sparkling waters of the river, that he neglected to send a detachment back over the battleground to recover the dead and wounded. Instead he ordered the Legion to build a fortified encampment for the night. Eventually the Kentucky volunteers straggled in; as Wayne perhaps expected, they and their horses—bogged down by swamps and bewildered by the maze of toppled trees—had missed out on the entire action.

9

Major William Campbell, commander of Fort Miamis, sent a curt note inquiring why the Legion was camped under his guns; Wayne responded that the muzzles of his small arms had announced a full and satisfactory answer during the glorious rout of a horde of savages in the vicinity the previous morning. The next day Wayne provoked Campbell more by approaching within pistol shot to inspect the fort's defenses.

"Don't come any closer," Campbell cautioned in a quickly scrawled note. "I won't have our flag or my honor insulted. You have brought our two nations, Sir, to the brink of war."

"This fort is situated on territory in the possession of the United States," Wayne wrote back. "I demand an immediate surrender of the garrison."

"I shall never abandon this post until so ordered by his Majesty, King George of Great Britain," Campbell replied. "I must warn you again, Sir, of dire consequences if any of your men venture within the range my guns."

Flames lingered near fuses, as artillerymen waited for the order to fire, but fortunately for both countries the only shots exchanged were espistulary gasconades between two blustering commanders.

Wayne told his men to slash, burn, and destroy everything in sight. The soldiers whooped and yelled as they cut down all the crops, made bonfires of the stacked hay, girdled the fruit trees, and torched every dwelling, including McKee's house and store. Some dug up graves, taking scalps and other trophies. Within hours the lush countryside became a char-black and ash-gray wasteland.

The next day the Legion reconnoitered the battlefield in order to collect and bury the dead—a grisly procedure, since many of the corpses showed the effects of being left to the hot sun and happy vultures. Drums and trumpets sounded the funeral dirge, cannons fired, and the triumphant army marched back to Fort Defiance.

Although his men had fought bravely in the battle, Wilkinson was beside himself with indignation—to think that the laurels of victory should be bestowed upon the brow of that undeserving blockhead! How could such folly and incapacity be so outlandishly rewarded? Only a concurrence of fortunate contingencies, a concatenation of accidents, a run of pure dumb luck could explain such unmerited success. He would have to write at length to his friends to explain these egregious events. He would have to revise his plans and plot anew.

Wayne was determined to present his victory in the most grandiose terms possible. When Antoine Lasselle, a French trader, was found after the battle, dressed and painted like an Indian and armed with a double-barreled fusil, he had been placed before a Court of Inquiry to determine if he could be executed as a spy. Even though he had been forced against his will to fight and his gun had not been fired, what infuriated Wayne was his statement that only 900 warriors had been engaged.

"Where is the rascal?" Wayne demanded as he strode up to the prison door.

"There, Sir," replied the guard.

"You damned infernal villain," Wayne roared, "I'll cut off your head!"

Wells, who knew Lasselle from Kekionga, spoke up in his behalf. "He's a good man, General. He's ransomed captives and given them clothes. Once at Kekionga, I saw him pay two hundred dollars to save a man from a slow death at the stake."

"What happened then?" Wayne asked.

"He was tomahawked, Sir."

"I wish they hadn't washed that fellow's face," Wayne insisted. "If the Court of Inquiry could have seen him painted like a savage, they'd have known his true colors. Keep him in irons."

With a little coaxing from Wells, Lasselle came up with numbers more to Wayne's liking: he now recalled 1,500 warriors and 250 British militia too! Wayne still preferred the report of a British drummer boy, who deserted with the gratifying estimate that 2,000 had been engaged.

"It really *was* only 900," Lasselle insisted to Wells repeatedly, stroking his own precious neck as he spoke. "Little Turtle told me himself, the morning before the battle. He said it wasn't enough and that they would lose."

Wells longed to see Little Turtle and he missed his beloved Sweet Breeze, but because his wound continued to fester he was more or less confined to the fort while others scouted the territory and skirmished on occasion with small parties of hostiles.

Although the army had been victorious, the soldiers of the Legion were deeply depressed by a regimen of hard duty and scant allowance. The whiskey supply had run out some time ago. Cooling temperatures and inadequate diet also brought on the fever and ague. By mid September, after the army had consumed almost all of the remaining vegetables in the area, and Fort Defiance had been strengthened to his satisfaction, Wayne ordered the Legion to march downriver to Kekionga. He also sent the Delaware squaw Wells and his men had captured in August back to her people with a long talk urging all the tribes to seek peace.

"If the British approach this place," Wayne told Major Thomas Hunt, the fort's commandant, "lift your breech to them."

"What then?" the baffled officer asked.

"Why, tell them to kiss your arse!" Wayne shouted, delighted with his wit.

After a three-day march over rough terrain the Legion arrived at Kekionga. Wells's heart sank. The beautiful open area where the Miami, Shawnee, and Delaware villages once stood, surrounded by miles of cornfields, was now covered with waist-high grass, thickets of bushes, and scrub crabapple and plum trees. The charred timbers of a few cabins were visible above the resurgent undergrowth. Wayne selected an elevated spot of land—on the south bank of the Maumee across from the ruins of Kekionga—with a commanding view of the confluence of the St. Marys and St. Joseph rivers.

One October morning Tappan Lasselle arrived, bringing three Americans to exchange for his brother, the long-suffering Antoine.

Wells experienced a sudden flood of memories as he inspected the redeemed captives. One was a young girl, about thirteen, who had been taken by a war party three years ago along the Muskingum; she reminded him of his sister Elizabeth. Tappan reported that the warriors and their families were encamped at Swan Creek, up the Maumee near Lake Erie, where the British had promised to provide for them over the winter. In the spring, he predicted, all the tribes would come in and seek peace.

Wayne smiled at this confirmation of his great victory.

"I haven't done with your services yet," he said. "I'll need you to interpret at the treaty."

"I'll do my best," Wells replied, although his thoughts at the time were elsewhere. He planned to return to Kentucky soon to see Sweet Breeze. He'd been away too long.

Ten days later on the 4th anniversary of Harmar's Defeat, John Hamtramck took command of the new fort, which as yet consisted only of four walls of barracks and a blockhouse. The men fired fifteen rounds, gave three cheers, and the colonel announced jubilantly that the former Miami stronghold of Kekionga henceforth would be known as "Fort Wayne."

The Treaty of Greene Ville

1

On the march from Fort Wayne to Fort Greene Ville, the Legion was overtaken one afternoon by a small, ragged band of Indians carrying a white flag. When William Wells rode forward to translate, he did not recognize them. Then he saw that they were The Soldier, his son The Sleepy One, and a few warriors— Sweating, Buckfeet, The Cat, and his good friend Thin Raccoon; their gaunt faces and haggard eyes, matched by their scraggy horses, presented a picture of defeat.

The Soldier had only sad stories to tell. The Porcupine and No Nose had died the previous winter, and he had become headman of the remnants of the tribe. Wells recalled the first time he set foot in his Indian father's lodge at Snake-fish Town and No Nose had offered her drunken welcome. Now he would never be able to thank his adoptive parents for being so good to him. He thought with regret of his last glimpse of them, paddling in frightened haste away—from him, and the Kentucky militia he had mistakenly guided to the Mississinewa River. Others in the village had died recently from small pox. The Soldier himself had narrowly escaped death two winters ago, during the trip to Philadelphia to deliver Putnam's Treaty for ratification. The chiefs had met with President Washington in early February 1793, but shortly afterwards a sickness spread among them, killing nine, including The Names of the Beautiful Animals Invoked By Our Ancestors. To make matters worse, all of Wells's efforts at Vincennes had come to nothing. The Senate had rejected the treaty—because it acknowledged the Indians' right to keep or sell their own lands—and The Soldier had returned to the warpath, taking part in the ill-advised attack on Fort Recovery.

Several days later, when the Legion made its triumphal entry at Fort Greene Ville to a many-gunned salute and sustained cheers, a delegation of Wyandots was waiting to speak with Wayne. They also wanted peace. A half-breed named Abraham Williams had brought a speech from The Crane, chief at Sandusky. After three of their war chiefs had been killed at Fallen Timbers, power in the tribe had passed back to the peace faction. Wells's feelings about his former life at Snake-fish Town were so ambivalent that it was difficult for him to ask about his wife and son; Thin Raccoon told him that Speaks in Dreams was the liveliest boy in the village and that Laughing Eyes lived with The Muskrat, whose first wife Brings Joy had died. Although Thin Raccoon never accused Wells of leaving his family, his eyes could not hide the hurt. As if in apology, Wells loaded their lean horses with all the provisions they could carry to their village at the mouth of the Mississinewa and assured his former tribesmen that he would see them in the summer. Had he stayed with the Miami, Wells knew he would have been the one seeking terms. That he had acted prudently by abandoning a lost cause brought him little satisfaction.

Williams informed Wayne that Governor Simcoe was still telling the chiefs that they were entitled to the Ohio River boundary and that the British were prepared to support them. Joseph Brant had advised the warriors "to amuse the Americans with a prospect of peace" until they could collect in force to fall upon them early in the spring. The hostiles were to appear bearing white flags and proposing peace, but this was only a ruse. Colonel McKee was also busy at Swan Creek, feeding the Indians and promising British arms and assistance. The chiefs, however, had seen too many British promises broken and were deeply divided.

"They're playing an artful game," Wells confided to Wayne. "The Wyandot at Sandusky have come in because their corn fields are within striking distance of the Legion."

"I'll keep two hostages here and send the rest back with my terms," Wayne replied. "We shall see how seriously inclined for peace they are."

2

In November, Wayne gave Wells permission to visit his wife and daughter in Kentucky. Ann was already walking and could say that she was hungry in two languages. Sweet Breeze understood that they were safer with Sam Wells and his family, especially during the winter, yet she begged her husband to come back for them in the spring. Wells promised that he would. She had taken to wearing linen and muslin dresses now and served him tea from a Staffordshire pot every afternoon. They had never slept together in a bed with sheets before, in a room to themselves; by the time he left after Christmas, Sweet Breeze was pregnant.

During Wells's absence, Isaac Zane, captured as a boy by the Wyandot and now the chief of his own small village, had returned to Greene Ville in December to reaffirm his tribe's commitment to peace. As the winter turned more severe and British provisions at Swan Creek dwindled, more Indians, wrapped in tattered blankets against the biting winds, appeared at the fort.

In January, Antoine Lasselle, whose trading company hoped to capitalize on the prospect of peace with the Americans, arrived with a contingent of Ottawa, Chippewa, Potawatomi, and Sac tribesmen; they were joined later in the month by five men from Pacan's band of Miami, led by The Wildcat, who preferred the name his French father had given him, Jean Baptiste Richardville. As a sign of good faith they had brought in two women taken at St. Clair's Defeat. To reciprocate, Wayne released a squaw he held hostage and provided food and drink. That night the drunken Indians fought among themselves and two were killed.

At a council a few days later, Wells translated between Wayne and the different tribes.

"Six years ago the United States signed a peace treaty with various chiefs at the mouth of the Muskingum, but since that time there has been nothing but war and the roads have run red with blood. My repeated offers to end the fighting were rejected. I can assure you that I am invested with the full power to make a peace, with you and with all the tribes, which should last as long as water runs and trees grow."

The chiefs grunted "ho-ah" in approval and passed around a string of white wampum. They said they would give their answer shortly, but first they would like something to drink; Wayne gave his consent and a decanter of brandy appeared.

"The bayonet is the proper instrument for removing the film from the eyes and opening the ears of the savages," Wayne gloated to Wells that evening. "It has another quality as well—its glitter dispels the darkness and lets in the light!"

The close collaboration between Wayne and Wells was based on a mixture of mutual respect and selfish interest. Although he was reluctant to admit it, Wayne knew in his heart that he owed his great victory, in part, to Wells's shrewd advice and that the upcoming peace depended in large measure on his skilled interpreter's powers of persuasion and knowledge of the Indians. Perhaps Wells saw in Wayne a man to replace the fathers he had lost; certainly he wanted to please his commander-in-chief and he knew which side his bread was buttered on.

"I think they're sincere this time," Wells said, "even if it's their bellies talking. They need the promise of a peace agreement before the spring planting."

"By God I hope so," Wayne replied in all earnestness. "I am as sick of this execrable war as any man—the meekest Quaker not excepted. If we can conclude a peace, I shall at last go home."

The next day Richardville suggested that the treaty be held at Fort Wayne in mid-June; Wayne countered by insisting on Fort Greene Ville, a place unstained by blood.

"I know you are sincere in your desire for peace," Wayne said. "After you have agreed to lay down your arms, you will be permitted to go where you please. The gates of our forts shall be open to you since we will all be brothers. I propose that the articles signed at Muskingum serve as the basis for the treaty. Each of you will receive a copy."

Richardville presented Wayne with an exquisitely beaded string of wampum, saying, "This is from the ladies of my village to the ladies of your village." A preliminary agreement was signed, followed by a feast that became another drunken frolic.

In February Blue Jacket and Buckongahelas agreed to a grand council of all the tribes in June. Blue Jacket told Wayne that McKee's son Thomas, who had been making him a new scarlet coat with gold epaulets, was so angry when he learned that Blue Jacket was going over to the Americans that he threw the epaulets in the fire. Wayne gave the Shawnee war chief a fancy blue American officer's coat and secretly promised him a pension of $300 a year if he proved a faithful friend and worked for peace.

Finally, in March, the aged Miami civil chief Dappled Fawn said the Miami would come to the treaty. He insisted, however, that he did not know the sentiments of Little Turtle. Wells brooded over the matter. What if the British had finally given him the assurances of military assistance he had sought for so many years? If that were true, perhaps the war would continue.

3

Secretary of War Henry Knox wrote to Wayne urging him to welcome the Indians at the treaty with kindness, even liberality, since the national character was at stake. "It is a melancholy reflection that our modes of population have been more destructive of the Indian natives than the conduct of the conquerors of Mexico and Peru. The evidence of this is the utter extirpation of nearly all the Indians in the most populous parts of the Union. A future historian may mark this destruction of the human race in sable colors."

Wayne's men had spent the months leading up to the treaty strengthening the oak walls of Fort Greene Ville. A large council house was built on a bluff overlooking the creek, with a shingled roof and open sides, which not only provided ventilation during hot summer days but also gave the riflemen of the Legion a clear line of fire—just in case.

In May, Wells and Little Turtle's eldest son, Black Loon, traveled to Louisville so they could bring Sweet Breeze and Ann back to Greene Ville. The trip went smoothly and Sweet Breeze, now visibly pregnant, was happily reunited with her mother and father. Wells only visited on occasion; it might look suspicious if he spent too much time with the Miami.

When enough Delaware, Ottawa, Potawatomi, and Eel-river tribesmen were gathered by mid-June, Wayne formally lit the council fire and smoked the calumet. One sunny morning in late June, Dappled Fawn, Little Turtle, and seventeen Miami arrived. Wayne greeted them and warned the assembled Indians not to be alarmed by the firing of guns and the occasional explosion of fireworks, since the Fourth of July was approaching. He turned over several outlying redoubts to the various tribes, who established their camps in the vicinity of the fort.

A week later, Dappled Fawn assured Wayne that he and the other chiefs felt satisfied. "As it is a cool day," he added, "we hope you will give us some drink. You promised to treat us well and we expect to be treated as warriors. We wish you to give your brothers a glass of wine; and we should like some mutton and pork, occasionally."

Wells glanced over at Wayne to see how he received this sly gibe at his hospitality; the general continued to smile, even when The Sun, a Potawatomi chief, noted: "We get but a small allowance—we eat it in the morning and are hungry at night. The days are long—we have nothing to do—we become uneasy and wish for home."

"Pork, we have none," Wayne admitted graciously, since he wanted no man to question his bounty. "The few sheep we have are for the comfort of our sick and occasionally for our officers. Your sick shall most cheerfully share with mine, and I will, with pleasure, share what I have with you. I will give the chiefs of each nation a sheep for their use and some drink for themselves and their people, this afternoon, to make their hearts glad and dry their tears. Now we will have a glass of wine together—I wish to see you all happy and content."

Although some grumbling about the lack of enough rum, brandy, or whiskey to get drunk on persisted among the Indians, Wells was satisifed that Wayne was doing his best, within his means, to keep the tribesmen comfortable, and Little Turtle, who had almost reconciled himself to the necessity of making peace with the Americans, spoke up in favor of waiting calmly until the Shawnee and Wyandot arrived. In private, when Wells was not present, Wayne took a harsher line with selected chiefs, telling them that the Legion had the power to drive them all into the sea.

4

Under a merciless mid-July sun, the council was opened, the council-fire uncovered, and the interpreters sworn in. William Wells would speak for all the Wabash tribes—the Miami, Eel River, Wea, Piankshaw, Kickapoo and Kaskaskia.

"Younger Brothers!" Wayne announced. "These interpreters have called the Great Spirit to witness that they will faithfully interpret all the speeches made by me to you, and by you to me; and the Great Spirit will punish them severely hereafter, if they do not religiously fulfill their sacred promise."

As Wells spoke Wayne's words, it was as if he had heard them for the first time. He felt the weight of his responsibility. In effect, the council would take place through the medium of his voice and depend upon his ability to speak truly.

"This is the calumet of peace of The Fifteen Fires of the United States of America," Wayne continued. "I shall now present it to The Soldier, who first took us by the hand, as I do not know yet which nation among you is in future to have the precedence. The next were the Wyandot, who came forward last fall; then the Ottawa, Chippewa, Potawatomi, and Sac, followed by the Delaware. The treaty of Fort Harmor of 1789, concluded at the mouth of the Muskingum with Governor St. Clair, was founded upon principles of equity and justice. I therefore propose it as a foundation for a lasting treaty of peace."

Little Turtle said, "I must tell you, that I am ignorant of what was done at that treaty."

Wayne struggled to keep his composure at this first sign of opposition but promised to respond: "In two days I will explain the treaty of Muskingum, of which some plead ignorance."

On Monday, Wayne presented Little Turtle with strings of white wampum to symbolize the purity of his heart and then read and explained the treaty of Muskingum. The next day a Chippewa chief said, "You have made the terms of the treaty clear and I now wish to bury the hatchet on behalf of the Three Fires, even though my people were never compensated for their land."

His speech raised the touchy issue of the overlapping claims various tribes made to the territory north of the Ohio. The Crane tried to defuse the question by appealing to Wayne. "I hope you will explain how the country first came into your hands," he said, thus suggesting that the United States was now the rightful owner. "These words of our brothers, claiming in this manner these lands, are alarming to us."

Wayne saw the building tension and suggested a postponement until the next day: Before the council was adjourned, however, Little Turtle addressed Wayne:

"Elder brother! The lands on the Wabash, and in this country, belong to my people. I now take the opportunity to inform my brothers of the United States and others present, that these lands were disposed of without our knowledge or consent."

When Wells translated Little Turtle's words to Wayne, he could see the general's face redden. If Little Turtle wanted to debate which land was owned by what tribe, Wells thought, the entire peace process could collapse. Laying claim to Miami territory was indeed Little Turtle's intention, which was made plain the next day when he spoke:

"General Wayne! I hope you will pay attention to what I now say. You have pointed out to us the boundary line between the Indians and the United States; but I now take the liberty to inform you, that that line cuts off from the Miami a large portion of country, which has been enjoyed by my forefathers, undisturbed and without dispute, from time immemorial. The prints of my ancestors' dwellings are everywhere to be seen in this portion. It is well known by all my brothers present that my forefather kindled the first fire at Detroit; from thence he extended his line from the headwaters of the Scioto to its mouth; then down the Ohio to the mouth of the Wabash; and finally to Chicago, on Lake Michigan, where I first saw my elder brothers, the Shawnee.

"I have now informed you of the boundaries of the Miami nation, where the Great Spirit placed my forefather a long time ago, and charged him not to sell, or part with his lands, but to preserve them for his posterity. This charge has been handed down to me. I was much surprised to find that my other brothers differed so much from me on this subject; for their conduct would lead me to suppose that the Great Spirit and their forefathers had not given them the same charge that was given to me, but on the contrary, had directed them to sell their lands to any white man who wore a hat, as soon as he should ask it of them. I came with an expectation of hearing you say good things, but I have not yet heard what I had expected."

Little Turtle then faced the assembled chiefs. "I expected, in this council, that our minds would have been made up, and that we should speak with one voice. I am sorry to observe that you are rather unsettled and hasty in your conduct."

Wells observed how Little Turtle's caustic words, which clearly questioned the legitimacy of past treaties and the present all-too-easy capitulation of the chiefs, upset Wayne and caused consternation among the other Indians. In an effort to avoid a crisis, The Crane, who had lost the use of one arm at Fallen Timbers, rose and addressed Wayne, resorting to a set of time-honored metaphors to calm the troubled waters: "I now take the tomahawk, which the English gave me, out of your head and bury it beneath a great tree. I now tell you, that no one in particular can justly claim this ground— it belongs, in common, to us all. Now, I wipe your body clean of all the blood, I wipe the tears from your eyes, I open your ears and throat and place your heart in its proper position; I clear away all dark clouds so that the sun may shine; I gather all the bones of your warriors that lie scattered and bury them in one sacred place. I speak not from my lips but from my heart. We here are all of one mind. The treaty of Muskingum was based on the fairest principles and is binding between us. You might have taken all our lands; but you pitied us, and let us hold part. We now establish a lasting peace. Be strong, brothers, and fulfill your agreements."

In the hope that The Crane's words had soothed Little Turtle's ruffled feelings, General Wayne forced a smile and quickly adjourned the council until the following afternoon.

5

"Who does this Little Turtle think he is?" Wayne raged at Wells that evening. I've got all my ducks in a row and he stands up and puts the treaties into question. Will the chiefs support Little Turtle and what should I say to refute him?"

"The chiefs are divided," Wells said. "They don't like it that a war chief like Little Turtle took charge today and they resent how the Miami stand aloof and yet claim most of the territory. The peace chiefs blame the war chiefs for the bloodshed; they want to conduct a treaty in the traditional way and regain their power."

"What does that mean?"

"You saw some of it today when The Crane spoke," Wells explained. "After a tribe has been defeated, it is traditional to bury the hatchet, cover the dead, and humble yourself to the victor, begging for his pity and protection. I think The Crane and the other peace chiefs plan to make you their father, instead of the British, in the hope that you will take care of your children the way the French once did."

"What about Little Turtle?"

"He's for peace, but he don't trust the Americans. He wants justice, not pity."

"What you said about the French gives me an idea," Wayne said. "Didn't the Miami sell some of their lands to them?"

"French traders have been along the Wabash for a long time," Wells admitted, "from Kekionga to Vincennes."

The next day, as Wells had predicted, the Chippewa peace chief Bad Bird attempted to return to the prescribed peace rituals of contrite supplication.

"If we Indians acted wrong, it was our father the British who urged us to do bad deeds," he said. "With this belt I cover all the slain, together with our evil actions. When I look upward, I see the sky serene and happy; when I look on earth, I see all my children wandering in misery and distress. When I show you this belt, I point out to you your children at one end of it; and mine at the other; and I ask The Fifteen Fires to have pity on my helpless offspring. I do not speak to you about lands; for why should I? You have told us we might hunt upon your lands. You need not fear any injury from us—we will for the future live and hunt in peace and happiness."

Other chiefs of The Three Fires rose to support what seemed to the Americans to be an abject capitulation; Wayne was pleased: "I promise to send a little liquor to all of you this evening and I shall invite all the chiefs in due rotation to share my table."

Blue Jacket, Wells observed, was making it abundantly clear that he, as most of the chiefs, had resolved to win Wayne's good graces by isolating Little Turtle and his challenge to the treaty's legitimacy. He sat with the Wyandot and Delaware and requested Wayne to direct his words to The Crane, peace chief of the Wyandot, before they were translated to the other nations.

Wayne thanked the Three Fires for burying the hatchet. "It will give infinite pleasure to General Washington, the Great Chief of The Fifteen Fires, when I inform him," he said and promised them compensation for their lands. Next he turned his attention to Little Turtle and presented a well-rehearsed rebuttal to the chief's definition of Miami territory:

"These boundaries enclose a very large space of country indeed; they embrace, if I mistake not, all the lands on which all the nations now present live, as well as those which have been ceded to the United States. Little Turtle says the prints of his forefather's houses are everywhere to be seen within these boundaries. Younger Brother! It is true these prints are to be observed, but at the same time we discover the marks of French possessions throughout this country, established long before we were born. Next these lands were given to the British, who must now relinquish them to the United States, so that we, the French, and the Indians will be all as one people."

Wayne named the various trading posts and old forts the French and British had erected at Detroit, Vincennces, Ouiatanon, Chicago, Kekionga, Au Glaize, Roche de Bout, and Sandusky:

"It appears to me, that if the Great Spirit, as you say, charged your forefathers to preserve their lands entire, for their posterity, they have paid very little regard to the sacred injunction, for I see they have parted with those lands to your fathers the French—and the English are now, or have been, in possession of them all: therefore, I think the charge urged against the Ottawa, Chippewa, and other Indians comes with bad grace indeed, from the very people who, perhaps, set them the example," he said sarcastically. "The English and the French both wore hats, and yet your forefathers sold them portions of your lands. Now you shall receive from the United States further compensation for the lands you have ceded to them by former treaties."

Then Wayne delivered what Wells determined was the *coup de grace*, presenting first the terms of the Treaty of Paris of 1783, in which Britain surrendered control of the Northwest Territory, and then the recently completed Jay Treaty, in which Britain agreed to evacuate all its western posts. This last treaty effectively dashed any lingering hopes that Britain might still come to the defense of the Indians. Little Turtle, Wells noted, looked shattered.

"We have nothing to do but bury the hatchet," Wayne said with a closing flourish, "and draw a veil over past misfortunes."

On Monday Wayne read and explained the ten articles of the treaty, using a map to illustrate the proposed boundaries. In addition, the United States claimed sixteen reservations, mostly former trading posts within Indian territory. Again, as Wells had forseen, the peace chiefs made no objection. Speaking on their behalf, The Crane thanked Wayne for his moderation and humanity and urged all the tribes to sign the treaty without delay.

Only Little Turtle stood up in favor of more reflection and meditation: "Listen, you chiefs and warriors, to what I am about to say to you! This is a business of the greatest consequence for us all; it is an affair to which no *one* among us can give an answer. Therefore, I hope that we will take time to consider the subject, that we will unite in our opinion and express it unanimously. Perhaps our brothers, the Shawnees from Detroit, may arrive in time to give us their assistance. You chiefs present are men of sense and understanding: this occasion calls for your serious deliberation."

6

Even though Little Turtle pleaded with the Indians to put up a united front against Wayne's dictated terms, the divisions among the tribes and between the peace and war chiefs within each tribe were too deep to be bridged. Wells knew that he had strengthened Wayne's hand by telling him about French and British posts within land claimed by the Miami, now he wanted to help Little Turtle criticize the treaty at Fort Harmar, but neither he nor Little Turtle had been there; thus Little Turtle did not have enough facts, or the backing from other chiefs, to mount a strong case against it. He could only raise objections and maneuver for minor concessions.

The peace chiefs, on the other hand, continued their counter strategy of throwing themselves on the mercy of the Americans and hoping for the best.

The Crane, for example, presented a speech to Wayne, written by Isaac Williams: "We shall never be happy or contented, if you do not take us under your powerful wings. You are master of the lands. We leave the disposal of the country wholly in your breast. Take pity on us and settle the present business as you think proper."

In response, Little Turtle once more rose to his feet. There he stood, face to face with Wayne, with Wells between them, deeply split in his sympathies, translating. Whenever he spoke the chief's sentences, Wells warmed to his passionate defense of his people and the justice of his cause; but when he spoke, in turn, for Wayne, he also found himself swayed by the power of his argument. The chief wore only a breech clout, diamond-patterned moccasins, a bear claw necklace, brass arm bands and ear hoops, and a tuft of feathers in his hair; Wells was dressed in fringed buckskin and a coonskin cap; Wayne looked immaculate in his polished boots, white satin pants, blue general's coat with silver buttons and golden epaulets, powdered wig, and tricorn hat.

"Elder brother!" Little Turtle said. "You have told us to speak our minds freely; we now do it. This line takes in the greater and best parts of your brothers' hunting ground. You take too much of our lands away and confine our young men within limits too contracted. The Miami, the owners of those lands, and all Indians present, wish you to run the line from Fort Recovery along the road to Fort Hamilton." He then turned to the map and pointed. "Here is the road we wish to be the boundary between us. What lies to the east, we wish to be yours; that to the west, we would desire to be ours.

"Elder brother!   Listen to me with attention.   The Miami villages were occupied by traders, but we never sold land there to the French or English. These people were seen by our forefathers first at Detroit; afterwards we saw them at the Miami village—that glorious gate which your younger brothers had the happiness to own, and through which all the good words of our chiefs had to pass, from the north to the south, and from the east to the west."

He then urged the general to keep his reservation there on the south side of the river where Fort Wayne stood, so that the Miami could return to the site of Kekionga, and he suggested that the Miami and the United States jointly control the valuable Little River portage to the Wabash.

The next day other Wabash tribes—the Kickapoo, Kaskaskia, and Wea—asked Little Turtle to speak for them, to see if he could soften Wayne's terms.

For his part, Wayne wouldn't budge on the boundary he had proposed, which included the game-rich Whiteriver Valley, responding to Little Turtle's objection by stating that the seventh article of the treaty granted all the Indians the liberty to hunt within territory ceded to the United States. Neither did he want to share any profits from the portage with the Miami, since they would receive in compensation an annuity of one thousand dollars.

"Let the tribes settle peacefully any differences they might have. Now I want the articles of the treaty read a second time; then I will ask each nation individually, starting with the Chippewa, to state if they approve and are ready to sign."

One by one, a chief for each tribe said yes, including Dappled Fawn for the Miami. Wells watched as Little Turtle, with folded arms, sat in silence.

7

It took several days for copies of the treaty to be engrossed for signing; during that time the Indians were encouraged to eat, drink, and rejoice. The noted Shawnee orator Red Pole arrived with eighty-eight warriors; his appearance revived Little Turtle's fleeting hopes that resistance to the treaty might yet be possible. Red Pole, however, quickly aligned himself with his cousin Blue Jacket, who had announced that he was no longer a war chief.

In early August the articles of the treaty were read for a third time and all the chiefs were asked to sign the copies. Richardville and Dappled Fawn signed for the Miami from Kekionga and The Soldier signed for the Eel River tribe. All the principal chiefs, on behalf of 1,130 Indians there assembled, stepped forward and made their marks.

Only Little Turtle refused to sign.

That evening, as Little Turtle was eating in his lodge, his wife, Setting Sun, suddenly slumped over and died on the spot. Her untimely death was seen as a bad omen by the other Indian tribes— a further reason to shun the outspoken Miami war chief. Sweet Breeze was despondent over the loss of her mother and moaned throughout the funeral service, which was conducted by the Reverend David Jones, Wayne's Baptist chaplain, with Wells translating to a small gathering of mourners seated on skins and blankets. Afterwards soldiers paraded and fired a three-gun salute; a Miami medicine man chanted and the Legion's fife and drum corps played military music as she was lowered into her grave. Little Turtle turned and walked alone into the woods.

For a week no one saw him; the rumor spread that he had returned to the warpath. Wayne took advantage of his absence to solidify his mastery over the other chiefs.

"Listen, all you sachems, chiefs, and warriors!" he said. "Lift up your eyes, and behold these instruments of writing, to which the Wyandot, Delaware, Shawnee, Ottawa, Chippewa, Potawatomi, Miami, Eel River, Wea, Kickapoo, Piankeshaw, and Kaskaskia have set their hands and seals, that they may be passed down to your children's children, as a memorial of the happy peace thereby established. When your posterity shall view these records, they will know that you were the great people that accomplished this blessed work to ensure their peace and happiness. The next business will be the distribution of the goods and presents promised in the treaty."

True to Wells's prediction, The Crane then stepped forward and said, "Brothers, listen. I inform you all that we do now, and will henceforth, acknowledge the United States of America to be our father—you must call them brothers no more. An impartial father regards his children equally, as well those who are ordinary as those who are more handsome; therefore, should any of your children come to you crying in distress, have pity on them and relieve their wants. Be strong, brothers, and obey our father; always listen to him when he speaks and follow his advice. I now deliver this wampum, in the presence of all of you, as a token of our now being the children of The Fifteen Fires."

"I now adopt you," Wayne said, "in the name of the President of the Fifteen Great Fires of America." As Wells repeated Wayne's statement in Miami, he realized that while the general assumed that this honor enhanced his patriarchal authority, the Indians believed that it only increased his paternal responsibility to look after them.

Even the great Delaware war chief Buckongahelas, who had frowned all through the lengthy negotiations, took this occasion to speak: "All who know me," he said, "know me to be a man and a warrior; I now declare that I will, for the future, be as strong and steady a friend to the United States as I have in the past been an active enemy."

A few days later Little Turtle reappeared and told Wells he wanted to meet Wayne in private. The three men smoked the calumet for a long time in silence before Little Turtle turned to Wayne with woeful eyes and began to speak.

"I have had time to look closely at the treaty," he said. "No article has escaped my serious deliberation. I am a man who says sincerely what he thinks; if during our talks I spoke hard words, I hope you will understand I was only doing my duty to myself and my people."

"You should sign the treaty," Wayne said. "All the other chiefs have."

"If I am forced to," Little Turtle replied calmly, "I will."

"I didn't mean that," Wayne insisted. "I want your free consent."

"I do not think my hand should do a thing my heart does not approve of," Little Turtle said in a brooding voice. Wells could not repeat the words without sharing the sentiment behind them.

"For this treaty to have a chance to last," Wayne said, "it needs your mark on it. I'd like to consider you a friend of the United States."

"If I sign, I will return to my home near Fort Wayne," Little Turtle replied. "My father will have daily proof of my friendship."

"I can assure you that the United States will provide for you," Wayne said. "If you sign we will send you to Philadelphia to meet President Washington and receive his personal thanks."

"Would you let this man accompany me and live with the Miami as our interpreter?"

The general glanced over at Wells, who nodded, surprised by this turn of events.

"Yes, of course," Wayne said, "I can arrange that."

Little Turtle hesitated a moment, then took up a quill, dipped it in ink, and made his mark at the spot Wayne indicated.

"I have been the last to sign this treaty," Little Turtle said solemnly. "I now give my word that I shall be the last to break it."

Philadelphia

1

In September 1796, William Wells, Little Turtle, and The Soldier traveled from Fort Wayne to Detroit, the assembly point for a delegation of chiefs going to Philadelphia to meet President Washington.   Two months earlier, in compliance with the Jay Treaty, Britain had relinquished the town to Colonel Hamtramck's American forces. It had taken over a year for the wound to Wells's wrist to heal; he still had only partial use of his right hand. His days as a warrior and a scout, for whichever side, were over. General Wayne, now in constant pain from the gout, had promised to write a letter of recommendation for him to James McHenry, the Secretary of War, detailing Wells's service to the United States and urging that he be rewarded with a pension.

Little Turtle had been to Detroit many times to trade furs with the French and demand military support from the British. The small settlement was packed inside oak-post palisades under the shadow of the once formidable but now run-down Fort Lernault.   The wooden houses were mostly dingy cabins with sloping roofs, dormer windows, stone chimneys, and front porches that made the already narrow streets narrower. Most of the troops were stationed at the Citadel, a three-story barracks facing a picketed parade ground a short walk from the fort. A handful of substantial two-story homes along Saint Anne Street were owned by prominent fur traders, like John Askin, whose tannery by the river, along with the nearby slaughterhouse and wharves, contributed to the smell of death that hung over the dirty cramped town like an evil omen.

By day the constricted streets thronged with horse-drawn carts and a motley medley of people. Most prevalent were the French fur trappers of the *pays d'en haut* in their brilliantly hued shirts, blue cloth sashes, and red bandanas; the women wore short skirts over long petticoats and protected their faces from the sun with wide-brimmed straw hats. The prosperous British merchants persisted in powdering their hair and sported long-tailed coats with lace at wrists and throat; their knee breeches, vests, and shoes flaunted flashy silver buckles and buttons. In addition to the soldiers, the only other Americans on the scene were a few frontiersmen in buckskin. The wealthier families owned African or Pawnee slaves, many of whom worked at the docks. Hundreds of Indians loaded with peltry, reed mats, casks of maple sugar, and other products set up shop wherever they pleased and bartered with passersby. Colonel Hamtramck had restricted the sale of liquor to soldiers and Indians alike, but many of both reeled drunkenly through the streets laughing one minute and fighting the next. Since Pontiac's surprise attack in 1763, all Indians were banned from town at dusk and the massive gates were swung shut behind them. Wells, Little Turtle, and The Soldier camped on the Commons below the town, where the last mosquitoes of the summer did their damage and the odor of cow pies blended with the stench from the wharves.

When it came time to depart, Little Turtle had second thoughts. Blue Jacket made it plain that he considered himself the leader of the delegation; he constantly curried favor with Wayne and Hamtramck, insisting that *he* had triumphed over St. Clair while denying his role in the defeat at Fallen Timbers. The Shawnee had always put more warriors in the field against the Americans than the Miami, and there was no denying that Blue Jacket was a ferocious fighter, but Wells knew that Little Turtle could not stand his boasting or his blatant efforts to get the Americans to honor him as the British had. Nor could he forgive the fact that Blue Jacket had not confronted Wayne at the peace treaty in order to defend Indian rights to the land.

"I have told The Soldier that I will not go to Philadelphia," Little Turtle informed Wells bitterly. "He can speak for me and for the Miami. He knows my heart and so do you."

Without Little Turtle or Egushaway, the Ottawa leader who had died, or Buckongahelas, who had retired, Blue Jacket and the eloquent Shawnee peace chief Red Pole were clearly in charge. The Soldier would represent all the Wabash tribes, even though he was a war chief and a man of few words. Wells was happy to be reunited with Christopher Miller, interpreter for the Shawnee.

After weeks of muddy roads, axle-breaking mountains, and shabby towns with their pig-strewn streets and flea-bitten inns, Philadelphia appeared to Wells's weary eyes as a miracle of cleanliness and order. Thanks to Benjamin Franklin, and other like-minded men of the Enlightenment who believed in civic virtue, William Penn's original plan had become poplar-lined streets laid out in a perfect grid and paved with cobblestones. The north-south ones were numbered sequentially starting near the Delaware River; the east-west ones were named after the local trees, except for High Street, the hundred-feet-wide main avenue where a colonnaded market, a cornucopia of foodstuffs and flower stalls, was located. Because of raised brick sidewalks lined with wooden posts, pedestrians were protected from the passing carriages and wagons as well as the refuse in the free-flowing gutters. Public pumps for water were situated at uniform intervals. Every morning the tranquility of the city was interrupted by the cries of black boys offering their services as chimney sweeps. In the evening the streets were lighted by four-sided, ventilated, whale-oil lamps—one of Franklin's many useful inventions, along with his cast-iron stove and lightning rod—and the spiel of the oyster venders was heard. Patrolling night watchmen called out the time and reported the weather.

The downtown, a few blocks from the extensive docks along the river, consisted mainly of two-story red brick row houses and small retail stores punctuated by a few soaring church spires and the marble facades of neoclassical public buildings. Most of the private homes had white shutters and tile roofs; the various stores, otherwise identical to the houses, were distinguished by their display windows and intricately painted signboards swinging gently in the breeze. The government buildings were clustered on or near Chestnut Street, between Fifth and Sixth. Independence Hall, City Hall, Congress Hall, the American Philosophical Society, and the Philadelphia Library formed a coherent architectural group, next to the delightful State Garden with its gravel paths, shady trees, abundant flowerbeds, and well-placed benches.

Wells liked to sit there and survey the spectrum of people. Due to the reign of terror in Paris and the bloody revolt in Santo Domingo, adamant Royalists, outflanked revolutionaries, and ousted plantation owners by the thousands were seeking asylum in America; each day arriving ships added to the steady influx of Irish redemptioners, British indentured servants, Scotch adventurers, German farmers, and a host of other European émigrés as well. The plain Quakers, once the mainstay of the city, were now the exception rather than the rule: Wells found the men in their round hats and cloth coats and the women in their black bonnets and homespun dresses drab in comparison to their more fashionable neighbors in silken waistcoats and satin breeches. Of course not all kept to the simple ways of the past; many a pretty pale-faced Quaker girl now let her ringlets fall to her shoulders, decorated her bonnet with bright ribbons, and substituted linen and muslin for linsey-woolsey. Several affluent Quaker men took up powdered hair, lacy ruffles, and silver buckles—these apostates were known as "wet Quakers."

The docks were an even better place to savor the diversity of the city. Wells had never realized before how many different jobs there were. The shipyards swarmed with artisans—some freed slaves who had learned a trade—rope makers, riggers, caulkers, coopers, carpenters, sail makers, shipwrights, blacksmiths, painters. As he watched the cargos from the tall-masted ships being unloaded in large barrels and crates, and the contents piled along the wide wharf or stacked in the huge warehouses before being carted off by draymen to stores and customers, Wells marveled at the world's plenty. How many useful and pleasing things there were! To see so much unexpected and unimagined bounty was to discover a new set of wants and desires.

2

After securing their lodging at a nearby inn, the delegation went to the office of James McHenry, the Secretary of War. In contrast to the omnipresent red brick, his office was a two-story frame house painted white, an easy walk from Congress Hall. A handful of clerks and copyists, none with expertise in Indian Affairs, handled the paperwork. McHenry, a pleasant-faced man with a friendly smile, shook each chief's hand vigorously to convey his warm welcome. Red Pole, with Christopher Miller translating, spoke first:

"We have traveled a great distance to see President Washington. For too long we listened to the lies of the British; now we have discovered our error, made peace with the Fifteen Fires, and listen only to our great Father. We wish to speak with him and hear what advice he has for us in order to keep the path of peace open between our people and the United States. We hope that we can see him soon, for we would like to return home before the deep snows come."

"Red Pole speaks for us all," Blue Jacket announced before proceeding to celebrate himself. "The British have honored me as a great warrior and gave me this commission as proof of it. I now break it and pledge my service to the United States."

He gave the tattered parchment to McHenry, who handled it gingerly, understanding that a suitable replacement was expected.

"I will communicate your words to the President," McHenry assured them. "I hope that he will find the leisure to meet with you Tuesday next."

Washington intended to remain aloof from any negotiations with the Indians, receiving them only on ceremonial occasions and letting McHenry handle all the difficult details. Just as a gentleman never dueled with a denizen of the lower orders, so Washington considered it beneath his dignity to dicker with aborigines. A few days later McHenry, through Wells and the other interpreters, read a speech from the President that urged them to abide by the Treaty of Greene Ville and never sell their lands to individuals. In return, the Indians and their posterity would receive an annual quantity of goods. To prevent fraud, each tribe was to tell its agent which persons should receive the goods and oversee their distribution. To ensure the friendship of the United States, they should also prevent bad Indians from stealing the frontier settlers' horses.

"Your lands are good," the President wrote. "Upon these you may raise horses and cattle, by the sale of which you may procure the conveniences and necessaries of life in greater abundance, and with less trouble than you do at present. You may also, by a little more industry, raise more corn and other grain, as well for your families, as for the support of your stock in winter. I hope the Nations will maturely reflect upon this subject, and adopt what cannot fail to make them happier. When the Government shall be informed that they have taken this wise course, and are sincerely desirous to be aided in it, they may rely upon receiving all necessary assistance."

The Indians listened to the message with signs of approval, but Wells made it clear to McHenry that they would consider it an insult if they were not allowed to speak to the President in person. The twelve-man delegation was invited to Washington's home that evening for dinner; McHenry explained that it was strictly a social occasion, not a time for oratory. They could give their speeches the following day; the President would then respond after due deliberation.

Washington's Fifth Street house, on loan from the debt-ridden financier Robert Morris, was a wide, three-story building of dark red brick with dormer windows in the attic. Two tall lampposts stood sentinel in the front and a six-foot-high brick wall surrounded the grounds, which included shade trees, a garden, slave quarters, stables, and a carriage house. A white servant in livery at the door ushered Wells and The Soldier down the columned entrance hall, where the key to the Bastille (a gift from Lafayette) was prominently displayed, and into the spacious mahogany-finished first-floor dining room, in the back part of the house. The Soldier and some of the other chiefs preferred their traditional moccasins, leggings, buckskin shirt, and blanket, but two or three had adopted white dress. Blue Jacket had exchanged his scarlet British officer's coat for an American one befitting his name. Wells wore pantaloons and a linen shirt with ruffles. McHenry, Vice President John Adams, and a few government officials and army officers stood in one corner, sipping Madeira and exchanging pleasantries.

When Washington entered the room, a hush fell on the gathering—the great man walked among them. Wells stared with unabashed curiosity. He was a towering oak of a man, almost a head taller than anyone in the room, and a giant when he stood beside short, portly John Adams. As McHenry introduced the guests, the President would make a slight bow but not shake hands, speak briefly in welcome, converse for a moment, and then move on. He was dressed in a black velvet coat and breeches with shiny silver knee buckles, a pearl-colored vest, yellow kid gloves; a ceremonial sword snug in a white leather scabbard hung by his side, its glittering hilt visible beneath his coat; he kept a cocked hat tucked under his left arm.

Wells scrutinized Washington carefully. That his head was too small for his large body made him appear taller than he was—almost six-feet-four-inches. He had unusually big hands and feet, broad shoulders but a shallow chest, and the sag of age showed in his heavy hips and softening stomach; still, he moved with remarkable ease and grace, as some large men can; and when he gestured with his free hand, it was with the precision of a polished actor.

Washington's face was a study in contrasts: although he wore his hair powdered white, to hide the gray, Wells could detect he was in the presence of a fellow redhead. Perhaps it was the ruddy cheeks, or what appeared to be freckles—which on closer inspection proved to be smallpox scars—on his strong, prominent nose, or was it the bluish gray of his penetrating eyes? They were small and set widely apart within large sockets and beneath a massive brow that accentuated the skull beneath the skin. A defective set of false teeth compressed his thin lips and wide mouth, constricting his frown of gravitas into a grimace. Washington prided himself on never revealing his true feelings, but to Wells he looked like a man whose teeth hurt.

Washington knew he could govern the country, because he had already accomplished the more demanding task of governing his own fiery temperament. He saw himself as a dutiful, deserving son and his country as his true father—thus he strove all his life to be about his father's business and win his approval. He had crafted himself into an icon, a symbol, a paragon upon whom all could depend. It was the *idea* of Washington that held the country together—he provided the needed image of public service and private integrity. As head of a government based on classical models, he made a conscious effort *never* to be compared to Caesar, but rather to Cato—Caesar was power, Cato virtue. For Washington to maintain his image of civic virtue incarnate, it was essential that a discreet silence be maintained about what was happening west of the Appalachians to Indians and south of the Mason Dixon line to slaves.

"May I present William Wells," McHenry said, "the man General Wayne spoke so highly of during the Fallen Timbers campaign."

"Ah, yes, your name is familiar to me," Washington replied solemnly. "Colonel Hamtramck mentioned you in his letters and General Putnam said you had done him good service."

"It's a honor to meet you, Mr. President," Wells said, hoping to strike the correct note of deference.

"Tell me, do you think the Indians will take my advice and become tillers of the soil?" Washington fixed Wells with an intent gaze.

"I don't know, Sir," Wells admitted. "You see, the women…"

"I ask no more of them than I do of myself," Washington interrupted. "In a few months I shall retire to Mount Vernon. There I shall tend to my flocks and fields."

"Like Cincinnatus retrieving his plow," McHenry suggested.

"Not exactly," Washington remarked. "That task is for others."

"The Indians are sincere about wanting to live in peace," Wells stated.

"We all must submit to events we cannot prevent," Washington said with calm deliberation. "They must learn to accept the inevitable, abandon hunting, and take up husbandry. If they will not change, theirs can only be a poor and perishing life. The future of this country lies in the West—that is the great stage where we shall display our character and act out our destiny. If you can teach the Indians to adopt our ways, Mr. Wells, you will do a great service to our country, otherwise…"

At that point Washington fell into an awkward silence that was finally broken by the signal that dinner was served.

In an effort to foster good fellowship the Indians and whites were interspersed around the table; often that meant, as in the case of Wells and The Soldier, that the interpreters were not sitting close enough to the appropriate chiefs to translate, thus the diners could only muster a smattering of small talk. Washington's farewell address, recently published in the local papers, had warned his countrymen to moderate the fury of partisan factions and to steer clear of permanent alliances with foreign powers. When this topic was brought up, Washington seemed compelled to shake off his gloom and explain himself.

"We are a young country and must establish our character," he said with measured conviction. "It is sheer folly for one nation to look for disinterested favors from another. We must show the powers of Europe that we are for *ourselves* and not *for others*. We must act for *our* benefit, not for theirs. We must demonstrate that we don't need them and are capable of governing ourselves. Those incapable of doing so are mere slaves made for a master."

The allusion to slavery, even in metaphor, put a damper on the conversation; Washington once again fell into a melancholy silence that lasted through the rest of the meal. Wells noted that he began absentmindedly drumming on the edge of the table with his knife and fork, as if trying to summon the martial music of glory days gone by.

The next afternoon the chiefs were allowed to address Washington in person. As usual, Red Pole spoke eloquently about the desire of the Indians to live at peace with the United States; he asked that the treaty line be changed to the Great Miami River, while Blue Jacket elaborated on his previous remarks to McHenry, telling how British agents had deceived him into fighting against the Americans. Once again he displayed the document he received from Sr. John Johnston, the British Superintendent of Indian Affairs, which he now dramatically cast aside, asked for a similar testimonial from the United States, and shook Washington's hand. When it was The Soldier's turn, Wells stood uneasily between him and the President to interpret.

"I speak for the Miami, Eel River, Wea, Potawatomi, Kickapoo, and Kaskaskia tribes. All of those nations are pleased, in general, with the treaty, but wish the line to be altered if possible as Red Pole has already stated. This is not a great change, but it permits us to keep vital hunting grounds. We who live on the Wabash love our land and do not desire to part with it for anything."

The Soldier then handed the President a belt of white beads.

"The nations have asked me," he continued, "to request that this man live among us, because we believe he could be of great service in keeping the peace and giving us good advice. We will provide a spot for him to live as well as for anyone sent to us to teach us how to farm."

Wells felt awkward singing his own praises, but he spoke forcefully, hoping Washington would grant The Soldier's request.

The Black Chief of the Chippewa and Asimethe of the Potawatomi also said they wanted the boundary altered and Wells as an agent. Finally, Red Pole in an act of solidarity requested that the absent Little Turtle receive the same presents promised to all the other chiefs, including a rifle, a saddle, a bridle, a sword, a medal, and a coat. Washington shook hands with each of the chiefs and interpreters—Wells felt the force of his mighty grip—and McHenry informed them that the President's official reply would be forthcoming in a few days.

3

Peale's Museum, "a Repository of Natural Curiosities," occupied three large rooms on the ground floor of Philosophical Hall. Charles Willson Peale was a self-taught child of the Enlightenment. A silversmith, watchmaker, and jack-of-all-trades, he was an accomplished painter, ardent naturalist, and insatiable curator—as well as an indefatigable begetter of sons, each named after a famous artist. When the museum overflowed his house, he had moved it to these more spacious quarters.

The Soldier had come down with the flu and was confined to the inn; along with the other two interpreters, Wells accompanied the chiefs to the museum. A huge mangy stuffed buffalo standing inside the entrance elicited startled sounds from the Indians before they realized it was dead. One of Peale's many skills was making hand-carved models that replicated the musculature of each animal and filled out its preserved skin to animated perfection. He also painted detailed backdrops that recreated the appropriate habitat for a given exhibit. Many of the animals of North America were on display—a moose, a black bear, a panther, a wolf, a porcupine, a possum with nine young hanging by their tails from a miniature tree—but what most interested the Indians were those they had never seen before: a jackal, a mongoose, a duck-billed platypus, a live hyena from Bengal in a cage. They found the rows of stuffed exotic birds in floor-to-ceiling cases equally astonishing, marveling at the resplendent plumage of Chinese pheasants, scarlet curlews of Cayenne, toucans, cockatoos, spoonbills—even an albatross from the South Seas and a rare specimen of the extinct heath hen from New England. High above the exhibits perched a live bald eagle; a hand-painted sign on its cage read: FEED ME DAILY FOR 100 YEARS.

The multitudinous mishmash of the place set Wells's head spinning, as the natural history exhibits of sponges and shells, rocks and corals, bats and butterflies yielded to freakish curiosities: a seventeen-foot hammerhead shark, a four-foot paddlefish with a sword-like snout, a petrified snake from Fort Pitt, a six-foot-tall Chinese fan, a four-inch shoe for a merchant's wife from Canton, a piece of the Bastille, a chip from the Coronation Chair in Westminster Abbey, lava from Mount Vesuvius, the trigger-finger of the notorious murderer Broilman, a feathered cloak and headdress from the Friendly Isles, a bamboo bow and quiver (a gift of an African prince turned faithful slave named Jambo), the Koran in Arabic, a two-headed pig, a five-legged cow with two tails, the massive, mysterious bones of the *Incognitum Americanus*... Peale believed that his museum conveyed the benevolent harmony of nature and the wisdom of the Creator, but Wells was overwhelmed with a dizzy sense of abundance verging on chaos.

He was brought up short at the next exhibit; with a shock of recognition he realized he was looking at several peace pipes smoked and wampum belts exchanged at the Treaty of Greene Ville. Why were they here? Who brought them? Could it have been General Wayne? What would the Indians feel if they saw that their prized possessions were already artifacts?

At that moment he was interrupted by a commotion in the other room. What he discovered was one more wonder that somehow did not seem incongruous in that place: Blue Jacket, Red Pole, and the other chiefs, hands on their weapons, were standing face to face with about forty Creek, Cherokee, Choctaw, and Chickasaw, who also happened to be in Philadelphia to see the President. Furthermore, a Cherokee named Humorous Fellow had just snatched one of Peale's prize live rattlesnakes from its glass case, cut out its heart with his knife, and eaten it! Peale, a tall, long-nosed, thin-faced cadaverous man, whose usual manner somehow suggested a cheerful undertaker, was visibly upset, which only added to the tension between the rival Indians exchanging taunts and daring each other to fight.

Fortunately, Wells recognized The Mountain Leader, a Chickasaw chief he had scouted with under Wayne; Red Pole also had friends among the Cherokee. In a short time cooler heads prevailed. After a brief discussion, the chiefs realized that this chance meeting might prove serendipitous and decided to hold a formal council the next day. The incorrigibly optimistic Peale was overjoyed with this turn of events and offered a room in his museum for the occasion. At the council, the various chiefs expressed their desire for peace and unity. A delighted McHenry promised to inform Washington of the results; Peal credited the benign influence of his museum.

On December 7th Wells witnessed Washington's final congressional address. A master of magnificent entrances and magnanimous exits, the President arrived in style: at noon, six bay horses pranced up the street pulling a flower-draped, cream-colored carriage, with cupids painted on the panels and six footmen in white coats trimmed in scarlet clinging to the sides. Hat in hand Washington mounted the steps of Congress Hall, paused at the entrance, and turned toward the crowd, giving everyone an opportunity to gaze at him. He stood still for a suspended moment, looking out over the people's heads, as if he were posing for posterity and wished to exchange his aging flesh for ageless marble.

From the upper gallery Wells saw Washington ascend the podium in front of a semi-circle of seated legislators, take his speech out of his coat pocket, retrieve his spectacles from his vest pocket, remove them with studied slowness from their case, place them on his nose, and begin to read:

"Measures calculated to insure a continuance of the friendship of the Indians, and to preserve peace along the extent of our interior frontier, have been adopted, guarding on the one hand our advanced settlements from the predatory incursions of those unruly individuals who cannot be restrained by their tribes; and, on the other hand, protecting the rights secured to the Indians by treaty; drawing them nearer to the civilized state; and inspiring them with correct conceptions of the power and justice of the Government."

The rest of the speech discussed the recent treaties with Great Britain and Spain that secured the frontier forts and opened the Mississippi to commerce. To protect United States seaman abroad and preserve our neutrality among the European powers, the President called for the creation of a navy. Domestically, he favored encouraging manufactures while not neglecting the primary importance of agriculture. To encourage unity and security, he proposed the establishment of a national university, where the best of the country's youth could learn the science of government; as well as a military academy, where they could learn the art of war. He recommended a pay raise for the congressmen and urged them to extinguish the national debt. Finally, he asked the Supreme Ruler of the Universe to continue extending his providential care over the United States, protecting and preserving its virtue, happiness, and liberty.

Everyone was silent during the speech and only stood to applaud at the end, when Washington bowed once and walked from the chamber. Wells felt moved by the solemnity of the moment.

The next day, the chiefs heard McHenry read the President's response to their talks. Since the Senate had already ratified the Treaty of Greene Ville, Washington said that the terms were inviolate and the boundaries could not be changed. As proof of his personal regard, however, he wanted to give all the chiefs, including Little Turtle, presents as a testimonial of his affection. "He has told you," McHenry stated, "that when you shall show a sincere desire to raise stock, and to improve in husbandry, that the United States will assist you, and he has no objection to Mr. Wells residing on the Wabash. He now wishes you a good journey and a safe arrival at your respective nations."

Afterwards, Wells met privately with McHenry.

"Does this mean that I will be the Indian agent to the Miami?"

"That hasn't been decided yet," McHenry said. "The current budget does not fund such a position. The President wants men he can trust, like his old friend Benjamin Hawkins, who will represent the United States to the southern tribes."

"I have done good service," Wells insisted. "Do you doubt my loyalty?"

"Certainly not," McHenry assured him a little too heartily, "but we are faced with a delicate situation, keeping the Indians at peace while leading them from the savage to the civilized state. If they can learn to support themselves on a smaller circumference of ground, our frontier settlements can proceed unimpeded—do you understand?"

"Yes, Sir, I believe I do."

"Good. I've drawn up a short statement that the President and I would like you to sign."

He placed a piece of paper on his desk and motioned for Wells to sit down and read it: *I promise for what I have received and for what I may receive to promote to the extent of my power the interest of the United States with the northwestern Indians.* McHenry then counted out $300, laid the money on the table, and asked almost jokingly, "You don't have any problem signing that, do you?"

Wells hesitated, said that he didn't, and signed his name.

4

William Wells was back in Pittsburgh, a year later, bound again for Philadelphia, only this time with Little Turtle, whose Miami tribesmen had roundly criticized him for letting his rivalry with Blue Jacket prevent his negotiating in person with Washington to revise the Treaty of Greene Ville. To make amends, Little Turtle had vowed to argue his people's case with the new President, John Adams. Wells wanted to clarify his own status; he still didn't know if he was officially the Indian agent or whether he would receive any more payments. Besides, he had a growing family to support; Sweet Breeze had given birth to their first son, William Wayne, named for the general, who had died the previous December.

Wells and Little Turtle stayed at the Black Bear Inn on a public square called the Diamond, where the foundations of a new courthouse were visible. Although Pittsburgh was taking the first steps toward becoming a major merchandising and manufacturing center, the old frontier post was still in evidence. Outside the numerous taverns drunken whites and Indians vied for wallowing space in the muddy, garbage-strewn streets with hordes of stinking pigs and howling dogs—if they weren't snoring in the arms of some poor pox-ridden doxy. Wells thought that the stench of the place was even more pungent than Detroit; to the odors of privies, pigsties, stables, slaughterhouses, and scum-covered ponds was added the pervasive smell of coal smoke, the local fuel of choice, which was plentiful in nearby hills and streams.

A new prosperity could be seen in the trade goods brought on packhorses and in Conestoga wagons from Philadelphia and Baltimore as well as the keelboats and barges from New Orleans unloading their prized cargoes at the docks. Peace with the Indians and the promise of free, or at least cheap, land brought thousands of prospective settlers streaming across the mountains; for a dollar a foot they could purchase a flatboat and ride the spring floods down the Ohio—without the fear of the unknown and the dangers of Indian attack that the Wells family had faced twenty years earlier.

The easy availability of coal stimulated industry; William Turnbull, owner of the only stone house in town, had established the region's first iron furnace on Jacob's Creek, near Wells's birthplace; and James O'Hara, who made a fortune outfitting Wayne's army, had started a glass factory on the south side of the Monongahela across from The Point. At the boat yard plans were underway to build ocean-going ships that would put Pittsburgh on the world's map. Even some inklings of culture were in evidence; in 1786 John Scull began publishing a newspaper, *The Pittsburgh Gazette,* and in 1793 he printed the third volume of Hugh Henry Breckenridge's cervantine novel, *Modern Chivalry.*

Little Turtle fell ill on the wind-swept, mud-rutted road to Philadelphia. When they reached the city in December, Wells went immediately to the office of Secretary of War McHenry, who brought them to the home of his former mentor, the renowned Dr. Benjamin Rush, on Walnut Street. Upon being introduced to Little Turtle, Rush bowed, took the chief's hand, and said, "I hope you aren't feeling too badly, Sir."

As Wells recounted Little Turtle's symptoms, a combination of winter flu and recurrent gout, Rush nodded and prescribed his favorite cure-all—bloodletting—which the chief submitted to without complaint, while the doctor kept an eye on the filling basin and a finger on his pulse. Then Rush suggested a warm footbath and questioned Wells about Little Turtle's habits.

"How much does he drink?"

"Depends on how much is available," Wells replied, "but he's rarely drunk, if that's what you're getting at."

"Is he married?"

"Several times," Wells said.

"Oh, I'm sorry, have his wives died?"

"Two did."

"You mean he has…"

"He's a great chief; he's entitled to more than one."

"Tell him that immoderate indulgence in transports of Venus can ruin a man's health."

"I'll tell him," Wells said with a skeptical shrug, "but I don't think he'll believe you."

"And does he eat to excess?"

"Whenever he gets a chance."

"I know the aborigines prefer the cold bath," Rush said, as he poured more hot water onto Little Turtle's feet, "but it is fatal for smallpox and harmful for flu."

"Have you got a cure for smallpox?" Wells asked. "That could save a lot of Indian lives."

"Not a cure, but a preventative," Rush said. "Would Little Turtle be willing to try it?"

Rush had learned the Suttonian method of inoculation in London and brought it back to Philadelphia. When the doctor explained that he would induce a mild case of the disease to prevent a more serious occurrence later, Wells had his doubts, but Little Turtle, who had seen smallpox ravage his people, wanted to take the risk once his flu was over.

During the fall the Federalist press had reopened old wounds by launching a series of attacks on Rush's conduct during the devastating yellow fever epidemic of 1793. "Doctor Sangrado," the partisan journalist William Cobbett called him, "a quack who would fill Mambrino's helmet with blood if he could." Naturally, all this was on Rush's mind when Wells and Little Turtle visited him in January for his smallpox inoculation.

Rush prepared his trusty lancet and made a slight puncture in Little Turtle's left arm, just enough to produce a single drop of blood. No bandage was placed over the cut; for two days the chief was to drink no wine or spirits and eat only vegetables. If he felt feverish, he was to return for more bloodletting.

"I have had to endure the rancor of rival physicians," Rush complained, "and I assure you, there is no species of hatred more demonical than the *odium medicum*."

The epidemic had begun in August of 1793, at the height of a humid summer and about the time several ships docked from Santo Domingo. As the disease spread across the city and the death toll mounted, Rush had abandoned his conventional remedies—vinegar-soaked blankets and cold baths—for massive emetics, purgatives, and bloodlettings, until his poor patients were drained of what little strength they had left. Miraculously, some survived; this convinced the dedicated doctor that his brutal cures were benign.

When he wasn't bemoaning his martyrdom and comparing himself to Jeremiah, Rush was a very pleasant man with a lively mind; he took a genuine interest in Little Turtle, asking him about Miami beliefs and customs. One day in late January he introduced his twelve-year-old son James to him. The chief dubbed the boy "Wagamongua," or White Loon, after a son of his sister he had adopted. Rush also took Wells and Little Turtle to a house on Third Street to meet the Polish patriot Thaddeus Kosciuszko, who, after serving as an engineer in the American Revolution, had carried the struggle for independence to his native Poland; on his return visit to America, he was still nursing his wounds from fighting the Russians and being imprisoned in St. Petersburg. Kosciuszko's head and left knee were bandaged and his hip was impaired; he received people while stretched out in a bed that almost filled his small room. Rush, Wells, and Little Turtle waited in a tiny antechamber until his other visitors left.

A man of strong emotions, Kosciuszko wept with joy to see Rush. "These are more honorable than being shot in the arse," he told his old comrade, jovially comparing his current state to his only injury during the American Revolution.

"You'll be up walking in no time," Rush assured him, "and every step you take will remind you of your bravery."

"Is this the man you have been telling me about?" Kosciuszko propped himself higher on his pillow. Because of his bitter experiences fighting for his beloved Poland, he admired any man who stood up for the underdog; he looked at Little Turtle as another brave patriot defending a worthy cause.

Wells told the story of how long and hard the Miami had fought for their land and freedom. When Little Turtle then presented him with an intricately designed pipe tomahawk, Kosciuszko was moved; he motioned for Rush to retrieve a battered leather case wrapped in a sea otter skin stashed under the bed. He took out a brace of silver-mounted dueling pistols, with gold touchholes, which he presented to Little Turtle, along with a *bourka,* a sleeveless cloak brought to Poland by the Tartars.

"I have carried these pistols on many battlefields. I have fought on two continents in defense of the weak, the wronged, and the oppressed. Use them to shoot dead the first man who comes to subjugate you or steal your country."

As Wells translated, Little Turtle smiled at the irony of this tardy advice; he was greatly pleased with the gift and told Wells to tell him so. As the conversation continued, the chief happened to pick up a pair of spectacles, which startled him by how sharply they improved his sight. He had seen such glasses before, and even tried some on, but these were the first that clearly worked. When Kosciuszko saw the lively interest on the chief's face, he offered them to him.

Wells had rarely seen Little Turtle so enthused; he could hardly contain his delight as he cried out in Miami, "You have given me new eyes!"

5

When Little Turtle's health improved, James McHenry explained that President Adams was preoccupied with foreign affairs and couldn't see the chief until early February. Why not settle in and enjoy the sights? Winter weather made the mountains impassable until spring anyway. On Wednesdays and Saturdays Wells took Little Turtle to the grand market, stretching for three blocks down High Street. Farm wagons arrived the previous evening and by dawn all their produce would be on display. The arcades were a convenient place to walk on cold, snowy days; in spite of the crowds, everything was subdued and orderly. Wells and Little Turtle marveled at the variety of fish, flesh, and fowl, as well as fruits and vegetables, baked goods and dairy products, coal and firewood, even horse feed and flowers. At one end of the market a wizened black man wearing a purple turban sold fresh game—possums, squirrels, rabbits, raccoons—already skinned and hanging by hooks; he had a large bucket packed with live snapping turtles that he would chop up on the spot for soup. The market was a good place for eyeing women. The wealthier ones arrived in private carriages and strolled casually from stall to stall making their selections, followed by a servant carrying a basket. Wells and Little Turtle were not alone in this male sport; French émigrés in particular hung around and in hushed tones debated the merits of various shy, bonneted beauties, or openly flirted with curly haired coquettes as they sashayed by.

It was here that Wells met Count Volney. The renowned French savant asked whether he might interview them about Indian customs for his next book; he took them to his lodgings that overlooked the market and began talking about his impressions of America.

Constantin-Francois Chasseboeuf, Comte de Volney, was the son of a wealthy lawyer in Anjou; although he had received a fine medical training, he resolved to make mankind his vocation and set out to see the world and its peoples. After learning Arabic at a Coptic monastery in Cairo, Volney explored the pyramids, wandered the ruins of Baalbek in Syria, and lived among Bedouin tribesmen and Corsican peasants. *Voyage en Syrie et en Egypte (1787)* and *les ruines, ou meditations sur les revolutions des empires (1791)* established Volney among the enlightened thinkers in France and his utopian belief in the universal brotherhood of man made him an early supporter of the Revolution; as the Terror spread and the threat of the guillotine neared, his enthusiasm waned; imprisoned for a year, he saved his neck by escaping to America.

"I thought Revolution could be effected by reason," Volney told Wells, "but I was wrong. Once unleashed, it is a mad beast; the only way to stop the frenzy of bloodletting is to impose an absolute tyranny, worse than whatever ruler you plotted to overthrow. Yes, liberty has been banished from Europe, with its incessant strife and endless wars, but here in America, the land of freedom, it will find a new and better home. Here, protected by an ocean, I feel safe."

Although Volney spoke in favor of reason, Wells observed, he was actually a man of passion, quick to pick a quarrel, forever seeking a new enthusiasm or lamenting an old regret. As he talked he swung between euphoria and despair, seldom realizing that his opinion of the moment often contradicted his previous sentence. He looked every inch the haughty French aristocrat, with his silken ruffles at throat and wrists, sleek velvet suit and languid posture. He was a tall, slender, finely formed man with a narrow oblong face, a high forehead, a prominent Provençal nose, mild blue eyes, and a small mouth, delicate but determined.

Volney questioned them about the soil and climate of the United States, the subject he was studying, but over the following weeks they met ten times and discussed a wide range of topics. Wells also helped him compile a list of Miami words.

Wells and Little Turtle each wore a round hat, a blue suit, and pantaloons; Volney was curious to know if the chief found these American clothes comfortable.

"At first, they were too confining," Little Turtle replied, "now I like them well enough because they protect me from the cold."

Wells and Little Turtle rolled up their sleeves and the three men compared skin color and texture. Volney even made a check of each man's pulse.

"His skin is as soft and fair as a Parisian's!" Volney was equally startled to see how dark Wells's skin was, telling him that he looked like an Andalusian.

"I have seen Spaniards in Louisiana," Little Turtle said, "and their skins were the same as ours, but why should they be different? The sun, the father of colors, burns us all. That is why our faces are darker than our bodies."

"Your face resembles those Chinese Tartars the Dutch ambassador brought to Philadelphia," Volney told Little Turtle. "I suppose that's not surprising; your people originated in Asia."

He brought out a large map and spread it on the table, explaining how the Indians migrated long ago across the Bering Strait to the Aleutian isles. Little Turtle scrutinized the map with obvious interest, recognizing the Great Lakes as well as the Ohio and Wabash rivers, but he questioned Volney's theory.

"If these Tartars look like us, they could have journeyed from here. Is there proof it did not happen that way instead? Their fathers could have been born on *our* soil."

Volney chose not to reply and switched the conversation to differing appearances among the Indian nations.

"We know every tribe at first sight," Little Turtle said. "The shape, color, knees, legs, and feet are all signs. From a single footprint I can distinguish not only between men, women, and children, but also tribes. You whites are easy to spot, you turn your toes out, while we Indians walk straight, although some walk more on the heel, some on the toes."

At the end of the session Volney had Wells ask Little Turtle if he needed anything. The chief responded promptly, "A bath."

The French, too, found the American custom of rarely bathing offensive; Volney took Wells and Little Turtle to the home of a compatriot on South Front Street, who had installed seven sheet iron tubs in his home; for a subscription of eight dollars a month, a man could bathe there as often as he wished.

At another meeting, Volney asked Wells why so many white captives preferred the savage life to that of civilization. This was a question close to Wells's heart.

"That's more common among the French Canadians, who marry, have families, and enjoy an idle life," Wells explained. "The British don't do that; they find Indian women unattractive. For Americans, the appeal is greatest if you're captured as a boy. To have nothing to do but play in the woods is what all children desire, and it's not hard to adapt to the hardships, because everyone shares them the same. I myself was taken at thirteen, and I was very well treated, but I never completely forgot my white family, so I finally decided to return home.

"Among us, a man may live comfortably in the present and also lay up something for his old age. Among the Indians, that's hard to do, especially now when hunting's poor and the cornfields are destroyed. Even if a man could store up possessions, his tribesmen wouldn't let him. Were Little Turtle to return home and die tomorrow, all his presents, clothes, hats, trinkets, would be scrambled for by his countrymen, and there'd be nothing left for his wife and children. He gets his power and prestige, you see, not from what he owns, but from what he can give away.

"Now life's even harder for the Indians." Wells became more animated, as if he were trying to justify his own actions. "They're stalked by disease and early death. Everybody thinks about dying; they're exposed to a thousand dangers and realize their lives are as frail as clay pots and just as easily broken. A father can't protect his children; sometimes he falls into despair and doesn't even provide for them. Suicide is common. I've seen a few simply lie down and die because they had no hope for the future. Others destroy themselves with drink."

"When I was in Vincennes," Volney replied, "I saw a drunken savage stab his wife four times with a knife. I had planned on spending a few months among them, as I had among the Bedouins, but I saw that there was no Arabian hospitality among them, only anarchy."

Wells didn't know if he would take it that far; indeed, he had the feeling that Volney was construing his remarks into a general indictment of Indian life (Volney insisted on the term *sauvage*) that Wells had not intended. Didn't he see that Little Turtle was as enlightened as he was?

On another visit, while Wells and Volney conversed in English, Little Turtle, as was his custom, wandered over to the window, where he used a small piece of brass wire on a short round stick to pluck facial hair. Noting his lively interest in the street scene below, Voleny asked the chief if he would prefer to remain in Philadelphia. Little Turtle walked back and forth across the room, giving the question serious consideration:

"Yes, I am accustomed to what I find here. My clothes are warm and comfortable. These houses are well made to keep out wind and rain. This market provides everything a person could want, without the need to hunt for food in the woods. I must admit, when I consider these things, you whites are better off than we are. Here I am deaf and dumb. I do not talk the language. When I walk the streets, I see everybody is busy about something: one makes shoes and another, hats, a third sells cloth, and all live by their work. I ask myself, which of these things can I do? Not one. I can make a bow, catch fish, kill deer, and go to war, but none of these things are done here. To learn would take time, success would be uncertain, and I am old. Were I to stay, I would be an idle piece of furniture, useless to myself, to you, and to my nation. I do not wish to be a piece of useless wood. I must go back!"

"We won't be able to return until the spring," Wells explained. "If he delayed any longer, he'd lose credit with his countrymen. At home, he must resume his former habits, and be careful to praise and give presents to those left behind, for fear of wounding their pride. Back in his village on the Eel River, the chief has a home made of logs, good clothes, he drinks tea and coffee, he has a cow, and his wife makes butter. But he doesn't dare flaunt these things. Little Turtle's first cow was killed out of jealousy, but he had to act as if he didn't know who did it."

"Is there no hope then," Volney earnestly enquired, "for the savages to abandon their barbarian ways?"

"The Miami are better off than they were a hundred years ago," Wells said. "Their captives and the French traders have planted peach and apple trees and taught them to breed chickens, pigs, even cows. Some are as improved as the Creek and Choctaw. The question is whether the men can learn to farm."

Little Turtle had returned to gazing out the window. To regain his attention, Volney told him about living among the Bedouins, who numbered two and a half million and were spread over a country the size of Ohio, yet they were kept in subjection by five or six thousand Turkish horseman. Volney expected the chief to respond with fiery indignation; instead he stroked his chin and said, "No doubt they have pleasures of their own kind."

"What do you find so remarkable outside the window?" Volney asked, changing the subject.

"Two things," Little Turtle replied, "the number of white people and the variety of their faces. Their skins are ten shades between black and white; their foreheads, noses, mouths, and chins are of various shapes and sizes; their hair and eyes are several colors—all these differences puzzle me very much."

Philadelphia, Volney noted, was a port drawing people from all over the world.

"The numbers are what trouble me most," Little Turtle added. "More than two lives, of eighty years each, have not gone by since the whites first set foot among us, yet already they swarm like flies. You whites can support yourselves on a small space of ground, while we must have large fields and forests to sustain the deer we live on. No wonder the whites drive us every year farther and farther before them, from the sea to the Mississippi. If things do not greatly change, we red men will disappear very shortly."

6

Wells and Little Turtle stayed at the Cross Keys Tavern, with its distinctive double-hipped roof, at Fourth and Chestnut Streets near Congress Hall. One night they walked two blocks to the New Theater to watch a performance of *Romeo and Juliet.* The building was unimposing on the outside; only a long wooden awning to protect the entering audience marked it off from its brick neighbors. The interior, however, was spacious; neither Wells nor Little Turtle had ever seen so large a room; three elliptical gallery tiers of fifteen boxes each held over 700 people and thirteen rows of benches in the parquet seated 400 more. The gilded Corinthian columns that held up the galleries and divided the boxes were festooned with crimson ribbons; the gray walls were decorated with golden scrolls. Thirty musicians filled the orchestra pit in front of the huge stage, which was lighted by oil lamps that were dimmed during the night scenes.

Since the play began an hour late, Wells and Little Turtle, seated on a bench toward the front, had plenty of time to survey the crowd. The American aristocracy, dressed in their finest, preferred the prime boxes; to amuse themselves a few of these self-appointed "gallery gods" singled out a pantaloon-clad democrat below and demanded that he doff his hat to them—if he refused, they pelted him with insults and apples; free blacks, prostitutes, and others of low caste or coin were confined to the upper tier. Most surprising of all, Wells looked across the wide hall and saw, sitting with solemn dignity in a separate box, a delegation of Wyandot chiefs in full tribal regalia.

When the curtain opened at seven, Wells noted on the wall above the stage a motto: "The Eagle suffers little birds to sing," a sly, Shakespearian reference to a Quaker campaign to shut down the theater; they had been prevented among others by Anthony Wayne, who had shared with Washington a love of drama. This was the first play Wells or Little Turtle had ever seen and they found it fascinating, although Wells, in spite of his linguistic gifts, was hard pressed to catch, let alone translate into Miami, the Bard's rich feast of language. What he didn't miss was the verbal melody; he never knew before that words could strike such modulated chords. Little Turtle heard it too, sometimes grunting his pleasure at the sounds before Wells provided the sense.

The celebrated English actress Mrs. Merry, who had made her debut on the American stage as Juliet two years earlier, was noted for her melodious voice and lovely face, which conveyed emotions from rage to pathos; Mr. Moreton, in turn, captured Romeo's passionate haste and intensity; Mr. Bernard, a fine comic actor, played Mercutio. The first act, where Romeo and Juliet fall in love at first sight, was followed by a masquerade and a dance. The sword fights excited Little Turtle most, and when the dying Mercutio, his voice rising as his life failed, cried out three times "a plague on both your houses!" the chief was moved, as if hearing an echo from his own past. At intermission, the store in the lobby did a brisk business in wine and porter; by the time the play ended with a funeral procession and a dirge, many in the audience were drunk. The interlude that followed, a comic opera entitled *The Agreeable Surprise,* was spiced with cuss words; the ladies turned their backs to the stage and pretended they weren't listening. The entertainment concluded at midnight. After the deaths of Mercutio and Tybalt, Little Turtle's interest waned; when Romeo's banishment threatened to bring on disaster, the puzzled chief whispered to Wells, "Why not find another girl?"

Another evening they attended Ricketts's circus in an amphitheater across from Oeller's Hotel. The interior, painted a dreary gray and black, dulled the illumination of hundreds of candles suspended from iron rings. John Ricketts himself performed some breathtaking equestrian mounts, dismounts, and jumps that Wells and Little Turtle both wished they were still limber enough to attempt, before simultaneously riding two horses, a foot on each back, while juggling oranges in the air; then he did the same feat backwards, and, at the end, skewered each falling fruit in turn on the point of his short sword as the crowd broke into tumultuous applause. After some clowns in motley tumbled about and told jokes, Signor Spinacuta danced on a tightrope and his gorgeous wife, her quasi-diaphanous costume clinging to her voluptuous figure, gracefully mimed a series of tragic heroines from history.

Wells and Little Turtle's meetings with McHenry and President Adams in early February were anticlimactic and inconclusive. Although Washington may have feigned a lack of interest in Indian affairs, Wells felt certain he knew that what happened west of the mountains held the key to America's future. Adams, on the other hand, really wasn't interested in and rarely gave a thought to the frontier. His mind was fixated on the relationship between Old and New England as well as the threat of war with France, who, since the Jay Treaty, had accused the United States of aligning with England. Wells browsed through the newspapers almost every day. They were filled with dispatches from Europe about General Napoleon Bonaparte's military conquests, and everyone was anxiously awaiting a report from the three United States commissioners sent to negotiate with foreign minister Talleyrand and the Directory in Paris.

His Rotundity, as his enemies dubbed Adams behind his back, was a short, corpulent man with the chubby face of a smug bishop fond of the bottle; he was bald to the top of his head and his frizzy hair flared out on the sides as if each strand were determined to go its separate way; he wore a dark suit cut in the French fashion of the previous decade. He had sharp, wary eyes under lowering brows and he kept his small mouth pinched firmly as Little Turtle stated his case for revising the Treaty of Greene Ville. Adams took Washington's position that the boundaries could not be changed, but he sympathized with the chief's desire to teach his people to farm, even though he had nothing concrete to offer in terms of government assistance and was vague about whether Wells would receive a salary as an Indian agent. As he listened attentively to Little Turtle's eloquent words, Adams seemed to realize that the Miami chief was a remarkable man, yet this insight didn't shake his conviction that the less thought given to Indian affairs the more likely those problems would go away.

After the brief meeting with the President ended, the ever-pleasant-but-less-than-competent McHenry shrugged, apologized for the administration's lack of decisiveness, and informed Wells and Little Turtle that they were invited to dine that evening as guests of Senator Bingham.

Located on the west side of Third Street above Spruce, the wide, three-story Bingham home had been modeled on the Duke of Manchester's mansion in London, only it was even larger. The Senator was one of the wealthiest men in America, his charming wife Anne was the uncrowned queen of Federalist society, and their home was the most opulent and ostentatious in Philadelphia. The big brick house and extensive grounds—including an orchard, an English garden interspersed with statuary, and a conservatory— were surrounded by a seven-foot-high wooden wall painted white; two gates with wrought iron tracery gave access to the semicircular gravel carriage way that led to the front door; a low stoop of tessellated marble yielded to the mosaic floor in the entrance hall, where busts of Voltaire, Rousseau, and Franklin stared blindly from their pedestals. A footman in livery asked the name of each guest and motioned with a gloved hand toward the magnificent, freestanding staircase of white marble ascending to the drawing room and banquet hall.

"Chief Little Turtle of the Miami and Captain William Wells" was called out in succession as the two men mounted the steps. The tall, folding doors at the entrance to the drawing room were covered with mirrors; as the butler announced their names once more, they mistook the image of their hosts for reality and bowed by mistake to their reflection.

Mrs. Bingham may not have been a perfect beauty, her nose and chin were too elongated for that, and perhaps her rouge was a bit thick, but she had the most pleasing face and captivating manner Wells had ever encountered. There was a birdlike quality to her lively glances beneath delicately arched brows, as if nothing escaped her notice, and her warm smile of welcome was memorable. Her powdered hair, bejeweled with diamond sprigs and artificial flowers, was elaborately piled to Wells's height. She wore a black velvet gown with ermine trimming whose deep décolletage revealed a goodly portion of her bosom; her diamond earrings and necklace vied with the sparkle in her eyes. Although he was dressed in silks and satins, including a scarlet coat with gold buttons, Mr. Bingham paled in comparison.

Philadelphia society, which aped a year late the fashions of France and England, was in the midst of a change of style. Some of the women, like Mrs. Bingham, still preferred ornate headdresses, high-heeled shoes, and low-cut gowns, while others now allowed their hair to fall in ringlets to their shoulders, wore low-heeled slippers and floor-length muslin dresses with short puff sleeves and a raised waist just beneath the breasts. This was meant to suggest a classical Greco-Roman simplicity, but to Wells it made the ladies look pregnant. The men had begun to exchange their brightly colored silk waistcoats, satin breeches, and silver buckles for short, dark coats with high collars. Dress swords were no longer au courant, nor were wrist ruffles, and some, like Wells and Little Turtle, wore pantaloons with laced shoes.

The well-appointed rooms of the Bingham house struck a note of rococo exuberance. There were curvilinear Chippendale chairs, tall Windsor armchairs, richly grained mahogany highboys, and chest-on-chests with canted corners, applied rosettes, and flame finals. The pictorial carpet in the drawing room as well as the sofa, settee, love seat, and armchairs were superb Gobelin from Paris. The wallpaper designs suggested Raphael's artwork in the Vatican. Italian paintings hung in the hallways, the library displayed British authors in Moroccan bindings, and the mantels, above sculptured fireplaces, were lined with bric-a-brac and objects d'art from various lands. A long banquet table, draped in damask and decorated with Sevres porcelain figurines and fresh flowers from the conservatory, featured a handsome set of Queen's ware, cream-colored with a dark chocolate edging; the Bingham crest—an eagle rising from a rock—was etched on each piece. The chairs, with lyre-shaped backs and yellow silk seats, were imported from Seddons in London. The serpentine-front sideboard, cut-glass decanters, and shining silverware spread on top in resplendent array, dazzled Wells's eyes as he took his place and the dinner began.

Ever since he had come to Philadelphia, Wells had noticed a puzzling pattern: people would invariably ask how he liked the city, expecting in response nothing but lavish praise, but almost never did they ask him anything about his life among the Miami. He sensed that the question they secretly wanted to ask—how many men had he killed and scalped?—paralyzed their tongues; even his passing remarks about the frontier engendered visible discomfort and furtive looks. It was the same with Little Turtle. Were people simply not curious, or did they already know that any answer Wells might give would only disturb their complacency?

Not surprisingly, therefore, Wells and Little Turtle found themselves eating in silence; Wells had the impression that they had been invited to dinner only as a courtesy to President Adams, who, as the guest of honor, once he had imbibed enough Madeira, began to hold forth, in his outspoken and tactless way, on Federalist society's favorite topics—sex and politics.

Mrs. Bingham, as at home in Versailles, the Hague, and London as Philadelphia, relished risqué wit and did what she could to foster lively repartee at her table. Wells was sitting close enough to overhear a conversation among Mrs. Bingham, her husband, Adams, Henry Clymer, and his lovely wife Mary, Mrs. Bingham's sister.

"Do you admire her?" Mrs. Bingham inquired of Adams regarding a certain Miss M., the reigning talk of the town.

"No, she is too painted."

"Ah, did you ever see an angel that wasn't?" she replied.

"Madame, *you* are a swan," Adams said, striving for savoir-faire, "she is a goose in comparison."

"Mr. President, you flatter me."

"I only speak the truth."

"Then you are making *game* of me."

"Or is he speaking *fowl-ly?*" Mr. Bingham added with a droll smile.

The guests laughed and clapped.

"She is merely a coquette," Henry Clymer said, returning to Miss M, "a light wine everybody tastes but nobody buys."

"Some coquettes come at a high price," Mr. Bingham said.

"I assume you allude to Mr. Hamilton and Mrs. Reynolds."

"Not exclusively, but I fear that example fits."

"That bastard brat of a Scotch peddler will destroy us yet," Adams blurted out. "He's as debauched as old Franklin and as ambitious as Oliver Cromwell. There aren't whores enough in this city to draw off all that man's secretions!"

"I think he is a very great man," Mrs. Bingham protested.

"That may be so, but not all great men are good; we must always fear the intrigues of artful and designing men—without public virtue our republic is doomed."

"He has done this country good service from the Revolution on," Mr. Bingham said, coming to the defense of an old family friend and ally.

"Quite so, to hear him tell it," Adams replied curtly. "The true story of our Revolution is lost forever. The history books will say that Franklin's electric rod struck the ground and out sprang George Washington, fully formed. Let me tell you, it was a patched and piebald policy then, as it is now. We had to improvise as we went along, do you see? The trick was to get thirteen clocks to strike at once—imagine the difficulties!"

"We are in as deep a dilemma today." Mr. Bingham said.

"What with the open assaults of France and the secret plots of England," Adams stated with growing animation, "we are caught between a hawk and a buzzard. One day we will have to beat down John Bull's pride—Britain will never be our friend until we are her master. And as to France, I know not what to make of a republic of thirty thousand atheists. Absolute power, I fear, intoxicates kings and sans culottes alike. Dragons' teeth have been sewn in France and come up monsters, and now throats are cut by their own folly."

Wells couldn't take his eyes off the red-faced man as he expressed his vehement opinions.

"Capet has lost his *caput*," Mr. Bingham offered, "and now he's *kaput*."

"Please, let us speak no more of the dismal butcheries in France," Mrs. Bingham pleaded, stifling the titters of laughter over her husband's word play, which to Wells was sheer gibberish.

"If only the newspapers would let us forget," George Clymer replied.

"Let the jackasses bray as they will," Adams said. "I take no notice of their billingsgate."

"What if they go too far?" Mary Clymer asked.

"First slanders, next seditions, then civil war with all her hissing snakes." As Adams made his dire prediction he raised one trembling hand in the air.

"But haven't we reached that point already," Henry Clymer insisted.

"A few bold strokes will silence the scoundrels," Adams warned. His sudden anger reminded Wells of Anthony Wayne's rages. "Arrogance shall be made to feel a curb. At least I never hired scribblers to defame my rivals, unlike some others I could name."

"Mr. Jefferson is safely ensconced on his mountain top where he sees no evil," Mr. Bingham remarked.

"And does none," Mrs. Bingham added with studied irony.

"Ah, that is the question," Adams said, his tone implying that he knew the answer.

"Thank goodness a benevolent Providence watches over us," Mary Clymer chimed in, her face beaming.

"We are not a chosen people," Adams responded in measured tones. "I believe that honor is reserved for the Jews. We must make wise decisions and forge our own way. Life is a game of leapfrog, some men advance as others fall behind. We are born to equal rights not equal abilities, success, and influence. As long as prosperity exists, it will accumulate in individuals and families. The snowball grows as it rolls. That is why I have always favored a Senate of the rich, the well born, and the able. How I love to dine with persons of virtue and beauty," Adams added, smiling at Mrs. Bingham, "who have perfected the arts of elegance."

Wells wondered where he and Little Turtle would fit in the President's ideal society.

"Mr. President, you flatter me again," Mrs. Bingham replied with a smile, "but don't let the middling sort hear you."

"I trust I am not without the popular touch," Adams continued. "After all, it was I, not Mr. Jefferson, who was elected. I see myself as the Sancho Panza of American politics. I prefer the real to the ideal. Need I say what that makes Jefferson? I believe he will break his lance if he mistakes our national bank for a windmill. We must not allow our republic to degenerate into a mere democracy at the mercy of the lowest dregs of the mob. Democracy is Lovelace and the people are Clarissa, who will live to regret listening to sugared words."

"But we have enjoyed listening to *you*," Mrs. Bingham said with a bright smile. "All these literary allusions, gracious, how well read you are!"

"Ah, madam, now it's you who are flattering me!"

As the echo of the President's words faded, Wells knew he would never be at home in this artificial world of flaunted erudition and clever word play. He questioned once again the wisdom of his decision to bury Blacksnake. Would he ever again feel as accepted and as alive as he had when he was a boy living in Snake-fish Town? At the same time, something within him wanted to own a big house and play the gracious host to people who, like it or not, had to defer to *him*.

7

Winter lasted deep into March that year and so Wells and Little Turtle remained in Philadelphia for another month. On snowy days they liked to walk the streets to watch sleighing parties, accompanied by fiddlers and pulled by jingling horses, glide by. Free blacks made up about one-tenth of the city's population; most lived near the docks or in the working class suburbs of Southwark and Northern Liberties. On Sundays they would dress in their best for church and, weather permitting, afterwards promenade and have picnics; Wells admired the women, striking in their pale pink outfits with white kid gloves; a few donned chignons made from white women's hair. Some of the French émigrés from Santo Domingo even had the nerve to flaunt their black mistresses in public.

Philadelphia had a tavern on every corner and Wells spent a lot of time taking Little Turtle from bar to bar in quest of the perfect porter. City Tavern, on South Street near Walnut, was their most respectable destination; here local merchants had lunch, read newspapers from Europe (albeit a month or more out of date), and studied the book on what ships were arriving and departing. In the evenings they sometimes wandered into the seedy side of town, down by the docks. Along Water Street—a narrow, crooked, malodorous lane next to the wharves—many slovenly, pockmarked prostitutes, the so-called frail ladies of Philadelphia, and numerous bawdyhouses were to be found. Those who wished to sample their draggle-tail favors could purchase condoms at Moreau de St. Mery's bookstore on Front Street; for anyone who did not avail himself of these "French preventatives," the newspapers were filled with ads for venereal cures.

On occasion Wells and Little Turtle headed for Helltown, a squalid set of blocks north of Arch Street near the Delaware River. This was a favorite haunt of sailors, who sought out the toughest bars, especially The Three Jolly Irishmen on the northwest corner of Race and Water Streets. Fights were a nightly event there. These battles often replicated the conflict raging in Europe and on the high seas; supporters of Britain wore black cockades and shouted "God save the King!" while French partisans sported tri-colored cockades, sang the *Marseillaise,* and cried out, "Long live the guillotine!" Among the Americans, Hamiltonian Federalists sided with Britain, Jeffersonian Republicans favored France; when the factions met in the form of rowdy gangs, words swiftly led to blows and a bloody donnybrook ensued.

In February, Wells and Little Turtle visited Peale's Museum accompanied by Volney, who, upon stepping inside, declared, "This is the temple of God! Here is nothing but Truth and Reason!" This was music in Peale's ears, and he enthusiastically provided them with a guided tour. Little Turtle, who had an insatiable curiosity about the world's variety, was captivated by the displays of stuffed birds and animals. He was brought up short, however, by a *trompe l'oeil* painting of two of Peale's teenage sons, Raphaelle and Titian, ascending a staircase.

"That's quite an eye-fooler, isn't it?" Peale said with delight. "President Washington himself doffed his hat and bowed, mistaking the image for reality."

Peale had heightened the illusion by placing the picture inside an oak doorframe with a projecting step at the bottom. The accuracy of the deception was made even more apparent when Wells and Little Turtle turned around and saw young Titian in person, his pet blacksnake at his feet, standing behind them.

Peale led them to an exhibit of the races of man he had completed the previous summer. Wells and Little Turtle found themselves staring at ten life-size wax figures in native costume: a Carib, an Eskimo, a Gold Coast African, a family group from the Sandwich Isles, a Chinese laborer in his circular hat, and a mandarin in a red, silken gown; most astonishing of all, there stood likenesses of Blue Jacket and Red Pole. Peale had made models of them to commemorate the peace agreement reached in his museum. He then showed them his portrait of Joseph Brant, which hung in his gallery of great Americans.

Little Turtle gazed at all this with a combination of wonder and consternation. He was not especially superstitious, but stealing a man's image troubled him; at the same time, he didn't like the idea that Brant and Blue Jacket were considered important enough to be on display while he was not. Wells, for his part, looked on with a feeling of sadness. To him, those paintings were epitaphs. Nonetheless, at their next meeting with Secretary of War James McHenry, Wells asked if Peale could paint the chief's portrait.

"An excellent idea," McHenry, who fancied himself a patron of the arts, enthused, "but Gilbert Stuart is the better man for the job. I'll send him a note at the first opportunity."

McHenry and President Adams were so preoccupied by the crisis with France that Wells and Little Turtle never did manage to accomplish very much during their lengthy stay in Philadelphia. Whether Wells would be named Indian Agent or the government would make a serious effort to help the Miami become farmers remained in limbo. French privateers continued to seize the cargoes of neutral ships, compelling Adams to send a message to Congress urging that all American vessels should be armed. When a set of coded diplomatic dispatches arrived from Paris, they told a sordid tale of intrigue. The French had been contemptuous from the first of the American delegation, refusing to acknowledge their credentials and, ultimately, demanding a bribe, or *douceur,* for foreign minister Talleyrand. "How much do you expect us to pay?" John Marshall asked and was told, "You must pay a great deal, as much as you *can* pay." Finally, an exasperated Charles Pinckney, the same man who had failed to negotiate a treaty with the Indians in 1793, had said, "No! No! Not a sixpence!" The people of the United States were infuriated by these disclosures, fervid rumors of war with France swept the country, and President Adams enjoyed a transitory moment of widespread and ardent popular approval.

During their last weeks in the city, Wells and Little Turtle made several trips to Gilbert Stuart's studio in Germantown, where the Miami chief sat for his portrait. The renowned artist's bloodshot eyes, blotchy cheeks, purple-veined nose, and potbelly attested to his heavy drinking. The walls of his studio in a two-story stone barn behind his house were lined with casks of wine, brandy, and gin, and he sipped from a silver cup as he scrutinized Little Turtle's face, noting both the color of his skin and the bone structure beneath. The floor of his workroom was ankle-deep in torn canvases and broken picture frames.

An intense, talkative man, Stuart flitted about his studio like a high-strung squirrel simultaneously trying to chatter and gather nuts. He styled himself a wit and thought lively conversation was the best way to keep the features of his subjects properly animated. In order to fit Little Turtle into his busy schedule, he had agreed to paint the chief at the same time he finished up a portrait of a prosperous Irish merchant named Eamon O'Brien. During the rare intervals when Stuart stopped talking, the two men exchanged quips and mocking comments. One day, when Little Turtle fell into a meditative silence, the Irishman boasted to Wells that he had bested the chief at last, but Little Turtle replied with a smile, "He's mistaken; I was only thinking of asking this man to paint us both on one board where we could stand face to face and exchange insults forever."

Stuart laughed at this, wiped his hands on his snuff-encrusted, paint-smeared smock, and took another sip of brandy.

"I returned to America to paint Washington," Stuart explained. "I knew that I could make my fortune selling his portraits. But what a difficult subject he proved to be. There is something ferocious about that man; I swear if he were born in the forest he would have been the most savage warrior of them all. No offense intended to the chief, who looks like a wise and mild philosopher in comparison. The President is an aloof man, stiff as a board; he's a pain in the arse to paint."

Little Turtle sat on a stool in front of a gray sheet hung on the wall. Wells watched with great interest as Stuart took a lot of time preparing his paints, grinding his colors with oil on an agate slab before placing them on his palette; he then spat on each pigment and mixed it in with a rapid, circular motion of his knife. Because of a tremor in his hand, he could only paint in short, precise dabs of his brush at the canvas, which, bit by bit, became an astonishingly vivid portrait that caught not only the exact flesh tone and facial expression but also the vital essence of his subject.

Noting Wells's look of appreciation for his craft, Stuart added, "When I was in London, Benny West told his students, 'Yellow and white there,' and he made a streak, 'red and white there,' another streak, 'brown and red there for a warm shadow,' another streak, 'red and yellow there,' yet another streak. But nature doesn't color in streaks. Look at my hand, see how the colors are matted and mingled, yet all is clear as silver. You can't learn from a master. You have to see for yourself. Benny used to say, 'It's no use trying to steal Stuart's colors; if you want to paint as he does you must steal his eyes! He nails the face to the canvas!'

"What a damned business is this of a portrait painter! They bring me a potato and expect I will paint a peach. After I had finished one portrait, the lady said, 'Why, Mr. Stuart, you have painted me with my mouth open.' 'Madam,' I replied, 'your mouth is always open.' A true artist paints what nature presents him with. I don't do full-lengths, I do faces; and I don't do flattery either, I capture character. Let tailors worry about the cut of a coat, I don't alter to please; I copy the works of God!"

When he wasn't sipping from his silver cup, Stuart took snuff from an outsized golden snuffbox. Feeling Wells's intent gaze upon him, he said, "Snuff-taking is a pernicious, vile, dirty habit. I don't advise it, but I was born in a snuff mill, so I can't help myself." When he returned to his work, he saw that Little Turtle had begun to fidget and make faces at his Irish rival, thus breaking the artist's concentration.

"I say, Captain Wells, tell Mr. Little Turtle to please, please be still," Stuart said in high-strung exasperation. "Confound it, man, tell him not to stir for his life!"

Part III

*...our settlements will gradually circumscribe
& approach the Indians, & they will in time
either incorporate with us as citizens of the
US or remove beyond the Mississippi.... We
presume that our strength & their weakness
is now so visible that they must see we have
only to shut our hand to crush them.... You
will also perceive how sacredly it must be kept
within your breast, and especially how improper
to be understood by the Indians. In their
interests & tranquility it is best they should
see only the present page of their history.*

—Thomas Jefferson to
William Henry Harrison

Washington City

1

Main Poche was drunk again. Despite William Wells's watchful eye, at every town on their way to Washington in the fall of 1808 the Potawatomi war chief contrived to stash one more whiskey keg in his capacious saddlebags. At Wheeling he had brandished his tomahawk in the face of a startled tavern owner and demanded drink; at Bedford he had come up behind a woman out walking, grabbed a handful of her hair, and threatened to sever it from her skull, and now in Chambersburg he was staggering down the muddy street, shouting in broken English that the land was his and all Long Knives must die. Wells quickly intervened to prevent trouble, but often Main Poche proved to be unmanageable. What started in Fort Wayne as a diplomatic mission to redeem Wells's reputation and preserve peace was turning sour before he had even reached Washington and spoken to President Jefferson.

A confrontation with Main Poche, drunk or sober, could be unnerving. Huge, muscular, ferocious-featured, he was dressed from head to toe in animal skins, his face painted half-red, half-black, a bear-claw necklace on his chest, a hawk's head entwined in his hair, and a belt of scalps about his waist. His French name referred to the fact that he had been born with only one good hand; his left, in lieu of a thumb and fingers, ended in a stub. Rather than a handicap, he saw this deformity as a sign of spiritual power. The most bloodthirsty warrior among the Potawatomi, he was also a revered shaman in the secret Midewiwin society, a fire-handler, a sorcerer whose strong medicine made him invincible in battle. He had long been a scourge to the Osage across the Mississippi.

For months Wells had been writing letters to Secretary Dearborn requesting permission to come to Washington and discuss the frontier situation face to face. During his controversial career at Fort Wayne over the past ten years, Wells had made enemies, including Governor William Henry Harrison, the Shawnee Prophet and his brother Tecumseh, the factor at Fort Wayne John Johnston, and various disgruntled chiefs, dispirited warriors, land-hungry settlers, and greedy traders. Several of these had made their displeasure known to Dearborn and President Jefferson. Wells was suspected of conspiring with Little Turtle, lining his own pockets, forging documents, slandering the Shawnee, and misleading the government. He had switched sides too many times to be trusted. He was probably the best-hated man in Indiana Territory. His tenure as Indian Agent to the Miami at Fort Wayne was hanging by a slender thread.

When permission to visit Washington came on September 19, 1808, Wells welcomed the chance to clear himself. He dispatched a runner to contact Main Poche, who showed up two weeks later with his youngest wife, Black Bird and his wife, and Mad Sturgeon. Little Turtle and The Wildcat—also known by his father's name, Richardville—would represent the Miami; the Delaware chief would be The Beaver; the veteran diplomat Captain Hendrick Aupaumut of the Stockbridge Indians also agreed to come. Wells would serve as interpreter for all of them.

Back in the hard winter of 1804-1805, Sweet Breeze had contracted influenza. Though Wells rushed the fort's doctor to her bedside, his ministrations, as well as the conjurations of a Miami medicine man, had done no good and she, like so many other Indians, faded fast and died. Their shared grief made the bond between Wells and Little Turtle even stronger. Wells had sent his three daughters—Ann, Rebecca, and Polly—to live with his brother Sam in Louisville and be educated by his sister Elizabeth, who lived as a nun at nearby Bardstown, Kentucky. Eleven-year-old William Wayne had stayed with his father, and now, after much pleading, he too would travel to the new federal city on the banks of the Potomac and meet President Jefferson.

2

The French architect Pierre Charles L'Enfant had envisioned Washington as a magnificent city on a grand scale, with a sunburst of broad avenues, lined with stately brick townhouses, that would radiate from the widely separated Capitol and Presidential Palace, cut diagonal paths across the grid pattern of lettered or numbered streets, and pause at interspersed public squares or circles, each designed by a different State, which would feature heroic statuary, memorial columns, luxuriant gardens, and ornate fountains. Below the hills selected to display the monumental public buildings, on the tidal flatlands beside the Potomac, a vast, tree-shaded promenade, based on the Avenue des Tuileries in Paris, would provide a village green for the strolling citizenry in all their finery to see and be seen. L'Enfant assumed the city would draw a talented population from the provinces and supersede Philadelphia, New York, Baltimore, and Boston as the political, cultural, and commercial center of the rapidly growing nation.

Washington was a puzzling higgledy-piggledy travesty of a town, with clusters of houses randomly scattered here and there across a variegated landscape of marshes, pastures, and forests. It was, in effect, several small villages, close together but rarely in contact, bounded on the south and north by two attractive towns— Alexandria and Georgetown. The minimal commercial interests were concentrated at Greenleaf's Point; another cluster of cheap wooden houses and assorted dives was located at the Navy Yard, where many of the town's black population, both slave and free, worked at the dry docks making gunboats. Cabinet members and their staffs lived near the president's house and worked in two sprawling brick buildings flanking it, while the legislators congregated in a dozen boarding houses on Capitol Hill. The congressmen ate mess around long tables, bunked two to a room, and, other than an Oyster House, a few taverns, and good fishing and quail shooting along the Tiber, found little to do besides get on each other's nerves and yearn for the day when they could return home. In retrospect, Philadelphia tantalized their imaginations as a lost paradise of milk and honey.

When Wells and his Indian delegation arrived in late December, 1808, they stayed at the Pennsylvania House on Pennsylvania Avenue, designed to be a grand boulevard but still a rutted, stump-pocked road, where on rainy days carriages sunk to their hubs in clinging yellow mud. Wells took his son to see the still unfinished Capitol. The oval Senate Chamber, featuring carved friezes and fluted columns with "corncob" capitals, was nearing completion. A makeshift wooden portico crossed the gap between the two ponderous piles of hewn stone that formed the matching wings—the neoclassical domed rotunda that would serve as the centerpiece of the imposing edifice was still only a dream in architect Benjamin Latrobe's head. The projected location of the Supreme Court remained a bramble patch; the disregarded judges sought temporary quarters in Stelle's Tavern on Carroll Row.

The imperial pretensions of this parody of a city invited scorn from foreign diplomats condemned to endure a residency in so dreary a backwater. The English ambassador Andrew Merry found

it worse than the worst parts of Spain.   The Irish poet Thomas
Moore put the city's deficiencies into couplets:

> *This fam'd metropolis, where fancy sees*
> *Squares in morasses, obelisks in trees;*
> *Which second sighted seers e'en now adorn*
> *With shrines unbuilt and heroes yet unborn.*
> *Though now but woods and Jefferson they see,*
> *Where streets should run, and sages ought to be.*

Jefferson, who had no love of cities in the first place, seemed never
to notice what was lacking; he looked, one wag remarked, "like a
pelican in the wilderness."   He rather liked the town's remoteness,
its sequestered situation, for he had devised his own ways there to
exercise control.   Although dismissed years before, L'Enfant stayed
on, living hand-to-mouth, too proud to beg, a spectral presence
taking twilight walks with his small mangy dog through this city
that fell far short of his generous vision, this embryo Rome to which
few roads led.

3

Wells was not adept at the intrigue his position, as middleman
between the conflicting demands of the Indians and the government,
apparently required.   Although he was the Indian Agent for the
government, he also considered himself an unofficial ambassador,
along with Little Turtle, for the Miami.   His ambition was to
preserve their lands and protect their interests, while fostering Little
Turtle's and his own advancement; if that came at the expense of
other tribes, or the United States, then so be it.   His maneuvers in
the past on behalf of the Miami, especially Little Turtle's faction,
had created dissension within that tribe, caused the government to
question his loyalty, and put his job in jeopardy.

Wells knew that a major reason for bringing Indian leaders to
Washington was to awe them with the power and population of the
United States.   Just as crucial, in his mind, was the need for officials
in government to see *them* as real people, representing various
tribes, not savage abstractions living somewhere west of the
Appalachians.   In this, Little Turtle was always Wells's trump card.
The Miami chief, who had been to Washington before, never failed
to impress the national leaders, who were pleasantly surprised to
encounter so sophisticated and charming a man.   Little Turtle was
truly curious about the white world.   He admired those aspects of it
he considered superior to his own.   If only his fellow Indians
realized what a treasure he was, Wells thought.   If the Miami would

unify around him, giving him the support he needed so that he spoke with the voice of a unified people, the government might put the entire civilization program in his hands.

Jefferson, for his part, never seemed to notice the sinister consequences of his Indian policy. In theory it sounded lovely: two peoples, born in the same land, would blend into one people. Indian men would become farmers; Indian women would switch from farming to sewing and weaving; the vast forests, no longer needed for the hunt, would be sold off to settlers; and the resulting big happy family would be fruitful and multiply. In practice it was a policy of land grabbing in the name of doing good; the Indians would be accepted as brothers only if they ceased to be Indians. The trading posts, intended to provide them goods at cost in order to undersell British traders, were designed to put tribal leaders into debt and thus coerce them into surrendering land for cash.

In his first inaugural, Jefferson had made the celebrated statement, "We are all federalists, we are all republicans," which sounded to the nation like a note of reconciliation; but to Jefferson, who wanted all Americans to be of one heart and one mind, it meant everybody had better become Republican—or else. The same was true of his Indian policy; the tribesmen had better abandon their traditional native habits and habitat and behave like white men—or else. Wells and Little Turtle believed that, slowly over time, the Indians might be willing to accept these necessary changes, yet neither Jefferson nor the nation was in the mood to give them time.

Thomas Jefferson was a lawyer by training and a romantic idealist by temperament; sophistic logic-chopping on behalf of the cause *de jour* came all too easily to his pen. He was a man who believed that what he said and wrote outweighed what he did, that smooth words could pave over a bumpy world; above all, he was a man whose fame rested on declarations more than actions. Not surprisingly, he placed his confidence in verbal affirmations or denials—in spite of the evidence. Thus he was able to blind himself to the malign effects of his Indian policy and insist with a benign smile that all was for the best. He saw the quirks and proclivities of his own nature as natural laws binding on all men. What Jefferson regarded as self-evident truths often sprung from murky motives he failed to recognize.

4

On December 21, 1808, Jefferson gave Little Turtle and the other chiefs his response to the speeches they had presented to him a week earlier. In the seven years since he had last seen him, Wells had come to view the President with wary, jaded eyes. He braced himself to hear fine-sounding words that concealed an insidious policy. Jefferson stood in front of a mahogany table in the Blue Room, one hand touching a multi-colored globe on a slender cherry-wood pedestal. Wells noted that he had aged considerably. His once sandy red hair and even his blue eyes were faded to a tired gray; his freckled face looked blotchy. He wore an ill-fitting brown coat with brass buttons over a threadbare, scarlet waistcoat, and green velveteen breeches. He was six-feet, two-inches tall, with long arms and legs and large wrists, but to Wells he did not give an impression of grace or strength. He stood stiffly, shambled when he walked, and slouched in his chair. He was an awkward, angular man, ill at ease in his body, which seemed to have a will of its own. His voice was almost a whisper.

Jefferson rehearsed the events that had culminated in the Treaty of Greenville and promised the Indians that he would continue the friendship practiced by presidents Washington and Adams. Then he warned against British influence:

"My children, the English persuade you to hunt, supply you with spirituous liquors, and are now endeavoring to engage you in war against us. You possess reason as we do, and you will judge for yourselves which of us advise you as friends. Their course has worn you down to your present numbers, but temperance, peace, and agriculture will raise you up to be what your forefathers were and prepare you to possess property, live under regular laws, join us in our government, and mix with us in society, so that your blood and ours united will spread again over this great island."

As he spoke Jefferson's words in Miami, Delaware, and Potawatomi, Wells, in spite of his skepticism, could not help responding to the president's grand vision of America's future. Wells was no friend of the British; he had been warning both the Indians and the government about them for years; and, as someone who had been scorned as a "squaw man" on occasion, he shared Jefferson's hope for a mixed-blood nation; nevertheless, he knew that words like "property" and "regular laws" presented a real threat to tribal lands.

"My children," Jefferson repeated in closing, "this is the last time I shall speak to you as your father, it is the last counsel I shall give." He assured them that his successor, James Madison, would have the same friendly disposition towards them as he had had, and promised that he would continue to pray to the Great Spirit for their happiness.

Then Jefferson held individual audiences with each of the chiefs, starting with Little Turtle, who was dressed in a fine blue coat with epaulettes; three silver medals, gifts of Wayne, Washington, and Adams, hung on his chest. A broad red sash bound his waist and he kept his hat, ornamented by a red feather, tucked under his left arm.

"My son, it is always with pleasure that I receive you here and take you by the hand," the President said, his face beaming with benevolence, "and assure you of my friendship to your nation and of my personal respect and esteem for you."

Although Jefferson was fond of Little Turtle, his words cloyed on Wells's tongue as the topic turned to the Miami and their land: "It is a sincere solicitude for their welfare which has induced us, from time to time, to warn them of the decay of their nation by continuing to rely on the chase for food, and to press them before they are reduced too low, to begin the culture of the earth and the raising of domestic animals. A little of their land in corn and cattle will feed them much better than the whole of it in deer and buffalo, which will be scarcer every year. I have, therefore, always believed it an act of friendship to our red brethren whenever they wished to sell a portion of their lands, to be ready to buy whether we wanted them or not, because the price enables them to improve the lands they retain, and turning their industry from hunting to agriculture, the same exertions will support them more plentifully."

Wells and Little Turtle managed to keep a straight face at the qualifying phrase "whether we wanted them or not," since both knew that the American hunger for land was insatiable. In response to Little Turtle's complaint that the Ottawa and Wyandot had recently sold Miami land in Michigan without the chief's permission, Jefferson deferred any final decision until he had more facts. Although Little Turtle was not pleased by this delaying tactic, the two men parted amiably after Wells conveyed a presidential invitation to dinner later in the week.

Wells faced a much more difficult task of translating between Jefferson and Main Poche. The huge Potawatomi, barely sober, was outfitted for war from head to toe and maintained a fearsome scowl on his painted face. The lone American soldier who escorted the Indian delegation from place to place kept a anxious eye on the tomahawk and scalping knife jutting from Main Poche's belt of human hair. Several days earlier the chief had told the President the same thing Wells had heard the previous April when he had visited Fort Wayne: that the United States had no more business meddling in his business than he had meddling in theirs; if he wanted to go fight the Osage, what was that to the whites? Jefferson, trying to hide his exasperation behind soothing words, pointed out that the Osage had not attacked the Potawatomi, that if Main Poche fought them he would endanger American settlers and shipping on the Mississippi, and that war among the Indians only served to destroy them. Wells was certain that Main Poche would not budge; he had seen the President and was not impressed; he wanted a sword and a silver medal, and he wanted to go home.

The last interview was with Captain Hendrick Aupaumut. Wells had already suggested to Dearborn that the Mohican chief and Little Turtle ought to be in charge of the civilization plan, replacing William Kirk, who had badly overspent his budget in order to achieve a limited success among the Shawnee. Jefferson saw in Captain Hendrick a kindred spirit and launched again into the benefits the Indians would receive if they changed their lives:

"My children, it depends on yourselves alone to become a numerous and great people. Nothing is so easy as to learn to cultivate the earth; all your women understand it, and we are always ready to teach you how to make ploughs, hoes, and necessary utensils. If the men will take the labor of the earth from the women they will learn to spin and weave and to clothe their families. Once you have property, you will want laws and magistrates to protect your property and persons, and to punish those among you who commit crimes. You will find our laws are good for this purpose; you will wish to live under them, you will unite yourselves with us, join in our great councils and form one people with us, and we shall all be Americans; you will mix with us by marriage, your blood will run in our veins and will spread with us over this great island."

Afterwards, Jefferson signed a deposition in which Little Turtle acknowledged that the Miami had granted the Delaware, Mohican, and Munsey the right to occupy the disputed land on the White River forever—but not the right to sell it. Having spent the afternoon speaking Jefferson's smooth words, where only the discerning eye could see the steel claw beneath the velvet glove, Wells felt dispirited. Jefferson believed his own words, but did he? Would civilization save the Miami or destroy them?

We are all Americans, Wells thought. *We are all Indians*.

5

Jefferson's cult of republican simplicity was premised on the need of the new country to be the opposite of what he thought British rule had been: aristocratic, authoritarian, extravagant, militaristic, corrupt. Like many Americans, Jefferson defined freedom as an escape from authority. It was his deepest wish to never be in a position where somebody told him what to do or how to behave. He wanted to be free to follow his own whim and pursue his own happiness. Anything less, he saw as slavery.

Frugality was the order of the day in his administration. He wanted to extinguish the national debt, eliminate taxes, and replace the standing army with local militias. He pictured a decentralized rural republic, without a capital city of consequence, where individuals and States would go their own ways without interference from the government. His Secretary of the Treasury Albert Gallatin, a genius at finance, would oversee the economy, curtailing spending until the federal budget showed a surplus. The job of reducing the military and overseeing Indian affairs was given to Secretary of War Henry Dearborn, a battle-tested veteran of the Revolution. His most significant experience with Indians was Sullivan's Campaign of 1779; the colonial troops had marched up the Susquehanna and Genesee Rivers, into the heartland of the Iroquois, destroying every village, cornfield, and orchard they could find.

Dearborn had seen the skulls of dead soldiers, each bearing the mark of the tomahawk. Oh, yes, he knew what savage barbarity those inhuman hellhounds were capable of. If they could not be civilized, their days on earth were numbered. But if they could be taught the arts of progress, what a pleasant prospect for every benevolent mind!

As Secretary of War, Dearborn reduced the army and drastically weakened the navy, replacing frigates with cheaper gunboats that were worthless against British men-of-war. The militia, now the first line of defense, was inadequately trained and equipped. Expenditures for the national defense soon dropped below a million dollars a year. This policy of austerity proved to be penny wise but pound foolish, since, in 1803, war had resumed on the continent. Neither England nor France wanted the United States to trade with the other, and America's flimsy military was in no position to resist either of them.

As a last ditch effort to avoid armed conflict, Jefferson signed an Embargo Act, prohibiting American commerce with any belligerent nation. Jefferson was resorting to the type of despotic rule he had always denounced. The 10th Congress was also making a belated effort to restore the depleted strength of the army. This situation was very much on Dearborn's mind, since he, like most Americans, saw European affairs as far more important than clashes between settlers and Indians across the Appalachians.   The newspapers Wells saw in Washington were filled with accounts of Napoleon's battles and British blockades; citizens had yet to hear of the Shawnee Prophet or his brother Tecumseh.

The Louisiana Purchase, which more than doubled the size of the country, had a profound effect on Jefferson's Indian policy, inciting him to press the chiefs for the land bordering the great interior waterways, the Ohio and Mississippi, while opening up a vast territory in the west for the removal of hostile tribes who rejected the President's plans to civilize them.

Like Washington and Adams before him, Jefferson had misplaced his trust in James Wilkinson. Already Commander-in-Chief of the United States army, Wilkinson was put in charge of the new Louisiana Territory, while, as a spy for Spain, he plotted to send Commanche warriors to cut off the Lewis and Clark expedition.   Next he conspired with Jefferson's former Vice President Aaron Burr, out of favor in the East after shooting Alexander Hamilton in a duel, to pursue imperial dreams in the West. Wells considered Wilkinson a friend; it was to him that he first wrote, in the name of Little Turtle, to protest Harrison's 1804 treaty with the Delaware that had sold land belonging to the Miami. Wilkinson had passed his letter on to Dearborn and Harrison, causing Wells problems with his superiors. After many years of seeking a personal interview with Dearborn to clear his name and strengthen his position, Wells finally had the opportunity.

They met at the Secretary of War's office in one of the brick buildings flanking the White House.   Wells felt uncomfortable speaking on his own behalf—he was usually the medium through which other men conversed—and the skepticism in Dearborn's look did not put him at ease. The sixty-seven-year-old Secretary of War was six-feet tall and stoutly built, with a craggy face as solid as the rocks that lined the Maine coast. He had a pursed, almost feminine mouth, a large, hooked nose, and small, close-set, light blue eyes that maintained a wry gaze beneath arched brows; his white hair was tufted on top in a way that suggested a perturbed rooster.

"I am not unmindful of your past services," Dearborn began, "but you must know that I have lost much confidence in your probity and integrity. As agent you have three main responsibilities:

preserving the peace among the Indians, furthering the civilization program, and facilitating the purchase of their lands. Do I make myself clear?"

"Yes, Sir," Wells said, the blood rising to his cheeks. "I have done those things."

"Let me finish. For several years you have been very intent on making money. You have evinced considerable jealousy when anyone interfered with your agency, and, in the case of Mr. William Kirk, you improperly blocked his benevolent efforts to teach the Indians agriculture. You have been accused of inciting distrust among the Indians and being more a partisan of the Miami nation than an agent of the United States. You have been playing a foolish double game, Mr. Wells; your cunning intrigues are well known to us. I have repeatedly tried to impress upon you the necessity to change your conduct and place yourself in harmony with your government, but you have persisted in deviating from that course."

Expecting harsh criticism, Wells had prepared a spirited defense to stave off his dismissal. Although he had an ear for languages, he was uncomfortably aware that he lacked formal training and that his own speech often slipped into slang.

"I knew Mr. Kirk would never of succeeded," Wells asserted while trying to maintain his composure. "The year before, Little Turtle formed a plan he intended to lay before the President; Mr. Kirk learned of it, presented it as his own, and got six thousand dollars to put it into effect. Before he even arrived in Fort Wayne, he'd spent half of it, without any benefit to the Indians. This was when followers were flocking to the Shawnee Prophet and British emissaries were out among the tribes. Prejudice against the United States was very high. Mr. Kirk showed up at a very bad time. I done everything in my power to support him, but to no purpose. That man's own conceit sowed the seeds of discord at my agency; he intrigued among the Indians and accused me of obstructing him. He may be a Quaker, but he sure ain't one of the best sort."

"I've heard all of this before, Mr. Wells. No subterfuge on your part can extenuate the fact that you made Mr. Kirk unwelcome at your agency and forced him to go elsewhere. If the Prophet is so dangerous, then how is it that Mr. Kirk did succeed among the Shawnee? One of two things must be true: either you possess no useful influence with the chiefs or you make improper use of whatever power you do possess. In either case, you cannot be considered as well qualified for the position you hold."

"It's always been the first wish of my heart to promote the civilizing of the Indians," Wells insisted. "But now they're too much scattered to civilize them. The nations should be gathered together in one spot. A man should be employed that's acquainted with their customs and possesses influence among them. They won't trust a stranger."

"I think I know exactly the man you mean," Dearborn replied sardonically.

"We need to unite all the scattered branches of the Miami at Fort Wayne. The Shawnee and Potawatomi should be contracted there too. I could execute the views of the President among these Indians better than anybody else. Captain Hendrick and Little Turtle would be in charge, teaching the Indians how to farm. Until the tribes are together under leaders they respect, they'll never be civilized. You might as well say that corn will grow in the woods without clearing any ground."

"How much do you estimate that all this will cost?"

"I have it right here, Sir," Wells said, presenting a paper lined with figures. "Three thousand six hundred dollars a year, six hundred dollars per tribe. That covers the cost of workmen, fences, farming utensils, and livestock. Mr. Kick couldn't do half as much with double that amount."

Wells had finally found an argument that resonated with the thrifty New Englander. Although Kirk had accomplished a lot in Black Hoof's Shawnee village, fencing fields and raising good crops, he had also consistently overspent his budget.

"The melioration of the condition of the aborigines, which would soften down the ferocity of their manners, would be pleasing, even in contemplation, to every good mind. I have been impressed with Capt. Hendrick," Dearborn admitted. "I believe he is the right man to encourage agriculture, the domestic arts, and sound morals. If the savages can be taught to be sober, honest, faithful workmen, then they will have a place in our republic. In regard to him, you have made a good suggestion; I am going to ask you to deliver this notice of dismissal to Mr. Kirk."

Wells could hardly believe his ears; he watched with a satisfied smile as the Secretary of War scrawled out official orders, sealed them with a wax stamp, and handed them to him.

"But that still does not resolve the problems at your agency." Dearborn looked at Wells sharply. "Why have you brought this Potawatomi, Main Poche, with you? The fellow is simply impossible!"

"He's the greatest warrior in the West," Wells explained earnestly. "He has considerable influence among the tribes; he's capable of igniting the blaze the Prophet intends to strike. If he was our enemy he'd be very dangerous. That's why I've tried to win him to our side as a counterpoise to the Shawnee Imposter."

"That is all very good," Dearborn retorted, "but it seems to me that you've failed, and at a very great cost. You spent far more than you should have this past winter."

"Sir, the Indians were positively perishing. Almost every day somebody starved. That was why I issued more provisions than usual. The Indians at my agency had raised plenty of corn; those who followed the Prophet neglected their fields and had nothing, and no Indian will allow another to go hungry as long as he has anything to eat, but before long their food was gone, too."

"People who will do nothing for themselves have no claim on our generosity," Dearborn said sternly.

"I've been governed by economy," Wells insisted, "but we've got to stop the British."

"You're certain this Shawnee Prophet is their tool?"

"I've sent my spies and know his intentions. His followers are religiously mad and believe all he tells them; they dance and sing and neglect their families. The Prophet's brother, Tecumseh, has met with the British at Malden; he plots to kill any chief who signs away more Indian land."

"Do you think, then, that the Indians are preparing for war?"

"The way to quiet the Indians is either by force or liberal policy. The Prophet would like a war, but unless he can get the western Indians and the British to join him, I don't expect one. Most of his followers care more about finding the way to heaven than taking the warpath. And since he left Greenville and settled at Tippecanoe, his strength is down. What he wants is to destroy rival chiefs and become first chief himself. His movement provides a pretext for large numbers of Indians to travel around and meet together; that's alarmed our frontiers. I think he should be punished for his insolence and his followers lured away by good treatment."

"With respect to this Prophet, the President wonders if perhaps the chiefs could not resolve the matter in their own way."

"You mean kill him?"

"I didn't say that."

"His death would only inflame his warriors. Let me point out, Sir, that the Indians at my agency have remained loyal to the United States. No man has rendered this country more service than myself.

Nobody can serve it better in future. I'll do my best to forward the wishes of the President among the Indians."

"This is no time to push your pretensions with me, Mr. Wells."

"I only want to assure you of my devotion to the views of government," Wells said, fearing he had undercut the good impression he intended to make.

"We have been over that," Dearborn said with exasperation. "I don't like scolding and will say no more."

6

Indian delegations in Washington were a regular feature of the Jefferson administration, combining official meetings with various entertainments.   Since 1805, when the Osage had been paid in whiskey to perform a war dance in public and their chief later had been found dead in his bed from overdrinking, the sale of spirituous liquors to Indians had been forbidden.   Nevertheless, Main Poche and his young wife had come up with a keg and remained in their room, boycotting all social functions.   Wells took his son, Little Turtle, and the other chiefs to the theater to watch rope dancing and church services to hear the music; they visited Capitol Hill, sat in the balcony, and saw the legislators at work.   His old friend John Pope, now a senator from Kentucky, had won approval for a resolution awarding Wells preemption rights to 320 acres in Fort Wayne.   The Senator asked William Wayne what he wanted to be when he grew up.

"A soldier," the boy promptly replied.   "Papa said he'd buy me a uniform."

"When you're old enough, you let me know," Pope said.   "I'll nominate you for our new military academy at West Point."

Wells felt a sense of accomplishment; his talk with Dearborn had secured his job and now he owned land where Kekionga once stood.

The capstone of a visit to Washington was dinner at the President's House.   Wells and Little Turtle had eaten there on a previous trip and looked forward to doing it again.   Jefferson's dinners were the quintessence of social life in the nation's capital. To receive one of his hand-written invitations was to have a seat at the epicenter of government.   Especially now that the racing season was over, as were the Marine Band's outdoor concerts, there was simply nothing else of interest to do in the dreary, undeveloped town except play endless card games of whist and loo.   Savvy insiders knew that the President's power, especially over Congress, hinged on the exquisite concoctions of his French chef and his well-stocked wine cellar. Jefferson used his dinners to display his cosmopolitan tastes, charm his guests, and place them in his debt. In the case of the Indians, an opportunity to break bread with the President was seen as a chance for them to participate in the arts of civilization. Everyone sat at a circular table in order to converse face to face, although usually the chiefs could only watch in puzzlement without comprehending what was said; the hope was that they would be favorably impressed by the sophisticated spectacle.

Since Jefferson was a widower, he often asked Dolley Madison to serve as his hostess. Celebrated for her exuberance and graciousness, she was regarded as the unofficial "Queen of Hearts"; in her captivating presence people from ambassadors to indentured servants felt at ease. She was undaunted at the prospect of entertaining Indians, which she had done many times before. Once when some braves sat on the floor to smoke a pipe, she joined them and took snuff. On this occasion she was accompanied by her good friend from Baltimore, the bewitching Betsey Patterson Bonaparte, whose whirlwind courtship by and marriage to Napoleon's youngest brother, Jerome, followed in rapid succession by the emperor's ordering their union annulled in Paris, the birth of her son, nicknamed "Bo" for Bonaparte, in England, and her return to America, had made her the most talked about woman of her time. For the past five years her scanty costumes, selected from her trousseau of the latest French fashions, had been the scandal of Washington society.

The presence of a few attractive and refined American ladies was very much in keeping with Jefferson's assumptions about civilization. He condemned Indian men for brutalizing their squaws and keeping them in submission. The fair sex, he believed, had been formed by nature for male attentions and domestic felicities, but Indian women worked in the fields like slaves, while all their men were free to hunt and fight. Thus the Indians could maintain a standing army—one of the things Jefferson and his fellow Republicans dreaded most. In practice, Jefferson, like many of his contemporaries, had kept his own wife pregnant until complications following a childbirth killed her. But since he wished to give his Indian guests a taste of genteel society, who better to exemplify that devoutly to be wished for state than Dolley Madison and Betsey Bonaparte?

Betsey's embroidered muslin wedding gown, over a single diaphanous chemise, was, one eyewitness claimed, skimpy enough to put in his vest pocket. When Jefferson invited the newlyweds to dinner, he had offended the English ambassador Anthony Merry by escorting nineteen-year-old Betsey to the table, an honor he had not extended on a previous occasion to Merry's wife. This was because Jefferson insisted on replacing traditional diplomatic protocol with a new principle of equity, or *pele mele,* with no person taking precedence over another. The British delivered a formal complaint, but the President replied that Mrs. Merry should either accept the new rule or sup alone. This seemingly minor tiff, exacerbated by Betsey's presence in Washington, soured the Merrys on America and widened the rift between the two countries. Betsey's next appearance, at a select party hosted by Mrs. Robert Smith, won her the sobriquet of Madame Eve. Men and boys gathered around her splendid equipage and gaped in the open windows of the house, while the invited guests cast furtive glances at her sarcenet and crepe fig leaf of a dress, which set off her many charms to advantage.

The décolleté dresses that Betsey wore, designed by the celebrated *couturieres* Leroy and Leger and popularized by Josephine Bonaparte, were de rigueur in Paris salons. On this side of the Atlantic they were shocking. The low-cut, high-waisted gown she had chosen for Jefferson's dinner was of a thin muslin, lightly dampened to cling to her shape; slender and sleeveless, almost transparent, it draped down without a plait or a crease to her gilded slippers; she wore a diadem of seed pearls and amethysts in her dark, curly hair, a garnet necklace at her bosom, and pendant diamond earrings; the overall effect was that of a Greek goddess—a Venus, a Diana, perhaps even an Aspasia casting her spell on Pericles. Although he was accustomed to being around half-naked women, Wells had never encountered anyone like this. He could not help but notice her petite, classically proportioned body, yet something in her small, oval face finally left men flabbergasted. She certainly set the standard of beauty in her day; there was an ambiguity in her look, however, that held most men back, a cold and calculating reserve; those who dared to approach her were often rebuffed by her tart tongue.

It was a tribute to Dolley Madison's self-confidence and savoir-faire that she did not mind playing second fiddle to her friend from Baltimore. After all, she was considered a beauty in her own right—bright-eyed, buxom, convivial, and quick-witted. She was dressed in a robe of pink satin, trimmed in ermine, and wore a lovely pearl necklace; Wells had no difficulty locating her in the room because two towering bird-of-paradise plumes that topped her characteristic mameluke turban could be seen bobbing and swaying as she passed among the guests, greeting each person with equal enthusiasm. More than one chief must have eyed her outlandish headdress with envy.

James Madison did not like his wife's turbans; Dolley did; the turbans stayed. Although already selected as Jefferson's successor to the presidency, he was accustomed to being overshadowed by his vivacious wife. A small, frail man who always wore a powdered wig and dressed in black, the habitual morose expression on his sallow, wizened face was suggestive of a schoolmaster. The young Washington Irving dismissed him as "a withered apple-John." Only those fortunate enough to engage him in serious conversation encountered the acute mind that had shaped the Constitution and enjoyed his host of anecdotes about the foibles of the nation's founders.

As usual, Main Poche and his wife stayed away. Black Bird came clad in buckskin, while the other chiefs donned dark blue coats with epaulettes and pantaloons; Black Bird's wife, assisted by Mrs. Dearborn, was dressed in a short gown and petticoats of brightly colored, large-patterned chintz. Wells wore his high-collared, gold-embroidered, peacock blue captain's jacket and secured his long, graying hair by a black ribbon around the queue in back. His son sported a soldier's suit to match his father's.

Jefferson stood, arms folded, in the octagonal reception hall and greeted each guest with a bow before passing them on to Dolley. Four large sideboards in the dining room were laden with refreshments, including fine wines and punch in a silver urn. The Marine Band in their scarlet uniforms played "The President's March" and sang "Just like love in yonder rose." At four o'clock sharp everyone took a seat, except the President himself, who oversaw the presentation of the main courses, which included round of beef, loin of veal, lamb chops, roast turkey, and a new Italian dish called macaroni. Later, after a leisurely meal spiced with spirited conversation, there would be sweet wines, fruits, cheeses, pastries, and ice cream served up in a flaky crust.

"I once knew Outacite, the great orator of the Cherokee," Jefferson stated. "He was often at my father's house. My daughters married descendants of Pocahontas."

Wells had some trouble conveying the meaning of all this to the chiefs, since neither he nor they had heard of Pocahontas, but they nodded anyway to be polite.

"As you suggested last time we was here, Mr. President," Wells said, "me and Little Turtle contacted Doctor Thornton and told him a bunch of basic Miami words."

"Splendid!   That's splendid," Jefferson exclaimed, his countenance brightening. Here was a topic he loved to discourse on. "I lament that we have suffered so many tribes to extinquish without recording at least the rudiments of their language. That's why I have begun my own collection."

"Do you really believe the Indians are doomed?" Dolley burst out, casting a nervous glance around. "Surely a benevolent God would not permit such a thing!"

"Quite a few tribes in Virginia have completely vanished," Jefferson sadly admitted, "but the annihilation of an entire species is unthinkable. The economy of Nature and a benign Deity would never permit any complete species to become extinct. Somewhere in the west I believe the great hairy mammoth yet roams free. No, my dear Dolley, the American aborigines are no more likely to disappear from this continent than the passenger pigeons."

Wells didn't even try to translate the President's remarks, especially into three different tongues. He was sick of saying words that seemed to acquire a reality of their own, in spite of what he knew to be the actual case. He realized from experience that the idea was not for the Indians to talk themselves, but rather to sit in silence and witness a civilized conversation.

"I must ask you, Captain Wells, a friend of mine is simply dying to know," Betsey interjected, "is it true that the savages are Anthropophagi?"

"Ma'am?" Wells replied in puzzlement.

"Do they eat people, for food?"

Betsey's inquiry sent a tingle of excitement around the table.

"No, not for food," Wells said slowly, basking in the knowledge that all eyes were fixed on him. "For strength. Sometimes when they kill a warrior known for his bravery they eat his heart to gain his strength."

A lull fell over the conversation, a pause in the chewing, as the white guests avoided looking at what was on their forks.

To change the subject Dolley asked the President, "Won't you miss this house?"

"I long for the tranquility of Monticello," Jefferson responded with feeling. "No prisoner released from his chains can feel such relief as I shall shaking off the shackles of power. I will retire to the solitude of my study, repose in the bosom of my family, and never set foot in Washington again."

"Surely you plan to travel?" Betsey insisted. "Won't you return to Europe?"

"Never. What I wish, if my health and my wealth permit, is to take a flatboat and descend the Ohio and Mississippi to New Orleans. In all these years, I have never ventured west of Staunton, Virginia. Before I die, I should like to see the West."

Wells, with childhood memories of floating down the Ohio flashing through his mind, couldn't quite picture the President at ease on a flatboat, while Betsey looked perturbed at his answer.

"I can never be satisfied in America," she said. "I am out of my element here. As soon as there is peace in Europe, I will find some means of returning."

"What about your son?" Dolley asked.

"Of course he shall come too. Bo shall never be an American; he is a French citizen, he should be educated there; he shall be brought up a Catholic, the royal religion of Kings. Because of his name, my son has rank and distinction; his rightful place is in the first society of Europe."

Although Betsey's son was only three, it was clear that she was already planning to present him in courtly circles on the continent and marry him off to the highest bidder.

"I married for position, not love," Betsey continued. "Anyone who marries for love is a fool. Love in a cottage is even out of fashion in novels. I was sacrificed by Napoleon for political considerations. That's why I accepted his offer of support over Jerome's. I prefer to be sheltered under the wing of an eagle to hanging from the bill of a goose!"

"Our sky is always clear," Jefferson said with a serene smile, "that of Europe is always cloudy. The hope of the world is here. You are still young and beautiful, your husband has remarried, why don't you?"

"That, Mr. President, is exactly what my father says. I loathe Baltimore, I would rather die than spend the rest of my days there. I would rather be the wife of a Bonaparte for an hour than vegetate as a housewife in that horrid place. The men there are all merchants, and commerce, though it may fill the purse, clogs the brain. Beyond their counting houses they possess not a single idea. And the women, they have babies simply to kill time. I should be positively entombed there. Nature never intended me for such obscurity."

"Oh my dear, you're not obscure at all," Dolley gaily protested. "People have seen a great deal of you!"

That brought general laughter, as well as a smile, even the hint of a blush, to Betsey's face. Gazing across the table at this woman of great beauty and biting wit, feeling the heat engendered by fine wine and sudden desire, Wells tried to picture what it would be like to propose to her. She sneered at love in a cottage, what would she say to love in a wigwam? What was Fort Wayne compared to Paris? Nevertheless, Wells believed he was rising in the world; he had consorted with chiefs, fought both with and against generals, and dined with presidents; perhaps the time had come to find a respectable wife—maybe even a lady.

7

On the day before Christmas, Wells called at Dearborn's office, finding only a clerk who could not answer his questions. What should he do now? Main Poche was demanding five horses as presents. Wells didn't even know how to dispose of the ten horses the delegation already had. He also intended to suggest again that the Shawnee and Wea should be concentrated at his agency in Fort Wayne, and he wanted back pay for trips he had taken to assist Governor Harrison with two treaties. Finally, he needed permission to visit his children in Kentucky. Although Wells thought he had made a favorable impression, he still wasn't sure the Secretary of War realized how indispensable he was.

Early in the evening the delegation arrived at their lodgings near Baltimore where George Ellicott, a Quaker leader, was waiting to invite them to Christmas dinner at his house. Main Poche announced gruffly that he was not going.

"I can promise a warm welcome and kind treatment," Ellicott insisted.

"You are white, why should I trust you?" Main Poche demanded.

"Do not speak to him in that way," Little Turtle protested. "You are too big a man to give so small a display of Indian manners."

Any reference to his imposing size made Main Poche laugh, but he still declared that he and his wife would not go.

On the other hand, Black Bird threw himself into preparations for the dinner with great gusto. While his wife held a small mirror and commented on the work in progress, the Potawatomi proceeded to blacken his face and then add a deep dash of vermilion on each cheek. His hair hung down in a heavy bang in front and was tied in back with buckskin thongs and dusted with red paint. He placed eagle feathers in his hair and, as a precaution against the cold, he donned the coat of a grizzly bear he had killed on a hunting expedition to the Stony Mountains. His wife wore an Indian-style dress made of blue cloth and a hat of multicolored ribbons and feathers. Her moccasins were beautifully embroidered with moose hair and porcupine quills, and her bead earrings touched her shoulders. She wrapped herself in a lovely Makinaw blanket. The other chiefs wore the blue coats they received in Washington as well as leggings and moccasins.

George Elliott lived in an H-shaped, double house made from locally quarried granite, with a wide front porch facing the Patapsco River. His brother Jonathan's home stood adjacent to it.

Wells made all the introductions, with Little Turtle setting an especially gracious tone; then the group sat down to a simple dinner of hominy. Several of the chiefs had suffered a bout of diarrhea after feasting at Jefferson's table and now this basic Indian dish was a welcome relief.

George Ellicott had long been active in Quaker missions to the Indians and was a gifted amateur astronomer. Once night fell, he took his guests up to a gabled room on the third floor and showed them his telescopes as well as his prized terrestrial and celestial globes. Little Turtle was fascinated; the spectacles he had received from Koscuisko had shattered years ago and now he wondered if a pair of glasses might be made that would enable him to see the farthest stars.

The conversation, as usual, centered on how best to help the Indians become civilized. Little Turtle didn't hesitate to praise the obvious benefits of the white way of life, but he had become increasingly frustrated with ineffectual efforts to aid his people.

"Do not speak to me of your superiority," he said, "if you cannot furnish me with the means by which my nation can attain the same advantages."

Because of Mr. Kirk's bad reports, the Quakers had been reluctant to send another mission to the Miami, but Little Turtle's charm and frankness quickly won them over.

"What sort of assistance dost thou seek?" Ellicott asked.

"We need a mill to grind our flour," the chief replied, "and a better blacksmith shop to mend our tools."

The next day the delegation took a hike along the Patapsco River to inspect several mills. Main Poche and his wife came along, although they spent their time gathering hickory nuts and persimmons. Ellicott's Mills was built down in The Hollow, surrounded by seven hills; most of the buildings—the mills, the Quaker meeting house, a general store, a small inn, a row of houses—were made of granite. The Indians, who knew from experience that even the most substantial wooden structures were constantly rotting away, couldn't resist touching the hard, abrasive, dark-gray blocks of stone as they walked along the main street. Although they had come to see the gristmill, the ironworks with its furnace and rolling mills drew their amazed attention. So this was how the whites made metal!

After a week in Baltimore, where Mad Sturgeon fought off a bout of flu, the delegation headed to the West, with the exception of The Beaver, who decided to return to Washington. Somewhere along the way to Wheeling, Main Poche obtained another keg and, in a drunken rage, began to threaten people. When the other chiefs attempted to calm him down, he raised his war club and vowed to kill any man who tried to stop him. A tense standoff ensued, with Little Turtle issuing a stern warning to Main Poche to shut up or die. That night, Wells heard bloodcurdling screams. He raced down the hall of the small inn and burst in a door, only to find Main Poche, scalping knife in hand, straddling his wife and vowing not only to slit her throat but also to drink her blood and eat her flesh. Assisted by the other chiefs, Wells pulled the crazed Potawatomi off his trembling, glazed-eyed wife and placed him under guard until he was sober enough to travel.

Wells had left a letter for Dearborn in Washington, asking him to send his instructions to Chambersburg. When no word came, Wells did what he thought best. At Pittsburgh he put the delegation on a boat to Cincinnati. An uneasy peace prevailed on the trip down the river; Little Turtle and Main Poche were not on speaking terms. Wells could hardly wait to get rid of the Potawatomi war chief. He had wasted a year of his life trying to tame that insufferable rogue! After watching so many of his efforts fail, Wells was tired of living with Indians. He felt edgy and irritable. He longed to get away. He needed a change.

In Cincinnati, he purchased a set of fresh horses; Little Turtle would lead the delegation back to Fort Wayne. Wells watched them ride off with relief and then he and his son took a boat to Louisville. Sam now had a two-story, eight-room brick house and a thriving plantation. Wells barely recognized his own daughters. It had been more than a year since he had seen them. They were dressed as little ladies in fluffy petticoats and their dark hair was done up in ringlets and ribbons.

"Papa! Papa!" they cried as he lifted all three in his arms in a mighty hug.

William Wells was now legendary in Kentucky. As the threat of actual Indian attacks disappeared, the idea of a man who had been captured by the Miami, fought as a warrior in their greatest triumphs, but switched sides to serve as head scout in Wayne's decisive victory at Fallen Timbers—all this had gained a romantic luster. Over the years, tales were told around Kentucky fireplaces of daring deeds that Wells may or may not have performed.

One person enthralled by his aura was twenty-year-old Mary Geiger, whose father Frederick had been a long-time Middletown neighbor, hunting buddy, and militia companion of Sam. Her brother Jacob had married Sam's eldest daughter Margaret, and Mary was a close friend of Sam's eighteen-year-old daughter Rebekah, who still called Wells "Uncle Billy." Wells had noticed how lovely Mary was on a previous visit and how her eyes brightened as she heard the stories of his adventures. Here was a man who had fought toe-to-toe with savages in dark forests and met face-to-face with George Washington and Thomas Jefferson!

Wells and Mary soon found themselves at the center of a conspiracy of giggling girls, as Sam's daughters, Rebekah and Ann, joined Wells's daughters, Ann, Rebecca, and Polly, in teasing Mary that she should set her cap for the famous frontiersman. Not only were the girls fascinated by romance, they had also, thanks to Wells's devout sister Elizabeth, gotten religion. They said grace before dinner and sang spirituals in the parlor.

Mary had refined features—warm brown eyes, a pert button nose, and thin lips, slightly up-turned at the corners in an incipient smile, although she rarely laughed. She wore her abundant auburn hair piled high on her head and favored low-cut dresses. She saw Wells as an experienced man of action, someone who could make a decision and shape her life.

When they took walks together, there would often be long silences—was it because strong emotions tied their tongues or did they have so little in common there was nothing to say? Or was it because Wells, used for so long to speak the words of others, was at a loss to find his own? Mary was a headstrong girl who wanted to be pampered and said her father was too strict with her. Wells was a man in a hurry to find a new wife.

"It is so dull here," she told Wells one day as they strolled by the river. "I don't want to marry a farmer. All the men here talk about is land, crops, and breeding horses."

Wells looked up at overcast skies warning of cold rains that would turn to snow in the night and wondered how to respond.

"I have to go away soon," he said.

"Yes, I know. What is Fort Wayne like?"

"I think it's a beautiful spot." Wells glanced at her sideways, trying to read her expression. "Would you like to see it?"

"I would, with you."

There was a tense silence while Wells continued to stare at the horizon.

"As my wife?"

And so it was decided. Two weeks later, on March 7, 1809, they were married at the Middletown Presbyterian Church, Reverend James Vance presiding.

"I suppose you've never been with a white woman before," Mary said on their wedding night, as sounds of merriment still filled the house from the revelers below.

Wells realized that this was a crucial point for her; she knew of Sweet Breeze, not Laughing Eyes, nor that he had fathered a daughter with White Swan since Sweet Breeze's death, to say nothing of a brief dalliance in Ohio with a certain Mrs. Willis.

"You're the first, Polly," he lied, calling her by his preferred term of endearment.

"I'm glad," she murmured, hugging him closer, "and I'll be the last."

After a few days of farewell visits, the newlyweds returned to Fort Wayne accompanied by Wells's children as well as Rebekah, who had always wanted to visit. Wells saw how raw and meager the place looked in his disappointed bride's eyes. His rotting cabin, the slave shacks in back, the muddy roads, the empty fields, the log houses of French Town, the old fort, the bare trees whipped by the last winds of winter—it all looked bleak and barren, utterly lacking in civilizing amenities; the ragged, begging, drunken Indians, a constant presence in the town and around the fort, were the last straw. Mary broke down and wept and stared at her new husband with shining, reproachful eyes.

In spring, when the first flowers came out, Mary felt somewhat better and vowed she would make him a good wife. Rebekah, in particular, made a conscientious effort to revive Mary's spirts; she helped with the housework and served as a sympathetic confidant when Wells was preoccupied or absent. Wells was grateful to his niece for what she had done; he promised his wife that he would try to pay more attention to her needs and build her a proper house. One day in mid-April there was a knock on the door; John Johnston, the Fort Wayne factor who had been away in Ohio, entered the front room wearing a smug smile and presented a letter. It was the long-awaited message from Dearborn, but it did not respond to, let alone mention, Wells's requests. Instead it stated that Johnston was now the Indian agent and that he, William Wells, was henceforth dismissed from government service.

William Henry Harrison

1

William Wells blamed John Johnston for his dismissal. For the past seven years their relationship had been acrimonious. A devout believer in the chain of command, Johnston disapproved of the fact that Wells reported to the Secretary of War as well as to Governor Harrison and frowned at his intimate ties with the Indians. Born in Ireland in 1775, Johnston had left County Donegal at age eleven and immigrated to Pennsylvania to make his fortune, but his early efforts ended in failure. As a packhorse master during the Fallen Timbers campaign, he was sacked from the service and docked three months pay when he lost fifty-five horses due to neglect. In Philadelphia he labored for scant wages as a scrivener for the state Supreme Court before moving to Washington to clerk in the War Department, where his claims of success in business and his masonic connections persuaded Henry Dearborn to select him as head of the Indian trading factory at Fort Wayne. A methodical, fastidious man, straight-laced and strong-willed, he prided himself on his patriotism and good digestion. More narrow-minded than mean-spirited, he did not know what to make of Wells, a man tainted with savagery, whose morality and loyalty were suspect.

The two men had a confrontation when Wells came to Johnston's house to settle the agency accounts and turn over any government property in his possession, including the tools of the Indian Department carpenter.

"Why did you fire him?" Wells demanded, taking up the cause of his friend.

"His services were no longer necessary," Johnston stated with finality. Wells had to admit that Johnston appeared to have ability. He was over six feet tall and looked even taller because he held his head up and his shoulders back, as if he considered slouching a sin. A pair of gray, appraising eyes took the measure of all they surveyed while a supercilious smile, almost a smirk, counted up the costs. Over the years he had trained himself to replace his thick Irish brogue with the inflections of an English gentleman. "He was hired to work for the government, not you, and so I discharged him as a supernumerary and useless person."

"What the hell do you know about what's useful to the Indians?" Wells sneered. "He built the Council House, people's homes, he's helped clear land and fence off fields—he even built *your* damn house!"

"And what about yours?" Johnston raised a disdainful eyebrow. "It is my impression that he mainly worked for you."

"You just hate to see me better myself, don't you? That's why you've conspired behind my back to get my job."

"I know you're spreading rumors to that effect," Johnston replied with forced calm, "but you're wrong. I've already written to the War Department to establish my innocence. I assure you I have never disparaged your conduct to Secretary Dearborn."

"You sure complained to Harrison," Wells asserted. "He told me so himself."

"That was because I found your protest of the Delaware Treaty most improper. Really, Mr. Wells, I often ask myself which side you are on."

"I'm on the side of justice," Wells declared. "I know the treatment I've received was cruel and unjust. What exactly do you think I've done that's so damn bad?"

"I've observed you for years," Johnston said, "and I know how cunning and persistent you can be when you feel your interests are at stake. If you're guilty of dishonest practices, as the Indians often say, I'm sure that would be almost impossible to prove. You speak so many languages, how could I possibly keep track of your intrigues? Frankly, since the death of Sweet Breeze your behavior has been deplorable and tales I've heard of your exploits as a Miami warrior have chilled my blood."

"I wouldn't mind spilling some blood right now." Wells locked eyes with Johnston before he stomped out the door.

Given his mixed motives, Wells's dismissal was inevitable. He was no longer the obedient young man eager to please and striving to prove himself. The passing years had sharpened his edges and hardened his heart; a fiery temper and a stubborn streak rendered him constitutionally unable to abide by rules or adopt the notions of others. He had always taken pride in his daring and audacity, his willingness to take risks. He had pledged himself to serve a government whose policies he questioned. A man of many loyalties, no wonder he was often seen as having too few. As Indian Agent he had often found himself standing on a shrinking middle ground, torn by conflicting emotions, vacillating between the incompatible needs of the long-suffering Indians and the rapidly advancing settlers. This ambiguous situation fostered a devious side to his character, usually in the service of what he conceived to be his and Little Turtle's interests.

What exasperated him the most was that even his best-intentioned schemes failed to work out as expected. At the treaty of Greenville he had gained recognition for the people of Snake-fish Town as a separate Eel River tribe entitled to annuities, but this only served to destroy them, since many moved to Vincennes and wasted their money on drink. Now that he was a peace chief, Little Turtle needed presents to distribute as proof of his power. In return for helping Harrison negotiate treaties, Wells had arranged for the chief to receive a personal annuity, a house, even a slave; what Little Turtle accepted as gifts that acknowledged his high status, however, Harrison saw as bribes to ensure his cooperation and other Indians resented as signs of betrayal. Indeed, the privileges Little Turtle enjoyed, including his trips east to visit various Presidents, caused the Miami to split into factions. Wells had resisted William Kirk and the Quakers' civilization project because he thought that if Little Turtle controlled the program he would regain lost prestige; instead the government had lost faith in his own allegiance.

When Elijah Tyson and a delegation of Baltimore Friends arrived at Fort Wayne in May to reconsider their civilization program, Wells guided them to the Mississinewa, seeing it as an opportunity to reinstate himself in their good graces. It was one of those spring days that play a medley of all weathers: the morning was cold and windy with a steady rain; by afternoon the sky cleared, the sun came out, and a warm breeze from the south carried the promise of summer. White Loon's village was beautifully situated near the mouth of the river, with a hundred acres freshly planted in corn, potatoes, watermelons, and cucumbers, but it was the women who had done this work while the men sulked because of the failed hunt.

"Our game is vanishing," White Loon lamented. "Soon the animals will all be gone and we will either have to move or cut down the trees for pastures and fields."

The Miami on the Mississinewa were not receptive to offers of assistance; the women mocked any man who picked up a hoe and everybody took offense when Tyson suggested that their horses ought to be put to work plowing.

That same day a drunken Indian, grieving over the death of his daughter, stabbed his equally drunken wife in the neck for falling off her horse. He sat beside her body, wrapped in blood-soaked calico, until her relatives came to claim it.

"Kill me if you wish," the whiskey-fuddled husband said.

Wells was able to gather enough gifts to appease her family and save the man's life; he knew similar scenes were being acted out all over Indian country. Alcoholism had became so rampant that many men hunted merely to buy whiskey. When the annuities were distributed unscrupulous traders hid kegs at predetermined spots in the woods and the Indians would rush off for a drunken frolic that lasted until their money was gone. As Indian Agent, there was little Wells could do to prevent this destructive behavior; when he was short of cash, he had even abetted it. Five Medals, Little Turtle's Potawatomi ally, sometimes came to Wells's door and pleaded, "Give me lum or I get sick."

Wells and the Quaker delegation proceeded to Turtletown on the Eel River. There Wells learned that the Wea held him responsible for moldy blankets they had received in the past and that The Beaver had accused him of confiscating $400 of the Delaware annuities, which actually had been withheld by the government as payment for stolen horses. Wells was preoccupied by his appeal to William Eustis, the newly appointed Secretary of War, as he and the delegation rode back to Fort Wayne.

Once she had adjusted to frontier life, Wells's young wife proved to be remarkably resilient in the face of adversity. As he paced the puncheon floor of their cabin, berating his enemies, rebutting hypothetical charges, and predicting their financial ruin, she compressed her lips in sympathy and said, "Write to him, Will, surely Mr. Eustis'll believe you."

"Do you think so, Polly?" Wells would ask, and return to his pacing and cursing.

The presence of Wells's daughters and his visiting niece Rebekah went a long way toward lifting Polly's spirits. While Wells's son William Wayne was off playing soldiers and Indians, the young women liked to shop and socialize in French Town, on the site of the old trading post along the north side of the river. They quickly became acquainted with the three lovely Chapeteau sisters; the most beautiful, Angelique, was called "Golden Hair" by the Miami. Married to traders in the town, they were as fond as the French settlers of old had been of singing and dancing. At one frolic, attended by officers of the fort, the vivacious Rebekah caught the eye of Nathan Heald, the garrison commander and a good friend of Wells. He came a-calling every day thereafter until she returned in early June to Kentucky.

In late May the Shawnee Prophet and a few men arrived in Fort Wayne to size up the new Indian Agent, wheedle supplies, and blame their past troubles on Wells, who, for his part, attempted to goad the man he saw as an imposter into showing his true colors. He was certain that the Prophet and Tecumseh were biding their time until they had enough well-armed warriors and British assistance to attack the settlements. The newly appointed Indian agent didn't share Wells's views; Johnston came away from his talks with the Prophet convinced of his desire for peace.

Wells spent much of June collecting affidavits and composing a letter to Eustis explaining the injustice done to him and pleading for his reinstatement, either as Indian Agent or as head of the civilization program. Attestations to his mastery of Indian languages and customs and his great influence among them, as well as his honesty in distributing annuities, were provided by the blacksmith, the recently fired carpenter, the army surgeon, and the garrison commander. They called Wells "the most proper person" to be in charge of Indian Affairs at Fort Wayne.

"I always believed that the many important services I have rendered the United States," Wells wrote, "would certainly entitle me to be heard before I was condemned."

When Wells's packet arrived in July, the Secretary of War was not impressed; he noted that it contained "sundry testimonials corroborating his pretensions" and filed it away unanswered.

2

In 1801, when twenty-seven-year-old William Henry Harrison had arrived in Vincennes as the first governor of the newly created Indiana Territory, he had been appalled by the condition of the Indians. The Piankashaw were the most depraved set of wretches he had ever seen, and the raggedy Wea, Kaskaskia, and Eel River Indians weren't any better. They seemed to make a special point of killing their old chiefs; those who weren't undone by drink often suffered the ravages of smallpox and other infectious diseases. To make matters worse, white squatters and Kentucky long hunters encroached on their lands, depleted their game, and, on occasion, shot them down with impunity—since no jury would punish a white man for murdering an Indian. Others fell to the rapacity of traders, who plied them with whiskey, stole their peltries, and left them to starve.

Scion of a distinguished Virginia family of landed gentry, whose brick mansion, Berkeley, fronted the James River near Westover, with a grandfather who had been struck dead by lightning and a father who signed the Declaration of Independence, Harrison was sure he was destiny's child. As a boy he filled his adolescent head with visions of the glorious exploits of Roman proconsuls and their valiant legions. After his father died, he stopped dabbling in medicine with Dr. Rush in Philadelphia and enlisted in the army. Harrison, when he was General Wayne's aide-de-camp, had first met Wells in 1793. The two remained on friendly terms until parting ways after the Treaty of Greenville. Harrison left the army and tried his hand at farming and running a distillery, but he longed for a larger stage to display his talents. He was appointed Secretary of the Northwest Territory and defeated the son of Arthur St. Clair by one vote to become a delegate to Congress, where he helped draft a land law that enabled western settlers to purchase 320 acres at two dollars an acre. This measure proved to be so popular that President Adams saw fit to name the ambitious and articulate young man governor of Indiana Territory.

As governor Harrison used his patronage to surround himself with sycophants and soon possessed almost despotic power in the territory; he could pardon any offense, favor any friend, and had a free hand to negotiate with the Indians. His liberal land policies encouraged new settlers and he obliged the slave owners by circumventing the law. In 1803, Jefferson commissioned Harrison to make treaties with the Indians and sent him secret instructions on how to proceed: "The crisis is pressing. Whatever can now be obtained must be obtained quickly. The occupation of New Orleans, hourly expected by the French, is already felt like a light breeze to the Indians. You know the sentiments they entertain of that nation. Under the hope of their protection, they will immediately stiffen against cessions of lands to us. We had therefore better do at once what can now be done." Harrison took Jefferson's urgency seriously. The essentially military strategy was to purchase lands on both banks of the Ohio and Mississippi in order to secure supply lines, strengthen American settlements, encircle Indian territory, and curtail foreign intrigues.

By threatening to withhold annuities, Harrison drew over 1,000 Indians to a treaty negotiation at Fort Wayne. At first Little Turtle and Wells had resisted Harrison's overtures; finally, in return for a

$150 personal annuity for the chief, they used their influence to back a slightly modified version of the plan. The offended Shawnee walked out of the conference; but in the end Harrison, with the strong backing of friendly Potawatomi chiefs and the support of Wells and Little Turtle, got his way. The Vincennes Tract and the valuable salt springs on Saline Creek became American property; in return, the Indians would receive only an annual shipment of salt.

Another conference was held in the summer of 1805 at Grouseland, Harrison's newly erected Georgian mansion in Vincennes. A portrait of Benjamin Harrison hung over the hand-carved mantle in the large reception room and a semicircular spiral staircase led to the numerous bedrooms on the second floor. "My nursery fills faster than my strongbox," Harrison had quipped to Wells, as if they were still old friends, but he was in no joking mood when the two men met privately in the governor's study.

"I don't want you to put words in the mouth of Little Turtle," Harrison had told Wells bluntly before the negotiations. "It is not your function to speak for the Indians. You have pledged your loyalty to the United States. If you want to keep your job, then I expect your full and energetic cooperation so that this upcoming treaty will have a fortuitous conclusion. Do I make myself clear?"

Knowing that his future as an Indian Agent was at stake, Wells had done his best to fulfill Harrison's wishes. The treaty stipulated that the Miami, Wea, and Eel Rivers were the sole owners of the Wabash and its waters above the Vincennes Tract. In return, all the tribes who signed received an increase in their annuities; Little Turtle had $50 added to his yearly pension as well as the promise of a slave, which Wells later brought back from Kentucky

In three years Harrison had purchased more than sixty-million acres at less than a penny an acre, much to the dissatisfaction of the Indians in general, especially of the Shawnees, who had been insulted by the governor and denied any increase in their annuities. To retain their own influence, Wells and Little Turtle had collaborated with Harrison and had precious little to show for their efforts other than the hatred of many tribesmen.

3

A few days before he learned of his dismissal, Wells had written to Governor Harrison offering his services for another purchase. The land in question was Wea territory, part of the sacred Wabash Valley that Wells had pledged always to preserve for the Miami; now he needed to establish credit with Harrison and Secretary of

War Eustis. Wells thought that this treaty would save the Wea, who, because of their proximity to the traders in Vincennes, were being destroyed by drink. The sale of their homeland would compel them to move closer to Fort Wayne, perhaps joining Little Turtle's village on the Eel River, thus strengthening the chief's hand among the Miami.

Harrison had long coveted this land. Much of the territory he had already bought was low-lying, marshy prairie, while the Wea lands were higher, dryer, richly timbered in places, and very fertile. Wells reported that the Shawnee Prophet was losing followers and contemplating an exodus across the Mississippi; the time was ripe to push for cessions. In February of 1809 Illinois had become a separate territory, as had Michigan four years before; if Harrison wanted statehood for Indiana, he had to acquire additional land in order to lure more settlers. Over the years, the governor's popularity had begun to wane; many former allies now lived in Illinois, and an infusion of Quaker emigrants from the Carolinas into the Whitewater Valley had invigorated an antislavery, pro-self-government opposition party that styled themselves "democrats." Nothing would revitalize the governor's support like the availability of good, cheap land.

In September Harrison arrived in Fort Wayne, accompanied by his secretary, interpreter, manservant, and French guide. Wells found that Harrison had hardly aged since he had last seen him. Although now in his mid-thirties, he still possessed a boyish quality that suggested he was playing at the serious position he held. A hank of hair black as a raven's wing flapped down his forehead, almost reaching his right eye; an unusually large nose dominated his narrow, egg-shaped face. He had firm lips and a strong jaw, implying an assurance that verged on conceit; his lean form and the quick glitter in his dark eyes reminded Wells a Great Blue Heron stalking the shallows for easy prey. His enemies called him a moral chameleon for his facility at manipulating people to do his bidding.

Wells translated Harrison's usual speech about how much better off the Indians would be if they stopped hunting and started farming, and he pictured the advantages the Wea would gain by selling their lands and joining their Miami brethren. "The Miami Nation would be more respectable and formidable," he said, "if its scattered members were concentrated in the center of their country." When he had finished, Little Turtle told Harrison that the Indians would give careful consideration to his proposal.

"They are resolved not to part with another foot of land," Wells reported later that evening.

"Do you think they mean it?"

"Can't say for certain," Wells replied, "but they sure said some hard words."

"Directed at whom?"

"At you for proposing the treaty and at Little Turtle for supporting it."

"At least we have the backing of the Potawatomi."

"They don't like that either." Wells shook his head. "At Grouseland you promised that only the Miami owned the Wabash; now hundreds of Potawatomi and Delaware are involved. You haven't even invited the Wea, and it's their land you want to buy."

"What else could I do?" Harrison pleaded disingenuously. "If I excluded the other tribes, they would be resentful and seek satisfaction from the Miami. I did it for their own good, to protect them. This way they all will get more annuities."

"What about the Wyandot and Shawnee? Where are they?"

"The United States considers them refugee tribes, at least in Indiana Territory. Imagine the problems I would have if the Shawnee Prophet and Tecumseh were here! The whole point of recognizing the Miami's ownership of the Wabash was to refute Tecumseh's claim that no chief has the right to sell tribal land."

"Little Turtle don't want any tribe to benefit from the sale of Miami land except the Miami themselves."

"Do you think they're resisting the treaty in the hope of driving up the price?"

"That may be," Wells said, without admitting that he himself had suggested to Little Turtle that the Miami might profit by driving a hard bargain. "They know that white settlers are buying up old Indian lands for two dollars an acre. They want the same deal. If you sweetened the pot some they might come around."

"I hope for your sake, Captain Wells, that you aren't encouraging them to make extravagant demands. I've never been informed of the reasons for your dismissal, but I do know that doubts were raised in the past about your handling of money. Yesterday the Delaware told me that you'd stolen four-hundred dollars of their annuities."

"Here's the proof that's a lie," Wells promptly replied. "This letter from Secretary Dearborn says he withheld the money to pay for stolen horses. I can honestly assure you I committed no crime;

my dismissal was unjust; I was slandered by my enemies. You know what that's like."

Harrison glanced at the letter and acknowledged its validity. "I will make immediate restitution to the Delaware," he announced, fixing his sharp eyes on Wells. "I want you to talk to Little Turtle and any other Indians you can influence. If you can help me complete this treaty, I'll do what I can to see that you're reinstated in the Indian Department. Agreed?"

"I have always done my best to further the views of government," Wells asserted, trying to find an official phrase that concealed his conflicting hopes and doubts.

When the negotiations began, Harrison told the Indians that their increased annuities would enable them to clothe their women and children and purchase cattle and hogs to substitute for the uncertainties of the hunt. The next day the Indians gave their reply. The Potawatomi, boldly seconded by the Delaware, were vehemently in favor of the treaty, but the Miami balked and offered objections. Little Turtle wanted more compensation. The Potawatomi, in desperate need of provisions, and the Delaware, still bitter over their humiliation at the Treaty of Grouseland, outnumbered the Miami and Eel River Indians by four to one at the conference. They made no secret that they expected the Miami to sell lands for their benefit, but the Mississinewa chiefs remained recalcitrant and refused to comply.

After three days of wrangling, Harrison made another attempt to win them over.

"Is there some evil spirit amongst us," he inquired, "that has set brothers against brothers and children against their father? The wind I hear has blown from the North, no good has ever yet come from that quarter."

He then blamed the British for sending bad birds among them and urged the tribes to seek common ground.

"Miamis, be not offended with your brothers the Potawatomi, take pity on their women and children. Potawatomi, do not suffer your own distress and your love for your Father to make you angry with your brothers the Miami. My children, the Miami, what disconcerts you? Have you not always received justice from the hands of your Father? What is it he asks of you? Nothing but what you can spare. I know that you have long desired to have your brothers the Wea alongside you. Bring your scattered members together and you will be strong."

Harrison insisted that no treaty could be made unless all the tribes consented. "I wish to hear you speak with one voice the dictates of our heart. This is the first request your new Father President Madison has ever made of you. It will be the last. He wants no more land. He will *never* make another proposition to you to sell your lands."

Little Turtle apologized that the Miami were not in agreement with the Potawatomi and Delaware and said they would meet to resolve the matter. That evening Wells talked with Little Turtle, White Loon, and his boyhood friend The Sleepy One, who, since his father The Soldier had died, was chief of the Eel River village on the Wabash. They agreed to go along with Harrison's wishes; the Mississinewa Miami refused.

When the tribes met again, The Owl declared that the Miami would never consent to sell another foot of their land. At that, a great roar of outrage and defiance went up from a host of Potawatomi warriors; they brandished their weapons and threatened to drive the Miami into the lake, but the Miami remained adamant about not selling land on the Wabash.

"If Harrison will meet your price," Wells repeatedly told any Indians who would listen, "I think you should treat."

"We love our lands," The Owl told the assembled Indians. "We are determined never to sell them. The land on the Wabash belongs to our younger brothers, the Wea. We have nothing more to say."

Wells observed that as Harrison listened his face reddened and his jaw tightened. In reply to the Miami refusal to sell Wea land, the governor went off on a two-hour harangue. By the time he finished translating, Wells had a scratchy throat and a raspy voice. Harrison reviewed the long and honorable history of American conduct toward the Indians, contrasting it with the perfidious intrigues of the British. He swore that the United States considered all its treaties as solemn and sacred engagements that they would never violate.

Much of this rhetoric stuck in Wells's craw; he knew from experience that Harrison's version of frontier history was slanted; yet he had to stifle his anger to render a faithful translation.

Winamac (The Catfish), a Potawatomi chief Harrison had been cultivating for years, stood to express his support. "Father, all that you have said is good. You asked for land, we will give it to you. We your children consider the land as belonging to us all, not to one nation alone. We know that everything you have said is true."

When they heard these words, the Mississinewa Miami stormed out. Seeing the disgust on their faces as they left, Wells felt certain that the treaty was doomed.

"They will never sign," he told Harrison. "You might as well go back to Vincennes."

"I intend to get at the root of this matter," Harrison replied. "Their tenacity is astonishing, but I don't think the cause of their obstinacy is the money or their loyalty to the Wea. I mean to find out what's really on their minds."

Early the next morning Harrison went to the camp of the Mississinewa Miami without bringing Wells, taking instead Joseph Barron, who spoke the language passably.

"What are your objections to the treaty?" Harrison demanded.

"Father, here are your own words," The Sleepy One said, presenting him with a copy of the Treaty of Grouseland. "In this paper you promised that the Miami have always owned the Wabash. Why then do you want to purchase it from others?"

"It was the Miami," Harrison insisted, "who wanted the other tribes consulted. I must admit, I did not expect the Potawatomi to be so assertive. That was not my intention. The Miami own all the land watered by the Wabash; if you wish, I will give the compensation for it only to you, but that might offend the other tribes who have participated in this treaty expecting a reward."

These statements met with general approval, as did The Owl's reiteration of his long-standing grievances about Wells cheating him of money and taking his whiskey and Little Turtle receiving too much government support.

"Why do you listen to them more than us?" he challenged.

"I am listening now," Harrison replied, understanding what was expected of him. "I hereby declare that Pecan and the other Mississinewa chiefs are the real representatives of the Miami and I shall always consider them as such. Does that satisfy you?"

"We have heard your words," Pecan said, his aged face breaking into a smile. "You can now return to the fort and shortly we will come to you with good news."

That afternoon the treaty was signed, with an additional article affirming that the Wabash belonged to the Miami, Wea, and Eel Rivers and increasing their compensation. Wells observed that when the Potawatomi, whose collective influence had ultimately compelled the Miami to negotiate, saw that there were too few presents, they took offense and refused to touch any gifts. Why was Harrison favoring the Miami? they complained. The Potawatomi were his most faithful children. To defuse the situation, Wells suggested giving them an advance on their next year's annuities; this expedient seemed to satisfy them, although some still went away with nothing to show for their efforts.

Harrison didn't tell Wells about the bargain he had struck with the Mississinewa Miami—no doubt he would find out later. As promised, however, he did send a letter to Secretary of War Eustis.

"I think from Wells's former services (which I personally know were very great in the Indian war) he deserves a hearing, & if his removal has been occasioned by misrepresentations, & a vacancy should occur in the Indian Department, the government would find their account in placing him in it."

4

Wells encouraged the Indians to protest the very treaty he had helped to bring about. He had earned a recommendation from Harrison for his services, but the results of the treaty were not what he anticipated. Instead of regaining lost status with the Miami, Little Turtle had been condemned for surrendering tribal territory and deposed by the Mississinewa chiefs. Wells was not alone in his opposition. None of the Indian tribes were happy with the sale of lands along the Wabash or the incursion of settlers from Ohio. Even while the treaty was underway, a rumor had spread among the Indians at Fort Wayne that President Madison hadn't requested the purchase; rather Harrison merely wanted the lands for his own use and to regain his lost popularity.

No Indian was angrier than Tecumseh. The militant brother of the Shawnee Prophet had been working for years to build a confederacy among all the young warriors, north and south, pledged never to sell any land without the consent of every tribe—and, when the time was ripe, to repel the hated American settlers with force. More than any other event, the Fort Wayne Treaty of 1809 fueled Tecumseh's burning rage and brought more determined braves into his camp at Tippecanoe.

Although Harrison urged Eustis to rehire him, Wells heard nothing from Washington. And so he wrote on his own behalf; this time claiming that the government owed him thousands of dollars in back pay—not the best argument to sway Eustis, who was as parsimonious as Dearborn had been. When John Johnston learned that Wells was trying to get his old job back, he sent a letter to the Secretary of War, stating that Wells was an unprincipled man, guilty of defrauding the Miami, Wea, and Eel Rivers of their annuities.

The government had justly deprived him of his office, he asserted, since, except for Little Turtle, his dismissal did not excite displeasure among the chiefs. Johnston also wrote to Harrison, blaming Wells for spreading false rumors and fostering discontent among the Indians following the treaty.

As the months dragged on and Wells moped around the house, Polly's spirits sagged, her rosy complexion lost its luster, and a frown clamped down on her mouth.

"I have been deprived of an office I purchased with my own blood!" Wells asserted.

"I know, Will, I know," Polly said soothingly, with a weary, defeated look in her eyes. "Give it time, we'll get by."

"How? That's what I'd like to know. That smug scoundrel Johnston is getting more money than I ever did, now he's hired Abraham Ash to be his interpreter, at a dollar a day. When I was agent, who did the interpreting? Me. And what did I get for it? Not one red cent!"

"It isn't right."

"You're goddamned right it isn't. I don't blame the government; it's my enemies, here in the territory, acting in concealment, that have done all the damage; I know who they are. I've a mind to call Johnston a few choice names in public, issue a challenge. If he accepts, I'll tell you this, that son-of-a-bitch will be flyblown by sundown."

"I wish you wouldn't talk that way, Will. It only makes things worse."

"How in hell can they get any worse than they are right now?"

"We'll get by," Polly repeated without conviction. She was pregnant, expecting a child in January, and the little cash Wells had squirreled away might not see them through another year.

"I don't want to get by," Wells growled. "I want justice."

When Johnston informed Harrison that Wells was to blame for the dissatisfaction over the treaty, the governor had second thoughts about his previous recommendation. He wrote to Eustis again in early December, reviewing Wells's outstanding service to his country during Wayne's campaign and recapitulating the problems he had had with him after the Delaware treaty of 1804. Harrison said he had accepted the aid of Wells and Little Turtle at the Treaty of Fort Wayne because, if he hadn't, he feared they might thwart his intentions. Their zeal in promoting the treaty was commendable, but their behavior since then had been highly improper. All things considered, Harrison still thought that it would be better to hire

Wells than to endure his intrigues, but only in a subordinate situation. Eustis concurred with Harrison, authorizing him to appoint Wells as Indian Interpreter, under the governor's immediate control, in a position where his services would be the most useful. Upon receiving these instructions, Harrison wrote to Johnston to see if he approved.

On a leave of absence to restore his poor health, Johnston had been in Lancaster and Philadelphia since November. When he returned to Fort Wayne in June, he read Harrison's letter for the first time and immediately replied. During his travels through Ohio he had learned disturbing news about Tecumseh. After visiting her relations in Tippecanoe, Abraham Ash's Potawatomi wife had informed Johnston's assistant John Shaw that the Shawnee Prophet and Tecumseh had been plotting for three years to launch a surprise attack on all the major frontier towns, forts, and trading posts. The British were directly involved, urging the Indians to take up the tomahawk because the Americans consistently cheated them. All the warriors lacked were the supplies to sustain a campaign.

Having warned of Tecumseh's conspiracy, Johnston then turned to the persistent problem of Little Turtle and William Wells; his intention was to destroy, once and for all, the reputations of both men. All the trouble with the Indians over the treaty, he reiterated, originated with Wells, as did any other mischief among the Miami. Johnston stated that as agent he planned to cherish the Mississinewa chiefs, because Little Turtle was contemptible, in the eyes of his fellow Indians, and should not be sent ever again to represent them in Washington—he had been there too often already. As for Wells, he was too unprincipled to be employed anywhere, except as an interpreter in Vincennes, where Harrison could keep an eye on him. At Fort Wayne, he was nothing but a pest, unsuitable to any honest purpose.

"He has so long traveled in the crooked, miry paths of intrigue and deception," Johnston wrote, "that he never could be made to retrace his steps, and pursue a straight, fair, and honorable course, such as might be creditable to himself and useful to his country."

Tecumseh

1

Often during the winter and early spring, when disease ravaged the Indians, William Wells would receive reports of witch hunts from the eleven villages strung along the White River. Back in 1802 he had heard that a Shawnee shaman ordered the executions of two old hags he accused of transforming themselves into night owls and inflicting a fatal coughing sickness on the people. The next year an elderly Delaware woman named Beata, muttering to herself about the lack of game, encountered in the woods an apparition who told her, "I am your grandfather. You must live again as you lived before the white people came. At present the deer are under the earth. If you do what I have told you, they will once more come out." Beata had more visions that called upon the Indians to maintain their ancient customs and stop killing each other. The Delaware at Chestnut Tree Place built a council house where sacrifices were held, people recited their dreams while shaking a turtle shell rattle, and Beata, exhorting them to live properly, exposed the witches among them.

The spring of 1805 was especially trying for the Delaware. A hard winter had been followed by devastating floods that swept away the split-rail fencing around the cornfields and ruined the crops. After that came hunger and epidemics. In May, while Sweet Breeze was succumbing to influenza at Fort Wayne, the Delaware war chief Buckongahelas died of a bilious fever. No man so great could die of natural causes; he must have been cursed by secret enemies; suspicion focused on another old chief, Tetepachsit, who feared for his life.

Tecumseh's band of Shawnee occupied one of the White River villages. His brother, Loud Mouth, was a notoriously lazy, uncouth drunkard. A blustering braggart with a mean streak, he beat his wives and offended his friends with his unruly tongue; in sharp contrast to Tecumseh, he was an inept hunter and warrior, having fled from the field at Fallen Timbers. To gain respect, he had apprenticed himself to the noted shaman Change of Feathers and, upon the medicine man's death, had assumed his office; but all his ministrations to combat the insidious sicknesses were in vain. As the death toll mounted through the summer of 1805, and the search for evil sorcerers intensified, he fell into a deep despondency, sought oblivion through drink, and became even more surly and difficult. One evening he was lighting his pipe, when suddenly he dropped to the floor. After his wife failed to revive him, she sent for her relatives, who determined that he was dead. As they were preparing his body for burial, they heard a groan and watched in amazement as he regained consciousness.

"I have seen the Master of Life," were his first words. "He has shown me the true path."

The incipient Shawnee Prophet had more visions; he began to gather a following and formulate a creed. The Indians were to return to the old ways; they should exchange white people's clothing for buckskin; discard flints and start fires with sticks; kill their cows, hogs, and chickens (but not horses); braves should shave their heads to a scalplock and hunt only with bows and arrows (although guns should be kept in good repair); stop selling their furs and barter only for necessities; no one should eat bread or pork or, above all, drink whiskey. Indians intermarried with non-Indians should leave their partners; an Indian husband should take only one wife and treat her well; if he struck her for behaving badly, they should look each other in the face and laugh about it, and not bear lasting grudges. Everyone was to make a public confession of past sins and follow the Prophet's teachings. A fire was to be kindled in every lodge, which should never go out lest the inhabitants die. Regular sacrifices should be offered and tribal rituals observed. The Indians should dance and pray daily, morning and evening. The old medicine bags should be destroyed and persons guilty of witchcraft killed. Anyone who rejected the new rules should be cut off. Indians should consider the English, French, and Spanish as friends, but keep away from the Americans. Devout followers would bring the good news to other tribes; they would carry four strings of sacred beans and, by stroking them in the proper manner, converts could "shake the hand of the Prophet." A new village would be built near Greenville where believers could gather to worship the Master of Life and live in a way pleasing to Him.

In March of 1806, the Prophet arrived in Chestnut Tree Place, where Billy Wells had been brought twenty-two years earlier as a captive. The people sat in a circle and the inquisition began. The Prophet identified two old chiefs, Tetepachsit and Hockingpomsga, both signers of the Treaty of Greenville, as witches. Tied to a stake and tortured with fire, Tetapachsit implicated an old Indian named Joshua, interpreter for the nearby Moravian missionaries, who was also killed. Ann Charity, an elderly woman once baptized by the Brethren, was burned on the spot; Billy Patterson, a half-breed well-known to William Wells, was hacked to death by tomahawks.

When it came to executing Hockingpomsga, the Prophet encountered unexpected resistance. The old chief's friends stepped forward, raised their weapons, and threatened to kill anyone who touched him. Harsh threats were exchanged and for a moment, before cooler heads prevailed, it looked like a bloody internecine struggle would break out. This counterrevolution stopped the slaughter, at least for the time being, yet it left the Delaware deeply divided, young against old, just like the Shawnee. No longer welcome on the White River, Tecumseh and his brother, who were rapidly becoming catalysts of Indian discontent, decided to move their village to Ohio.

2

When William Wells learned that a new Shawnee seer had emerged who believed he had been selected by the Great Spirit to destroy witches, and that old chief Tetapachsit and several other miserable wretches had been condemned to the flames in the Delaware towns, he immediately wrote to William Henry Harrison in Vincennes. The governor, in turn, sent a message to the Indians on the White River, warning them of the imposter in their midst: "Who is this pretended prophet who dares to speak in the name of the Great Creator? If he is really a prophet, ask him to cause the sun to stand still—the moon to alter its course—or the dead to rise from their graves. If he does these things, you may then believe that he has been sent by God."

The Prophet accepted Harrison's challenge and predicted that at noon on June 16, 1806, he would use his power to blacken the sun. On the designated day, hundreds of Indians gathered to witness the miracle; they could hear the Prophet praying in his lodge. Just before noon he stepped out, pointed to the sun, and commanded it to paint its face black. Moments later a dark disk passed across the sun, casting an eerie twilight over the earth.

"Did I not speak the truth?" the Prophet demanded. "See, the sun is dark!"

Then he ordered the sun to shine again, and lo, it did, sending a wave of awe through the crowd. As word of these wondrous things spread, Indians from near and far made pilgrimages to visit the Prophet.

It did not take Wells long to figure out the truth. An eclipse of the sun had been predicted; astronomers from Harvard had come west that spring to set up observation stations in the Midwest. A British agent posing as a trader at Greenville had told the Prophet exactly when the event would transpire, thus enabling him to call Harrison's bluff and enhance his prestige.

Soon Wells received many complaints from white settlers and friendly Shawnee about the Prophet's followers at Greenville. He wrote to Secretary of War Dearborn that it was imperative to order their removal, especially since the village was not in Indian territory but in Ohio. During the winter and spring, a steady stream of pilgrims bound for Greenville passed through Fort Wayne, often in a half-starving condition, and Wells was compelled to feed them. He did so reluctantly, telling them he would give them more food if they heeded his advice and went home. Nevertheless, the pilgrims kept coming.

Frustrated with Dearborn's indecisivenss, Wells decided to take the initiative. In April of 1807, he sent Anthony Shane, a half-breed who had grown up in the same village as the Prophet, to Greenville to demand that the town be abandoned.

Wells and Tecumseh had met on occasion over the years, but they had never been friends; in fact, after Wells abandoned the Miami, they had become enemies, and so Tecumseh did not take kindly to Shane's mission.

"Go back to Fort Wayne and tell Captain Wells," he said, "that my fire is kindled on the spot appointed by the Great Spirit; if he has anything to say to me, *he* must come *here*—I shall expect him in six days from this time."

Wells was not about to lose face by acceding to Tecumseh's demands; he sent Shane back to Greenville with another message that only served to enrage both brothers.

"These lands are ours," Tecumseh said at the conclusion of a long speech that recapitulated all the past injustices done to his people by the Long Knives. "No one has the right to remove us, because we were the first owners. The Great Spirit sees no boundaries and neither do we. If the President of the Seventeen Fires has something important to tell me, he must send a man of note. I have nothing more to say to Captain Wells."

"We will not speak to a squaw man like Wells," the Prophet added. "Why does not the President come? I will talk to him. Tell him that I can bring darkness—I can put the sun under my feet. What other man can do this?"

This challenge to his authority infruiated Wells; he was tempted to go to Greenville himself, but Shane finally convinced him that the risk was too great.

The situation in Ohio worsened in May when the mutilated body of a settler was found along a tributary of the Mad River; a tuft of human hair, a deer-hoof rattle, and a war club decorated with black feathers had been placed on his back. The Prophet and Black Hoof accused each other's warriors of the crime. Governor Tiffin sent two emissaries to Greenville to investigate. Along with Blue Jacket, Tecumseh accompanied them to the small settlement of Springfield for a face-to-face confrontation with Black Hoof, which failed to settle the matter, since the murder was actually done by the Potawatomi to avenge a previous killing. In a later meeting at Chillicothe, the state capital, Blue Jacket blamed Wells for any tension between the Shawnee and their white neighbors.

"Brothers, the disturber of our peace is at Fort Wayne," Blue Jacket asserted. "He is a bad man. I want you to take him away and replace him with a good man."

"We hate him," Tecumseh vehemently added. "When the Indians travel to our village, he sets doors to stop them. 'Why go to hear the Prophet?' he asks. He is possessed by the devil. I would rather see a dog with mange than see him. When we want to speak with him, he insults us and treats us like dogs."

The chiefs were told that the President had appointed Wells and only he could remove him. If they could support their charges, they should present their evidence.

Thus Wells once more found himself in the middle; to the Shawnee he provided a convenient scapegoat for their problems with the white settlers of Ohio, while the United States government, preoccupied by the conflict in Europe, did not welcome his dire warnings about trouble brewing on the frontier.

"The Indians are religiously mad," Wells wrote to Eustis, "and believe all the Shawnee Prophet says to them and his intentions are not friendly to peace.... No time should be lost in sending this villain and his insolent band off the lands of the United States."

Wells was certain that neither stern words nor wampum beads would accomplish the removal of the Prophet and his followers from Greenville; he urged the governor of Ohio to order the state militia to compel them to leave by destroying their houses and cornfields. When that suggestion failed, Wells sent a delegation of chiefs to confront the Prophet, but they were rebuffed. Governor Harrison was reluctant to act; he preferred to keep an eye on the Prophet at Greenville—even though, as Wells pointed out, the Indians now had a pretext to gather in large numbers, march close to the settlements, and steal horses.

After Wells returned from his ill-fated trip to Washington— shortly before a smug-faced John Johnston appeared at his doorstep with the letter that ended his career as Indian Agent—he had filed his last official assessment of the Prophet, who had moved from Greenville to a site on the Wabash called Tippecanoe. Wells reported that many Indians had abandoned the Prophet, leaving him with less than a hundred warriors.

"With this handful of men," Wells wrote to Harrison in April of 1809, "I am sure he will attempt nothing. At the same time, it is and always has been my opinion that he only wanted power to make him dangerous."

3

Just when the Prophet's strength was dwindling, Harrison's greedy, land-grabbing Treaty of Fort Wayne in September fanned the flames of Indian discontent anew. In the spring of 1810, as soon as the grass was high enough to feed their horses, hundreds of warriors began arriving at Tippecanoe. They came not only as converts to the new religion but also as fighters for Tecumseh, whose exhortations that no land should be sold without the consent of all the tribes and that the affairs of the Indians should be in the hands of the warriors, not the repudiated government chiefs, fell on sympathetic ears. Thus, in the name of unity, Tecumseh was dividing the old from the young, the peaceful from the hostile, and setting the stage for a showdown.

The name "Tecumseh" had a powerful mystical meaning, suggesting a supernatural panther, often invisible to human sight, either crouching along a path for prey or streaking across the sky like a shooting star. He was from a long line of honored warriors. Back in 1782, when George Rogers Clark's frontiersmen attacked his Shawnee village, the young Tecumseh had panicked and run from his first battle, leaving a wounded brother behind—never again. Although he did not participate in either Harmar's or St. Clair's Defeat, he quickly distinguished himself as a fearless fighter and formidable war chief during raids into Kentucky. While his brother the Prophet urged a return to traditional spiritual ways, Tecumseh's militant vision, which he had tirelessly pursued for years, was to form a confederacy of warriors pledged to defend what remained of their ancestral lands.

At Tippecanoe in June of 1810 Tecumseh stopped a boat carrying eight barrels of annuity salt for the Kickapoo. The enraged war chief grabbed the French boat-master by the hair and shook him violently and cursed him. A Vincennes trader, Michel Brouillette, was called an "American dog" and his house was plundered.

When Harrison learned of this challenge to his authority he sent first Toussaint Dubois then his trusted interpreter, Joseph Barron, to investigate. Barron's visit to Tippecanoe in late July caused apprehension among some of the warriors, who feared he was scouting out their town for Harrison's advancing army, but the Prophet was only filled with scorn.

"Why do you come?" he demanded. "Brouillette was here; he was a spy. Dubois was here; he was a spy. Now you have come. You, too, are a spy." He pointed to the ground at Barron's feet and added, "There is your grave, look on it!"

Fortunately, Tecumseh intervened and asked to hear Harrison's message. Barron told him that the governor declared that the lands he had purchased were sold by their rightful owners, and if he, Tecumseh, had just cause for complaint, he should come see him, present his case, and the land would be restored or a proper compensation given.

Tecumseh arrived in Vincennes on August 12th, accompanied by some seventy-five painted warriors, who camped on the banks of the Wabash above the town. Having sat at the feet of tribal elders as a boy, where he learned to recite with pride the history of the Shawnee, Tecumseh was an eloquent speaker.

"Listen," Tecumseh told Harrison. "When the French came they adopted us as their children and treated us well. They gave us presents and asked for nothing in return. At first, the British treated us the same way; then they put the tomahawk in our hands and many of our people died. Now the Seventeen Fires say they will be our father, and we will be protected; let me remind you of the promises you have made in the past. Was Cornstalk protected when he was murdered at your fort? Was Moluntha protected when he was killed at his village? Were the Moravian Indians safe in their town when the Long Knives came? Since the peace at Greenville, you have killed our people and taken our lands. How can we remain at peace with you if this bad conduct continues?

"I want to unite the Indians as one nation; you want to divide us; you take tribes aside and advise them against me. At

Tippecanoe, we have tried to level all distinctions, destroy the village chiefs who have done bad deeds, and give power to the warriors. We do not accept the treaty of Fort Wayne; the Wea were not present; it was made through the threats of Winamac and signed by chiefs who do not represent us. *None* of our lands can be bought without the consent of *all* the tribes. In two or three moons we shall hold a great council; we shall call those chiefs that sold the land; they shall suffer for what they have done.

"I did not come here to receive presents from you," Tecumseh added. "If you offer me some, I will not take them. If I took them, you would say that I have sold you land. Why should we trust you? How can we have confidence in any white people? When Jesus Christ came upon the earth, you killed him and nailed him to a cross. You thought he was dead, but you were mistaken. I tell you that the Great Spirit inspires me and everything I have said to you is the truth."

Harrison's face reddened at Tecumseh's accusations; when it was his turn to reply he was agitated and spoke more rapidly than usual. He began his standard speech about how humanely the United States had treated the Indians, but the moment he started defending the treaty of Fort Wayne, Tecumseh rose, put his hand on his pipe-tomahawk, and shouted, "You lie, that is false," and launched a tirade of his own, directing his invective specifically at Harrison and Winamac, who was sitting behind the governor; he spoke so fast that Barron was hard pressed to translate his words.

John Gibson, Secretary of the Territory, understood Shawnee, and, realizing the imminent danger of the situation, told Lieutenant Jesse Jennings, "Those fellows intend mischief, bring up the guard with shouldered arms," which act caused the three-dozen warriors assembled on the grass beside Tecumseh to jump to their feet, grasping war clubs, tomahawks, and spears. Winamac recharged his pistol, a few onlookers drew their dirks, others raced back to their homes to get guns. For a suspended moment there was a precarious standoff, accentuated by a pervasive silence and the hair-trigger tempers of the antagonists.

Harrison unsheathed his dress sword and spoke with forced calm to Tecumseh, "Since you have behaved badly, I will put out the council fire and not confer with you again. You and your men are still under my protection, but you must leave immediately." Then he turned on his heel and walked back to his house.

Tecumseh regretted his rash behavior, sent an apology, and requested a private conference with the governor. That night,

Captain Peter Jones paraded his company with fixed bayonets through the streets of the alarmed town. When he met with Harrison the next day, Tecumseh blamed any misunderstandings on two Americans who had visited Tippecanoe, one last winter and the other that summer; they told him the governor had purchased the land against the President's wishes, many opposed the new purchase, and if the Indians would refuse their treaty annuities, the governor's scheme would be exposed and he would be replaced by a good man who would restore their lands. The man who came in the winter, he noted, was at the treaty of Fort Wayne and knew how the Indians were cheated there. He said his visit must be kept secret or he would be hanged. The other said another treaty was planned, but if Tecumseh went to see the governor and made a loud protest he might be able to block it.

Afterwards, Harrison sought to identify the two villainous white men who had met secretly with Tecumseh. He quickly concluded that the one from Vincennes must be none other than his archrival, William McIntosh, a Scotch Tory who for a long time had led an faction against him. But who was the person at Fort Wayne? On second thought, the answer was easy. Who in the past had found fault with Harrison's Indian policy? Who had connived to turn the Miami against him?

"The person alluded to by Tecumseh as giving him information from the Treaty of Fort Wayne," Harrison wrote to Eustis on August 22nd, "is beyond all doubt—William Wells!"

4

During the fall of 1810, William Wells found himself at the center of a maelstrom, blaming him for their troubles seemed to be the only common ground whites and Indians alike could find. When over 1,700 Indians gathered at Fort Wayne in October, John Johnston noted that the Miami were reluctant to come to the council. When they finally arrived, he informed them of Tecumseh's meeting with Harrison. Without mentioning Wells, he told the Miami that certain individuals had been conspiring to have the governor removed from office and warned that such inappropriate actions had no chance of success; whoever advised that course was a bad man; it was a damnable lie that Harrison had purchased their land without the consent of the President.

The next day Pecan, as spokesman for the Miami on the Mississinewa, said, "The Wea are not satisfied with the treaty; there is not enough room for them on this side of the new line. We, the

Miami, are not happy either. We were forced to sign the treaty because the Potawatomi held tomahawks over our heads. We have determined that the treaty must be broken; we do not want to receive any annuities from it this year."

Always flustered by any opposition to his will, Johnston took offense and chided the Indians as if they were spoiled children.

"You no longer talk like our friends, but as followers of the Prophet. It is his voice I hear. Your father is tired of listening to his children speak in fear; when his patience is exhausted, he will send his troops up the Wabash. The treaty was a fair one; you will never regain that land; soon it will be surveyed and settled."

"If you want to hold that land," Pecan warned, "you will have to build a bridge across it."

"Never threaten the United States," Johnston snapped back. "If necessary, we will build a bridge of warriors with rifles in their hands. General Wayne may be dead, but there are many brave men who can take his place."

Johnston gave annuities to those chiefs who would accept them. Only The Sleepy One, chief of the Eel River tribe, who claimed that Wells still owned him from last year, and some thirty of the most militant of the Mississinewa Miami refused and left to seek their supplies from the British at Fort Malden.

Later, The Owl confirmed Johnston's notion that Wells and Little Turtle were the cause of Miami resistance to the treaty.

In October, Wells had gone to Kentucky to solicit the aid of his old friend John Pope, now a United States Senator, to get his job back. Eustis had approved the hiring of Wells as an interpreter the previous January, but Harrison's second thoughts and Johnston's obdurate opposition had effectively blocked his reappointment for almost a year. Johnston now took advantage of Wells's absence from Fort Wayne to restate in a letter to Eustis his loathing for the man he had replaced:

> *The Agency was disgraced and contemptible in his*
> *hands and since his dismissal, although I did nothing*
> *to bring it about, he has done every thing that a bad*
> *man could do, to render the Indians disaffected to the*
> *public cause, and to destroy my influence among them.*
> *In short, there does not exist a worst man. This evil*
> *disposed man was taken prisoner by the Indians at*
> *15 years old, some time after we find him on the Ohio*
> *River under the pretense of being a white man lost*
> *in the woods, inveigling boats to shore and murdering*

> *and plundering the defenseless emigrants descending
> that river. The next place we find him was on the
> memorable 4th of November 1791, fighting with
> the savages against his American brethren under
> St. Clair. To use Wells's own account he killed and
> scalped that day until he could not raise his arms to
> his head. Previous to General Wayne's campaign in
> 1794, he was induced from the temptation of gain
> to join the American Army as a spy. His services
> were highly useful but he was well rewarded for them.*

Johnston asserted that Wells had amassed a personal fortune of $50,000, based largely on money he had defrauded from the government. Even if Wells were honest, Johnston argued, he wasn't educated enough to keep accounts or carry on the necessary correspondence: "his ignorance of letters ought to be an insurmountable objection." It would be, he concluded, "a serious evil to saddle the Indians again with such a rapacious and unprincipled character as Wells."

Harrison remained convinced that Wells was part of a scheme concocted by William McIntosh to arouse the Indians and topple the governor. During his years in Vincennes, Harrison had learned to switch the onus for the miserable condition of the Indians from the inroads of American civilization to the inadequacies of Indian character. He questioned whether Jefferson's policy, insidious as its effects were, wasn't too mild. The savage, Harrison decided, did not desire peace; he was only happy under the influence of some powerful stimulus, such as the intense thrills of combat or the chase. If he hunted in the winter, he must fight in the summer. By encouraging the Indians to live at peace with each other, Jefferson had only induced them to go to war against the whites. Now the only answer was to meet force with superior force. If Wells and McIntosh had encouraged the Indians to resist the government, then they, too, would be crushed.

In November of 1810, Harrison delivered his annual message to the Legislature in Vincennes. The Prophet, Harrison asserted, would not have gained his dangerous influence were it not for British agents and disaffected Americans. These persons were the ones who raised a clamor about the treaty at Fort Wayne, claiming that pressure had been applied to the Miami, the real owners of the land. Although Wells and McIntosh were never mentioned by name, Harrison was maneuvering to bring them to justice once he had sufficient proof. Convinced that the objections to the Treaty of

Fort Wayne were the product of a nefarious conspiracy, he remained blind to the flaws of the treaty itself. He was so deluded that he proposed another treaty: "Is one of the fairest portions of the globe to remain in a state of nature, the haunt of a few wretched savages, when it seems destined by the Creator to support a large population, and be the seat of civilization, science, and true religion?"

Of course the answer from the assembled legislators was a resounding "yes," but Wells, when he learned of Harrison's plans, could smell disaster ahead like a distant rain.

5

In the spring of 1811, there was an ominous mass migration of squirrels, fleeing from the north to the south. On his way to Vincennes in early April, William Wells watched hundreds swimming the Wabash; so many drowned in the attempt that the shore was strewn with small, bedraggled bodies. That month, too, a large comet appeared in northern skies. Rumors were rife in the Indian villages about what these strange signs might portend.

Wells had been summoned to Vincennes to testify for William Henry Harrison in his suit of slander against his old antagonist William McIntosh. Over the winter Harrison had decided that Wells could be useful after all. Dissatisfaction among the Indians had made them highly susceptible to Tecumseh's claim that their lands were the common property of all the tribes. Since the fertile upper Wabash valley would soon be in dispute, the best method of stopping Tecumseh's grand design was to support the Miami as the owners of that country. The chief who most strongly believed that his tribesmen should be the sole proprietors of their land was Little Turtle; the only proven way to influence him was through Wells. Therefore, Harrison reasoned, why not let bygones be bygones and find a way to reinstate him? The charges against him had been brought by his known enemies, such as The Owl and John Johnston; Harrison had not been able to find any evidence that Wells had conspired with McIntosh.

The moment John Johnston learned that Harrison planned to reappoint Wells, he renewed his attack; he warned Eustis in February that Wells was fomenting discontent among the Miami on the Mississinewa, questioning the motives of government Indian policy and the abilities of those who made it. How could Harrison even consider relying on Wells again, Johnston asked, when the governor himself had called him "the most dangerous unprincipled man in the Indian Country"?

Wells had not sat idle while this heated debate about his future was raging. In November he traveled to Washington and met with Secretary of War Eustis. Stating that Johnston planned to resign as Indian Agent at Fort Wayne, Wells asked for his old job back; he was strongly supported in this by Senator John Pope and other influential Kentucky friends. Eustis replied that he was certain Dearborn had sufficient cause to order his removal. Back in January, however, he had approved hiring him as an interpreter, provided Governor Harrison did not object. Wells assured Eustis that his differences with Harrison were settled and the governor now required his services.

Finally, in February 1811, Harrison had informed Wells that he was employed in the Indian Department, at $365 a year, but in an unspecified capacity, with no tribe under his control and no power to act on his own initiative. Having been batted back and forth by bureaucrats for two years, Wells was once again on the government payrole. That was where matters stood in April when Wells rode into Vincennes on the hope that his testimony would fully restore him to the governor's good graces.

William McIntosh, the largest landowner in the area, was outspoken in his criticism of the governor's conduct. He said that the treaty of Greenville had been dominated by the powerful Potawatomi; that Harrison had stacked the negotiations with chiefs of his own choosing; that defrauding the Indians of their land had strengthened the confederacy led by the Shawnee Prophet and Tecumseh. When Harrison learned of these accusations—which, if true, might ruin his present reputation and his anticipated place in history—he brought an action of slander against McIntosh, demanding $9,000 in damages.

McIntosh's attorney argued that his client had indeed publically questioned the governor's Indian policy, but he had done so hypothetically: McIntosh had stated that *if* the governor had done such and so, *then* and in that case he ought to be deprived of the honor and emoluments of his office. Harrison's Cincinnati lawyer brushed aside these grammatical niceties and dismissed the defense's argument as a mere *protestando,* namely an oblique, not a direct denial of the accusations, and thus entirely nugatory, or, in Sir. Edward Coke's phrase, "The exclusion of a conclusion." Hence, the case stood and would go to trial.

In spite of feeling guilty about his complicity in the Fort Wayne treaty, Wells was one of twenty-five witnesses who appeared on Harrison's behalf before a crowded courtroom.

"I've been at a lot of treaties," Wells testified, speaking the words that he knew were expected of him. "I saw nothing on the governor's part that was objectionable. In fact, his conduct was exemplary; he explained the terms fully several times and the Miami signed of their own free will, not because of pressure from the Potawatomi."

The trial lasted all day; many facets of Harrison's conduct in office were rigorously examined, but the verdict was never in doubt. Within the hour, McIntosh was found guilty of speaking defamatory words and Harrison was awarded $4,000, which would be raised by selling the defendant's possessions and property.

Afterwards, a vindicated Harrison was in an expansive mood.

"You're all invited to McCandless' Tavern," he announced to the smiling circle of witnesses and jurymen. "Drinks are on me."

Wells welcomed the invitation; he needed to wash the bad taste out of his mouth. It seemed that everything he did to reinstate himself only made his situation worse.

A few days later Harrison met with Wells in private.

"I want to thank you personally for your forthright testimony," Harrison said with a solemnity that banished any sense of irony. He paused and then spoke again with obvious relish. "We made that rascally calumniator McIntosh beg for mercy!"

"I was glad to help," Wells replied.

"Yes, yes, of course, I appreciate that. I have never doubted your talents. Now I would like to ask a further service of you."

Wells stood in suspense, staring intently at the governor in an effort to read his thoughts.

"Renegade Potawatomi warriors have been running amok in the west. Last July, they raided a settlement in Missouri and stole some deerskins, buffalo robes, and horses. Captain William Cole and five others found the abandoned peltry, but that night they were ambushed while they were sleeping. Cole and three of his men were killed and their camp was plundered; the culprits fled back to Main Poche's village on the Kankakee. Later they were seen at Tippecanoe."

"Are you sure they're Main Poche's men?"

"I'm not, but isn't he their greatest war chief?"

"He is that."

"Hasn't he always been a part of the Prophet's confederacy?"

"Only on his own terms," Wells admitted from hard-won experience. "He always does exactly what he wants. Last fall he raided the Osage and got wounded pretty bad. He's been holed up in a village near Lake Peoria all winter recovering."

"All right, then, let's leave Main Poche out of this for now. What I want you to do is go to Tippecanoe and see what you can find out about the Cole ambush and the stolen horses. While you're there, inspect the village and bring me your estimation of Tecumseh's strength and intentions. I plan to establish a strong post and display a respectable force on the Wabash."

"I know they're up to no good," Wells replied, "but right now they're not in any condition to make trouble. Their numbers are down and they're short of food."

"The more abject their misery, the more those half-starved savages resent our prosperity." Harrison spoke in an overwrought voice. "They are the most treacherous, cunning rascals on earth, fickle, heedless of futurity, they will cut down the tree to get the fruit and kill a teeming doe for a present feast. They are capable of the rashest of actions. I believe a crisis is fast approaching."

"I would have destroyed that scoundrel the Prophet years ago," Wells boasted, unaware of how much he had begun to echo his old commander Mad Anthony Wayne. Years of frustration at his thwarted efforts to shape Indian policy had left Wells thirsting for a good fight. He was tired of speaking other men's words and wanted once again to be a man of action. "If you want, I could lead a force against the Indians myself."

"That won't be necessary," Harrison replied briskly.

"Can I take John Conner with me?" Wells asked. "I sent him to Tippecanoe a couple of years ago to recover some stolen horses."

"Certainly, and report back to me as soon as possible. You will find me not ungrateful for what you have accomplished. I plan to write to Mr. Eustis on your behalf."

"Thank you, Sir," Wells said, already weighing the risks and calculating the benefits of his new assignment. "My only desire is to serve my country," he added, employing his favorite formula.

Harrison did write to Eustis, praising Wells's superior abilities while once more expressing concerns about working with a man of such questionable character and suspect loyalties: "Could I be allowed to dispose of Wells as I thought proper, my first wish would be to place him in the interior of our settlements, where he would never see & scarcely hear of an Indian."

6

Tippecanoe, also known as Prophetstown, was situated in an extensive clearing on the north bank of the Wabash below the mouth of the Tippecanoe River. The town was laid out more symmetrically than most Indian villages, with rows of bark-sided wigwams running from the riverbank up a gradual bluff to an adjoining prairie. In addition to the usual long council house, a sizeable log-and-bark House of Strangers stood at the water's edge and, on higher ground, a small, solidly built structure served as the Prophet's medicine lodge, with a dais in front where he often sat to receive pilgrims from faraway tribes. In spite of the Prophet's injunctions, a few farm animals were visible; extensive cornfields spread along the bottomlands.

Despite their past animosities, the Shawnee brothers greeted Wells and Conner cordially and treated them with the respect due to visiting dignitaries, offering them food and drink before smoking pipes and beginning serious talks. Conner's life had been in many respects a duplicate of Wells's; he had grown up among the Delaware, married into the tribe, and devoted much of his time as a trader and interpreter to protecting their interests. Yet he had never stirred up the bursts of controversy that always swirled around Wells; whites and Indians alike welcomed his company and the two men had cooperated on various projects in the past.

The contrast between Tecumseh and his brother could not have been more marked. Even though his visions had given the Prophet the power and veneration he had always longed for, Wells felt immediately that something suspect and unsavory emanated from the man now called The Open Door. Seasoned as he was, Wells couldn't help but recoil at the unnerving spectacle of his maimed right eye, which he had put out himself in a boyhood accident with a bow and arrow. Often he covered it with a black patch; when he didn't, as on this occasion, the upper lid drooped down to almost cover the iris, leaving only a blood-streaked sliver, reminiscent of a sunset, in view. The cheek on that side retained a permanently discolored bulge, giving his face a lopsided look. He wore a mustache that accented the scowl on his wide mouth. His head was wrapped in a gray, silken turban, dotted with black spots; his cheeks were daubed with red lines that suggested deep scratches; he wore a silver nose bob, a silver gorgon at his neck, and pendant earrings that touched his collarbone. The general effect was of a sulky, morose man with a chip on each shoulder.

Tecumseh was five feet nine, about an inch taller and two years older than Wells; he had a broad chest, strong shoulders, and muscular limbs. His movements bespoke energy and resolution, even though he walked bow-legged with a slight limp, having once broken his thigh while hunting buffalo. He dressed in fringed buckskin, his treasured silver-mounted pipe tomahawk, leather-sheathed knife, and otter-skin pouch at his belt; a large silver George the Third medallion hung from his neck on a multi-colored string of wampum, three small silver coronets served as a nose bob, and a single white feather, dipped in red at the top, adorned his hair. He had a copper-tan complexion, relatively light for an Indian, and his eyes were a rare hazel, deep-set beneath a high forehead and thick black brows. They were his most striking feature—alight with intelligence and flashes of insight, darting from here to there in a quest for more information, then pausing to submit someone to a sustained stare that seemed to absorb the very soul—Wells could hardly keep himself from flinching under his unrelenting gaze.

He was by any standards a handsome man. No wonder women were drawn to him, although he showed little interest in them. He had taken and rejected wife after wife at whim (one was discarded after she failed to pluck a turkey properly) and fathered one son—clearly his mind was elsewhere. Once, back in Greenville, he offered a white neighbor fifty silver broaches to mate with his teenage daughter. Women had their uses but were not essential to achieving his grand design.

"I thought the British supplied you with every necessity," Wells remarked sardonically. "Why do your warriors kill our settlers and steal their furs and horses?"

"I never spoke to the British," the Prophet insisted, pausing to pack his pipe from his skunk-skin tobacco pouch, "and I never sent for any Indians. They came here themselves to listen to the word of the Great Spirit."

"What I hear is that you claim to be God."

"I have the power to cause and cure illness," the Prophet declared. "I know a witch when I see one. I have put my foot on the sun. I lead all who believe from darkness to light."

Because of his bad eye, Wells had the impression that he was winking at him. "If it's true you're God," Wells drawled, "you shouldn't steal horses. Governor Harrison hangs horse thieves."

"You might as well cut a man's throat as take his horse," John Conner added. "How else can he work his fields and support his family?"

"I have no fear of the Americans," the Prophet brashly remarked, tapping out his pipe. "They are nothing but the scum of the Great Sea where the Evil Serpent dwells; long ago they were blown like froth into the woods by a strong east wind." At that point he rose from his mat, bent forward and slightly to one side, farted loudly, smacked his hand on his backside, and sneered, "I care no more for the white man than that. If Harrison comes here, we will overthrow his men as easily as that basin of water," which he then kicked aside before walking away.

Tecumseh had been sitting quietly and listening intently. Now he turned his full attention to Wells and Conner.

"The Potawatomi warriors who killed the white people and stole horses were not under my control. I am sorry for what they did." His regret sounded genuine.

"Then you must know who they are," Wells observed.

"They are not ashamed of their deeds," Tecumseh replied. "Mad Sturgeon and his band were here, but they have returned to the west. You must seek them there. I can give you four of the captured horses. If I find more, I will return them."

Tecumseh spoke with unadorned directness, as though to equivocate during a formal parley were beneath him. Still, Wells knew, his show of honesty could serve to hide a deeper deception.

"I have received several reports that you plot in secret to attack the settlements," Wells said. "You must know that the soldiers of the Seventeen Fires are as numerous as the trees in the forest; if you start a war you will be destroyed."

"They do not think we are sufficiently good to live," Tecumseh said with sudden bitterness. "We are driven before them like dry leaves in a winter wind. Should we sit patiently on our mats and wait to be murdered as our fathers were? Or should we unite, form one body, one heart, and protect our country and the graves of our ancestors? I hear in every breeze the voices of our dead fathers calling to us to take a stand. We do not fear the white soldiers; they make fat targets to shoot at; they are afraid to die and we are not. Our lives are in the hands of the Great Spirit; we are determined to defend our lands; if it is his wish we will leave our bones to whiten upon them."

"What about the treaty?" Wells persisted. "Will you let the surveyors mark the boundary?"

"The Great Spirit sees no boundaries and neither do we—there is nothing to survey. We do not recognize that pretended treaty.

You were there, you participated, you know very well it was not fair. Those who signed had lost their senses."

"Harrison did not give the Indians any whiskey until the treaty was completed."

"Their thirst was enough," Tecumseh replied sternly. "If the surveyors come they will survey no more. We will not permit white settlement on our lands."

"Listen to me," Wells earnestly pleaded, pausing at every word for emphasis. "Resistance is impossible. There are too many soldiers, too many guns; you can only lose. What you hope to accomplish will never take place."

"It will come sooner than you think." Tecumseh spoke with calm assurance, giving Wells a sustained, probing look that appeared to combine triumph with sadness. "It will not be long; if you are lucky, you might live long enough to see it."

7

In the late spring, after Wells had returned to Fort Wayne, the Wea frightened the surveyors off their land and the Prophet seized the salt annuity Harrison had sent by pirogue to Tippecanoe.

"Tell the governor not to be angry," he said. "We did not receive any salt last year and now I have two thousand men to feed."

Harrison sent a message that demanded satisfaction for seizing the salt and warned about the consequences of starting a war: "Brothers, I am myself of the Long Knife fire; as soon as they hear my voice, you will see swarms of hunting shirt men pouring forth, as numerous as the mosquitoes on the shores of the Wabash; brothers, take care of their stings."

Tecumseh had been absent from Tippecanoe when the salt was taken; now he promised to come to Vincennes in order to ease Harrison's heart and wash away all the bad stories that had been circulating. The governor welcomed his visit, but insisted that he bring only a few warriors.

For over a year Harrison's constant theme with Secretary of War Eustis was a request for a strong force to march up the Wabash and demand the dispersion of the people gathered at Tippecanoe. Preoccupied by problems with England, France, and Spain, President Madison had no desire for warfare with the Indians, but he left the actual statement of his policies to Eustis, who knew nothing of the frontier and answered Harrison's militant entreaties with equivocations, which Harrison brushed aside. He had read his Julius Caesar well enough to know that sometimes the road to Rome led through Gaul. When Madison and the rest of the Revolutionary generation died off, who better to head the nation than the man who had rid the Northwest Territory of Tecumseh's band of savages?

Tecumseh's arrival above Vincennes in late July with more than a hundred warriors alarmed the residents. Harrison called out the militia and a detachment of dragoons. On July 30, 1811, the two men met in an arbor near his house, Grouseland. Tecumseh's warriors left their guns in their camp and carried only scalping knives, tomahawks, and war clubs while armed dragoons stood guard around the governor and the militia paraded conspicuously through the streets.

In Harrison's opening address he mentioned the murders in Illinois Territory and the spreading fear among the settlers. The governor stated that the Treaty of Fort Wayne was not subject to negotiation; any complaints Tecumseh might have on that score should be made in person to President Madison. He then demanded to know why the salt was seized.

"I was not present," Tecumseh explained. "Why has this action upset you?"

"It is a violation of a treaty and an insult to this government."

"You are a difficult man to please," Tecumseh remarked calmly. "Last year you were angry when we rejected the salt; this year it is because we took it."

At that point a sudden thunderstorm forced a postponement of the meeting. On the following afternoon the Wea chief, The Orator, asserted that Winamac and his Potawatomi warriors had held the tomahawk over the head of the Miami who signed the Treaty of Fort Wayne. Harrison strenuously denied this accusation and then turned his attention once more to Tecumseh.

"If you want to live in peace with us," Harrison said, "you can show your friendship by a single act: surrender to us the Potawatomi who killed Captain Cole and the others on the Missouri."

"I told Captain Wells and I tell you, they were not under my command."

"They were seen at Tippecanoe."

"Yes, but they have returned to their own country."

"If you know where they are," Harrison said, "then you should bring them to me."

"Perhaps they should be forgiven what they have done," Tecumseh said in a conciliatory voice. "I and my people have had to forgive many murders the whites have committed against us. Settlers were killed in Illinois, so were my people. I have often taken the tomahawk out of the hands of warriors who wanted to avenge these deaths. I have worked long and hard to unite the northern tribes under my direction. This should not alarm you; we intend nothing but peace. When the Seventeen Fires united, we did not complain. Why should you complain when we follow your example? We want our people and your people to live at peace with each other. I am about to set out on a long journey to the southern tribes; I will invite them to join us as one united people. When I return in the spring, we can resolve all our differences."

"What about the surveyors?" Harrison insisted.

"I want the present boundaries to stay as they are," Tecumseh said. "In the fall we expect a large number of Wyandot and Mingo at Tippecanoe. They will need that area as a hunting ground. They might kill the cattle and hogs of any new settlers, and that would only produce more trouble. I want everything to remain as it is until my return. There should be no new settlements by the whites; none of my people will seek to revenge past injuries. When I return I will go see President Madison and I will discuss everything with him. Now I give you this wampum to cover the dead."

By the time Tecumseh had finished talking it was early evening. Harrison pointed to the sky and said that the moon would fall to the earth before President Madison would suffer his people to be murdered with impunity—and that he would put his warriors in petticoats sooner than he would give up a country which he had acquired fairly.

A few days later Tecumseh again assured Harrison of his peaceful intentions; then, accompanied by twenty of his men, he set off down the Wabash for the South.

8

If Tecumseh had intended his visit to Vincennes as a gesture of reconciliation that would preserve the status quo while he recruited warriors among the Choctaw, Creek, and Cherokee, he had badly miscalculated. His absence gave Harrison a perfect opportunity to break up his confederacy. Ironically, the governor was so impressed with Tecumseh's abilities that he felt compelled to take decisive action before he could return and assert his remarkable leadership.

Harrison's plan was to present all the tribes with a set of preemptory demands that would force them to choose sides and show their allegiance. They must turn over the Potawatomi warriors who had been raiding the frontiers and require everyone who had joined the Prophet to renounce him. The Miami, in particular, must

322   *Blacksnake's Path*

order the Prophet and his followers off their land. Any tribe that failed to comply would be exterminated or driven across the Mississippi. By mid-September Harrison would march up the Wabash, build a fort on the site of the former Wea towns, and cross into Indian Territory for a showdown with the people of Prophetstown. President Madison should rest assured, Harrison told Eustis, that these measures would preserve the peace.

Harrison's message to the Miami was blunt. A dark cloud hung over the Wabash and thunder sounded. Soon the storm would burst over their heads. The time of decision had arrived.

When a trader in Vincennes brought this message to Fort Wayne, Wells knew that it would cause a furor among the Miami. What had they done to arouse the governor's ire? Why this sudden uncompromising militancy? In his letters to Eustis, Wells contradicted Harrison, reporting that the sporadic Indian raids in Illinois were not a part of Tecumseh's conspiracy; they had been committed by renegade Iowa, Menominee, and Potawatomi warriors, who, returning from a failed attack on the Osage, had taken out their frustration by killing a few settlers. The Prophet, he stated, did not have as strong an influence over the Indians as many supposed; any support he did have among the Miami was because of John Johnston's mismanagement as Indian factor and agent at Fort Wayne. He had, in effect, resigned his post months ago and moved to Piqua, in Ohio, leaving John Shaw, a well-intentioned Quaker, to look after things in his absence. If a better-qualified person were appointed, Wells argued, the Miami would no longer heed the words of the Prophet.

In early September, 350 Miami gathered in front of the public store at Fort Wayne to hear Wells translate Harrison's message. The next morning they assembled again to give their response.

The Orator denied that his people were walking a bad path and wondered at Harrison's unprovoked anger.

"Father—we the Miami are not a passionate people: we are not made angry as easily as it appears you are! Our hearts are as heavy as the earth! Our minds are not easily irritated. We don't tell people we are angry with them for light causes; if we flew into a rage for no reason, we would appear contemptible in the eyes of others. We hope you will say no more that you are angry with us, or you will make yourself contemptible to others. We are determined to keep our lands; if they are invaded, we will be angry but once and defend them to the last man."

When it was Little Turtle's turn to speak, Wells had to help him to his feet. Almost incapacitated by the gout, he was a shadow of his former self and far less able to assert his leadership; Harrison's belligerent message had only added to his distress.

"Father—you have told us you would draw a line; that your children would stand on one side and the Prophet on the other. We the Miami wish to be considered in the same light by you as we were at the Treaty of Greenville; we still hold fast to that treaty which united us, Miami and Potawatomi, to the Seventeen Fires.

"Father—listen to what I have to say! Do not bloody our ground, if you can avoid it. Let the Prophet be requested, in mild terms, to comply with your wishes and avoid, if possible, the spilling of blood. The lands on the Wabash are ours. We have not placed the Prophet there; on the contrary, we tried to stop him. What he has done was without our permission. We are not pleased by his actions, but you should have no reason to doubt our friendship. That is all I have to say. My words are few but my meaning is great. I ask you to pay attention to what I have said."

The chiefs met for most of the night, debating whether The Orator had spoken too harshly or Little Turtle too softly

"Our tomahawks shall fall upon the heads of any Miami who accept annuities from the Seventeen Fires this fall," The Orator declared with the vociferous backing of many of the young Miami warriors. "Little Turtle will be the first to die."

"Kill me if you wish," Little Turtle answered, a spark of defiance in his eyes. "I know I will not see many more winters, but if you seek my death know that I will not die alone."

Little Turtle's warriors shouted their approval and for a tense moment it appeared that the Miami would slaughter each other. The next day Wells watched The Orator and his followers leave for Fort Malden to ask the British for arms and ammunition.

After they left, Wells met with He Who Sits Quietly, head chief of the Potawatomi, Five Medals, and Little Turtle; he persuaded them to send a joint message to Harrison affirming their commitment to peace.

"It is true that some of our foolish young men have been deluded by the Shawnee Prophet," Little Turtle admitted with regret, "and made to follow a path that is filled with thorns and briers. We pray that you will have pity on these foolish people, forgive them the crimes they have committed, and incline your heart to be kind to your red brethren."

9

At the same time William Wells was working to preserve the peace, Harrison was in Louisville talking to Sam Wells and making preparations for war.   Anti-British feeling was running high in Kentucky and people were calling not only for an attack on Prophetstown but also an invasion of Canada.   Sam promised Harrison a hundred mounted riflemen, experienced Indian fighters all, once the harvest was over in October.   Harrison then crossed the river to Jeffersonville to greet Lieutenant John Boyd's 4th Regiment, which had been raised in New England and recently stationed in Pittsburgh.   They were a sight to see in their brass-buttoned, swallow-tailed coats, skin-tight pants, and high, stovepipe hats with a red, white, and blue cockade on top.

As soon as Tecumseh had left for the South, Harrison launched a campaign to gain government support for a confrontation with the Prophet.   In his correspondence with Eustis, Harrison defended his aggressive strategy.

Harrison's final instructions from Eustis prohibited starting a war with Britain, but left fighting the Indians to Harrison's discretion.   Wells, back in Fort Wayne, had been deliberately left out of Harrison's plans and would not learn of his preemptory strike until it was well underway.

Harrison's troops, comprised of Boyd's trained but untested regiment, companies of local militia, and a body of dragoons under Major Jo Daviess, a Kentucky fire-eater whose craving for glory even exceeded that of his commander, marched to Terre Haute, the site of a former Wea village.

On October 27th Major Daviess broke a bottle of bourbon on the main gate to christen Fort Harrison.   A few days later Sam arrived with two mounted companies—one led by William Wells's father-in-law Frederick Geiger—of rifle-toting, buckskin-clad Indian fighters, each with a big knife and a small axe in his belt.   Harrison, sporting a long calico hunting shirt and a round beaver hat with an ostrich plume, made Sam a Major in charge of the Kentuckians.   Then the army headed into Indian country.

On a misty morning in early November the troops came in sight of Prophetstown.   They were met by Chief White Horse carrying a white flag.   He expressed surprise at their hostile advance, since the Prophet had sent chiefs Catfish and Little Eyes to negotiate; unfortunately they had sought the army on the wrong side of the Wabash.   Harrison vowed that he would not attack the village if the Prophet accepted his stated demands; the two sides agreed to a truce

until a conference could be held the following day. When Harrison
inquired about a well-watered place to camp, the chief suggested
some high ground a mile to the northwest.

Back at Tippecanoe a debate raged among the Indians whether
they should flee, fight, or negotiate. Many Kickapoo, Winnebago,
and Potawatomi warriors were eager for battle; those who wanted to
hear what Harrison had to say were shouted down. The Prophet
wavered, uncertain what to do; he knew that Tecumseh had
admonished him to keep the peace until his return, but his visions
told him that now was the time for a surprise attack. A captured
black army cook had been brought to the village; under threat of
death, he swore that Harrison's plan was not to negotiate but to
deceive the Indians and destroy the village. This information
emboldened the warriors to take action. The Prophet in a vision had
seen the Americans fall; half would be dead the moment the battle
began and the other half would wander about blindly in the dark like
crazy men. Harrison himself would be riding a white horse; if he
were killed the rest could be shot down like so many pigeons.
Moved by this prophecy, the warriors blackened their faces for
battle and dipped the tips of their arrows and the muzzles of their
guns in a magic potion the Prophet had prepared to guarantee
victory.

The attack came in the darkest corner of the night. Rain clouds
covered the moon; the only light was the gleam of scattered
campfires; the sentries could not see three feet ahead in the cold,
murky drizzle. The brunt of it was directed at Frederick Geiger's
company on the far northwest corner of the camp. A sentry was
killed near the captain's tent; he and a few of his men instantly
engaged in hand-to-hand combat. Geiger discharged his pistol into
the breast of one warrior trying to tomahawk him and received a
bullet wound in the arm. Soon all was confusion as Kentuckians
and Indians fought furiously in the dark. In the first frenzy of battle
a dozen raw recruits on the left side of Geiger's line broke and ran.
The Indians took advantage of this breach to fire on Barton's
company as well, shooting down three men tending the campfires.
In spite of the sudden onslaught of the Indians, most of Barton's and
Geiger's men formed quickly and held their lines; but on the right
two militia companies from Kentucky and Indiana retreated, leaving
Geiger's position exposed to enemy snipers on three sides.

Harrison was conferring with Sam Wells when the shooting
started. He ordered his servant to bring him his light-gray mare,
which could not be found, so he mounted a bay and rode toward

Geiger's company, where the fighting was most intense. When some Indians who had infiltrated the camp saw Harrison's aide on a white horse, they opened fire, killing him instantly. Waller Taylor, riding Harrison's mare, was also mistaken for the commander; a volley killed his horse and left him pinned beneath it.

Harrison ordered two infantry companies forward to support Geiger's position, which buckled but did not break. Meanwhile, the fighting had spread across the entire perimeter. The Indians fought with desperate tenacity, rushing up as close as possible, firing at point blank range, and then retreating just as rapidly to reload. Then all would be silent until at a whistled signal, or a deer-hoof rattle, they would surge forward again, yelling their war cries, while others crawled ahead on hands and knees in the high grass. One band found cover behind some oak trees, where they unleashed galling volleys at targets of opportunity. The soldiers did their best to put out the campfires that exposed their position, even though moving into the light to do so was often lethal. As musket balls smashed into the campfires, red-hot embers flew in all directions, briefly illuminating the field of battle.

Harrison rode back and forth in an effort to shore up his defenses and keep his lines intact. His commanding voice could be heard above the din, ordering companies to this flank or that.

"I wish to God you'd let me charge those god-damned savages," Major Daviess shouted, pointing at a clump of oak trees close by that harbored enemy snipers.

He urgently repeated his request three times before Harrison finally consented, "Take the dragoons and dislodge them."

Because of the dark, the confined space, and the swampy ground, Daviess's dragoons were dismounted; he selected eight men—too few for such a risky mission—and they proceeded Indian file, armed with pistol and sword, groping their way ahead. Dressed in a white blanket surtout, Daviess presented an obvious target; before he had advanced twenty feet several guns flashed; he twisted in his tracks and sunk to the ground, crying out, "I'm a dead man." One other dragoon was fatally hit, but three more ran up and fired, forcing the Indians to retreat.

For an hour the fighting in the dark remained intense; the Indians continued to rush forward, shoot, and withdraw, while Harrison's lines took steady casualties but held. Powder smoke drifted among the dripping trees like ghosts of the lost. When men were shot, some shrieked with pain, others said simply "Oh," as if they had forgotten something. Captain Spier Spencer had brought his twelve-year-old son along for his baptism of fire; the boy had watched in horror as his father was hit first in the head, then the legs, then the body before he died; his two lieutenants fell beside him. During lulls in the battle, the chant of the Prophet rang out:

> *We shall conquer if we are brave*
> *The water will wash them away*
> *The wind will blow them down*
> *Darkness will come upon them*
> *The Earth will cover them*

As the first streaks of sunlight penetrated the trees, the Indians, their supply of arrows and ammunition dwindling, retreated to Tippecanoe. When Sam Wells noted the enemy forces thinning, he gathered a group of Kentuckians and some regulars and mounted a charge against the Indians on one flank, driving them back into the swamp where they could not be pursued. Lieutenant Boyd, whose 4th Regiment had fought with great courage, launched a bayonet charge on another flank with similar results.

The early morning light revealed the bloody cost of victory; the bodies of the slain covered the ground. Forty soldiers were buried in two trenches, thirty more would die later of their wounds; the piteous cries of the injured filled the air.

Laughing soldiers took pot shots at a lone, badly wounded Potawatomi warrior, who was seen staggering across the prairie; he fell before he reached the cover of the trees; four Kentuckians went out and brought back his scalp, which they cut into equal parts and stuck on their ramrods as trophies. The same was done with the scalps of other dead Indians.

A Potawatomi chief was found still alive, his legs ripped by buckshot; the only thing that might save him was amputation, but he refused and said he would prefer to die. He placed the blame for the battle on the Prophet, who had promised that the soldiers would throw down their guns in a mad panic, but instead they had fought like devils. He was sure the Potawatomi would never again believe the Prophet's lying words.

The next day Sam Wells and his mounted riflemen were sent to inspect the town; it was deserted except for one old squaw who had been left to die. Since the army's beef cattle had been taken by the Indians, and the only alternative was to dine on horse flesh, the soldiers sacked the village for provisions. Anything that wasn't plunder was torched. By morning all that remained of Tippecanoe were smoldering ashes.

Fort Dearborn

1

At two o'clock on the morning of December 16, 1811, William Wells and his family in Fort Wayne were awoken by a sudden shuddering of the earth. They rushed from their house, which shook to its wooden foundations but remained standing. That was only the first of a series of massive quakes, all centered near the village of New Madrid, in Louisiana Territory. The shock sundered the ground into gaping fissures, caved in the riverbank, and flattened the town; the ruins were swept away by the surging currents of the Mississippi. Subsequent major quakes over the next two months cracked brick walls and toppled chimneys in Cincinnati, temporarily reversed the flow of the Mississippi above St. Louis, and rang church bells as far away as Boston. Whites and Indians alike pondered the portent of these mighty tremors.

Upon his return to the Wabash valley in early January, Tecumseh declared that the Great Spirit was stomping his foot in anger over what had happened at Tippecanoe. Certainly, *he* was infuriated with the Prophet for attacking Harrison in his absence. As though he were an earthquake embodied, Tecumseh grabbed a fistful of his brother's hair and shook him until his brains rattled.

"I ought to kill you," he hissed. "You deserve to die like a dog."

"I had a vision," the Prophet pleaded. "The Master of Life told me that the Big Knives would be blind in the dark while the warriors could see—but my magic was bad because my wife, who helped me prepare the sacred bowl, did not tell me she was in her blood moon."

Only a few of the followers Tecumseh had gathered so diligently over the years remained; Tippecanoe had been burned to the ground, the corn destroyed, and a hard winter had set in. The remnant camped on Wildcat Creek north of their ruined village, licked their wounds, and tried to survive until spring.

From early accounts of Tippecanoe, William Wells learned that Harrison had triumphed over 1,000 warriors, killing at least 100;

later he was told that barely 300 braves took part, less than thirty were slain, and the action was abandoned only because they ran out of arrows and ammunition. More than one participant now boasted that he was the equal of four white men.

Wells's first impulse was to gather some trusted Miami and lead another strike against that vile imposter the Prophet. What better way to rid the country of a notorious scoundrel, vindicate his own reputation, and solidify his position with the government? If he and his small band could accomplish something Harrison's army could not, what glory might be his! The Miami warriors, however, were less than enthusiastic about the project, and John Johnston was adamantly opposed, telling the Indians that Wells was actuated by sinister motives. Wells, in turn, angling for a challenge, accused Johnston of base and cowardly conduct.

Tippecanoe was the only important engagement on the northwest frontier in over twenty years that Wells had not participated in. It galled him that his brother Sam and his father-in-law Frederick Geiger, both in their fifties, had played prominent roles in the fight. Although he was only forty-one, he wondered if he was past his prime, on the downward path to death. How long had it been since he'd killed a man? For some reason, the question had begun to haunt him. He could still see the scene in his mind's eye: It was the day he'd been wounded, before the battle of Fallen Timbers, back in 1794—eighteen years ago; he'd gotten in a clean shot, as he was riding off, and seen a Delaware brave fall into the campfire. An old squaw screamed and a young man, probably the warrior's son, had loaded and aimed so fast he forgot to retract the ramrod, and *that* was what had shattered Wells's wrist. Why was he remembering those old stories? They came back so vividly—perhaps he should try to write them down.

Wells contemplated telling the story of his captivity and what living with the Miami on the Eel River was like when Fort Wayne was still Kekionga. He recalled the day The Porcupine told him that his new name would be Blacksnake, and that he would walk a winding path and think twisted thoughts. What a true prophecy that had proved to be. He could write about his friendship with Little Turtle and describe the chief's victories over generals Harmar and St. Clair; he might even tell about Laughing Eyes, Sweet Breeze, and other Indian women he had known—but then again, maybe not; Polly would read the manuscript and give him grief. Maybe he shouldn't be too personal. In fact, the more he thought about it, the less likely it seemed that white readers would understand his exploits as a Miami warrior. How could he explain why he had waylaid a flatboat on the Ohio? Or taken that man's scalp—what did they call him?—Filson. Or the boy under the bed—that was the worst. Best not to think about it. Best to forget.

Nevertheless, Wells did indeed begin to write that winter, but in a more general vein: *The Miami Nation is composed of the oldest inhabitants of this country. The Eel River tribe, the Wea, the Piankashaw and Kaskaskia, are branches or tribes of the Miami Nation, and all speak one language....* He completed a description of the manners and customs of the Miami and a brief account of the various battles the Indians fought in defense of their land north of the Ohio, then he put the manuscript aside. Perhaps it was still too soon to tell the story of his life. Besides, there wasn't time; Tecumseh had returned to the Wabash and the United States was on the verge of war.

Fortunately, Harrison was not aware that Wells had joined the chorus of criticism of what had transpired at Tippecanoe. First his aide Waller Taylor, although pinned beneath his horse during the battle, stated that confusion had prevailed because the troops had been lulled into a false sense of security by the Prophet's promise to parley; next Captain Boyd claimed that the dastardly conduct of the militia had caused the deaths of several officers, and that only the heroic exertions of the regulars and a few gallant Kentuckians led by Sam Wells had saved the day; then John Johnston and others published the Indian version of the how they had more than held their own against a vastly superior force. Harrison's critics in Vincennes pounced on these assertions and gave them wide play, mocking the governor turned commander and lamenting his incompetent response to the continuing Indian threat.

Sam Wells, for his part, defended Harrison's conduct; at a dinner he hosted in December for veterans of Tippecanoe at his plantation outside Louisville, they toasted the heroism and bravery of both the militia and regulars and appealed to the God of Mars and the Eagle of America to destroy the British Lion. The final toast— "May the starry flag of 1812 soon triumphantly fly over the ramparts of Quebec!"—was endorsed by seventeen cheers.

His future on the line, Harrison collected affidavits from as many officers as possible; unanimously they swore that their commander had chosen his ground wisely, prepared his troops properly, and that everyone—with the exception of two companies who broke and ran—had fought valiantly under his inspiring leadership. President Madison was not at all pleased with the governor's preemptive strike and urged him to make peace with the Indians as quickly as possible.

In an effort to buy time to rebuild his coalition, Tecumseh informed Harrison that he was willing to go to Washington. Other chiefs followed his example, humbly supplicating for peace.

"Father, I throw the tomahawk on the ground," the Wea chief Stone Eater stated. "All my people who were killed are as dirt, I think no more of them. The dead look from the ground toward their father and wish once more they could speak to him."

At first Harrison accepted these protestations of peace at face value and announced that his victory at Tippecanoe had ensured the tranquility of the frontier; he even assumed that elements of the friendly tribes—the Delaware, Miami, Eel River, Wea and Potawatomi—would help protect the settlements from renegades and drive the Prophet's followers away from Tippecanoe.

Reports from the frontier itself painted a different picture. White Pigeon, a Potawatomi chief lately at Fort Malden, said that the Indians intended to commence hostilities when the corn was two-feet high. Governor Edwards in Illinois Territory warned that the Winnebago, Potawatomi, and Kickapoo—the three tribes that had suffered the worst losses at Tippecanoe—would soon be seeking to avenge their dead. William Clark in St. Louis stated that Main Poche had promised his warriors that they would play a new game with the Americans come spring. Raids had already begun. Nine members of the O'Neal family were wiped out at the mouth of the Salt River and two Americans were killed at a trading post near Prairie de Chien.

Wells scoffed at Harrison's assumption that peace was at hand. In March he warned Eustis that Tecumseh was assembling all the Indians he could at Tippecanoe with an intention to attack the frontiers. Main Poche had concealed his warriors near Fort Malden and had sent runners to raise more on the Illinois River. Wells offered to lead a few hundred mounted riflemen—this time recruited from Kentucky—and put an end to the Prophet.

In early April the dire predictions came to pass: small war parties began to attack isolated cabins and kill whole families. From Sandusky Bay to the Mississippi the death toll mounted across the frontier, spreading panic among the settlers, who either forted up or fled for safety across the Ohio. Mad Sturgeon—the Potawatomi warrior Wells had pursued in the previous spring—and his men perpetrated some of the most gruesome murders. They burned a house and killed six members of the Hutson family as well as their hired man; eleven days later they butchered the Harriman family, including five small children, on the Embarrass River seven miles west of Vincennes.

Faced with such mayhem, albeit by renegades not under the control of Tecumseh, Harrison changed his tune. "Nothing but a rigorous Indian war with all its horrors will effect a peace with them," he wrote to Eustis, requesting prompt authorization to call up the Kentucky mounted militia and commence offensive action. Madison demurred; he had enough on his mind: imminent war with Great Britain.

In mid-April Wells was disturbed by a report he received from the Indian agent in Chicago, relating the murders of Liberty White and John Cardin at a cabin three miles from Fort Dearborn. White, an American, was singled out for special torment: he was shot twice in the body, stabbed seven times, his throat slit from ear to ear, the lower part of his face cut off from nose to chin, and scalped. Wells knew that a killing like that could only indicate a raging passion for revenge, and Fort Dearborn, the most exposed American garrison, was in the eye of the storm.

The commandant there, Nathan Heald, who had previously held the same position at Fort Wayne, was a friend of Wells. He did not like his new post and requested a leave of absence to visit his home in New Hampshire; on his return, he had stopped in Louisville and resumed his courtship of Rebekah Wells, Sam's daughter, who married him in May of 1811. The newlyweds, mounted on Kentucky thoroughbreds and accompanied by a slave girl named Cicely, had stopped at Fort Wayne to visit with Wells and his wife on the way to their new home in Chicago, which consisted of the fort and a few cabins belonging to fur traders.

Following the murders of White and Cardin, Fort Dearborn was in quasi state of siege; Heald didn't know for sure which tribe had committed the outrage—the Winnebago were the most likely suspects—and so he forbade any Indians to approach the garrison to barter or beg for provisions. If hostilities broke out in earnest in the western territories and England entered the fray, Wells was already contemplating what might be necessary to rescue his favorite niece.

2

Back in early March John Johnston had visited Washington to confirm his commission as Indian Agent to the Shawnee at Piqua, Ohio, lobby for the appointment of Benjamin Franklin Stickney as his replacement in Fort Wayne, and push for the removal, once again, of Wells. Stickney was not authorized to dismiss Wells; rather he was told to tolerate him, if possible, making use of his skills as an interpreter while denying him any say in Indian Affairs. Eustis wanted Harrison to decide how best to dispose of Wells—perhaps by transferring him to another outpost—since his services no longer were needed at Fort Wayne.

Upon receiving Eustis's new instructions, Harrison was reluctant to comply. Under the auspices of Little Turtle and Five Medals, Wells was deeply involved in arranging a major Indian council at Mississinewa in mid-May. Since these two chiefs were friendly with Wells and on the side of the United States, it would not be good policy to remove him at so critical a time.

Accompanied by his wife and children as well as fresh soldiers for the garrison, Stickney arrived in Fort Wayne in April. Wells put his best face on this unexpected event. He had experienced enough of life to know that the wheel of fortune took strange turns—why not adopt a policy of wait and see? What met his eyes was not promising. Stickney soon proved to be an absolute stickler for authority. He was something of an eccentric to boot; his male children, for example, were called "One," "Two," and "Three," while his daughters were named after States in the Union. Although he had lived at Upper Sandusky among the Wyandot, his knowledge of Indians was perfunctory, and of course he did not speak their language. In comparison to Stickney, Wells thought, John Johnston no longer looked quite so bad. Be that as it may, he was determined to walk a straight and narrow path with the new agent, never dreaming that the job he wished to keep had already been forfeited back in Washington.

Stickney held his first meeting at Fort Wayne with chiefs representing the Eel River, Miami, Potawatomi, and Wyandot. He told them that the Great White Father of the Seventeen Fires had granted peace to those who had raised the tomahawk against him; now he wanted a few chiefs to visit the Great Town and talk to him in person.

The spokesman for the tribes, The Sleepy One, was was well aware that he lacked the authority of his famous father The Soldier. A woebegone glance at Wells, who was translating, indicated that he was less than impressed by Stickney's strained attempt to talk like an Indian.

"Let the Kickapoo and Winnebago go to the Great Town," The Sleepy One suggested, "since they are the ones who offended you. It will be best for us not to go now; we could only tell our Great

Father a little, and perhaps it would not be the truth. We prefer to sit on our mats and keep bright the chain of friendship. Maybe we shall be ready in the fall. I have no more to say."

Stickney was clearly disconcerted by The Sleepy One's evasive reply, but he managed to mumble to Wells, "Tell him I am pleased with the wisdom of his speech and that I hope he will follow the course we are fixed upon."

That night Wells sent Little Turtle's youngest son, The Bear, to inform Stickney that four Potawatomi loyal to Tecumseh had stolen six horses, three belonging to Little Turtle, and taken them to Tippecanoe. That was his way, Wells knew, of demonstrating what he thought of the proposed peace. After delivering the message, The Bear asked for provisions and a little whiskey for his father, bedridden back in Turtletown with the gout.

Within the week Stickney was swamped with Indians begging for food.

"What am I supposed to do with these people?" he complained.

"Feed them," Wells said curtly.

"Why can't they feed themselves?"

"The cold winter killed the game and now they've eaten all their corn."

"Even if we feed them, they're doomed to die anyway. What's the point?"

"The point is that they're hungry."

"Very well," Stickney relented, "issue the minimum you deem necessary."

Wells liked to goad Stickney into taking pity, not only from compassion for the suffering Indians but also because it gave him satisfaction to watch someone else struggle with the problem of being generous on a miserly government budget.

One morning in early May a naked Indian, his flesh badly torn from underbrush and holding up his bloody left hand in his right as if in lamentation, came staggering into Fort Wayne. Wells recognized him as Stands in Smoke, the brother of Abraham Ash's Potawatomi wife; he told how he and two other men, two women, and one child had set out from Fort Wayne earlier in the week to buy whiskey at Fort Recovery: "The whiskey seller was not in his house, so we walked toward Greenville. Outside of the town two men met us and we exchanged signs of friendship with them and then camped for the night. When I awoke early the next morning, I saw a dozen men with guns advancing and shouted an alarm. At that moment, they opened fire, killing the two other men and hitting me in the arm. I escaped into the bushes and ran away."

"What about the women and the child?" Wells asked.

"I do not know," he replied. "I did not stop running until I reached this place."

It wasn't long before the parents of one of the dead men—the father's face grim with rage, the mother weeping loudly—confronted Stickney and demanded retribution.

Stickney told Wells to ask the distraught couple to control themselves; he could do nothing until the matter was investigated.

"Why should I suspend my anger?" the father demanded. "I know my son is innocent."

Wells translated the grief-stricken man's words and added, "You must cover the dead by giving presents. If you don't, the families will seek revenge."

"In that case, see to it."

Wells had the fort surgeon dress the wounds of Stands in Smoke and gave the relatives of the dead man a suit of clothes, a rifle, powder, lead, a little whiskey, and a substantial meal, which seemed to satisfy them. Wells could picture what had happened; it was a story often repeated on the frontier. The posse pursuing the Indians who killed and scalped a white man near Greenville had simply opened fire on some easier targets. Identifying the perpetrators would be easy, convicting them of murder, impossible. Stands in Smoke told Wells he would not forget what he had done, but such small acts of kindness couldn't stop the cycle of violence.

While Wells was acting to assuage the grief of the dead man's relatives, the Potawatomi chief Five Medals arrived in Fort Wayne, on his way to the Mississinewa council, and tried to educate Stickney about the history of Indian discontent.

"In one year less than ten, Governor Harrison came to Vincennes and told us that it was the wish of our Great Father that we should sell him land. We did not wish to offend, so we sold him land. Soon after, a man came to Detroit and bought more land. This alarmed us, and alarmed our young warriors more—they said their chiefs would sell all their land and ruin them. This destroyed the influence of the chiefs: since then, the young men have refused to obey us. At that time, the Shawnee Prophet began to preach and gained his influence: this has produced the mischief. I speak as the voice of the red people; I want you to communicate what I have said to our Great Father of the Seventeen Fires: tell it on paper, and make it strong!"

As he translated, Wells was moved by Five Medals's eloquence; Stickney saw it as mere whining and delivered in response a condescending lecture: "To make bargains today and unmake them tomorrow, or even to talk about it—belongs to children, not men. We cannot have our cake and eat it too. Nor can anything be done to restore to life those who have been killed. We must take things as they are: not as we would have them. No one has compelled you to sell your land, it was your voluntary act, and you have received goods for the land according to bargain. If this has diminished your authority, I am very sorry; for on the support of your authority depends your safety—and the safety of your young warriors as well as your women and children."

"Why does the government send men like this?" Five Medals grumbled to Wells afterwards. "He does not know how to talk."

"He thinks that because you call him father," Wells explained, "that he can speak to you as if you were a child."

"He is wrong, I am a man," Five Medals stated indignantly; then his face softened and he said to Wells in a lighter tone, "Do you have any whiskey?"

Wells had been working on the council at Mississinewa for over a month; since the government would not authorize him to lead an armed force against Tippecanoe, the best alternative for him to regain his lost prestige was to take the initiative in restoring the peace. More than 600 Indians from twelve tribes gathered at the Miami town at the mouth of the river in mid May and began a round of talks. Even Tecumseh had agreed to come; everyone waited anxiously to see what he had to say; whether there would be peace or war hinged on his words.

The first speaker was a Wyandot chief from Brownstown named Isadore Chaine; his father was a Frenchman and, indeed, Wells thought he acted more French than Indian. He had been in the area since February; sometimes he stayed at Wells's home and assisted in planning for the council. Although he was congenial, Wells did not fully trust him. In his opening remarks, however, Chaine presented a belt of white wampum and professed his dedication to the cause of peace:

"Younger brothers, we are sorry to see your path filled with thorns and briers, and your land covered with blood; our love for you has caused us to come and clean your path and wipe the blood off your land. Our determination to stop the effusion of blood has met with the approbation of our fathers, the British, who have advised all the red people to be quiet and not meddle in quarrels that may take place between white people."

Wells glared at Tecumseh to see how he would respond.

"We thank the Great Spirit that you take pity on us and our poor women and children. We have not brought these misfortunes on ourselves. Governor Harrison made war on my people in my absence. Our younger brothers the Potawatomi..." Tecumseh paused and pointed to where the chiefs of that tribe were sitting. "...in spite of our repeated counsel to them to live in peace with the Big Knives, would not listen to us. When I passed through Post Vincennes, I told the Big Knives to remain quiet until my return, when I would make a lasting peace. On my return I found my village in ashes. Had I been at home and heard of the advance of the Big Knives towards our village, I would have gone to meet them and, shaking them by the hand, asked them why they had come in such hostile guise, and there would have been no blood shed at that time.

"We are not to blame for the conduct of those we cannot control. Those I left at home (I cannot call them men) were a poor set of people, and their scuffle with the Big Knives I compare to a struggle between little children who only scratch each other's faces. The Kickapoo and Winnebago have since been to Post Vincennes and asked for peace, but the Potawatomi remain angry and have killed twenty-seven people. If these bad acts bring the Big Knives to our village to speak of peace, we will receive them; but if they come in a hostile manner, we will rise as one and defend ourselves like men, but we will never strike the first blow."

If Five Medals took Tecumseh's accusations against the Potawatomi personally, Wells thought, he did not show it; rather he calmly accepted responsibility for his people, while shifting the major part of the blame to Tecumseh's own brother:

"Some of our foolish young men, who no longer listen to their chiefs and follow the counsel of the Shawnee Prophet, have killed some of our white brothers this spring. We have no control over these vagabonds; they no longer belong to our nation; they should be found and put to death. If they have done bad deeds, it is because they have learned them from this pretended prophet."

"We defy any living creature to say we ever advised anyone, directly or indirectly, to make war on our white brothers," Tecumseh answered in anger. "It has constantly been our misfortune to have our views misrepresented to our white brothers." He then looked directly at Five Medals and added, "This has been done by false chiefs who no longer speak for their people and sell land that does not belong to them."

Suddenly a Delaware chief interrupted Tecumseh to defuse the volatile situation.

"We have not met at this place to listen to such words," he said. "The red people have been killing the whites, who now have guns in their hands and want retribution; this is no time to tell each other who has done this or that or to tell the Prophet he has given bad counsel; this is the time to join our hearts and hands together and proclaim peace throughout the land of the red people."

Chief Richardville, or Wildcat, speaking as the host of the council, gave his full support to this sentiment: "We, the Miami, have not hurt our white brothers since the treaty of Greenville. We will cheerfully join our red brothers for peace, but not in a war against the white people. The Potawatomi, Shawnee, Kickapoo, and Winnebago have murdered innocent white people. The white people are entitled to satisfaction. Let us do justice to our white brothers and expect it from them; by doing this, we shall ensure the future peace and happiness of our women and children."

Wells was pleased with the way the council ended and sent his translation of the proceedings to the former captive, Oliver Spencer, to put in the Cincinnati newspaper. If the vows of the chiefs to remain neutral in case of war between the United States and Britain and bring the Potawatomi renegades to justice were sincere, then Wells wanted credit for what had been accomplished.

When informed of the council's resolutions, Stickney was not impressed.

"Tell them they have one moon to give up their murderers, or our army will destroy them."

"I wouldn't threaten them," Wells cautioned. "Not when they're talking peace."

"It is not your place to offer unsolicited advice, or tell me what I should or should not do."

"Yes, Sir," Wells muttered. How he hated to defer to this self-satisifed man who occupied his rightful place! "There *is* one other issue I wished to mention. The garrison sutler requested a license to sell liquor and you refused him."

"What if I did?"

"You had no right to do that." Wells stood with his hands behind his back and delivered these words in a matter-of-fact tone.

"Who are you to tell me what my rights are?" Stickney snapped back, his voice rising. "I don't understand you, Wells. I thought you opposed the liquor trade."

"I certainly do. Those rascally traders from Ohio come up to the boundary line and sell whiskey by the keg to the poor Indians, who get drunk and then go off and commit mischief."

"Exactly."

"But you're never going to stop the trade entirely, and Bill Oliver is a good man. Do you think Five Medals would remain loyal if I didn't slip him a little whiskey every now and again?"

"Your way of doing business is not mine, Captain Wells. Good-day."

Shortly after the council at Mississinewa, Wells received the depressing news from Indian friends that all his hard work to foster peace had gone awry, the wheel had taken its last turn and hostilities were now imminent. Isadore Chaine had in fact been playing a double game; in his saddle bags were two belts of wampum, one white and one black; the former he presented to the council when he spoke, the latter he passed around in secret. Chaine had been sent by Matthew Elliott at Fort Malden to publicly favor peace while privately preparing Tecumseh and other pro-British warriors for the outbreak of hostilities. Chaine told the Indians that it would be foolish to remain neutral if war came. The Americans would not only attack the renegade Potawatomi; if they struck a blow, it would be against the whole. All the nations knew in their hearts that the Americans wanted to destroy the red people and take their country from them. Therefore, they should keep their eyes on their true father at Malden; when he gave the signal, but not before, they must strike, and strike hard.

3

President Madison sent his war message to Congress on June 1, 1812. From the moment they took power eleven years earlier, Jefferson's Republicans had reversed the policies of their Federalist predecessors; if Washington and Adams supported concord with Britain, a strong military, mercantile development, and a national bank, then Jefferson would befriend France, cut military spending, foster farming, and rescind the bank's charter. When fighting resumed between England and France in 1803, American ships and sailors were caught in the crossfire. In an effort to find an alternative to war and coerce Britain into concessions, Jefferson tried his ill-fated embargo. Madison, in turn, searched in vain for an effective policy. This daunting challenge was made more difficult by a Congress splintered into factions and a haughty stance on the part of the British, who were too preoccupied by Napoleon to negotiate with American diplomats in good faith.

By the spring of 1812 the United States had run out of options. Either they would have to submit to Britain blockading their ports, impressing their sailors, restricting maritime rights, and controlling markets—to say nothing of inciting Indians on the frontiers—or they could defend their honor, redeem the national character, and fight as free men. That was certainly how Henry Clay saw it, promising that the Kentucky militia alone would be sufficient to conquer Canada. Clay stacked the Foreign Relations Committee with his War Hawks; the Republicans, for once, united behind the cause; and Congress, by a mere sixty-one percent, voted for war. William Wells's boyhood friend "One Arm" John Pope of Kentucky, a staunch Republican, voted against the measure—he was promptly hanged in effigy in Lexington. Sam Wells, on the other hand, was elated, boasting, "We'll take the Canadys and be home before the first frost."

The country—militarily, materially, and mentally—was woefully unprepared for combat. A mosquito navy of a few dozen flimsy gunboats was to sink the mighty British armada that ruled the waves. A paper army, less than one-fifth of its authorized size of 35,000, was to defend the country's extensive coastline while conquering Canada in its spare time. Congress adjourned without funding the war, appointing competent generals to lead it, or bothering to warn the frontier posts that they were being left to the tender mercies of hostile Indians and their British allies.

Ironically, at the very time the Americans were rushing headlong into war, the British were pausing to question their uncompromising position. The threat of a two-front campaign and growing discontent within England itself were slowly but surely moving Parliament toward scrapping its laws against American shipping. In May, a madman assassinated Spencer Perceval, the author of the hated legislation; for a crucial month, while a new government was being formed, the motion for repeal was stalled. The vote was finally taken and approved on June 17th; the next day, ignorant of these hopeful developments, Madison signed his declaration of war; within the same week, Napoleon invaded Russia.

4

While distant events and untimely decisions were shaping his fate, William Wells, unaware he was a pawn in a great game beyond his control, brooded on what his next move should be to regain his position. Polly listened patiently as her husband rehearsed his grievances against the government, yet the more he explained his situation the less chance she saw for him to succeed.

"Why don't we go back to Kentucky, Will?" she suggested one day. "You've done all you can here; it would be a fresh start; you'd have a chance to be with your children."

"That would sure satisfy some bastards I could name," Wells retorted in anger, then began seriously to consider the idea. "I'd sure like to see my darling girls and spend more time with William Wayne. I suppose Sam would be pleased."

"I know it's what my father wants," Polly offered.

"Was all this his idea?" Wells eyed her suspiciously.

"No, Will, it was mine, but it would make him happy. I'm certain he'd help us out."

"I won't be beholden to any man, not even your father, and I hate to turn tail and run."

"Nobody would say you were running." Polly gave her husband an anguished glance. "People know you've tried. They'd understand."

"Some wouldn't," Wells said. "I know who's been plotting behind my back and smearing my name. Thanks to them, my reputation is ruined. Even if we went back to Kentucky, the rumors would follow me. I'd have a dark cloud over my head."

"Isn't there anybody you could talk to or write to?"

"All I do these days is talk and write," Wells complained. "No one listens to me. General Wayne did, at least usually. Have I ever told you about the time he didn't, and he moved his camp, and a tree fell on his tent?"

Polly nodded with a tired smile; she had heard that story often.

"Now all I do is talk, and I'm tired of it. I used to *do* things. Where would Wayne have been without me and my scouts? Why, if I hadn't been shot in the wrist, I would have showed everyone a thing or two at Fallen Timbers."

"You can't be a figher all your life, Will. Since you became an agent you've tried to help the Indians, you can be proud of that. You know Little Turtle's too ill to do much now, but he and his people still respect you. You've done what you could. It's time to say enough. It's time to go."

"I admit I've made mistakes," Wells continued, talking more to himself than to his wife. "I've done things I'm ashamed of. What man hasn't? But I done what I thought was right by my own lights, and damnit, *I was there*! I know what happened. I know for a fact that there are men sitting in high places who've got a lot more to be ashamed of than I do."

"You've done your best, Will," Polly pleaded. "When we get to Kentucky you'll be able to finish your memoirs and explain all that. You can tell your side of the story. I'll write to father and say we're coming."

When Frederick Geiger told Harrison that his daughter and her husband planned to move back to Kentucky, the governor, knowing Wells's services were essential, wrote to Stickney and told him to employ Wells in a way that made the best use of his abilities. Since Secretary of War Eustis had instructed him to have nothing to do with Wells, Stickney informed Harrison that he would not obey his order.

Stickney's smug reply infuriated Harrison, who dashed off a long letter to Eustis. The regulations of the War Department clearly stipulated that Indian Agents were under the authority of Harrison as Superintendent of Indian Affairs; in the public interest, Stickney's error should be corrected immediately. Even though Wells was a difficult man, Harrison understood that his talents were indispensable: Although many Indians hated him, he still had influence with a few important chiefs and he was a source of invaluable information. Harrison next sent a caustic letter to Stickney, calling him an ignorant, inexperienced, and outrageously insolent upstart who did not know his place or responsibilities. His dander up, Stickney mocked Harrison's claim to be a Minister Plenipotentiary of *vastly superior rank,* and restated his refusal to have anything to do with Wells, who, because of Harrison's intervention, remained in limbo at Fort Wayne.

Tecumseh arrived there in mid-June with ten of his warriors and announced that he was going to Fort Malden for powder and lead. Stickney warned that the government would view that as a hostile act, but Tecumseh insisted that his purpose was to urge the Wyandot, Chippewa, and Ottawa to accept a general peace.

"When you reach the Rapids of the Maumee," Stickney dryly remarked, "watch for General Hull and his army."

Tecumseh sneered and walked away without shaking hands. That evening he rode off with his men. Wells watched him go with trepidation; as the receding backs of the small band dissolved in twilight mist, he distinctly heard their defiant war-whoops.

In early July several hundred Indians gathered at Fort Wayne to learn whether Winamac and his warriors had been able to kill or capture the Potawatomi renegades terrorizing the frontier. Wells was not surprised to hear him report his failure; what Winamac did encounter at Peoria were runners from Tecumseh, carrying twists of tobacco and wampum painted red, a sign for all the tribes to take the warpath. That evening word reached Fort Wayne that the United States had declared war on Great Britain. At Wells's insistence, Stickney immediately sent an Indian runner to inform Nathan Heald at Fort Dearborn.

Wells brought the bad news to Little Turtle, who scowled and said he was not sorry his death would be soon. He now lived at Wells's house in order to receive treatment for his gout from the garrison surgeon. He didn't actually live *in* the house, preferring, he said, to die outdoors. It was clear that he was in his final days; no one knew that better, or took the fact with more composure and fortitude, than Little Turtle himself. A lean-to resembling a small hunting shelter had been constructed in Wells's flourishing orchard for the dying chief. His old wife and his younger one cared for him amiably; his children came to see him daily; he loved to have his youngest granddaughter, The Setting Sun, age two, sit in his lap and play at combing his hair.

Wells's children with Sweet Breeze—Ann, Rebecca, Mary, and William Wayne—home after a year of schooling in Kentucky, often sat with their grandfather, hoping he would tell stories; but he didn't talk much now, and the deep creases etched in his face hinted at the pain he never complained about. Polly, who was pregnant again, had been charmed like everyone else by the chief; with two-year-old Sammy toddling behind, she often brought him freshly baked bread.

After holding the warm, round loaf to his nose for a long time, he would say, "It smells good," break off a small piece, and nibble slowly.

"I always loved good food," he said to Wells the day he died.

"Good drink, too," Wells added, "and lots of sweets."

He nodded with satisfaction. "The doctor said that is the cause of my sickness."

"They say gout is a gentleman's disease," Wells noted.

Little Turtle pondered this and then replied, "I have always thought that I was a gentleman."

"You are more than that," Wells said, struggling to control his emotions. He thought back over the many years they had known each other. What a great war chief he had been and how hard he had worked for peace! "You are a noble man, the most noble I have ever known."

The chief understood the import of these words; he and Wells rarely spoke directly about their friendship. He smiled, as if in satisfaction at the praise, closed his eyes, and was quiet for such a long time that Wells was sure he was asleep. When he opened his eyes again, they were weaker, fading embers, and his voice was so low Wells had to bend forward to hear.

"We should cut off the pack horses," he said in an insistent whisper. "I know a good place along the Auglaize."

"Whose horses?" Wells asked.

"What?" Little Turtle looked bewildered, as if he didn't know he had been speaking.

"Whose horses?" Wells asked again. "You said the pack horses should be cut off."

"Ah," the chief said with recognition. "General Wayne's, if only we had attacked him there, when we had a chance. They should have listened to me."

"I might have stopped you," Wells reminded him. "My spies were everywhere."

Little Turtle studied that proposition before replying.

"That is true," he admitted, squinting at Wells. "You were on their side then."

"But maybe not," Wells granted, not just to be gracious to a dying friend, but because who can say what might have been? There certainly were days when Wayne's army was so strung out it was wide open for attack.

"Maybe not," the chief repeated slowly, as if savoring the taste of the syllables in his mouth; those were the last words he ever spoke.

Little Turtle died that evening; his relatives immediately began to prepare his body for burial the next day and Wells rode over to the fort to tell Captain Rhea.

Since the country was in a state of war and hundreds of Indians, including the Prophet and some ninety of his followers, were present at Fort Wayne, certain precautions were called for. In the morning a select squadron shouldered arms and, marching to muffled drums, crossed the river to Wells's house. Two men carrying a pine coffin and two shovels trudged behind.

A sad procession of friends and relatives brought Little Turtle to the old Kekionga burial ground just north of Wells's house. The chief, his hair neatly tied with a leather thong and his face painted red, had been dressed in his finest and decked out with silver earrings, armlets, anklets, medals, crosses, broaches, and beads. As the grave was being dug, his body was placed in the coffin; Little Turtle's wives, their faces blackened with charcoal, began to arrange the things he would need for his journey: a small copper kettle filled with corn and beans, a drinking cup, a spoon, a pocket knife, scissors, an ax, a hammer and awl, patch leather for his moccasins, a flintlock rifle, bullet molds and a bullet pouch, a pistol, a scalping knife, steel spurs, and the sword sent to him by President Washington. Not everything of value was to be buried with the chief; the medals he had received from American Presidents went to his surviving children; the brace of pistols presented to him by the Polish patriot Kosciusko were his gift to Wells.

Little Turtle's nephew, The Woods, gave a short talk.

"We are sorry that the Master of Life has taken our beloved leader away. We know that he has only gone on a long journey before us; in a short time we shall all have to travel the same spirit path to a land where we shall meet him again and be glad. Now we will cover the body of our departed friend and mourn him in the appropriate manner."

People stepped up one by one to sprinkle a pinch of tobacco on Little Turtle's body and place one hand on his chest. Wells looked into his dead friend's face for the last time, touched the place where his heart once beat, and thought how much the chief would have enjoyed the slabs of meat the women were roasting nearby. Then his eldest wife covered him with a blanket. The coffin was draped with an American flag and lowered into the grave. The soldiers fired a series of salutes, each one answered by a booming cannon shot from the fort; clumps of earth thudded down on the coffin lid like the sound of distant drums. Afterwards a feast was held outside the fort and the Indians performed a solemn dance reserved only for a man of great distinction.

Three days later the Prophet presented Stickney with a long belt of white wampum with a small purple spot in the middle.

"This end is Vincennes; that one, Fort Wayne; Tippecanoe is in the middle. When I was at Malden the British invited me to go to war; they said they would give my men plenty of guns, powder, and lead. I refused. They think we are their dogs, ready to run when they call and bite anyone they say. We want to live at peace with the Seventeen Fires; we relinquish all claim to the land sold in the treaty of 1809; all we ask is for some food for our women and children, and some powder and lead for our hunters. We beg you for pity, because you are a good man, not like the one in Vincennes, who is bad and talks with a crooked mouth."

With a mixture of astonishment and disgust, Wells watched Stickney fall for this blatant flattery. Why, all you had to do was look at their faces to know those Indians weren't interested in peace! The newly appointed agent invited them to a council at Piqua in August, passed out a small amount of food, but hesitated, at first, about providing them with ammunition. As a compromise he supplied powder and lead to the Delaware, who could then give it to whomever they pleased.

The Prophet thanked Stickney profusely and said that his people wanted him and not Harrison to have the honor of settling on the Wabash—a remark so disingenuous that it convinced Wells that something sinister was afoot.

The following day his suspicions were justified when an express—who in his haste had ridden his horse to death—arrived with a message from Tecumseh, telling his brother to flee with his followers towards the Mississippi. On the way they should strike Vincennes and do as much damage as they could. If Tecumseh survived the coming battle with the American army marching on Fort Malden, he would join them in the west. That night the Prophet ordered emissaries to ride quickly and spread the news—to make the most speed possible, they stole two of Wells's horses.

The next morning he stormed into Stickney's office.

"Those damn yellow thieving rascals took my finest riding horses," Wells seethed. "Kentucky thoroughbreds!"

"The Prophet has already informed me," Stickney calmly explained, "that two Kickapoo lads are missing—he feared they intended some mischief of this sort."

"And you swallowed that fat bait like a stupid carp!"

"I think it gives further proof of his honesty that he informed me about the bad apples he has in his basket."

"Bad apples my arse!" Wells shouted. "You're a damn fool. Those men were sent by the Prophet to steal my horses and ride west in to raise the Indians in Illinois Territory for war against us. Mark my words, if they do what Tecumseh wants, soon they will strike a heavy blow against the whites in that quarter."

Stickney gazed at Wells with detached bemusement—he knew how little credit the poor man's rash notions merited.

5

In early August Wells learned that Mackinac, the northernmost American garrison, had fallen without firing a gun. Surrounded by an overwhelming force of Indians and their British allies, the commander had no choice but to surrender. Wells feared that the same fate had already overtaken Fort Dearborn, when an Indian arrived and showed him a message from General Hull for Captain Heald:

> *Sir, It is with regret I order the evacuation of your post,*
> *owing to the want of provisions only, a neglect of the*
> *commandant at Detroit. You will therefore destroy*
> *all arms and ammunition, but the goods of the factory*
> *you may give to friendly Indians, who may be desirous*
> *of escorting you on to Fort Wayne, and to the poor and*
> *needy at your post. I am informed this day that Mackinac*
> *and the island of St. Joseph will be evacuated on account*
> *of the scarcity of provisions, and I hope in next to give you*
> *an account of the surrender of the British at Malden,*
> *as I expect 600 men here on the beginning of September.*

The words troubled Wells; he didn't like the pretense Mackinac had not been captured but evacuated; he was skeptical of Hull's expectation of taking Fort Malden; and who were these "friendly Indians" eager to provide safe passage to Fort Wayne? After consulting with Captain Rhea, Wells sent Winamac with the message to Fort Dearborn. As soon as he left he recruited his own escort of Miami warriors to rescue his niece and cover the retreat of Heald's garrison—if they were still alive.

Hull's Canadian campaign had been a disaster from the start. A short, fat, convivial man who liked his food well cooked and his bottle uncorked, Hull dreaded the horrors of war, especially if the enemy were bloody savages. He had marched his 2,000 men up to Detroit in early July, boldly crossed into Canada, and threatened Fort Malden. Then he stopped in his tracks and frittered away his advantage. While Hull dillydallied, his situation deteriorated. Because the British controlled Lake Erie and Tecumseh's warriors roamed the forests, his line of supply back to Ohio was vulnerable. With word of the surrender of Mackinac, Hull's worst nightmare suddenly seemed possible—hordes of savages from the north would descend on his army and butcher them all! When Tecumseh ambushed 150 Ohio militiamen at Brownstown, killing seventeen, and General Sam Wells's Kentucky reinforcements did not arrive, the plan to attack Malden was abandoned; within days Hull's demoralized army would turn tail, sneak back across the river in the dead of night, and hole up in Detroit.

One morning in early August, Wells, accompanied by sergeant Walter Jordan and thirty Miami warriors, left Fort Wayne. The previous day another message from Hull had arrived, authorizing Wells to guide the Fort Dearborn garrison to safety. Because Fort Wayne, too, might soon be in danger, James Logan, a loyal Shawnee brave, had come to take the women and children to Piqua, Ohio, including Wells's daughters Ann, Rebecca, and Mary. His wife refused to go; she would stay at the fort with William Wayne and young Sammy until her husband returned.

"You be careful now, Polly," Wells cautioned. "William Wayne, don't you leave the fort. I'll be back within the month."

"I'll wait for you, Will." She kissed him hard then turned away to hide her tears.

Wells took one lingering backward glance at his wife and sons before he and his men headed northwest through alternating stretches of dense forests, swampy bottoms, and luxurious prairies where grass grew taller than a man on horseback. Thriving cornfields and fine sugar trees bordered Five Medals's village on the Elkhart River. Stands in Smoke, his left hand still in a sling, now lived there. He told Wells that Winamac had revealed that Fort Dearborn was to be evacuated; word had quickly spread through the Potawatomi towns along the St. Joseph and Kankakee and many braves were rushing to the post to share in the spoils. Accompanied by Stands in Smoke, Wells and his men hastened on, hoping against hope that they would be in time.

Fort Dearborn was still standing—although surrounded by the campfires of hundreds of Indians, mainly warriors. Wells was greeted as a godsend by the beleaguered garrison; he was a man who possessed the knowledge of the Indians and the skill to deal with them in this moment of crisis. The Potawatomi and Winnebago, however, noted his arrival with sour faces; here was the brave but hated traitor who had betrayed his adopted people.

Wells had first visited Chicago back in the summer of 1803, when he led a squadron from Fort Wayne to help Captain John Whistler select a site, construct the fort, and conciliate the Indians. The Potawatomi had not been at all happy to have a garrison in the heart of their domain; they had relented only when Wells promised that more fur traders would come with better goods to barter.

Fort Dearborn was situated on a modest elevation several hundred yards from the lake and some twenty yards from the south bank of the Chicago. The water there was eighteen-feet deep, clogged with weeds, and sluggish, because a long sandbar blocked direct access to the lake; just below the fort the river made a sharp bend to the southeast and ran parallel to the shore for about a mile before its mouth widened into an easily waded outlet at a sandy point marked by a clump of stunted pine trees. A mile above the fort the river divided, one fork meandered north along the lake while the southern branch provided a portage, leading to the Illinois River and the Mississippi, which explained why Chicago had always been prized as a strategic location.

Four two-tier log barracks, enclosed by a double row of twelve-foot oak palisades, formed the sides of the quadrangular parade ground. Two sturdy blockhouses, jutting out on the fort's southeast and northwest corners, shared three small cannon that commanded both the inner and outer walls as well as the space between. The officers' quarters were on the south side, flanking the main gate that opened on a sweeping view of the shoreline and prairie; on the north side of the fort near the river an underground sally port could provide an escape passage in an emergency. The garrison had a well, a brick powder magazine, and a substantial stand of small arms.

On the heavily wooded north side of the river directly across from the fort stood the house of John Kinzie, the leading fur trader and only silversmith in the area; the original cabin of hewn logs was the oldest in Chicago. When Kinzie and his family came in 1804 he had enlarged it considerably, planted poplars and a garden surrounded by a picket fence, and added a veranda across the front that overlooked the grassland sloping down to the water and the fort on the opposite bank. Anyone wishing to cross the river, which was thirty-feet wide at that point, made use of a dugout canoe. The dozen other cabins in the vicinity were more humble affairs owned by French-Canadian fur traders with Indian wives or American farmers selling food to the garrison. Three warehouses next to the fort were for the factor and Indian agent.

Rebekah wept with joy to see her "Uncle Billy." Wells gave her a vigorous hug and, after providing for his men, followed Heald to a room where they could speak in confidence.

"When did Winamac arrive?" Wells asked anxiously.

"Three days ago."

"I was afraid of that. He should've gotten here sooner. We left five days after him and we had packhorses to slow us down."

"What took him so long?"

"He couldn't keep his damn mouth shut. He had to stop and talk. Now every Potawatomi from here to Detroit knows you've got to evacuate the fort."

"Hull's orders leave me no choice."

"What the hell does he know about the situation here? Hundreds of warriors are waiting for you to open that gate, and more will be coming every day. If I was you I'd hunker down and make a stand. This fort looks plenty strong to me. What do you have in the way of supplies? How long can you hold out?"

"Not long enough. Where would our relief come from? If Hull could only take Malden! Then some of these Indians might have second thoughts about who their friends were."

"Don't expect good news from that quarter," Wells said with regret. "Before I left I heard the northern Indians were descending on him like a swarm of angry bees."

"We'll call a council with the Indians tomorrow," Heald decided, looking sharply at Wells. "I'll need your help. I am honor bound to obey my orders. Perhaps you could arrange a truce with the chiefs to allow us safe passage. Everything we don't take will be theirs the day we leave, and any Indians who escort us to Fort Wayne will be rewarded."

"I'll do what I can," Wells promised, mustering resolve. "It's our best chance."

"God, I hope so," Heald replied with sudden passion. "I'd give anything to get out of this hell hole alive!"

"I'd sure rather be home in Polly's arms than settin' on my arse here until they starve us out. How's Rebekah takin' all this?"

"She's had a hard time of it. We lost our first child in May for want of a skilled midwife."

Wells nodded in sympathy. "What's the morale of the men?"

"Terrible! Dissention in the ranks ever since I arrived. And it's not my fault, Captain Whistler had the same problems."

"Who's to blame then?"

"It's John Kinzie and his crew," Heald said with scorn. "That damn man is cantankerous by nature; he spreads discord every chance he gets."

The next day Heald and Wells met with the Indians in a cleared area near the fort's main gate. Wells recognized many of the Potawatomi leaders. Black Partridge, He Who Sits Quietly, Peek of

Day, and Bread were peace chiefs Wells trusted, but control of the angry young warriors was in the hands of a set of war chiefs whose faces were already painted for battle. Prominent among these were the two chiefs that had accompanied Main Poche on Wells's ill-fated trip to Washington in 1809—Mad Sturgeon, notorious for his bloody raids in Illinois, and Black Bird, spokesman for the militant faction. Main Poche himself, Wells knew, was back at Fort Malden with Tecumseh.

After lengthy negotiations, the peace chiefs agreed to guarantee the safety of the settlers and soldiers in return for all the provisions and property in the abandoned fort, but the war chiefs also wanted arms, ammunition, and Kinzie's supply of whiskey. After glancing at Heald, Wells deliberately left the matter vague.

"You shall have everything in the fort that we don't take with us," Wells stated.

Black Bird and the other chiefs seemed to accept this, provided the distribution of the fort's goods was made the next day; they even promised Captain Heald's garrison a peaceful evacuation and a friendly escort to Fort Wayne.

That evening Wells, Kinzie, Heald, and Lieutenant Helm debated whether to destroy the fort's military supplies and whiskey.

"If we don't give them any arms or ammunition," Heald argued, "they'll accuse us of lying to them. They know we have stacks of muskets and kegs of powder."

"I didn't lie," Wells insisted. "I promised them what was left. You saw the faces of those warriors—do you want them to have more guns, and whiskey too? They'd slaughter us for sure!"

"If you abandon the fort, give away my goods, and destroy my whiskey, I'll be ruined," Kinzie grumbled. "Who's going to pay me for my lost business?"

"Better that than to lose your scalp," Wells said.

"The government might reimburse you," Heald suggested.

"They'll suspect we're up to something," Wells noted. "We better act in secret."

The men began staving in the tops of powder kegs and smashing muskets; Kinzie ventured out by the sally port to see if they could throw the powder in the water without being seen. Before he even reached the river, two warriors seized him.

"What is happening in the fort, Silver Man? We heard the sound of hammers and breaking wood." They eyed him with suspicion. "Why?"

"That is just the men opening some barrels of pork and flour for the trip," Kinzie replied with forced assurance.

The Indians were less than satisfied with the silversmith's answer, but they let him return to the fort, where it was decided that the powder, gun parts, and bags of shot, as well as the whiskey, should be dumped down the well. Soon the pungent smell of sour mash pervaded the parade ground and wafted over the walls.

On the afternoon of August 14th hundreds of Indians gathered outside the fort and the distribution of goods was made.

After the food, clothes, blankets, and other supplies were handed out, Black Bird confronted Wells. "Where is the whiskey? My men are thirsty. Where are our guns and powder?"

"There is no more powder," Wells said.

"I see that there is no powder *now,*" Black Bird asserted. "You destroyed all of it last night!" Several braves, naked to the waist, joined him, their tawny skins glistening in the hot sun and their faces streaked red and black for war.

Wells unwisely tried to make light of the situation. "I had a dream that the water-gods wanted it."

Black Bird scowled at Wells. "We have not painted our faces to fast. I also had a dream and the Great Spirit told me it would not be good for the Americans if they lied to us."

"I sometimes paint my face, too," Wells replied, "and the Great Spirit told me that I should fear no man."

"I am a man," Black Bird insisted with fierce pride. "You should fear *me!*"

"I once killed an Indian almost as ugly as you," Wells said with a sneer. "I believe he was your brother."

Heald noted the anger in the chief's face and became alarmed. "Control your tongue, Wells!" he said firmly and pulled him away. "People's lives are at stake here."

Wells shook loose from Heald's grip and began pacing the ground to cool his temper. An old squaw he recognized from Five Medals's village came up to him and said, "I like you, Captain Wells. Tomorrow I will be sad when I see the crows eating you."

Wells tried to shrug off her prophecy, but he could smell danger in the air. Late in the afternoon an Indian suddenly fired at an ox that was supposed to pull one of the baggage wagons during the evacuation of the fort the next morning. Wells was standing not far away when the beast gave a groan and dropped to its knees; he wondered if the shot might have been intended for him.

That evening Black Partridge sought out Wells and asked to meet with Heald. The chief handed the commandant the silver medal he had received from President Washington many years ago and said, "I promised you protection and I must break my word. Bad birds are whispering in the ears of our young men; a runner has just arrived with a red war belt from Main Poche; he says that the Indians have defeated Hull in five battles and trapped his army by the river. Mad Sturgeon tells his warriors now is the time to kill the Americans. If you leave the fort, you may all die."

Wells and Heald exchanged a long, agonized look. If only they hadn't destroyed the powder and passed out the provisions! It was too late; their only choice was to go, before more warriors arrived, and hope for the best.

"You must talk to the other peace chiefs," Wells urged. "Tell them to do everything in their power to control the young men. If we reach Fort Wayne in safety, everyone who helped us will be given many presents."

"Do you think he'll succeed?" Heald asked after the chief had left.

"If he don't," Wells said morosely, "we're both dead men."

6

Wells somehow managed to catch a few fitful hours of sleep before he awoke at dawn. After he had dressed, cleaned his weapons, and strapped on his shot pouch and powder horn, he moistened some ashes and defiantly blackened his face; if it was a battle they wanted, he'd show them that he could go as far into an Indian fight as any warrior—and die, if need be, in a blaze of glory. As he gazed in a small hand mirror at a faded image of Blacksnake he began to chant to himself the Miami war song:

> *Do not weep, women,*
> *We are ready to die.*
> *We are all brave men,*
> *None is braver than I!*

At half past nine the fort's main gate swung open and the solemn procession made its slow way down the road along the shore. As if to deepen the pervasive gloom, the four-man garrison band played the "Dead March" from Saul on fife and drum. Wells mounted on a thoroughbred and some Miami warriors on ponies led the way, followed by Heald and about sixty of his men; next came three large creaking wagons pulled by oxen; one carried Sukey Corbin, who was pregnant, the Heald's slave girl Cicely, nursing a baby boy, as well as other young children with their mothers walking beside them; the other two contained baggage and several invalid soldiers; the wagons were guarded by a dozen militia on foot; Rebekah Heald rode a beautiful, spirited thoroughbred, a gift from her father; a few younger women and older children were also on horseback; bringing up the rear were the rest of the Miami escort and a few packhorses. John Kinzie accompanied the procession; his family would go by water in a bateau.

It was a cloudless day and the hot sun sparkled off the whitecaps on the lake.   A large crowd of Potawatomi and Winnebago had gathered to watch the evacuation, including Stands in Smoke, but Wells noted that most of the warriors who had glared threateningly at him yesterday were nowhere in sight.   After advancing about a mile and a half, as Wells was approaching a grove of cottonwoods, his horse became skittish.   He saw the scalplocked heads of painted warriors popping up like turtles behind the dunes that loomed ahead of him, dividing the shoreline from the prairie.   No sooner had he turned his horse and started back to warn Heald, less than a hundred yards behind, than the air was shattered with war whoops and gunfire.   Knowing that this was not their fight, at the first volley Wells's Miami escort deserted him and rode off into the prairie.

"Form up and charge!" Wells shouted at the soldiers, pointing his pistol at the low sandy hills where the warriors were crouching. "Don't let them surround us!"

The men seemed to grasp instantly the gravity of their situation; they dropped their packs, fixed bayonets, and ran forward under a withering fire, driving the nearest Indians out of their protective cover in the dunes.   The warriors, however, had merely withdrawn to reload and regroup.   Reinforced by others, they quickly flanked Heald's men and began to pick them off from all sides; a few braves brandishing scalping knives and tomahawks rushed in and engaged in lethal hand-to-hand combat.   Within minutes, more than half of Heald's men lay dead in the sand.   The remnant that survived were forced to retreat into the prairie, where they made a last desperate stand against overwhelming odds before finally surrendering.

Meanwhile, Wells fired his pistols left and right, reloading as he galloped forward; he was hit once in the side, but he tightened his thighs on the flanks of his mount and remained on horseback.   Upon hearing piteous shrieks for mercy from the women and children in the wagons, who were now separated from the soldiers, he rode rapidly to their defense.   As he approached, he saw that the situation was hopeless. The militia, some distance from the wagons, had fired only one round before they were all killed, now a few warriors in a murderous frenzy were tomahawking the woman and children.

In spite of being wounded in both arms and one hand, Rebekah clung to her saddle; when she saw her uncle riding hard in her direction she felt a sudden surge of hope amid all the horror; but then Wells went down in a hail of bullets. He had been shot in the chest and was pinned by one leg beneath his dead horse. As he struggled to call to his niece, Wells coughed up blood. He knew that was his death warrant; he'd been shot in the lungs.

"Rebekah," he finally managed, "I'm done for. Tell Polly I did my best."

She saw Wells spitting blood and a band of warriors closing in; before she could ride away she was pulled kicking and screaming off her horse and captured.

Through blurry eyes in the shimmering heat Wells recognized He Who Sits Quietly, a Potawatomi peace chief who had tried to prevent the attack, standing among the Indians encircling him. Several warriors pointed their guns at Wells's head and watched him warily like a rattlesnake that might strike, yet no one fired. Perhaps it was because his pistols were lying on the sand beyond his reach; or maybe they wanted to save him for a slower death.

"Father, I want to live," Wells mumbled with great effort.

"My son, you can," the chief answered. But at that moment Black Bird and Mad Sturgeon came up, recognized Wells, and cocked their rifles.

Wells saw and understood. He made a circling motion over his head, pointed at his heart, and said, "Shoot away."

The fatal balls found their mark; Mad Sturgeon scalped Wells, picked up his two matching pistols, and handed them to his brother, Clear Day. Sergeant Jordan was dragged forward to meet the same fate, but a warrior named White Raccoon recognized him.

"Jordon, no hurt you," he said. "You gave me tobacco at Fort Wayne, but see what I do to your great captain."

He raised his battle axe and, with one deft swing, cut off Wells's head and stuck it firmly on a pole, waving it aloft in triumph. Then Black Bird slashed open Wells's chest, removed his heart, cut off a piece of it for each Indian in the circle, and shouted "Epeconier! Epeconier!"

"Wells dead," White Raccoon said to Jordan in exultation. "Him called Wild Carrot when a boy, as warrior, Blacksnake. He was brave man!"

Later that day Stands in Smoke wandered aimlessly through the battlefield strewn with some sixty slain, including fourteen women and children. *The Potawatomi will pay for this*, he thought. *The ghosts of these dead will haunt them. One day soon they will hear their women and children cry and not be able to protect them.* When he came near the wagons tipped over in the sand, he recognized Wells's mutilated body and retrieved one of his prized possessions, half hidden beneath his dead horse.

Four days later, on August 19th, Stands in Smoke was the first person to bring news of the massacre to Fort Wayne. Polly Wells was at home, rocking Sammy to sleep by the fireplace, when a tall, sad-eyed Indian unknown to her stepped into the room. They exchanged a long, silent glance. Then he placed on the plain wooden table a tomahawk—whose custom-carved hickory handle, engraved brass blade, and steel edge were unmistakable—and, still without speaking, he walked out the door to return to his people.

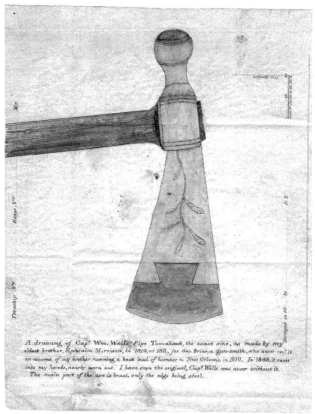

A drawing of Capt Wm. Wells's Pipe Tomahawk, the exact size, as made by my oldest brother, Ephraim Morrison, in 1810, or 1811, for Geo. Brier, a gun-smith, who never rec'd it on account of my brother running a boat load of lumber to New Orleans, in 1810. In 1848, it came into my hands, nearly worn out. I have seen the original, Capt Wells was never without it. The main part of the axe is brass, only the edge being steel.

Epilogue

The day after Wells died, General Hull surrendered Detroit to Tecumseh; the death of the great Shawnee war chief at the battle of the Thames, on October 5, 1813, marked the end of effective Indian resistance. Among those who claimed the honor, Richard Johnson of Kentucky rode his reputation ("Rumpsey Dumpsey, Rumpsey Dumpsey, Colonel Johnson killed Tecumseh") all the way to the Vice Presidency under Van Buren. The Prophet died in Kansas in 1836. Using the slogan "Tippecanoe and Tyler too," William Henry Harrison launched his log cabin campaign that won him the Presidency. Shunning a hat and coat in spite of a chilly March day with brisk winds, he delivered a prolix inaugural address that led directly to his death, a month later on April 4, 1841, from what his doctor called "a bilious pleurisy." Presidents Jefferson and Adams both died on July 4, 1825, the 50th anniversary of the Declaration of Independence. After years of hoodwinking his superiors and lining his pockets, General James Wilkinison died near Mexico City, December 28, 1825, from an overdose of laudanum taken to relieve acute diarrhea.

Polly Geiger Wells survived the siege of Fort Wayne in September of 1812 and gave birth to Yelverton Peyton Wells later that fall. In 1817 she married Robert Turner in Louisville, while his brother, Doctor William Turner, married William Wells's eldest daughter, Ann. Dr. Turner served briefly as the Indian agent in Fort Wayne; he died of drink in 1821. Ann died in 1834, leaving no children. Rebecca Wells married James Hackley, Jr., an officer at Fort Wayne; they had two children before they separated. Capt. Hackley hanged himself in 1831, and Rebecca died in 1834. Mary Wells married Judge James Wolcott in 1821; the couple lived in Fort Wayne until 1826, then moved to Maumee, Ohio; their home is now a family museum. William Wayne Wells graduated 4th in his class at West Point in 1821; he was promoted to first lieutenant in 1825, but heavy drinking compelled him to resign his commision in 1831; he died from cholera a year later at Erie, Pennsylvania. William Wells's illegitimate daughter Jane lived for a while with his other daughters, yet maintained her status as a Miami. In 1830 she married John Griggs and bore him six children during a relationship that lasted over fifty years. Sammy Wells was twenty-two when he died in 1832; Yelverton Peyton Wells married Maryann Scheble and died in his forties. After the loss of her second husband, Polly returned to her father's house in Middletown, Kentucky.

Following the siege of Fort Wayne, Harrison ordered the destruction of Turtletown on the Eel River and all the villages on the Mississinewa. After the War of 1812, the Miami resisted efforts to remove them, although they did sign treaties and sell land. Finally, in 1840, the Miami ceded "all their remaining lands in Indiana," and the majority of the tribe was compelled to move to Oklahoma in 1846. Nonetheless, a significant remnant remained behind, concentrated in the area around Peru, Indiana, where they remain to this day. Little Turtle's two sons and two daughters died before the removal; but their children lived on both in Indiana and Oklahoma. His youngest and favorite granddaughter, The Setting Sun, died in 1915 at the age of 105.

Although badly wounded, Rebekah and Nathan Heald survived the massacre and their subsequent captivity. They moved to Missouri, where they were joined in 1817 by Sam Wells, his second wife, and his large family. Sam Wells died in 1830 and is buried in O'Fallon, Missouri. Nathan Heald, still suffering from his wounds, died two years later. Rebekah lived until 1857; she wrote a memoir about her life in Kentucky, at Fort Dearborn, and about her beloved "Uncle Billy." The manuscript was lost during the Civil War when the Heald house was sacked by Union troops from Illinois. In 1882, the superintendent of the Kalamazoo Paper Company in Michigan discovered, in a bundle of papers recently sent from Fort Wayne, twenty-seven pages of foolscap in the same hand, apparently torn from a book, which proved to be a fragment of the memoir begun by William Wells, although this was not realized at the time. It contained speeches by Little Turtle and an account of the manners and customs of the Miami. It was published in Chicago as *The Fort Wayne Manuscript*. In it Wells wrote, "Few Indians will give an opinion respecting a future state. They say that those things are only enquired after by fools and the white people.... They generally celebrate the death of a distinguished chief or warrior by drinking, feasting, dancing, and singing."

359

Afterword & Notes

I would like to thank the Newberry Library in Chicago for awarding me a fellowship in 2002 to study their invaluable collections. I was the grateful recipient of summer research grants from Mount Saint Mary's University, whose library staff were also most helpful with inter-library loans. Over the years, friends, colleagues, and specialists in the field have generously given of their time and expertise to read my manuscript and offer their support and suggestions. I am deeply indebted to the following people: Frank Bergon, Holly Bergon, Tom Bligh, Andrew R. L. Cayton, Peter Dorsey, Robert Ducharme, Marshall Dunn, Arthur Goldwag, Simon Lipskar, Jack Vernon, Jim Vincent, and Richard White. Michele Rubin, my agent at The Writers House, has loyally represented my novel through revisions, rejections, and final acceptance. My sister and her husband, Alice and Lloyd Baker, helped sustain my interest in the history of the Old Northwest. My wife, Roser Caminals Heath, a Catalan novelist herself, read numerous drafts, giving me the benefit of her precise insights, and accompanied me to research sites throughout the Midwest. Without her love and lively spirit, this book could not have been written.

During the dozen years I spent researching and writing *Blacksnake's Path,* I visited some 33 archives and read more than 500 books and 300 articles. The sources mentioned below are highly selective and represent a fraction of those I consulted. The two most useful archival collections proved to be the 480 volumes of the Lymon C. Draper Papers at the Wisconsin Historical Society and the National Archives in Washington, D.C., especially the Records of the Office of the Secretary of War, who was in charge of Indian Affairs at the time. To chart my indebtedness to these archives would require a volume in itself. In addition, the Burton Collection at the Detroit Public Library, the Filson Club in Louisville, and the Fort Wayne library, as well as the Ohio and Indiana Historical Societies were indispensable. The best scholarly overview of the period is Richard White's magesterial *The Middle Ground: Indians, Empires, and Republics in the Great Lakes Region, 1650-1815.* Research on William Wells must begin with Paul A. Hutton's ground-breaking essay, "William Wells: Frontier Scout and Indian Agent," *Indiana Magazine of History* (1978): 184-220. The best book so far on Little Turtle and William Wells is Harry Lewis Carter, *The Life and Times of Little Turtle.* Research inquiries, comments on, or questions about my novel may be directed to my e-mail addresses: heath@msmary.edu or heath@hermes.hood.edu.

These notes mention a few key sources and briefly discuss how I, as both a novelist and a historican, have tried to dramatize my material.

The Ohio River: October 1788
The only evidence that Wells was involved in luring flatboats into ambushes was provided by one of his worst enemies, John Johnston (see pp. 310-11). What is certain is that white captives were used for this purpose and many flatboats on the Ohio River were attacked at this time.

Billy Wells
James Smith, author of a classic captivity narrative, lived on Jacobs Creek in 1779. The historical society in Dumfries, VA. was useful for the Wells family in Virginia. The Yahogania County Library, Unionville, PA., has information on Sam Wells and the Jacobs Creek settlement. See, Nicolas Creswell's journal and David McClure's diary. The trip down the Ohio by flatboat, the way many settlers headed West, is based on numerous sources. R. E. Banta, *The Ohio,* is the standard history.

Beargrass Stations
The Filson Club, Louisville, KY, is a wonderful archival source for information about the Beargrass settlements, especially the Robert E. McDowell Collection, the Pope Family Papers, and essays by Vincent J. Akers and Neal O. Hammon. See the Boone and Clark Papers, in Draper, and George H. Yater, *Two Hundreds Years at the Falls of the Ohio.*

Wild Carrot
The Garland Library of Narratives of North American Indian Captivities is a superb resource. The best captivity narratives for the period are James Smith, *Scoouwa,* Oliver Spencer, *The Indian Captivity of O. M. Spencer,* Larry L. Nelson, ed., *A History of Jonathan Adler,* John Tanner, *The Falcon,* Charles Johnson's "Narrative" in Richard VanDerBeets, ed., *Held Captive By Indians,* and John D. Hunter's *Manners and Customs...* See "The White Indians" in James Axtell's *The Invasion Within,* and *Women's Indian Captivity Narratives* (Penguin).

Vision Quest
Essential primary sources on the Miami Indians during the time Wells lived among them are C. C. Throwbridge, *Meearmeear Traditions* and Hiram Beckwith, ed., *The Fort Wayne Manuscript* (1884), which was compiled from writings by William Wells originally published in volumes 1 and 2 of *The Western Review and Miscellaneous Magazine* (1820). The Newberry Library has a typescript, Ayer Collection, vol. 10, #2, MS 689. The two standard histories of the Miami are Bert Anson, *The Miami Indians,* and Stewart Rafert, *The Miami Indians of Indiana.* See also, John Piatt Dunn's *True Indian Stories* and his histories of Indiana, as well as W. Vernon Kinietz, *Indians of the Western Great Lakes 1615-1760.*

Blacksnake

Two of the Miami's winter moons are based on the hunt for black bears. Chief Clarence Godfroy, *Miami Indian Stories,* contains engaging tales about bear hunts and other aspects of Miami life. As a boy, I was chased by a black bear and once found a six-foot blacksnake skin.

Warpath

The Draper Manuscripts contain a host of anecdotes about Indian attacks, especially in Kentucky and southern Ohio, as do the numerous primary sources at the Filson Club. My description of the attacks on the cabin and the flatboat are composites, the Kentucky counterattack is based on a real event. John Filson, author of *The Discovery and Settlement of Kentucky,* was killed by Indians while surveying land for what would become Cincinnati. Both Miami and Shawnee warriors were in the area, but no one knows who killed him. Wells probably went on the warpath with the Miami at this time, and so I have taken the tongue-in-cheek authorial liberty of having him lift Filson's scalp.

Laughing Eyes

The name of Wells's first Indian wife is not known. The courtship rituals I describe are true to Miami customs at the time. As depicted in the novel, John Hamtramck in Vincennes learned of Wells's whereabouts as a captive and Carty Wells, then Sam, paid him a visit at Snake-Fish Town.

Harmar's Defeat

Wiley Sword, *President Washington's Indian War,* is an overview. Harmar's Defeat is in dispute among scholars; some don't give Little Turtle as much credit as I do. One of the better attempts to make sense of the battle is Leroy V. Eid, "The Slaughter was Reciprocal: Josiah Harmar's Two Defeats, 1790," *Northwest Ohio Quarterly,* 65:2 (Spring 1992): 51-67. The Draper Colletion is essential for all the battles of this period.

St. Clair's Defeat

See, General Arthur St. Clair, *A Narrative of the Campaign Against the Indians.* A valuable account is William Denny, ed., "Military Journal of Major Ebenezer Denny...," *Historical Society of Pennsylvania Memoirs,* 7 (1860): 205-409. See also, William Henry Smith, ed., *The Saint Clair Papers,* 2 vols., William H. Guthman, *March of Massacre,* and Leroy V. Eid's essay in *The Journal of Military History,* 57 (Jan. 1993): 71-88.

Vincennes

See, Rowena Buell, ed., *The Memoirs of Rufus Putnam*; Paul A. W. Wallace, ed., *The Travels of John Heckewelder in Frontier America*: John Heckewelder, *History, Manners, and Customs of the Indian Nations.* Also,

Andrew Cayton, *Frontier Indiana*; August Derleth, *Vincennes: Portal to the West*; Judge Law, *The Colonial History of Vincennes.*

From **Au Glaize** *to* **Roche de Bout**

See, Helen Hornbeck Tanner, "The Glaize in 1792: A Composite Indian Community," *Ethnohistory,* 25: 1 (Winter 1978): 15-39; Milo O. Quaife, "Fort Wayne in 1790," Indiana Historical Society *Publications,* 7: 7 (1921): 208-61; and Dwight L. Smith, "William Wells and the Indian Council of 1793," *Indiana Magazine of History,* 56 (1960): 217-226.

Fallen Timbers

Alan D. Gaff, *Bayonetes in the Wilderness,* is the most detailed account and has an extensive bibliography, as does John Sugden's *Blue Jacket.* Richard C. Knopf, *Campaign Into the Wilderness,* 5 vols., collects primary sources. His edition of *Anthony Wayne: A Name in Arms* is useful for both the failed treaty negotitions and Fallen Timbers. See, Dwight L. Smith, ed., *With Captain Edward Miller on the Wayne Campaign.* The British side of the story can be followed in E. A. Cruikshank, ed., *The Correspondence of Lieutenant-Governor John Graves Simcoe* as well as Larry I. Nelson, *A Man of Distinction Among Them: Alexandere McKee and the Ohio Frontier,* Reginald Horsman, *Matthew Elliott,* and Robert S. Allen, *His Majesty's Indian Allies.* Microfilms of the Anthony Wayne Papers are at the Ohio Historical Society. Following his injury Wells disappears from the primary sources, with the exception of a participant's recollection, found in the Draper Papers, 5U 119-125, of his advising Wayne about tactics before the battle. Paul David Nelson, *Anthony Wayne: Soldier of the Early Republic,* is a recent biography.

Treaty of Greene Ville

The proceedings of the treaty are found in Erminie Wheeler Voegelin and Helen Hornbeck Tanner, *Indians of Ohio and Indiana Prior to 1795,* 2 vols. See also, Dwight L. Smith, "Wayne's Peace with the Indians of the Old Northwest, 1795," *Ohio Archaeological and Historical Quarterly,* 59 (1950): 239-255 and Frazer Ellis Wilson, "The Treaty of Greeneville," *OAHQ,* 12 (1903): 128-159. Transcripts of the treaty are available at the Garst Museum, Greenville, Ohio. I have condensed some of the speeches.

Philadelphia

Accounts of treaty negotiations in Philadelphia are to be found in the George Washington Papers, the John Adams Papers, American State Papers, and Records of the Office of the Secretary of War (National Archives). I have relied on the biographies and correspondence of the historical figures presented here—Washington, Adams, Benjamin Rush, Charles Willson Peale, Count Volney, Theodore Kosciusko, the Binghams, Gilbert Stuart, et. al.—to make sure they were in character and in voice. Wells and Little Turtle did meet with Rush, Peale, Volney (see his *A View of the Soil and Climate of the United States*), and Kosciusko; and Little Turtle did have his portrait (probably destroyed in the War of 1812) painted by Stuart; but the dinner at the Binghams' is my invention, although based on accurate descriptions of people, places, and styles of conversation. A lively general history of the city at this time is Carl and Jessica Bridenbaugh, *Rebels and Gentlemen: Philadelphia in the Age of Franklin.* See also, Richard G. Miller, *Philadelphia—Federalist City,* and Charles Coleman Sellers, *Mr. Peale's Museum,*

Washington City

Thomas Francek, ed., *The City of Washington,* Welhelmus Bogart Bryan, *A History of the National Capital,* and James Sterling Young, *The Washington Community, 1800-1828*; the city's high society is captured in Anne Hollingsworth Wharton's *Social Life in the Early Republic.* For Jefferson's Indian policy: Bernard W. Sheehan, *Seeds of Extinction,* and Anthony F. C. Wallace, *Jefferson and the Indians.* Joseph J. Ellis's books on the Founding Fathers are often insightful. Dolley Madison and Betsey Bonaparte were close friends during this period, and both were favored at Jefferson's table, but there is no record that they were present at a dinner with William Wells and Little Turtle. See, Eugene L. Didier, *The Life and Letters of Madame Bonapart*; David Stacton's *The Bonapartes* is a lively read. Gerald T. Hopkins, *A Mission to the Indians,* tells of Quaker participation in Jefferson's civilization program. Another fine account of missionary work is Isaac McCoy, *The Baptist Indian Missions.*

William Henry Harrison

Andrew R. L. Cayton, *Frontier Indiana,* is an excellent overview. John D. Barnhart and Dorothy L. Riker, *Indiana to 1816* is also of use. An early biography is Moses Dawson, *Historical Narrative of the Civil and Military Services of Major-General William Henry Harrison* (1824), the standard biography is Freeman Cleaves, *Old Tippecanoe.* Primary sources are collected in Douglas E. Clanin, ed., *The Papers of William Henry Harrison* (10 reels). For the Fort Wayne Treaty of 1809 see Peter Jones, *Journal of the Proceedings...* For the early years of Fort Wayne see Paul Woehrmann, *At the Headwaters of the Maumee,* Wallace Brice, *A History of Fort Wayne,* Gayle Thornbrough, ed., *Outpost on the Wabash,* Leonard U. Hill, *John Johnston and the Indians.* Wells's correspondence with Secretaries of War are in the National Archives Record Groups 75 and 107.

Tecumseh

John Sugden, *Tecumseh,* has an excellent bibliography. Bil Gilbert, *God Gave Us This Country,* R. David Edmunds, *Tecumseh and the Quest for Indian Leadership* and *The Shawenee Prophet* are also useful. James Alexander Thom, *Panther in the Sky,* and Allan W. Eckert, *A Sorrow in the Heart,* are well-researched novels. James H. Howard, *Shawnee,* and R. David Edmunds, *Potawatomis: Keepers of the Fire,* are standard histories.

Fort Dearborn

Milo M. Quaife, *Chicago and the Old Northwest, 1673*-1835, is an important source; see also, Mrs. John H. Kinzie, *Wau-Bun,* Joseph Kirkland, *The Chicago Massacre,* Robert B. McAfee, *History of the Late War in the Western Country,* and John Wentworth, *Early Chicago.* Two novels with good bibliographies are Jerry Crimmins, *Fort Dearborn,* and Allan W. Eckert, *Gateway of Empire.* Darius Heald's essential interview about William Wells is found in Draper 21S, 40-59.

Epilogue

For more information on William Wells's long-lost memoir about the Miami Indians see my forthcoming essay, "Re-reading *The Fort-Wayne Manuscript*: William Wells and the Miami Indians of the Old Northwest," *Indiana Magazine of History* (2010).

William Heath was born in Youngstown, Ohio, and grew up in the nearby town of Poland. He has a B.A. in history from Hiram College and an M.A. and Ph.D. in American Studies from Case Western Reserve University. He has taught in the English departments of Kenyon, Transylvania, and Vassar; from 1979-1981 he was a Fulbright professor at the University of Seville. In the spring of 2007, after twenty-five years of teaching at Mount Saint Mary's University, he retired as a professor emeritus. For seven years he was the editor of *The Monocacy Valley Review.* Presently he is the Libman Professor of Humanities at Hood College, where he teaches in the graduate program. He is the author of an award-winning novel about the civil rights movement in Mississippi, *The Children Bob Moses Led,* and a book of poems, *The Walking Man.* He has published over a hundred poems in literary magazines and anthologies, thirty reviews, and nine essays in scholarly reviews on Hawthorne, Melville, Twain, and William Styron, among others. He and his wife, Roser Caminals-Heath, who has published six novels set in her native Barcelona, live in Frederick, Maryland.

Made in the USA
Charleston, SC
16 November 2015